Inkbloom

Worldcon
2024

The World of Alyssia

Xelle 29 — *Night Ivy* (2022)

Xelle 29 — *Inkbloom* (2023)

Inkbloom

E.D.E. Bell

Atthis Arts
Detroit, Michigan

Inkbloom

Cover illustration by okenki
Book Design by E.D.E. Bell
Layout by G.C. Bell

Published by Atthis Arts, LLC
Detroit, Michigan
atthisarts.com

ISBN 978-1-945009-93-8

LCCN 2023937806

First Edition: Published May 2023

This book is dedicated to Tad, who sometimes sits
at my side and always likes when the window is open.

This book is dedicated to [illegible]

[illegible]

Contents

I will see you at the shore. Your cloak around me.

Deborah Reilly 1954-2023

Preface

You like Xeleanor! I'm so glad.

I do too. And, I've learned a little bit more about the origin of her name. My mom had told me she wanted to name me Eleanor and had been told no, by her mother. After reading the preface to *Night Ivy*, she clarified that my dad only ever had two names in mind for me: Emily or Emma, after his grandmother, Emma Miles, who I was fortunate enough to get to know a bit, at least in the way a great-grandmother can be known to a young child. I'm sure she was complicated, as I am, but my memories are simply nice.

I remember that she seemed to like me. I remember that she got out an oversized coloring book for me and my brother, and told us we were doing a good job with it. I remember that she smoked—a lot. I remember going to see her in the hospital before she died. I remember admiring the mid-century modern cats that now adorn my living room, bought for her by my grandma, Marilyn. And I remember that she tried to teach me to crochet, and then took the yarn and needle back, saying this wasn't for me. "You'll be good at something," she said. "But this isn't it."

Well, Great Gram, I'm a writer.

And I'm glad that my grandma, her daughter, knew in her lifetime that I was finally following my heart, and that she was glad for it.

Like that heart, my writing is nearly always composite, and as it's drawn (by necessity) from the patchwork of my brain, each new layer I learn . . . always somehow fits.

I was joyful when the title of this book occurred to me, and all at once (as with the previous and upcoming titles) I knew it was the one. My life, at the time of writing this book, was in bloom. The story, the words, bloomed in my mind. Opportunities and realizations opened around me, drawn from the secret garden I'd tended my whole life. The transient ink. The indelible stains. The glowing of the dream world in new ways. Seeing the shape of the void, and finding comfort within it. To continue to pull the threads I'd slowly traced in *Night Ivy* into something taking more of that shape.

I am so happy, and *so grateful,* to be able to continue this story. To weave my layers into Xelle's world. And hers into mine.

I must thank the community that is making this possible. The people who comprise my heart. My thanks, joy, and solidarity to my LeRoy (and Ann Arbor) family: Chris, Gwynn, Vance, Vera, Mura, Tad, and Xavier, who all take care of me in vastly different and equally organic ways. My appreciation to Camille Gooderham Campbell and Catherine Jones Payne for thoughtful and thought-inspiring edits, an extra bow to Stewart C Baker, Meghan Cusack, Art Luke, and Tessa Anouska, who pointed out every damn crack in this manuscript during the beta read, and to the absolutely essential proofreaders: Clara Ward and Minerva Cerridwen. Merci to ken, for the awesome, playfully goth cover. And extra hugs to the rest of my writing family (and chat friends! ♥) who lift me, who will not let me fall: Brandon O'Brien, Kella Campbell, Marie Bilodeau, Brandon Crilly, Marsalis, Ava Kelly, Ether Nepenthes, Jennifer Lee Rossman, Trish Matson, Paul Weimer, Oghenechovwe Donald Ekpeki, Tad Williams, Zig Zag Claybourne, Sienna Tristen, Avi Silver, Cat Rambo, and every one of you (so many more! I thought of so many of you writing this—I see you all!) who share in artistry and community together. Including, as always, to Gregory A. Wilson (*sunshine*)—I hope you find my quiet story at least as memorable as the last.

I am The Emily Reborn. I finally feel like me. I really love this book. I hope you will enjoy it.

Cheers and Best —
E.D.E. Bell
May 2023

Until Now

Hoping for additional access to resources used to study her craft (including the inkbloom blossoms she was secretly trying to grow in the hidden space she calls her nightgarden), Xeleanor Du'Tam, she or e, petitioned the Spire Mages of To'Arc (shorthand for Arc Tower) for the position of Mage. They informed her that, as she knew, she must pledge to To'Arc before being granted those privileges. Then, mysteriously, they asked if she would do something for them.

They sent her to To'Breath to learn more about a plot to discredit Mage Pelir before Pelir's presumed Ascension to the Crown of Helina at the time of the Current Crown Mage Jehanne's impending retirement.

On the way, Xelle wandered into the mountain foothills in search for some of the magically reactive obsidian she knew to be deposited there. There, she unexpectedly met a dragon, and then, even more unexpectedly, learned dragons could read eir mind. This dragon agreed to be called Thunder, and Xelle found them quickly forming a friendship, enough that Xelle said upon parting that if Thunder would wish it also, Xelle hoped to see zhem again. In response, Thunder imprinted a small sigil on eir forehead that e later learned was a magic connection to her friend.

Xelle learned little at To'Breath; the only point of interest was a brief encounter with a Mage named Thyra who was interested in the Ascension rumors. She did, however, spend a lot of time reading history books and made a friend, Kwill, to whom she grew close. Frustrated, she returned to To'Arc, and decided to try and determine on her own what might be going on. She learned that Spire Mage Kern had been influenced by an unknown group claiming to have cheated to cause Kern's adult cura (son), Tenne, to win a prestigious art grant. Xelle now calls this group the Hurts.

She also realized, through her sigil, that the dragons were in danger. Finding the Hurts crushing through the mountains with forces of magic, Xelle convinced the dragons to leave. When they did, they collapsed the cliff near which they had resided, covering the obsidian deposit within the rubble. The Hurts then tried to capture Xelle, but Thunder intervened, rescuing her and carrying her to To'Arc in view of the entire Tower, where Helia helped her from view and from questions. Still deeply rattled by the departure of her labmate, Ay'tea, for whom she'd just realized her deep feelings, Xelle let Helia, whom she'd been casually dating, know that she could not accept her implied offer of a more committed romantic relationship.

Xelle does not know what the goals of the Hurts are, but knows she needs to find out and restore the dragons to their home, without threat from this new and unpleasant group.

Believing now that Spire Mage Kern did not have ill intent toward the magesphere, she convinced him to take on a role of double agent. Meanwhile, Tenne is completing his year as a resident artist in the historic E'lle Gallery, as Xelle has asked him not to reveal that he was not the intended winner to avoid compromising Kern's efforts. Before departing To'Arc, the Crown Mage, Jehanne, cryptically offered that if Xelle needed someone to trust, she could trust Spire Mage We'le.

As for the Hurts, Xelle only knows that they are trying to exert power in the magesphere, trying to reach the dragons and/or their hoard of obsidian in some way. And she remembers what it felt like when they tried to take her away, against her will.

On her way to To'Ever, Xelle is currently taking a break in her homevillage of Tam (known for its forests, carpentry, small waterfall, and enthusiasm for tall ladder culture) to visit with her three parents, her nearby (and only) sibling, and his two young curas.

Inkbloom

Savanna Sheer

To'Arc
To'Ever
Mytil
Tam
To'Charm
To'Dust
Sharre
Alyssia

01 - *Home, in a way*

Xelle's room was now her parent's sewing nook. Not that it was really her room anymore; she'd moved out as a teenager and she was now twenty-nine years old. Which she'd just realized was almost thirty.

Thirty. This was not a big deal, and she needed to stop thinking about it. Or, maybe it was. It just felt like . . . In one's twenties, it was such a joy to be an adult. A real per. Finally independent yet infinitely young. Thirty would be an adult adult. Someone teens would see as old. Someone who saw teens as young. And proof the infinity thing hadn't lasted as long as she'd thought.

As for her old room, though mostly unrecognizable, not *everything* had been changed. The bed was still here (Na Lleyx had hurriedly removed several stacks of patterned fabric while assuring Xelle the sheets were recently cleaned) including the border of vines and leaves Xelle had carved (without permission) into the headboard when she was little. The scrunchy curtains from the starry purple fabric Xelle had picked herself still hung from the room's one window. And, to her complete delight, the metallic-printed poster illustrated with the completely offensive trend character of Firana, Stalker of Night—a busty, black-draped Mage knock-off—was still affixed to the ceiling. Xelle wondered if any of them had noticed it. Probably. How could they not? Respect, either way, to Firana.

Other than that, the room had been fitted with every size and color of shelves and drawers to neatly house her Na's sewing notions (Xelle found this term hilarious). Less neatly, fabrics and shreds and loose pins were strewn about the table, and, she hoped, only there. Xelle, who'd stashed most of her own things in her nightgarden at To'Arc, was basically living out of her backpack, which slumped, unimpressed, against the bed's foot. She stared up at Firana. "Sorry, friend of darkness, I have work to do. Stay cool."

A couple minutes later, Xelle emerged from the washroom, yanking on the side of her tunic that she'd somehow tucked into her pants. Her parents sat, rather picturesquely, around the round table, sipping from steaming cups of tea. They were framed neatly by the lines of stencils Na Lleyx had painted onto the walls longer ago than Xelle could remember, except that Xelle had always been told she'd helped.

Na Foose, still wearing an undyed sleep robe, jumped in eir seat. "I keep forgetting she's here." Not jumped, startled. Wiggled. Xelle knew that didn't really mean e'd forgotten, just that it continued to startle em in moments e wasn't considering it.

With a pointed side-eye, Na Vuia rose, filling a handled mug from another kettle and setting it in front of one of two empty chairs. Xelle slumped into it, glad for the coffee, and offering Na Foose a look she hoped was reassuring. "With Loren now, you'll need another chair." She took a sip, jumping, herself, a bit. Fira, they served it hot.

"Two chairs, if you're here," Na Lleyx murmured, adding a bit of lilt that Xelle knew entirely well. Ah, that explained the look. A talk was coming.

She imagined the picture that they saw: a perfect family, all together. Xeleanor and Hall, and Hall's curas. Not Xelle running off again. As it seemed they'd see it, or Na Lleyx. At least, any of her parents who felt that way kept it to themselves. Sort of.

She'd been by to see Hall not long after arriving. Loren was not a baby at all, but a toddling hu, currently perceived as rainbow gender by Hall, 'just like Ga Lleyx', he'd added. Xelle had gotten strong she vibes during her visit (same as Na Lleyx at the moment, actually), and had gone with that. And little Vallie! Talking and drawing. Asking Xelle how each drawing looked, as Vallie could see some shape and light, but not the lines she crafted lovingly onto each sheet.

Barely remembering when Hall was that little, it was really the first time Xelle had witnessed someone who had been a sweet baby now forming sentences, asking questions. A unique little spirit. She hadn't wanted to gush to Hall about it, but feeling this new connection to Vallie had really been . . . awesome.

Xelle hadn't yet given either of them the charms she'd brought from Old Vattam. She'd need to, soon, as whatever passive protests her parents were about to put up (and still avoiding her own unsettled feelings), she really needed to be on her way.

Na Vuia, ready for the day in a lace-trimmed black apron over a prim but comfortable burgundy dress, was pretending not to watch her, while Na Lleyx, in a quilted robe as colorful as Na Foose's sleepwear was plain, was diligently aligning a teaspoon against the pattern of the cup. Na Foose was at least trying to look like a per drinking tea in a normal manner, as in not waiting for whatever Xelle was about to say.

Ugh. She pushed the words out.

"I'll need to leave soon for To'Ever."

"Do you know you've already been there?" Na Foose chuckled, causing eir cup to rattle against the saucer, causing em to jump again slightly. Xelle, her hands clamped over the sides of her chair seat, stayed steady.

E meant the question humorously (Na Foose often struggled with appropriate humor and Xelle normally gave that understanding), but this was a worry of Xelle's, so she didn't love the note. Yes, she'd been there. Yes, she'd left. Now she was going there on another hunch. A way to help the dragons. These last days, all she'd really done was rationalize her hasty choice again and again. That if she were going to follow a hunch, it might as well be her own. Yet, why? Why was it settled, just because she'd said it once. Maybe she should take a step back.

"We'd like you here longer, Xeleanor," Na Lleyx said.

Not said. Positively whined. So much for passive.

"We never see you, at these Towers, whichever one you're at."

"I know, but I'm doing my thing." With a pang, she moved on from that. "Which is to say, you're welcome to visit me anytime. They allow that. I could take you on a tour."

An odd silence, punctuated only by the sipping of tea, followed. They worked here, from their home; it wasn't as if their schedules prohibited travel. Na Foose made coins well-enough from eir ghost-writing. Na Lleyx jumped from craft to craft, but kept busy on a solid mix of commissions and donations and gifts. Na Vuia, well, she mostly managed them, Xelle thought with a dark laugh. Xelle didn't quite mean that; she knew the ways Na Vuia worked. Quietly. Saving pers left and right without anyone ever knowing she'd done it. If Xelle were ever in trouble, it's Na Vuia she'd want on her side.

"We like to stay here. For our health," Na Vuia said, and that conversation was that.

"You're there on a whim, you said," Na Lleyx restarted, poking her to react.

A hunch, not a whim. She thought. She hoped. Ash-pile, it was a whim. But it wasn't like she had another plan. She missed To'Arc already, being honest, but the idea of a little space from it felt right. Or, maybe, necessary, she thought.

And no, Xelle had not told her parents about her telepathic dragon sigil and they had not asked about the new mark on her forehead. She'd have to tell them at some point—news even reached Tam eventually—but, for now, if this was a place Xelle could have space from that too, all the better.

She'd thought about what Crown Mage Jehanne said about covering the mark, but as she'd already been seen by so many with it, covering it felt like adding mystique. Why not let people wonder and then move along? Heh, she sounded like a Breath Mage. Perhaps a bit of their thought processes had rubbed off on her, after all.

"Na, you know how I talk," Xelle tried. "My brain is a whim."

"I don't even know what that means," Na Lleyx said, leaning back.

"I do," Na Foose muttered. "And so I know you could stay here a little longer, Xee. Your Na Lleyx would really like it. And—we're worried about you."

Worried? "Nas, I'm doing fine. The Tower switching is . . . me . . . it's not a *problem*."

"It's not your success we're worried about, it's . . ." E stared down at eir plate. "I think you should talk to her, Vuia."

Na Vuia's face tightened. "That was not yours to prompt."

"No. It's ours. And you see it as well as I do." Without further word, Na Foose rose and walked off. Without many places to go in the small house, e strode into the sewing room and firmly shut the door. Most definitely forgetting Xelle had been sleeping there.

With a wince and a shrug, Na Lleyx rose to follow em, closing the door more gently behind her.

And there it was, the pressure rising in her chest. Parental speech incoming. Thing was, Xelle was not a child. And she wasn't going to sit in her own flaming kitchen, or what used to be her kitchen, or her childhood kitchen, which actually made it worse, with pounding in her neck wondering what revelation or lecture her parent had in store. She turned, more defiantly than she wanted to, to look right at Na Vuia. Seeing Na Vuia mimic her expression, she dropped it.

"What," Xelle huffed. "You might as well, now."

Na Vuia sighed, and not a relaxed sigh. "They want me to tell you that I studied at To'Arc."

Xelle dropped her fork. But it didn't hit the table, as the waft of a cast swished by and grabbed it, setting it gently back to the mat. "I'm sorry!" Xelle blurted out; she'd not meant to drop it, or to cast. Then she realized what had just happened. That the cast had not been hers.

And every desire to prove herself mature flew out the window. Or actually . . . the door.

She flung it open, and lurching to her feet with a dramatic gesture not remotely required for Arc casting, she flung out strands of travel to the tree outside, pulling herself swiftly up to the lookout she'd built as a child, flying forward to land on its platform. ***Na Vuia knew casting.*** She knew casting all this time, and never once, never once showed it to Xelle. Never told her.

"Oh!" A voice called from below. "Impressive! Did you win, now?" Na Vuia breathed heavily, grunted some sort of heaving noise, and launched upward into the air, roughly and nearly not making the platform, but landing with a thump, before scooting in. Her apron caught on the wood, and with an annoyed expression, she untied the cord and swatted the whole thing away, guiding it back in through the house's open front door.

Now they were both sitting in a tree. Wonderful. Xelle glanced over, very much not trying to process anything that had just happened. "Um, you wanted to talk?"

"Are you done? We can keep going."

The last thing Xelle was going to admit was, before seeing the exertion on Na Vuia's face, she had been considering tying a couple threads to the branch above to make it look like she was floating. Now that felt . . . Anyway. "You wanted to talk? Or, the other Nas did?"

Na Vuia was reaching out to feel the small buds lining the old birch. "A late spring," she noted. "And yes. We're worried about you."

"About not pledging?" She really didn't want to have this talk.

Na Vuia looked annoyed. "No, you're fixated on it. About you pushing yourself too hard. We see it in your face. Something weighing your smile. Eyes pointed this way, and that way. They've taught you about material burnout, but there's more. There's you. What are you doing for yourself? Not your studies. You. Yourself."

Xelle didn't have anything for herself except herself; was Na Vuia just trying to make that hurt more? No, that was unfair, her parents always had her care at heart. But she felt downright sullen. *For a lot of reasons.* And she didn't want to talk about it, didn't want to think about it. She wanted to dress like Firana and go live in Mytil and tell edgy poems at the night market and let pers drop coins into her exaggerated cleavage. But she was not going to do that. She was going to To'Ever, where she would figure out inkblooms, learn better protection magic, decipher why hu were being terrible apparently both to dragons and each other, and then go meet with her dragon friends.

See. She had dragon friends.

"I'm being me now."

Na Vuia leaned back against the trunk. "I can think of no better first step, but part of being you you is caring for you you." Xelle made a face. "And," she continued, "whatever Lleyx says about missing you, and of course she does, we are not trying to pressure you to stay here forever. We wouldn't *do* that. Just maybe long enough to let that weight fall."

Xelle's weight could not fall while the dragons stayed away from their home at her urging. Not until she could give them what she'd promised: answers and an invitation back. And other reasons, too. Must be nice, having two spouses and a warm house and little babies to come over and roll around and then go home.

Also unfair. Xelle felt unfair. She *was* unfair.

She gazed out over the road leading to their home. It was still too chilly to be out like this, but pleasant in its own, teasing way. A breeze rustled the branches, and Xelle shivered a bit, involuntarily. "Cold shiver," she muttered by habit, not taking her eyes off of the road.

"I left the Tower because it wasn't me," Na Vuia added. "I figured you wouldn't want to ask. Wasn't dismissed. Just, left."

Magic was Xelle. She didn't see that as the Tower. Just, everyone else did. Her chest felt a little weight at the thought, like . . . well, like suddenly uncovering a new way to not be understood. It's not that she thought of herself as like any of her parents, but this disconnect with Na Vuia felt jarring. Yet, she also knew the tone of voice when Na Vuia didn't want to discuss something further.

"Then, you were born. Then Hall." She stopped.

Another breeze blew past. Then settled.

"I was planning on going over there today," Xelle said, breaking the silence. "To Hall's."

Na Vuia sighed a bit loudly. "He'd enjoy that. Now, we're proud of you, Xeleanor. And I told them, I didn't need to say anything. You're a grown per, my cura or not. But we care about you." As she extended her arms, Xelle leaned into them, finally letting herself relax against her parent's soft grasp. It had been so long since she'd relaxed against any hu. She wanted to hold longer, but . . . She let go.

"Thanks, Na." She let Na Vuia rub her back, and tried not to think about missing the closeness of touch.

"Anytime. Anytime. Now, help getting down? Before something happens that will be hard to explain back inside?"

Xelle smiled, and reaching easily into her material, she wrapped her arms around her parent and scooted off of the platform, lowering them down, together.

"Very smooth." Na Vuia sounded impressed, which Xelle tried not to dwell on. Or proud, maybe it was that. "If you're going to Hall's, I made cookies for the kids. Perhaps you'll take them with my greeting." Na Vuia hurried in through the front door, as if Xelle had already left.

And Xelle could not help but laugh as, while she was still brushing the dirt off of her pants, a small paper package floated its way out to her, along with her backpack.

"Thanks, Na," she called back into the house. And headed down the road.

"Sa Xelle," a little voice called as Xelle raised her hand toward the bell. The door swung open, and she lowered her arm, using it instead to sweep up the very big-kid looking child who grinned up at her, with a neatly wrapped black cap, not unlike something Xelle would wear. "Ga Vuia made cookies."

Without much sight, Vallie tended not to rely on what was in front of her. Xelle imagined that might be helpful if she ever wanted to study magic; half of first classes were spent opening one's focus.

"She did," Xelle agreed, walking with her into the house. "There's one for you both," she added, smiling at Hall who'd just walked into the room holding a toothbrush.

Xelle loved seeing her sibling as a parent, especially as it didn't seem to have changed him a bit. Today, he wore a casual blue shirt with an image of Tam's waterfall dye-painted onto it, and a fluffy set of gray pants over fuzzy black socks. His head was poorly covered with a plain undercap, enough that she could see wisps of bright orange crownhair from underneath. With strangers, one wouldn't be exactly certain whether a bright orange was fear, or excitement, or a range of nuances, but with her only sibling, she knew it meant he was flame-scorched happy here, raising these kids. She grinned, and set her bag next to the door.

"The Nas got on me," she said, plopping onto the couch with Vallie, as she glanced around looking for Loren. "Where's your sibling?" she asked.

"Loren is a goblin."

"A goblin?" Xelle gasped in feigned shock. "Where does this goblin live?"

"One, two, three," Vallie said, as Loren came tumbling out from under a draped blanket with a little squeak. Both kids laughed as Xelle leaned down to scoop Loren up to her other side. Loren wore a soft little romper with leg snaps. Her head uncovered, Xelle could see her crownhair was just starting to come in, that uniquely transparent sheen of baby crownhair that begged to be kissed.

"Hello, goblin!" Xelle gave Loren a brgly-sort of goblin noise, causing her to laugh.

Xelle didn't see herself parenting, but she was a flaming cool sarent, she thought with a slight gloat.

"Stay longer?" Hall said this through a mouth of toothpaste.

She knew he didn't mean here. "How did you know?"

He returned to his washroom, and Xelle wrestled the kids a bit waiting for him to reemerge.

No toothbrush this time, but Xelle noted he still hadn't put on a cap. She wondered how many visitors he actually had these days.

He plopped onto a squishy chair. "I mean, I get 'maybe you should get away some,' so it seemed only natural."

Xelle snorted. Then quieted, as this felt so odd to ask. "Did you know about Na Vuia? That she studied magic?"

Hall was silent a very long moment, his face still. He pointed at her. "It makes perfect sense, actually."

Xelle shook her head. "You did not know—and stop it! I didn't think you knew! Anyway, she's using it to tell me that I'm doing too much, or the Nas pushed her into it, really. They're worried about me. But I don't think it's just because I'm still studying. What do they care? It's because I'm switching again. Switching must be a sign something's wrong, right?"

"Is something wrong?"

She scrunched her face. "Keep a secret?"

"They hear everything," he reminded, his head tilting slightly toward the kids.

"I trust them." She winked at Vallie, adding a specific little side click. Vallie tried to imitate the sound, but with her little baby face (now kid, but still some baby), it came out more of a pop.

"I met dragons and this mark"—she pointed at eir forehead—"can help us communicate with each other. Like, the dragons know what I'm thinking."

Hall stared at her again, this time for longer. "You're . . . not kidding. Ash, Xella. Dragonfriend?"

Dragonfriend? Ooh, she liked that. "I guess."

"Dragons go *roar*," Vallie said, sweeping off the couch and rolling on the padded rug. Loren giggled.

"They do actually." She couldn't escape the image of Lightning glaring furiously at em and then throwing em down the hill, but probably not a good first story. "But they seem really nice. Anyway. As you can tell I have no idea what I'm doing, why I'm going anywhere, but whatever is on my mind, staying in Tam and staring up at Firana is not going to help."

"I can't with Firana." Hall walked over to the kitchen side of the room to get a cup. "You have the worst tastes."

"Sure." Hall's gibes never concerned her; he was solid for her always. Besides, Firana was not for the faint of heart. "So what do you think?"

He gestured toward her with the still-empty cup. "I think you are probably both right. You're a grown hu. Almost thirty? Eh? And I also think that Na Vuia is the wisest per I know, and if she expresses concern you ought to listen to her."

"What does that mean?" She flipped onto the floor and bounced Vallie up on her hands and feet, ignoring the thirty comment.

"It means go where you were going but be careful. Something feels off, you always have a place to come back to."

Her mind flashed to To'Arc, but of course he meant Tam.

Complicated. Complicated emotions. She'd think about that later. In fact! "Hey! I got you buds something in Vattam. Ack, sorry, Hall, I didn't get you something, just Loren and Vallie. Now I feel like a skip."

Hall chuckled and swooped out his arms. From where Xelle lay on the floor, it sort of looked like he was flying. "Everything I want, I have here. Besides, you brought cookies. And thankfully, not your own."

She sighed, rolling back over and crawling to her bag. "Also for the kids, Hall. Oh," she added, unwrapping the little package and seeing four cookies, neatly marked: V, L, H, and X. "I swear." Not that she was going to turn down a cookie.

"Eat at the table," Hall said, just as Xelle was about to unwrap hers. Not sure if that meant her as well, she grabbed the two gifts and pulled a side chair over to the sizable surface in the middle of the tiled half of the space.

"This is a nice table." She'd never really noted it.

"You don't want to know."

Her eyes widened. "No."

"Yes," he replied. "Rod. Look, when he moved out to Rich Hills, or whatever it's called, he had a big sale on his house here. Friend of the family, practically gave it to me."

"Practically," she confirmed. As Hall knew, Rod was not her favorite person growing up, and charging a young parent for a used table he was trying to get rid of did not improve her opinion of the blustering carpenter.

"Well, you said it was nice." He sat down, and for all his parently rules, practically shoved the cookie into his mouth. Xelle decided not to comment.

"So! I got the two of you little trinkets from a good luck shop in Vattam."

"Good luck?" Hall got out through the mouthful of soft cookie. "Not enchanted?"

Xelle winced. Hall had never been around Mages, so he didn't have the same sensitivity to things like turning the magic. Which giving someone an enchanted or even casted item without their consent would definitely be.

"No, just good luck." Fine. Once the Tower moveroom had dropped her off at Tam, she had cast detection on the items, just to be sure. Metal and stone. She'd checked.

Loren was engrossed in her cookie, but Vallie held her hand out expectantly.

"It's good to be patient," Hall said.

"It's fine; I'm glad she's excited," Xelle responded. A straight-mouthed glance from her sibling indicated perhaps she understood parenting etiquette as well as he knew the magesphere. Whatever. It was her gift.

"Ok, Vallie first. Now, I'll tell you, this shines with multilayered light, like a patina but somehow without one. It's the color of a brown-to-gold metal, but I can't quite pinpoint which one. Also, I don't know a lot about metal," she joked, as she put the small metal vine into Vallie's outstretched hand.

Vallie caressed it, and seemed without words. Finally, she looked toward Xelle. "Sa Xelle, I love this very much, but I want to see what you said. What is a patina?"

"It's like," Xelle tried, "when metal gets older and dulls, but with more color." That was terrible, but Vallie seemed satisfied.

"And for you, Loren." Xelle proffered the opalescent stone. "Vallie, you can look at this stone later, but I'll say it's flecked in every shade of white or soft rainbow or no color at all."

"Flecked means in little pieces," Hall added. As Loren grabbed the stone and slid it into her mouth. "Oh!" Hall lightly exclaimed. "A little young yet."

Before Xelle even had time to realize what had happened or worry about it, Hall had retrieved the stone, and was moving it in the light.

"Xelle, I know you walk with the Mage crowds, but this had to be expensive."

Xelle almost told him. That the shopkeeper had given that one for free, as long as she bought the other. But it wasn't really about value, if it was for luck, and Xelle really avoided talking about money, never knowing what might be rude.

"It's rare, I think. But it wasn't expensive, for me. Xe wanted me to have it. For Loren. Looks like you'll need to keep it safe, for now." Xelle felt a little silly, not having considered *eating it* as an option, but Hall didn't seem disturbed.

"Well," he did say, "I'm not going to tell you where to go, but you're welcome to stay and play goblin for a bit, do nothing, or whatever."

"Sa Xelle?" It was Vallie's little voice. She was holding the small metal sculpture over her heart, her fingers intertwined as though it was made for her grasp.

"Yes?" She was so cute. They were both so cute. How had time continued this way? What was Xelle doing?

"Thank you for my nopatina. I really like it. And . . . can you tell me about the dragons?"

02 - *The Weather at Ever*

If Xelle had considered the absolute discordance of yet again, a decade later, saying goodbye to her family in Tam and heading off toward To'Ever to seek an uncertain future, she never would have suggested the idea to Crown Mage Jehanne. But, she had done it, she had left, she had . . . Now she understood. She wanted to go back to To'Arc. But she couldn't. She could, but she couldn't. And now she was going to To'Ever. Again. And she could worry and worry until it consumed her, or she could keep on her way and navigate what would happen. As she always had, just with more complications now.

At least, though, something about the awkwardness of her parents' 'talk' and then spending the day with Hall and the kids had shaken some of the rigor around those uncertainties.

Xelle knew her rung was low. She couldn't explain to anyone how real it had been that she'd just made a life-changing decision without much (real) reason and then stuck with it. She couldn't talk about Ay'tea, or Helia, or Jehanne ('so the Crown Mage and I were chatting and she gave me this rare sword') or the details of her interactions with Thunder. She didn't really even want to say that she felt . . . bad. Weird. Off. Something. Because they'd tell her that was a reason to stay. And the one thing she just kind of knew was that she couldn't stay.

However, she'd at least spilled out a lot of things around the edges of all this to Hall, and she did have conversations that evening with each of her parents that had helped . . . not really ease the tension, but at least not let it hold so tight.

After learning Na Vuia had studied magic, they'd talked for a while about her studies and insights. Confirming Xelle's earlier sense,

Na Vuia kept a clear berth from any personal stories, sticking directly to magic itself, and her own thoughts about it. Discussing a subject with Na Vuia where it was quickly clear Xelle knew a great deal more, not just the result of more study, but a lot a lot more, was unsettling. Na Vuia knew everything. Did everything. When she'd never cared to study magic (in Xelle's view), the world had stayed in its place. But knowing that she had for a while, and that Xelle was intensely good at it compared to her parent's faded knowledge of perhaps some skill was different. It just was.

And on top of that, the discordance of Na Vuia not loving Tower life and so letting it go still sat heavy. Xelle had issues with Tower life too. But she couldn't let it go. Magic was part of her. She needed it. And the Towers, well, she kind of . . . loved them . . . too. Did Xelle have, like, a problem? Or were they just different?

Na Foose, now working a puzzle at the table, had mostly just wanted to listen. Not everything Xelle wanted to say, pers wanted to hear, so she took em up on the opportunity, and went on rather at length about nothing that was too important to say. (Being honest. Here, that is.) About her friend Kwillen she'd met at To'Breath, the work she'd done on logistics analysis (but not mentioning Ay'tea), her day in Old Vattam and how interesting it'd been.

She'd only mentioned the utility store briefly, but he'd (Na Foose didn't mind he on occasion and sometimes Xelle's mind went to it) been overly interested in that, wanting to hear all that she could remember of the crowded aisles and stacked gadgets. She'd liked seeing him so interested. He was so often withdrawn, but he sure loved hearing about that huge store. Na Lleyx would have asked about the gadgets themselves, thinking of any new way they could be used for sewing or woodworking or frames for sewing or whatever Na Lleyx was up to at the time. Na Foose, though, had the mind of a writer. What was it like there? Intimidating, or exciting? Echoey, muted? Any smells. (Yes! There had been smells of wood and oils and paints and Xelle had liked that bit of it a lot.)

Thus, after the emotionally complicated insights of Na Vuia's wisdom and then finding some peace with Na Foose's open ears and affinity for woodworking scents, Xelle was not braced for Na Lleyx's unsolicited life skills quiz. Xelle still didn't know what she'd done to have her parent suddenly run over the basics of everything from pipe repair to laundering (had she smelled?), but as some of the tips she had *not* known, she decided to stop being silently snide about it and just take a few notes. Including how to sew on a button without it either falling off or looking like it'd eaten the spool of thread.

Unlike with Hall, she hadn't broached the dragons with any of her parents. Not even a little. She knew she should have, but Hall had agreed to keep an eye on village gossip, and talk to them before they were caught unaware. Why this was such a relief was something she hadn't quite yet parsed. There were just some things too uncertain (too raw?) to know how to tell one's parents, she supposed. Even when that thing was amazing. Well, she considered, maybe that was it. Maybe there were some places where even the suggestion of a questioning reaction would land too hard.

Speaking of Hall, she'd passed through again on her way out, fighting unexpected tears at the idea of not seeing those little gems for so long again, at (only thought to herself) that nagging feeling of turning back into Imaginary Sa Xelle who is Not in Tam. Yet, Vallie kept her metal vine in hand and, while not seeming sad at all, had whispered at the doorway if sometime she could go with Xelle, a question Xelle hadn't known how to answer, so she'd responded with a hug. Loren was more interested in getting back inside for a bread Hall had baking.

Which left Xelle. Xelle alone, with a backpack, Essie, and a colorful, patched cloak Na Lleyx had demanded she take because she was inappropriately dressed to be out, and Xelle didn't want to explain that her previous cloak had been retired after a series of events culminating in being dropped off on the top of To'Arc by a dragon. "You've been down the high rim!" she'd scolded Xelle's way. To'Arc *was* high rim—near the edge but so was Tam, yet Na Lleyx remained convinced Xelle had forgotten how cold it was the way of To'Ever.

Well. She *had* forgotten how cold it was, and was grateful for the fuzzy cloak as she made her way, hiking through the forest (not totally amagically, leveraging the occasional help of what she now called her sling cast) toward the distantly familiar Ever Tower.

And again, the uneasy discordance of being almost thirty rather than almost twenty, and walking up that drive, and seeing the rough wood beams and sharp angles of To'Ever rather than the arches and colorfully segmented windows of To'Arc had her mind all in a haze by the time she walked to the Front Desk. The Ever Front Desk, she reminded herself.

"Xeleanor Du'Tam," she said. "I'm here—"

Suddenly totally unable to articulate what in Fira's flames she was doing here, she appeared to have just let out that she was here, as if she were some sort of dignitary they'd forgotten to escort from the village. Which made her even more rattled as the clerk started in surprise, ruffled through a stack of cards, and called back for a nondelay escort to the high floor.

"The high floors?" Xelle managed to say, now sounding like she was confused how Towers worked. "Perhaps a room, to put down my bag and cloak."

The clerk essentially ignored her, planting the idea that she was not the one being appeased here, and soon Xelle found herself tromping off behind a curt steward, the Tower Atrium opening into view.

Whatever was happening here, it felt like pure insult to have to hurry, fast-walking through the Ever Atrium at the moment of her return. Sure, she'd come back later, but she wanted to stop and feel it now. A tradition of hers, she supposed. The scents of wood and woodsy fragrance, the little balconies peeking out from many floors above, the long beams of rough-finished wood. She barely had time to run her hands over a low hedge marking the path, sneaking in a sniff of it to enjoy the fresh oils, when she was brought into a lift, and—

"High floor," the clerk repeated.

Ash, now she remembered. High floor. Not high floors. She thought the clerk had just abbreviated, but now she realized that was To'Arc speak, where the personal offices for Spire Mages were on the same level as each other, with several meeting and presentation areas above and below. Not here, where the highest floor was as highly restricted as it was dedicated. Fira, they were taking her to the Crown Mage.

No time to prepare. Was that bad? Was that good? Who was this per? When she was here, it was Avail. Avail, he or e, pretty old even then? Secretive. Gentle, she'd heard. Mysterious. She could barely picture him; short and thin, maybe? Wore a lot of white? Was he still here? She should have looked this up. Stopped in Vi'Ever and asked around.

Maybe she shouldn't have rubbed her hands through the evergreens. Maybe she shouldn't have stopped to rest without a seat in the forest, wearing her travel clothes.

Let into the office, clearly the Crown Mage's office, it was suddenly just the two of them. And yes, it was still Avail. Crown Mage Avail, she reminded herself. The doors clicked shut.

And all at once, Xelle was firmly back in the magesphere.

Maybe this was what Na Vuia had meant.

Avail stood to greet her, something she wouldn't have expected from her earlier time at To'Ever. Ok, not real short, just sort of shorter and without any sort of raised shoes or headwear. His cap of undyed linen was more of a cape in itself, tied around, billowing in three segments laced with gold threads behind him, over a rather plain (but fine) robe, with a few impressive-looking Mage chains. Sure, not *billowing*—there was no breeze and it was a sturdy fabric–but it did have some bounce as he moved. Hanging. She imagined him flying in the wind on some enchanted object, as they liked to do, here. It would billow then, certainly. Not specifically in the wind, just the motion itself, and some wind . . .

Crown Mage. Xelle. She bowed quickly, then thinking it was too quickly, stayed looking at the floor a little longer, then looked up. "Crown Mage Avail," she said, moving her hand in the sign of the Arc. Ash!

She curled it inward, in the sign of the Ever.

His wrinkled face showed no reaction, but instead of sitting down and peering at her behind his desk, he beckoned her over to two loungey green chairs, where they sat, gazing placidly at each other like they were meeting for tea, but the other guests had not yet arrived.

This was weird.

She'd never been to the high floors before, let alone the high *floor,* not when she was here, and curious, she glanced around. No one held as small but somehow as subtly luxurious offices as the Arc Spire Mages, but yet, the office of the Ever Crown Mage was not large, by what she imagined Crown Mage standards to be, and clearly didn't take up the entire floor. Like the rest of the Tower, the aesthetic leaned heavily on old wood and rectangular beams. His desk was gorgeous, the perfectly selected color and grain of the wood tastefully left unadorned, without carvings or inlays. Two ramps joined in a platform behind and well above his desk, offering what had to be a breathtaking view of the forest through a tall, beam-framed window of long-aged wood. Her eyes lingered on it. She knew she was avoiding the reality of now, and that it would not avoid her.

As he had not yet spoken and not sure what else to do, she drew her gaze back to the Mage. No expression. Well, he'd called her here. She leaned back with shaky breath (which was not supposed to be audible but probably was), and continued to take in the room, running her eyes along the tall bookcases on the two longer walls. He did have a lot of books; that spoke well of him. A variety of books, not long series of this or that, but a true collection, old and new and in various stages of slump. The other walls were painted with wispy lines of gold, not unlike the stencils in her parents' kitchen, but these clearly brushed by hand and with actual gold. Finally, she heard the rustle of his robes, as he flicked a hand, and a table walked their way, holding a large pitcher of what looked like cucumber water, and four tall, stylish glasses, secured by a handled metal frame.

"Jehanne and I were lovers," he said, picking up a glass.

What?

"Oh, that's nice. I like her very much," she said, stalling to figure out what the ash this was about. *I like her very much? Fira.*

"Which is to say, whatever you might be thinking to escape, I know you won't find it here."

Xelle leaned in. "I'm not here to escape anything."

"Oh?" He took a sip.

This annoyed her. A lot. Jarring her out of whatever fog she was in, in a way that, curiously, didn't rattle her mind in the moment. Crown Mage or not, he'd 'gamed on' the minute he went personal. Maybe he was *trying* to rattle something out of her, but then, even more reason for her to go in—especially if he was going to play he knew it all. *Which he did not.*

She pointed to her mark. "I am here to find out what is going on with the dragons, what hu have done to them, and how we undo it." Then, she said something she really shouldn't have. "And 'were' lovers? Not anymore, then?"

Avail nearly snorted. Nor did he answer. "If you are here to open doors long jammed shut, then I still puzzle to understand why? Why back? An old Study? Thrice moved Towers? Shall I put you on stair-scrubbing until I can coax you to pledge? To us, a Tower you left in short order? Surely you know we aren't a hotel. Or, am I overthinking it? Do you wish to apply to staff? Good carpenters are always in short supply."

There were times (all the time) when trying not to make a mistake caused Xelle no end of stress and worry and second return. And, a tiny voice told her, those would visit her later about this conversation. But Avail seemed eager for a diamondboard game with bold, rapid moves, and for now, Xelle decided one thing.

She was not a flatcap.

She crossed her arms. "Honestly? I have no idea why I blurted out I needed to be here to Crown Mage Jehanne and thus why I'm here, but apparently now I am. You've noticed. Clearly. You don't seem to be asking me to leave, and you wouldn't try and demand a pledge, even if I were qualified. You know what happened; where do you expect me to go? Where would you go?" Before realizing it, she'd opened her arms in a rather sweeping gesture. She tried to make it look intentional and tie it to her request.

"So, allow me to stay here with your blessing. Tacit, if not overt. Provide access to Mage libraries and resources. Call me a Mage. Or don't. Just . . . allow it. It's not about me, now. I want to find out how to help them, and help all of us. And by the way, if you know what our secret history is with the dragons or how it relates to the political roiling at Arc, any assists would be excellent. Crown Mage," she added, lowering her arms.

He laughed. "You ask for explanations more complicated than I am permitted to give. Will you pledge?" He appeared to know the answer. She shook her head. "Then I cannot have you here as a Study either, even with special access. You'd do no good; you'd disrupt our order." He tapped his chin. "An Apprentice."

"Apprentice?" She realized she'd said it aloud. Rather annoyedly. Yes, she knew the clause. A very specific clause, for those who'd been pulled, usually by a very important Mage, to do specific tasks. But . . . oh. That could work. "To you?"

"Oooh!" His eyes twinkled. "Bold and flattering. But no. To Mage Fepa."

"Mage Fepa," she repeated. The name meant nothing.

"Yes. He's one of the most well-connected Mages in our Tower." Avail cocked his head.

Well-connected. So that meant he did what he wanted. *Ah.* Xelle didn't think she liked this. But she thought she understood it. And it would give her what she needed, right?

"What access does an Apprentice have?" she prodded.

"Whatever access is ordered by one's Mage, based on said Mage's own access."

She nodded, slowly. Strangely, this whole Apprentice note took the juice out of what had been escalating to a much more interesting conversation. Avail's eyes gazed past her shoulders, and she didn't know much else to say that wouldn't mess up what was at least giving her a place to start. Well, one thing. "Are you willing, Crown Mage Avail, to provide me pointers regarding what hu did to the dragons?"

For the first time, he looked slightly annoyed. "I have done what I could here. I see it might be lost on you." He stood, returning to his desk. "Report to Mage Fepa, Apprentice Xeleanor."

That, she could tell, was that.

03 - *Cold out.*

Mage Fepa was an ash-hole. By which Xelle was able to quickly confirm Avail's intent, which was as decidedly bladed as it was generous. Fepa, as it were, didn't seem to actually do anything here other than take guests and be ambiguously essential. So Xelle's strategy, then, was to not let on that she realized that, puff up his ego, and see what access she could contrive. While minimizing her exposure to Mage Fepa, who, by the way, really, really, was an ash-hole.

A challenge, that. Since she didn't have any actual assignments, he assumed she'd be thrilled to dote around in the background of his equally obnoxious visitors, like a sculpture to be briefly admired and then ignored. A living sculpture of the one who'd met the dragon, simply honored to exist in his presence.

She'd put up with it enough to get by, and then once he'd seemed to forget she was even there but not enough to allow her to leave, she'd usually excuse herself, offering a feigned discomfort that wasn't . . . actually feigned, but needed to be expressed vaguely enough to keep the hu happy with her levels of admiration, all while hoping he hadn't noticed that other than his direct summons, she was doing her best to not be around him at all.

Then the question was, where to be. Fepa had not yet granted her access, Xelle did not want to set a precedent by working in the open library, and even with the ability to check out something to read or do, Xelle's assigned room was not a haven. It was rather . . . crappy. Tiny, no character, far from the nearest washroom, and not very high up the Tower.

For a Tower of enchantment, she was feeling a bit sour with old Avail.

Maybe she shouldn't. She knew how strict Tower guidelines were—at any Tower but no less here—and how much the order depended on assurance they were unwavering. Maybe she wasn't appreciating the gift he'd handed her.

But no. See. That was always her issue. Bladed gifts with a ribbon of groveling from the Mage Shop. This time delivered through a lingering inner belief that she probably prevented some really awful things from happening, both at To'Arc, and to the dragons, with unknown risks to the populace. Avail was the flame-tossed Crown Mage. Make your own rules. Anyway.

At least her room was solo (Fira, just the thought of it), and if she peered through the old leaded glass, she could see the vast high-rim forest (over a service shed) and see the little anima running around, and that made her happy. Missing the peace of her nightgarden already after a first week that felt like a month, at least she had a place sort of her own here, as she tried to remind herself in those moments when she felt as invisible as she was empty.

And yeah, invisible. Not what she'd expected at all. Unlike the crowds of whisperers and admirers alike that had watched her leave To'Arc, mostly, she found, pers here avoided her. Mages avoided her as much as they avoided anyone outside their circles, really. And the Studies were either afraid of her connections to dragons, perceived failure, the Amberborn network rumors (or whatever this really meant as surely the Ever Spire would never shelter someone they believed to be harmful), or Mage Fepa. Who knew. And without classes or a lab or appropriate social events (being neither a Study nor Mage), there wasn't much chance to make friends.

And so she was immediately grateful, like expecting a cold towel and finding a warmed one, to see someone she clearly recognized in the hallway, and to chase her down in hopefully what was not an awful way.

"Rayn?" she called forward.

Rayn turned around, cocked her head a long moment, and then

smiled warmly. “Vroomfriend! The paths wind heartward,” she said. “It’s good to see you.” Rayn glanced at where Xelle might wear insignia, but seemed too polite to ask.

“I’m an Apprentice,” she explained. “To Mage Fepa. And . . . I suppose we have some catching up to do.”

“Apprentice? Party Fepa?” Her eyes widened. “You’re the dragon—”

“Dragonfriend works for me.” Xelle wasn’t sure what people were calling her, and wasn’t yet ready for that conversation. “Or Xelle. It’s my name. But you know that. Or, maybe you don’t remember. I mean, it was just a few hours. That we talked, I mean. And I’m Xeleanor Du’Tam, she or e, that’s Xelle. And yes. It’s me.” She lifted her arms in a humorously exaggerated shrug, then lowered them when Rayn did not react. She had no idea why she was getting so arm-talky lately.

“So wait . . .” Rayn, her mouth suspended in place, seemed to be working through something. “That means you’re here now. Not Arc? What are . . .” Rayn jostled her sewn turban a touch, as if stirring her crownhair beneath. “This falls rather awkward, but I have a really important meeting and I—” She pointed. “Um. Meet me in the Study kitchen? A ring after dinner hour? Don’t eat. Or, do. Just, it’s less crowded then. I’ll cook something from home and we can talk. If you’d like?”

As Xelle nodded at the departing Study, she did have a moment of wondering whether someone would generically have an important meeting the moment she saw Xelle, but then, she’d invited her to dinner, so, anyway.

She was overthinking it. Rayn didn’t seem bothered. And Rayn had been walking quickly, and Xelle had stopped her. Also, why would she lie when she could just go on her way. Then Xelle felt bad for thinking it. Fira, when was the last time she’d talked to a hu?

And that evening, she did not eat, also curious what someone from Sharre would cook from home, as she had no idea, and peeked her way into the Study kitchen. The long, narrow room brought back a wave of déjà-vu that of course was not; it had just been so long and any memories here so faded. They hadn't updated the room in the last decade, either.

To her left stretched a long row of cabinets atop a counter with sinks and various cooking devices with a few pers wrapping up for the night. To her right, a dotting of small tables, mostly empty. From one, Rayn stood and walked toward Xelle, who realized she was holding out the decorative tin of spices. Ugh, she looked like she was presenting a gift of chocolates or something. But she didn't want the spices to spill so she just wiggled it in front of her a bit.

"No need to use these, but I got this spice sampler from Old Vattam. In case you'd like to use any."

Rayn gave her a skeptical squint, then relaxed, letting out a large sigh. "You really don't know. Fine." She reached for the tin.

"Sorry?" Xelle asked.

She waved off the implied question. "Let's say I know a lot about spices, and it would be a lovely conversation for another day. May I?" She gestured again to the tin.

Xelle had no idea what that was about, but she held out the sweetly painted container. Rayn did not take it, but opened it up, licked her finger, and stuck it one at a time into each small section, her eyes focused upward as she tasted each spice. "Funny," she said. "But this one would go perfectly with what I was going to make. Won't take much, at this strength." She took the tin from Xelle and walked it over to the counter, where she already had a couple of brightly painted bowls set up.

One held a soft dough that Rayn rolled out into columns and then pressed into small but charming shapes, only using a simple blade, but with skill as though she were a fine chef. As these rested, she mixed into the other bowl a blend of brown pastes and spices. Not a blacksauce, but seemingly a similar idea. With a grin, she finished with a pinch of the selected Old Vattam spice.

Xelle watched with interest as the sauce went into a warming pan and Rayn washed out both bowls. Evenly tapping the counter twice,

Rayn poured two glasses of water and took them to sit at a small adjacent table.

"And your path has wandered here," she said, before taking a long drink.

Path. Generous. "More like I impulsively decided and then stuck with it." She wasn't sure why Rayn chortled, but she continued. "Yes. I'm the dragonfriend." Xelle suddenly remembered she'd met Rayn just after receiving the sigil, but before knowing its meaning. Had Rayn commented on it then? She couldn't remember. "I'd just met one on my way to To'Breath. When we met. In the vroom." Rayn would know when they met; it was the only time they'd talked, before this. Except in the hallway. Anyway. Xelle sat across from her at the table.

"You did seem preoccupied," Rayn noted without much expression.

Xelle let that pass. "There are hu trying to reach the dragons for some reason. And the only thing I know about the reason is it's not a good one." Xelle was not ready to talk about how she knew that. The idea that someone covered her face, tried to take her somewhere without consent—probably do the same to a dragon—she'd not told anyone about those details. Her heart raced now, thinking about them. And when she did, she always felt the coarse burlap brushing over her lips, a feeling she was starting to realize she might never erase. She couldn't keep thinking about this now.

Rayn's face remained placid. No eyebrow. No questions. Xelle let that calm her, continuing as though just thinking about what to say. She tried not to stumble over her words. "The dragons have left where they were, for safety. Unhappily. And trusting me. The one who brought me back was protecting me, just getting me home." Her already-agitated heart pinged at calling To'Arc home so easily, and her next words spilled out a bit quickly. "And so I'm trying to figure out who these hu are, what they want, and what it has to do with the magesphere. While I can't really take on the magesphere, I just . . . can't rest . . . until I've sorted things with the dragons." This was all very honest. She'd said a lot.

"So you've arrived here to save all of us from something." The words weren't sarcastically spoken, at least.

"Sure." Xelle suddenly felt tired.

Seeming to note it, Rayn got up and uncorked a bottle, pouring one glass full and tipping a drop into a second. "If you'd enjoy," she said, setting them down and pulling the full glass toward herself. "No pressure if you don't drink wine; it's Sharre tradition to wet the glasses." Rayn looked uncomfortable as she said this, but Xelle had her own churning feelings about the idea of home, so she didn't want to press. "Otherwise, I'll set it back." Rayn motioned to the counter.

Not sure what to say, Xelle instead smelled the wine—it looked like wine, though it didn't really have much scent, which was unusual. She held the glass forward to allow Rayn to fill it and then hoped Rayn didn't think that she'd been testing it first, like seeing if it smelled proper. Moving to taste it and trying to look enthusiastic to do so (whatever that meant!), she found a light, welcome acidity. Like drinking the first light of morning. Finding that a rather poetic compliment that might save the moment, she repeated it aloud.

Rayn beamed. "Been keeping it for something special. It's from incity."

Pers out this way never referred to Sharre, Rayn's outward Charm Region hometown, as a city, reserving the term for Mytil, Vattam, and Wehj, (or Satta but only if one lived there), yet Xelle was fairly sure that's where she meant.

"It's really wonderful," Xelle confirmed. "Anyway, yes, so I arrived here, thinking things had just become . . . too much . . . at To'Arc, and your Crown Mage practically met me at the door, letting me know I'd be Apprenticed to Fepa. I'm still gathering myself a bit, but I plan to feel out whether I can continue my Arc practice in the open, determine what Ever magic I'd like to learn, and start combing the libraries."

She was glad Rayn did not ask her what she was combing the libraries for. Instead, she rose again, gently rolling the small dumplings down into the sauce, and giving the whole mix an artistic stir before tapping the spoon and returning it to its rest. She refilled her glass and sat back down. "We tend to drink more before dinner than with," she said with a shrug. "Like to let meals simmer. Unless the wrong sarent shows up, and then suddenly it's sat enough."

"A 'quick pickle guest', Na Vuia called it. My parent. Vuia, Lleyx, and Foose. I call them the Nas. I was just there."

"Your niblings?" Rayn inquired.

Xelle knew she must have broken into an uncharacteristically gratuitous smile, and it was nice for Rayn to remember about them. "Perfect. Well, and perfect." She sighed. "They were harder to leave than my Firana poster."

Rayn scooted in, wiggling the glass as though it was part of her hand. "You have a Firana poster? I grew up with one on my door. My ren took it down before I'd caught the moveroom."

"Ceiling," Xelle said. "The limited metal one. Still there. Credit to Na Lleyx's sewing room and the lack of need to look up."

"Vicious." Rayn nodded in admiration.

A sleepwear-clad Study, who'd just pulled what looked like a wrapped sandwich from the cooler, goggled as xe walked past. "That smells so good."

"Spices," Rayn called over. "Worth a try!" She turned back to Xelle. "So, Apprentice Xeleanor Du'Tam, Dragonfriend and Admi of Firana, Stalker of Night. You're on your way to Halina?"

Hardly. "I'll try it out for a while. The Apprentice thing. Go from there."

Rayn nodded, nearly sagely. "I'm glad to have caught you."

Her chest pinched. *Caught?* How was this catching? Unless . . . Was she about to lose her one friend here? Two hours would be a record even for Xelle.

"Yeah," Rayn said, glancing over at her, "I'm practically en route to Grand. Been campaigning for a Study exchange to wrap up my project, prior to pledging." She took a long drink.

Xelle's heart raced at the implication as much as the news, and she needed not to upset Rayn by letting that on. She'd learned to mask when her mind did such things, as pers tended to perceive it was about them.

So Rayn was about to become a Mage. Of course, she was, but . . . Not now. Also, she was leaving. But also, coming back soon. Study exchanges could be a fortnight, maybe a month?

And To'Grand, at that. Xelle had never been there, and she knew they were particularly fussy about visitors. "They're fussy about visitors, I've heard."

"Very much so," Rayn confirmed. "It's why I've decided to go as a Study, much harder to turn me away. And since I got Ever to hold off on my pledging, they tacked on a list of tasks. Nothing scandalous, just sneaky Tower stuff. I'll be gone six months, and back by the end of the year, to pledge."

Six months? Not outrageous for an exchange, but after Xelle's endless first week, it felt like forever, and Xelle set aside her fleeting hope of having a friend here entirely, trying to distract from the loss with a long sip from her glass.

Rayn seemed excited about traveling to To'Grand, and so Xelle let the conversation wander to that, as Rayn told her all that she'd learned and hoped to experience while there. In turn, as Xelle had learned some of the history of Grand Mages in her weeks at To'Breath, she shared what might be helpful to Rayn, which Rayn drank in with great interest, before rising to serve the dumplings, along with a refill of wine.

The dinner was as perfect as any that she'd had. She worried when she'd forgot Rayn was there and swiped her finger around the last of the sauce and stuck it into her mouth like a hoarded sweet. But then she remembered Rayn sticking her licked finger into Xelle's spices so she went in for another swipe. It really was that good.

Rayn looked entirely complimented and held out her bowl, as if Xelle might want to swipe it too. Too far! But they laughed, and Xelle helped her clean up.

The bottle was empty when Rayn yawned loudly. “Until next meet.”

“Until next meet,” Xelle repeated, and trudged up to bed.

04 - **ring ring**

Waking again never caused her room to grow in endearment. It wasn't as if there was anything *wrong* with the room, but she couldn't help but consider it a message from Avail that he did not love this entire arrangement. Well, she didn't love it either, and they would both need to get by. For now.

Xelle had not worn Kern's pendant since her arrival, but last night's dinner had at least kicked her into realizing she'd been slumping around all week, feeling lost, as in lost even from herself and her goals here. One of those depressions one doesn't notice until they realize the things they aren't doing. Xelle was still Xelle, was living in a Tower, and with Fepa finally signing her a pass, and hopefully running out of people to show her to, now had more time and some access.

She draped on the pendant.

Never having actually received a Mage call, she did not know how this worked. The locket wasn't enchanted, just an object of familiarity (a strong one; it had belonged to his late spouse), but did she need to wear the necklace longer to tune it in? She wasn't about to walk around the Tower with it, and have Spire Mage Kern Du'Arc pop up unexpectedly in the kitchen lobby. (Though that would cement her reputation here!)

Yeah, no. If she was going to leave it on a bit, she'd stay here. Without anything else to do in the awkwardly-shaped room, she gazed out of its unopenable little window, soon deciding no one would mind if she cast a wisp of Arc magic to at least clean the old thing off. Not dirt—she'd already wiped the inside—but to lessen the fog that had settled into the old, but by no means historically preservable, panes. Once done and her view clearer, she stood there, peering for birds, furry creatures, or anything other than the white, frozen ground and snow-covered trees. At least, with spring on its way, she would enjoy watching the forest emerge. She'd never had a view like this from Tam, out into the trees rather than just at their bases. Sure, she'd climbed the hills or sat atop the waterfall, but that took a hike. Here, she could look whenever she felt like it.

It started as a ringing in her ears.

She looked around, expecting wavering air, or an opening oval, like a floating painting, Kern's books neatly arrayed behind him. Her heart pinched at the thought; she wasn't really ready to see To'Arc right now, even just Kern's lofty little space, to which she held no affection.

The ringing continued to distract her, its impact elevating, and finally she tried thinking directly, *Yes, I'd like to talk to you.* Arc Magic ran, as though through her body, and into her dominant hand, and as if by instinct, she held it forward, willing a shape to emerge into view.

There he was, standing mid-air on an invisible floor and with no background to be seen, somehow fitting between the banged-up door and the shallow dresser in a way that would have felt very cramped in person. She looked ahead (not so far ahead) at Mage Kern, his cap tall and pointy, and his collar handsomely lined. He looked neither pleased nor distressed. Xelle wondered what he'd been through these weeks.

But, there he was. This was the time to ask.

Lowering her hand, she also bowed. He'd asked her to call him Kern, but that felt stranger now than it did then, so hopefully the bow would suffice.

"How does this work?" she asked. "Can you see me? Where I am?"

"I can see your room." He peered through, as he lowered his visage to appear standing on her floor. "I can also see you haven't won their favor, unless you're meeting me in a quaintly furnished closet."

They had not reached a joke place in their relationship.

"With advanced Arc instruction and practice," he went on after an awkward pause, "you would better control what is shown."

Yes, well she was here, with no ability to study Arc Magic except on her own without instruction, and he knew that.

"So how are things?" she asked, hoping it would convey how she felt about that. Also, she had no idea how this was supposed to work. Not the call, like, the scheming.

"Things are things," he answered. After a mutually unemotional gaze, he continued. "Meaning, the unrest has stabilized for now, but I don't have much to go on yet. Jehanne has announced a slight postponement in Ascension proceedings in order for her to resolve the sighting of a dragon at the Tower. More frankly, I presume, to take the chatter away from you and your supposed affiliation with the Amberborn. Jehanne is, as always, effective, and for now, the rumormongering seems to have slowed. Your escort here caused a great stir, and it seems the involved hu are laying low for a bit as well, to let that settle. Their plans will resume, I am sure." He shrugged. "They didn't go so far to give up now; I'm certain of that."

Xelle was still back on calling her delivery by dragon to the top of Arc Tower, then gliding descent down to the ice below, where she was dragged away by one of the lowest ranking Tower Mages, an 'escort'. That was quite a euphemism, even though she was glad he hadn't mentioned Helia.

Likewise, she suspected, the stir at To'Arc was more than simply stir. And as to the Hurts, it sounded like Kern was at least somewhat informed of their plans, unless he was speculating. She hoped it was the former. Kern's ability to make both groups think he was operating in their interest was key to anything they might be able to find out, together.

"Your relationship with . . ." She stopped herself from saying 'the Hurts'.

"My own." He spoke firmly.

Oddly, this reassured Xelle. If he was maintaining agency over his new . . . double-agency, it gave her more confidence he was stepping up. Something Jehanne had reminded her of, she'd since considered, was that Spire Mage Kern was not the sniveling flatcap they'd used him for. They'd taken advantage of his vulnerabilities, but he was where he was for reasons. Perhaps the Hurts would learn that, in time. Best for them if they stayed unaware for now.

Keeping all this to herself, Xelle nodded.

"Mages were sent into the mountains to learn what they could, based on your report," he continued.

The mention of Mages in the mountains made Xelle's heart pound, and for a moment, she worried. Would they approach the dragons directly? But, no, they wouldn't know where they'd gone. Kern meant to the place they'd been. The obsidian cliff, now covered in rubble, or perhaps rubble itself. Near the location of the machines, which she'd reported.

Xelle had told the Arc Spire much after her return. Where the dragons had been. That they'd left. That there had been machines, and ill-intended hu, and the shadow of strong magic. She'd said that there had been a large amount of obsidian, now covered by the dragons' last act before departing. And they'd all, by then, recognized her sigil.

She had left out three things. One, that she was linked to Thunder. (Maybe the sigil meant that but she hadn't confirmed it nor said which dragon.) Two, that she'd asked the dragons to leave. (This felt so complicated.) Three, that the hu had tried to capture her. (This had to have been relevant but she just . . . didn't want to say it.)

Kern seemed to realize she was distracted, and now he waited for her, albeit with a slightly impatient tilt to his otherwise impassive Spire Mage expression. Once she re-met his gaze, he continued. "Most of the area had been covered in the collapse, so there was little to find. At the end of the pathway leading up, large fuelstone machines had been abandoned."

That made sense; the machines were large and slow, and only not detected in the first place because no hu were there to notice them. "Was there magic? In the machines?" She remembered feeling that, but honestly the entire sequence of events had blurred greatly in her mind.

Except the feelings of the rough bag against her lips and of her shaking fingers gripping to the top of To'Arc. Those stayed clear.

By Kern's twitch of surprise at the question, she didn't think he was evading anything when he said no. He paused, then added, "One Mage insisted that a shadow of magic remained, but the others couldn't feel it. If you felt something there, the pers had taken it with them."

"The hu," she said, glad at the implication in his face that he seemed inclined to believe Xelle that magic *had* been in use.

Kern cocked his head. "Someone."

Xelle was going to have to watch what she said. She doubted she'd suddenly develop a new personality for totally safe (as in non-objectionable) quick responses, nor did she want to. But, to herself, she tried to envision almost a physical block. Don't say things about dragons without considering them first. Especially with a mental link to the dragons. Whatever these 'calls' would be with Kern, and however solidly (meaning magically) Kern might be able to remember them—an idea she instinctively and suddenly realized was probably true—caution, then. If things went the way she wanted them to, she might find herself with thoughts that weren't hers to share.

"Though my memories have blurred, I am certain that I felt magic there, of some kind, and that the magic I felt was not created by or emanating from the dragons," she said, measuring her words. "And not of the seven prongs. Not as I know them, having formally studied three."

At this, Kern's eyes flared.

For once, she didn't think it was about her Tower hopping. "I was there," she reiterated, "and yes, I sensed magic beyond what I could understand. When the dragons flew away, and kept moving away, I did not sense that shadow with them. It was not with them, whatever it was."

Kern nodded slowly. "The report concludes the machines were amagical in nature. As you saw them directly, you will know what I would otherwise not reveal. Four machines. The 'plow' and moveroom were of expensive make, but otherwise seemed to fulfill the functions they purported. The other two were transports."

Dragon-sized transports. Xelle had immediately suspected they were meant to restrain a dragon, not (or not only) to haul obsidian or anything else.

But she had just reminded herself not to offer dragon facts without consideration, and so she let the thought hang. Anyway, the Mages who went there—they'd have to have seen that too.

"The machines were dismantled and melted," Kern said.

Oh. She didn't know if that was good, or bad. She remembered the strength with which they moved. The force. "The fuelstones?" she asked.

"Fragmented. Against code."

There. So those huge fuelstones were not just of immense power and cost, they were forbidden. And already destroyed? Again, too much to parse while being watched by a Spire Mage. Xelle didn't even know there was a limit to fuelstone size (if that was the reason), but then, when would such a thing come up? Kern still watched, apprizing her. He didn't seem to have anything else to say, but he also did not disconnect. Then, she supposed, it was her turn.

"I just arrived here, at To'Ever," Xelle said. "Was with my family a bit. In the forest; you know where I'm from. I haven't had time to decide my approach, and so I have nothing else to pass along at this time." Realizing that might sound flippant or disrespectful of his own time, she hastily added, "I hadn't done this before. I wanted to make sure we could connect, that you knew I was here. And could pass along anything I might need." If she did get back to To'Arc, she was going to have to learn how to do this herself.

But now, that was not her priority. Reaching the dragons was. And that required her nightgarden.

"Fine." His tone had tensed. "Is there anything else?" he asked, glancing to his side as if perhaps there was a sound at the door she could not see.

Right now? No. *Oh!* One thing. "If I need to talk, how can I let you know?" Kern could reach out to her whenever she was wearing the locket, but she knew of no way to signal back.

For a moment, he looked openly annoyed, like a professor who'd just been given an absurd excuse for the incompletion of work. "If you're going to run around Alyssia playing Arc Mage, I suggest you figure that out." And with a flash of the Arc, and no time for Xelle to return it, the image blinked out.

"Flame-turned Fira," she said aloud, hoping he could hear it. And set that locket right back in its drawer. Now, another thing to do.

Except, no. She would get to that later. And if Mage Kern didn't want her sending singing messengers to To'Arc on his behalf, that was on him. This was not her priority, she repeated.

Xelle always had a swarm of thoughts and tasks in her mind; it was never possible to simply focus. But she knew her best way to make progress, in cases when possible, was to confirm to herself that nothing else was more important that a single task (or maybe two) and that way she could worry less that there was something else lagging behind. At least until she'd completed that task. Something like that. And now, she set a clear priority.

She had to get her inkblooms to grow.

Tenne's Da had finally called him, and it had been as awkward as flame.

Da flipped between talking like a worried nurse hovering over a just-awakened patient, sternly putting on his 'Arc Spire Mage Kern' voice, and acting like they were arranging to meet at the bar for some knockball. And since Da clearly wasn't going to tell him anything, Tenne decided he was a grown adult and cut the blah-blah talk off. "I want you to send me a Breath Mage," Tenne said, trying to imitate the Magey voice. "Someone we can trust."

"I have to know for what," Da had answered.

"So we're going to start sharing everything now?"

Da went silent. Maybe it was a rough hit, but honestly, Tenne was pissed. He was pissed, and embarrassed, and . . . Pissed.

That had ended the call basically right at that, leaving Tenne to his empty, guarded, room. Tenne had done what he'd always done. Returned to his art. For a few days, he sat around, working in his big loft room of the art gallery, wondering if Da was really going to leave him out like this.

Then, used to the dart-like casts of Arc Mages, it'd been super weird when he felt a random idea begin to settle in, right in the middle of a huge bite into a curry-laden mashed patty sandwich, that he should go open the secret door. And definitely not his own idea. Not being used to Breath Mages but definitely used to mageshit, he put down his sandwich and wiped his hands on his pants, cursing when he realized they were the white ones, and went to get the door.

The Mage had shrouded xyr face with a pretty cool-looking face veil, but Tenne got the vibe this per was, like, younger than he was. When Tenne explained what he needed, he thought he'd be given, like, a pouch of dust to throw at the gallery staff who would walk around in circles until he left, but the Mage said that would be 'turning the magic', and instead xe'd accompany Tenne through the offices.

At first, it wasn't even magic. They just stopped and started and peered around corners. Then kiddo-Mage had them sit behind a huge sofa, and they just sat there. Then Tenne started to feel tingly, but before he could ask about it, the Mage got up and made a hand-sign Tenne didn't know, but presumably meant 'pinch your lips and follow'. They walked past like, ten stewards, and no one noticed them, and then apparently the door was unlocked so they walked in.

"Move fast," was the instruction, and yeah, if Tenne was glowing with magic and might suddenly materialize in the middle of the offices with curry smears on his fancypants, he'd keep it snappy.

Tenne didn't know if he expected the Mage, to like, wait outside? But the Mage hovered, staring at him. Fira.

Shit, he didn't know how any of this worked. He moved over and whispered, "It'll go faster if you help. Where do you think they'd keep the–" He'd almost said the scoring, but maybe less information was better. "The records about the Prize."

The Mage, face still covered, moved over to a large wooden cabinet and pointed at a drawer labeled "E'lle Prize" in gold paint.

He opened it.

Five canvas rolls sat inside, each marked with the year of award. They'd done this more than five times, but maybe they moved them off to a dungeon somewhere. Dungeon of Doom, Tenne thought in a funny voice, laughing a bit. Either way, the Mage had gone back to standing near the door, and Tenne was hit with a blast of nerves. He gassed as he picked up the current year's volume. "Be blessed," he encanted.

A veiled Mage couldn't really shoot you a *look*, but the sharply turned head indicated he wasn't supposed to be talking in here. Or, uh, gassing. Right.

There was no seal on the bundle, just a fancy ribbon thingie that wound around it. So, he untied it, setting the ribbon to the side.

Tenne was shocked by the number of papers in the stack. It was just the applications, each with a lot of writing and numbers in different handwriting. No scoring or tally sheet, or final list or something. There were so many. He rummaged through them, trying to get a feel for what he was in for. Names, not just in Mytil, but from places he'd never heard of. Wait, Iyero was a real place? And where the ash was Feneil?

Then he saw the top sheet. Hu Tenne Cu'Arc, he – Winner. The old him. A kid of a Mage who didn't even have a home, because his only identity was a flame-crested Mage Tower, and wherever they'd been from before that wasn't important enough to mention.

Even Tenne knew his was not on top by coincidence, so maybe they'd been sorted by ranking. He hoped, with a blink of panic, they weren't random after that. This was a lot to sort through. Could he take them with him? They'd notice. And Da wasn't going to send a second Mage. He glanced up in worry, but the Mage seemed to be watching the door.

He pulled his sheet away. He didn't want to see. There was nothing on it anymore that would make this his.

Owi'neil Du'Hubo, he – ~~Finalist – Winner~~ – Disqualified

Hubo. Never heard of it; sounded like one of those mountain villages Da talked about. There was an address listed. In Mytil.

Tenne felt gross. He didn't want to see anything else. He put his sheet on top, rolled the cover back over and tied the ribbon, not as nicely but hopefully no one would notice, and set the bundle back in the drawer. Realizing the Mage was now over his shoulder, he stepped back as the Mage quickly removed the bundle, rewrapped it, and set it back, making it look the same as the others. Tenne felt another wave of magic, something going into the drawer. And then it was closed.

The Mage closed the door behind them with a click, and ushered Tenne to hurry. Again, they walked past stewards and clerks and a loudly complaining patron, and as they turned a corner, Tenne spun around, remembering to thank the Mage. "Hey, I—"

The Mage was already gone.

The address wasn't far. That bothered him; it felt bad. But at least he was used to sneaking out of art prison, so he felt pretty securely alone as he knocked on the inside door.

A hu opened it. He was tall. Tenne noticed this, because pers were rarely taller than him. "Owi'neil Du'Hubo?"

The hu squinted. "Something like that. Call me Owin. I know who you are," he rushed out. Then, he halfheartedly bowed. "Bon, to what do I owe this privilege?"

"You were supposed to win the art prize. Someone jacked it for me, and I don't know why."

Owin stared at him a long moment. A really long moment.

And slammed the door.

05 - *The Trials of Social Activity When No One is Like You*

Whatever strange arrangement she had here, this was still a Tower of Alyssia, and that came with a culture of relationships as much as regulations. She'd already resolved to follow process when she could, but she quickly realized her stay would be more *comfortable* if she made some effort to fit in socially. Not as in conform, but as in being friendly and acting like she lived here. Respecting Tower custom. Being known enough to receive more than tight grimaces in the hallways. Something like that.

Yet all this Tower's structures for socialization revolved around what you *were*, even more than at the somewhat more casual Arc Tower. Sure, anyone could interact in the village, but it was in the Tower where she needed contacts and ease. Staff functions were not to be attended by non-staff, unless invited as a guest. Many casters had personal relationships—friendships and family and such—with staff, but primarily via private gatherings: friends getting together, friends she did not have. Xelle could not attend Study functions, even as a guest; their limitation to Studies provided ease of mind of not having to behave around those of higher rank. And especially with Fepa show-and-telling her to anyone he could find, the only type of Mage events she could find herself in would be ones of extraordinary misery.

The Atrium was a place of solitude, the library a place of quiet, and food and drink were taken with friends; there was no equivalent of a village coffee shop in a Tower. (There should be!)

After wandering the Tower for options, she could only find one reasonable place to attempt some form of socializing, and it was the large first-floor room, off of the Atrium, simply known as the Lounge.

There was a Study Lounge on the second floor, but the otherwise undesignated Lounge allowed for teachers and students to meet outside of a classroom, or for visiting family to gather, or to host something like a game night that wouldn't disrupt anyone's concentration in the larger, more dedicated spaces, or smaller, more private ones.

Yet, after a couple of visits spent reading a fiction book and lifting her gaze if new pers walked in, she realized this was not going to work at all. First, pers weren't going to interrupt someone reading, especially one weirdly peering over the top of the book. Second, the designations of rank did not lower in this shared space. Studies gave her berth, and Mages invisibility. Third, she realized from some side glances that sitting alone in the Lounge was considered . . . odd. There were quieter and prettier places to relax.

One distinguishing feature of the spacious room was a broad window that opened to a clearing, with tall, unsegmented panels of thin, clear glass. Unusual not just for the large unobstructed panes, but also because most Ever Tower windows either looked directly at the forest, or into a garden. Keeping in mind, gardens at Ever Tower felt more like arboretums, or hedged walkways from a storytale, so for any view out to a clear-ish area, this was the place.

Yet there wasn't much to look at, even now with the snow mostly melted. With spring finally underway on the high rim, there was ground cover, squirrels, and a flurry of new bird activity in the trees beyond. Knowing not to trifle with squirrels, and with not much of a story behind staring at ground cover from a distance, Xelle checked out a set of binoculars and turned her Lounge visits into some sort of bird project, marking off and making notes about birds in an oversized, color-printed book she'd found in the village.

The first per to approach her was someone's parent, as she was quick to explain, as her adult cura, a new Study, hovered behind.

Xelle did not love this, but apparently the family was from a mountain village, incredibly excited to see the Tower for the first time, and not tuned into rank or status.

"Are you a bird-watcher?" she asked, taking the seat on the opposite side of the small table.

Ah, Xelle did love the seaward Ever Region. Where a per *did not sit next to you* if one could sit *near* you. "I was inspired by this window and clearing." She pointed. "It's been something to cheer me, as I'm new here and don't know many pers."

"Oh!" The young Study's parent poked him. "Do you know this Study? You could be friends."

"Ma," he muttered, glancing around uncomfortably. Not really wanting to get into her awkward Apprenticeship or parentally-poked friendship, Xelle hurriedly pushed over the book. "Here. You can mark in it, if you'd like."

"Just me?" he asked, stiltedly.

Great, she'd made it weirder. Wiggling to recover, she tried the first thing that came to mind. "Oh, no, I've been planning on setting it out here. We can all . . . add to it."

"Oh, that's pretty cool," he said. "Hi, I'm He'milo." His parent had already introduced him with he, but had simply called him "my cura".

He looked so young. A teenager, she felt sure. And Xelle had the feeling his own lack of adding "Study" or a placename was a sign of discomfort with her own status. Maybe with her age as well. She didn't push it.

"I'm Xelle. And yeah, let's make a cool catalogue."

"Oh, I'm so glad you have a friend!" He'milo's Ma interjected.

With the look the two exchanged, Xelle did not see them becoming friends, but she was glad for the kind smile. "I'm sure we'll get along fine," Xelle reassured her, throwing a knowing twitch of her nose to the teen.

A few more days passed, and the one new Study was still her primary interaction. Xelle sat, alone, staring out of the broad window.

Friends just weren't happening here. Her position held too much baggage. Or, the rumors about her. Surely all of it.

And the Studies were so young. Again, she could have friends at any age; she felt just as at ease with her niblings or with Old Ga (he went by that!) at the waterfall as anyone else. But there were commonalities pers of similar age shared, especially when one felt lonely. Experiences, and tiredness. And—these Studies felt so young.

She set a hand on the soft paper of the wide book, glad to see a few more markings on the open page, in another new handwriting. At least the bird book gave her a small connection. And a way to spread joy. For now, she'd take it.

It was going to have to happen. Why she hadn't thought about it, she didn't know. An intentional block, perhaps. A defense. But of course, not everyone here was younger.

"Xelle? It really is you!"

She turned to face a young Mage, smiling nervously. Why was xe nervous?

"Styli," Xelle said by rote. Realizing what she'd said, she now remembered. When she'd studied here, a decade ago, she and Styli had worked together in a lab. Styli had been from a village near Tam; she couldn't quite remember which one, just that at the time it'd been the sole reason they'd decided to work together. "She?" Xelle confirmed.

Styli nodded, yet her expression felt off.

Xelle scanned the hu quickly. Robes. A fuller face. A jeweled cap, one she'd never imagine on her fellow forester Study. *Oh. Fira.* Then, Xelle realized by her insignia, she wasn't even a *new* Mage.

"Mage Styli, forgive me the omission. I was caught off-guard. It's been—" Xelle realized she'd been about to ramble what a strange year it had been, but the Mage still didn't look comfortable.

"No, no," Styli assured, waving her off. "Don't worry about that. It's good to see you."

One thing they had been was decent friends. While she suspected that was not going to resume, she at least decided this conversation, not initiated by Xelle, could help get a few things out to the Tower before they parted ways.

"Thank you; so good to see you too!" Xelle said. "And congratulations; this is where I always saw you." Meaning as an Ever Mage. Not the hallway. And . . . in the far future, which apparently, was . . . now.

"Oh, yes, well, thank you." Styli's face warmed, the way Xelle just now remembered. Her smile was beautiful. And from a past that Xeleanor Du'Tam had left. She'd left it, she remembered. This wasn't on Styli.

The smile didn't last. "A lot is said about you," Styli said.

Well, then, enough for pleasantries.

"I am the dragonfriend, that's true," she started, watching Styli's eyes widen. "But I am not Amberborn, nor would I ever work against the interests of Alyssia."

Styli's warmth fully vanished, and now, Xelle saw not her forest-born friend, but an Ever Mage, holding that trained expression of no expression.

"It isn't Alyssia they say you work against. It's the magesphere."

Ash. This. And Xelle should not have to defend herself, without warning, stopped for prodding by someone who masked it as cheer. A little break snapped somewhere in her mind, and whatever this friend had been returned, now, to an abandoned past. "I work against none of us. Not the magesphere. Not the populace. Not Alyssia. My connection to the dragons was not sought after, nor did I understand it then. I am now riding the currents without portage. You will believe me, or you will not."

Styli's face was nearly a sneer, but perhaps without intent. "Who are you now?" she asked.

"I am Xeleanor Du'Tam. As I always was and always will be. And I could use some help, for the days I am here."

"Help with what?" Still, no expression.

In this moment, Xelle understood something she'd not understood before. Perhaps this was a thing that came with age, one of those things the teenage bird-watchers could not yet understand. About friendship. About family. That they were treasures. They were specific. They were forged. They were solid. The rest was something else. And Xelle was no longer a youth; she could respond and move forward.

Xelle measured her words. "I would like to be admitted to attend some Ever classes, without disruption. I give you my word, as a forestper, I am a protector." The word felt inadequate. Protect what? Protect good? Protect harm? But it was all she could think to say. No, not all. "And also, then, if you hear words against me, whisper a counterpoint. Whisper doubt, if you won't defend. When will the river carry a liar?" she asked.

Styli straightened. "It was good to see you, Xeleanor Du'Tam. I'm grateful that our paths crossed again." She bowed.

"Mage Styli Du'Ever," Xelle returned, with a deeper bow. "The needles fall thickest on the path to home."

The Mage said nothing else, but walked away.

And Xelle knew, they would not speak again.

Xelle found some comfort in music. Music was the sort of thing Xelle would forget to return to, yet when she did could not understand why she'd let it go.

In this case, she had a Study to thank. A young hu from Wehj, named Ebbia, who tried to make conversation with Xelle on her visits to the bird book. The stout young study wore elaborate, metal-accented headwraps over simple robes, which drew the eye to her face, which always felt warm even when unsmiling. Sometimes Xelle worried that the friendly Study was only talking to her out of an obligation to the lonely bird-hu dragonfriend Apprentice of dubious reputation, and other times Xelle was simply grateful that she did. Yet there was never a full sense of comfort. Finally, Xelle just asked.

"You don't need to talk to me only to be kind, though I appreciate it. I know my presence here is awkward."

"It is," Ebbia agreed. "I just know what it's like when no one else is like you."

Xelle was not going to pry, but Ebbia continued. "I'm from a supply town. It's nice. As a kid, my family, my friends, my classmates—everyone worked iron, and watched magipuck, and played magipuck, and raced carts. I tried to tell them, about wanting to learn magic, and they always laughed. Not at me. With me. They thought it was a joke."

For some reason, the idea returned to Xelle that her own parent had studied magic and never told her. That was different, and she wouldn't have raised it here.

"What did you do? To distract?"

Ebbia looked up. "Found things that were more easily shared. Like . . . " She held her mouth open in thought. "Like music. I learned that even very different pers can listen to music together, at least the public kind. And there's no conversation, no tripwire to misunderstanding or offense, or whatever else." She waited a moment, as if Xelle were supposed to ask something.

Xelle's mind spun, was there something about Wehj? Or a supply town? A type of music?

"There are concerts here, in the second-floor auditorium. Anyone who lives in the Tower can go—Studies, Mages, staff. You."

"Oh," she said, ignoring that. "How do I look them up?"

Ebbia walked her to the Front Desk, and showed how to request the schedule. Feeling overwhelmed at the clerk staring at her, she pointed to the one that first caught her eye. A brass band. Of Mages. She noted the day and time, and thanked the clerk. When she turned to thank the Study, she was already gone.

About that. While Xelle had meant what she said to Ebbia, about not needing to talk to her out of kindness alone, she still felt a rather painful drop of spirit when she realized the Study no longer visited when Xelle was there, and with her, the last others dwindled away. If Xelle was near the book, the Studies would wait.

While she was proud of the project she'd started and the joy it seemed to generate, Xelle spent less time around the book herself, to the point of nearly none. Instead, she glanced in happily as she saw a growing group gathered around the book, smiles on their young faces.

And, each week, she went to listen to the brass band. They were talented, and explored the range of their ensemble, including breaking to insert spoken word, including humor. As Ebbia had said, there, Xelle could listen not totally alone, but with others, together. Yet, no one looked her way. There, she could immerse. Forget. Almost.

Though she always found a spot in the back, where she could sit more freely, whatever chair was next to her always felt a specific, weighted emptiness. A cutout, of where she wished Ay'tea would have been.

He would have loved the music. She would have held his hand, now, without caution or shame. If he would have liked it. Whatever the nature of their friendship, certainly they could have held hands. They would have shared expressions, winked at the better jokes. Tapped fingers to the euphonious sounds that echoed in the acoustically deft space. He would have smiled. The emptiness would have felt full.

Xelle had to move on.

06 - Vessel, Thawed in Spring

She'd forgotten how cool spring was at To'Ever. She'd get used to it if she stayed, year by year, she knew, but this first reminder had her wearing the fuzzy poncho a little longer than she'd like her Na to know.

Two months of Tower bird-watching had warmed the ground and trees and brought a stencilbrush of deeply rich colors to the greens of the Ever Forest, but it had not, in any way, warmed her relationship with Mage Fepa.

He had, at least, continued to give her not *quite* library access, but a variety of temporary passes into specific sections including those only normally accessible by Mages. She had to be strategic about her requests, not wanting to make her focus decipherable. While getting into unauthorized Arc magic and rekindling dragon relations, she *really* didn't need Mage Fepa (or especially a librarian) questioning her business.

One thing Xelle had learned about during this past year was navigating libraries, and so, trying not to fret as each week clicked by, she visited the stacks like a nectarbird, in and out of sections, searching for the right flower.

In this case, an inkbloom. The phyta and its luminous blossoms were so sacred at To'Arc that you couldn't even find mentions of them in the Study sections of the library. (Surely there were books somewhere, but probably only available to advanced Mages.) Here at Ever and not under the watchful eyes of Arc Mages, she'd just hoped perhaps something might be let to slip.

On that subject, she was concerned about losing her edge in Arc Magic, and so she'd also dedicated several hours a day uniquely to its study. For a while, she'd been cramped in that little bedroom, hoping with the rules for an Apprentice unclear anyway, she'd get away with some practice. But now, with warmth striping the air, she traveled back into the forest, practicing in what she hoped was solitude. Hu-solitude, anyway.

She was shocked by how well these efforts proceeded. With ample resources, surrounded by rich green and the chorus of anima and phyta, and without the stress of assignments or errands or, well, friends, e was able to learn much and deeply.

Eir efforts felt nonsubstantive during each session, but a week here or there, and e'd consider eir progress with immense satisfaction.

Yet she was not going to spend time at Ever Tower without taking the opportunity to learn a more solid foundation in the ways of protection, and so, with what Xelle believed to be a quiet assist from Mage Styli, she convinced a few instructors to let her sit in on advanced classes, provided she stayed in the back and did not cast along with the Studies.

That was the hardest part, to her surprise. It seemed Xelle would be conditioned now to being a strange, unknown, presence in a room of Studies who nodded and tried to convey some warmth, but tried not to get associated with the odd Apprentice.

Yet, when the Mage and Studies cast together, it felt like a dance. E found emself watching with nearly visceral longing as the group studied and swayed in similar patterns, yearning to join them, even to walk the room and guide the motions of those struggling. To be part of an energy greater than emself.

Xelle could not. It had been a condition of her attendance. And so she stared, intently, trying to keep her eyes on the instructor, trying to keep some semblance of the demonstration smooth in the static of her mind.

She took notes, sure, but for Xelle, notes were a (necessary) way not to forget points of importance. Quantities, dates, names, or references. They were not a way to learn. She thought, again, of the brass band, of her own horn nestled in the Nas' attic. She hadn't learned to play by writing notes about the way one played. She'd learned by making music. By an instructor, in her case a neighbor, showing Xelle his technique, and then playing immediately herself, feeling the way to make the sounds flow not even in a similar manner, but building on that insight to play in Xelle's own manner.

Like the countermelodies she adored, casts of magic were the counterfabric of the world, yet to stitch one seamlessly required individual spirit, even in ensemble.

She realized she was drawing music notes on her notebook, and set her pencil down. Another thing. It was hard to follow a class where she couldn't interact. She'd be off on a daypath about brass instruments and the meaning of life, and . . . She was doing it again.

And again, the class would begin a cast. Again, they'd gasp as the reagent they used absorbed and the whole world changed, as even a small prickle of magic felt when you were in the midst of it. Xelle watched. And did not cast. And picked up her pencil again, turning it in her twitching fingers.

And so, after each morning's classes, she'd be practically burning to try what she'd seen, to remember the nuances of the Mage's motions and measures, the length of time of each step, the lilt of transition between them.

This required not just practice, but practice while it was still fresh-ish (sigh) in her mind, and so, she'd hurry to the forest, with hastily packed snacks in her bag. And there, for the first several hours, she'd ensure she'd moved through all her Ever practice before resuming her work with Arc.

Switching prongs at first was difficult, almost like stretching a limb a way it wasn't used to going. Yet, she quickly realized, it was not a *wrong* way, and so day after day in practice, she honed her skills. In both Ever and then in Arc.

Day after day of practice alone had also made her listless. Without a lab, she decided taking on a dedicated project might keep her motivated. And the thing was, Xelle had really liked having a good cloak. The cloak she'd borrowed from Na Lleyx was certainly distinctive, and the one she'd bought from Jaynel's was, well, actually famous (and hanging back in her nightgarden cabinet), so she decided she had time to prepare for next winter over the summer, and also try her hand at Mage-level enchantment. Whatever they called her here. "Apprenticenchantment," she said to a squirrel, who rolled aer eyes and bailed.

Using the pouch of coins Na Vuia had slipped into her pocket on the way out (thus far only dented by the bird book), she found a tailor in Vi'Ever with a style that she liked, and commissioned from him a cloak built exactly to her specifications.

With the masterpiece in hand (it was so good!), she began plotting out a plan to enchant it. Enchantments, of course, grew complicated quickly, and she'd not really heard of pers using them on something as fragile as cloth, and so she was taking small steps. Reading volumes on what she'd hoped to do, asking casual questions at events or around the village taverns— Despite the slow progress, thinking about working the next steps was what kept her at her morning classes, then her daily Ever practice, then some planning for her cloak, and then her daily Arc practice, and then occasionally checking by the bird book in the evening since that was somehow now her thing, and then getting to the library after dinner when it was less crowded.

And every night, before bed, she sent a message to Thunder. That she was working to help zhem return. That she would see zhem. There was never a response, not even a sensation. But the connection remained. It stayed with her now, all the time, like breathing.

This was a lot to balance, as the days turned into weeks, the routine always the same.

Yet, somehow, on all this, the one thing she didn't have to balance was being an Apprentice. Once he'd run out of pers to impress with her presence, the Mage had no use for her, no tasks. She'd ignore him completely unless she needed his access or passes or occasional other favors. Each time, she wondered if this was the moment when he'd stop and ask why she was here, or why he should do anything for her.

But Xelle consistently told him what an honor it was to learn from him, he'd tell her it certainly was, she'd get what she'd been looking for, and then she'd leave as quickly as possible.

And on the rare occasions someone new was around and he summoned her by, he bragged about her even more aggressively. No, not by name, but that the Tower was asking him to mentor particularly gifted and important Studies with distinctive affiliations. Visiting dignitaries of various sorts would gasp, "Is she *that one*?" and he would nod, his lip curled.

She knew in a lot of ways, she had it good, but Fira, this was not going to be a permanent arrangement.

That said, things were not going back to what they were.

Whatever path out of this Xelle would find, and whether or not the dragonfriend would ever fade from the minds of the magesphere, the dragons most certainly had not. They were talked about constantly now, here at least. In whispers inside the Tower, and loudly in the village. Discerned from the chatter in Vi'Ever, pers were now constantly hiking up, looking for dragon sightings or relics of some kind.

The magesphere had done well with the repellants of superstition and lore, so Xelle figured there must be discussions in the Spires, certainly here and at Arc. Yet, these casual hikers and thrill seekers would not reach the dragons, who remained far from amagic reach. As for magic reach, one would likely need to know where they were. And, Xelle, to her knowledge, was the only one who knew that information.

And, that, she was not telling.

Which, then, was why: Inkblooms took priority. Everything else, other decisions, next.

As summer class registration opened, she declined to enroll, at least for now, as she had plenty now to practice, a bit more time to do so, and the frustration of not finding anything to help her was enough to bear on top of watching classes she could not be in. So, now, she visited the library in the morning as well as the evening, searching again and again for any clue.

She found it in the take-bin.

The bin of old textbooks, not rare enough to be preserved, but too ragged to keep in circulation. Xelle had seen every use for these books, from Tower to Tower. Pages torn out and folded into holiday decorations, little paper birds still gleaming with crinkled illuminations. Books stacked and sealed with resin, to create step stools, tea tables, and bars. One creative Study at To'Frond had painstakingly cut out only the illustrations, and clearglued them to the walls of her room, in such a lovely fashion that when she'd pledged as Mage, they'd turned the room into a reservable reading nook.

Xelle wasn't even really searching here, she'd just stopped to shuffle through the stack, in case any were of artistic interest for "future projects". One of her drawers held a stack of such books already.

Phyta of Alyssia: Ga's Guide

As her sibling would have said, her first reaction to the withered tome was, "Who is this for?"

The text was far too detailed for entertainment. The size or layout wasn't designed to be viewed as art. It didn't contain the reagent information that would have interested a caster. So, then, a reference guide for the populace? But why would a scholar want a scientific guide to be presented with riddles and poems, from an apparently generic grandparent? She was intrigued by whatever backstory the lovely book held, even as she knew it was likely lost to time.

As she paged through the thick-papered volume, she saw a series of smudged notes. Cryptic references to reagents, and casts, measures and treatments, not just for one prong of magic, but for—

Trying not to appear too interested, she took it to the Mage on duty, flipping it a little in her hands. This would have absolutely have been incinerated at To'Arc, or dumped into a cellar. Even if what she'd seen turned out to be nothing, yeah, they'd never let it pass.

"This a Tower book?" she asked, in her best nonchalant tone.

"Ah, the well-loved charmer."

Hand it to a librarian. Xelle waited.

"Estate item. Populace title. Couldn't send it to the village with all the old casting notes, but couldn't bring myself to incinerate it either. Thought with all those pretty pictures, someone might use it for craft."

"Yeah, that's what I was thinking. It was just so unusual I wondered if it had a story."

"It surely did." The Mage smiled. "But the per who could have told us rose away, through Helina." She added a hand gesture that Xelle didn't know but was presumably about said Mage dying, and xyr . . . soul rising. Something.

The book fully and officially hers, she took it back to her room, bolted her door, and gazed down at a page about ninety percent through the book.

Inkbloom

The inkbloom (singular and plural due to its collective nature) is one of the most beautiful and elusive of flowers. There is little else that can be said.

Unlike the more elaborate and colorful illustrations, this one seemed to be done by someone who had never seen the phyta. A black and white outline, brushed over by a smear of watercolor blue. Then, underneath:

Gone too long
Gone too soon
Night, please take
In inkbloom

Next to that bizarre and unhelpful description, was written, barely legible as if someone had tried to rub it out:

Vessel, Thawed in Spring

Now, at least the other handwritten notes in the book, though clearly written to be referenced only by their author, referred to casts or measures that Xelle could comprehend and perhaps even follow.

But a thawed vessel? Sure, Xelle could have left vessels outside, then retrieved them in spring (things having just thawed recently, she did not want to wait a year to try this) but then what would she do with it? Plant the seeds in it? A specific vessel?

Did it just mean they only bloomed in spring? What if she went back now, and they were all in bloom?

It would never be that simple. And Xelle had tied threads of magic to the phyta, now, more than once—she thought she'd sense a fully-blooming garden, or even a change to what she'd left. Not just thought, she reminded herself. Maybe not knew, but . . . believed.

She'd been wanting to go check on them, but had been waiting until she had some sort of lead, but this was not a lot to go on. It could be a poetic reference, well, clearly, but she meant more the way people from Charm Region often spoke. Maybe 'thawed in spring' was a reagent, a low-warmed serum, familiar regionally.

It seemed like it could be anything.

Still, this was the first mention she'd seen of the flower in writing, and she was not just going to set it aside.

Also, singular and plural together. Not inkblooms. Inkbloom. Connection. That felt right.

What the ash was a spring-thawed vessel? Vessels were most popular at To'Breath, for the care or curing of potions. Had the answer been there all along? How much Tower-hopping could she do?

It was getting late. But tomorrow Xelle was going to have to start looking for casting books, and see which talked about vessels.

Whatever it was, she was going to find it.

07 - *A Sweet, Sad Song*

Xelle now knew way more about vessels than she'd ever wanted to know. And she'd been wrong that they were primarily a Breath focus, just more blatantly of a Breath focus. Or stereotypically? The point was, she thought of Breath, thought of potions, and thought of bottles. Putting it like that sounded ridiculous. But she'd certainly been biased by her own Tower experience. Arc was really the only Tower whose casts involved no vessels, and so the culture there did tend to dismiss them, or really any physical objects involved in a cast. (Xelle did not think this way, but she'd even heard the term "props" used and definitely not with respect.)

Frond, the previous place she'd studied, saw vessels as utilitarian objects for curing runepaints but without much care for the design (they were often recycled after use), and not as a 'thing'. Yet at the other five Towers, apparently, vessels, including their crafting and composition, were a thing. A big thing. And yes, that included at To'Breath, where the importance of incorporating a cast directly into a vessel did give the subject prominence. But it definitely didn't stop there.

Here at Ever Tower, with its high use of reagents, vessels were seen primarily as reagent storage, which was why Xelle had not considered their use as linked to casting. Yet she'd learned, once looking into it, that there was a great deal of reverence to their design, both in terms of preservation and definitely for aesthetics, for something that might sit on a shelf a long time, even placed in a position of view the way one would display a beautiful or important book. (Xelle had the sudden thought of enchanting a vessel, and now she was taking it all too far.) And not just for looks; many believed that the vessel that stored a reagent impacted the reagent's potency. There were even workshops dedicated to vessel-making and vessel selection. Workshops were limited to Mages, usually intended for those lower-ranking. And thus previously not within Xelle's span of attention.

To'Charm, she learned, often used capsules, (often rings or lockets!) to prolong the viability of their casts. At Grand, for which she'd only considered, what, wand sheathing (?), there were multiple entire lines of study and research dedicated to vessels to facilitate growth and power of intra-reflective casting, including for advanced generation of phyta. (Everyone had pots? She hadn't considered that vessel-ware?) And something she'd had no idea at all about, but now knew, was that vessels were considered absolutely *sacred* within To'Dust, though nothing she found got into why: whether it was part of their form of casting (which she still knew very little about), or more of a cultural art borne from life in the more barren Dust Region.

Xelle could open a vessel shop at this point. (Actually, "Container Store" sounded really fun.) If Apprenticing and saving dragons didn't work out, maybe that's where she'd end up. Or, she remembered, that idea for a Tower coffee shop. Which—she tapped her chin—could involve some lovely vessels.

Anyway. What she had found, nothing—*nothing*—about, were seasonal, frozen, or thawed vessels and what that had anything to do with a highly-reactive banned-ish Arc Magic flower.

Heading outside for another round of casting practice (she enjoyed the seasons, but the spring weather really was so, so nice) she was stopped by a clerk. "Xeleanor?"

Whether friendly or a slight, she truly appreciated the lack of title on that. "Yes?" She smiled.

"Mage Helia To'Arc has a message for you."

Helia! Surprised, delighted, and suddenly realizing in all her isolation she hadn't written to her friend, she reached out a hand for the message.

The clerk squinted, and as suddenly, Xelle also realized a clerk wouldn't track her down just to hand over mail. She lowered her hand.

"She's here for cross-Tower discussions with a set of ranking Mages. There's no time to visit, but she said if you went to the Atrium, they'll be there for a while longer and she'll find you. 'Don't interrupt the ceremony,' she said."

Xelle thanked the clerk profusely for the favor (apparently Helia had convinced the clerk to find her directly and leave no record of the message), and then just stood there as he left.

Helia. Here. Like her old life was still real. Like . . .

She longed to see her. More, a physical pounding flooded through her with unsteady sensations. Raw. Uneasy. Not excitement, but almost a fearful power and rush, pushing against a wall. She'd have to understand this later. Helia was here, and wanted to see her.

Hurrying to the Atrium without setting down her bag, she saw a formation of Mages, doing a normal goodwill-before-parting thing. Two young Mages were in the center, perhaps being awarded for a project? Not really caring, she scanned the congregating delegations.

Mage Fepa. Of course. He stood behind an Ever Spire Mage, and beside another Ever Mage, one of the newer ones. (Xelle reminded herself this just meant having reached that rank in the near-decade she'd been away.) Four other Ever Mages clustered around them. On the other side . . . Spire Mage Kern. Fira, that was on point. A couple of Mages she recognized, a couple she didn't. And there. Helia, looking her way without letting anyone know she was looking her way, wearing layered peach robes, a floral ombre headwrap, and enough jewelry to melt out a statuette. Ash, she always looked good.

Xelle beamed, as a cast reached her ear in Helia's whispered voice. "It's almost done, stay back there. You're kind of . . . well known." That was a bit real.

She almost sent a message back, but with the number and skill of Mages around her, including a certain Kern Du'Arc, Xelle took her friend's advice and slipped back behind one of the pillars, removing a bag of puffs she'd been planning to eat once in the forest.

They were kind of messy, and when Helia peeked around the pillar, Xelle was licking her fingers.

"I didn't write to you; I'm sorry!" Xelle unzipped Essie for a clothie, to more appropriately wipe her hands. She stood, and bowed. "Mage Helia!"

"Do you walk everywhere with your bag?" Helia put an hand over one hip.

"No, I was going outside. I practice there; my room's small. Sorry, I've just felt trapped here or exiled, or I don't know. I should have written. Fira, Hellie, it's good to see you."

Helia paused a moment, and then winked. "I'm sorry it can't be for long. Yes, I'm well. Yes, Bear is well. Yes, they still talk about you at Arc. Yes, I miss you. Also, what is this?"

Xelle glanced herself over. "A tunic and sweatpants? My vibe?" She shrugged, with a little extra drama for humor.

"No, this." She pointed to Xelle's pin.

"Oh." She despised that pin. 'The mark of sadness', she called it, but everyone got fussy if she didn't have it on. "It says I'm an Apprentice. Long story, another day, but maybe you met Fepa?"

Helia pulled her mouth back into an extended cringe. "My sympathies. Hey, I can't stay. I'll try to come back. And you always know where to find me. Not for pressure. For us. Xelle, I'm not upset at you."

Had she been worried about that? *Oh.*

In that moment, something came back. Something specific, and sharp, a welcome pain, if that was the right word. Maybe . . . Xelle felt a tiny piece less like a ghost, without ever realizing she'd felt as one. A sliver, back, like a shard of a broken mirror. "I'm so glad you said hi," she managed to get out. "I miss you too. Or, maybe, we can meet in Mytil sometime, once I can shake off being stuck here. I still have that place I'd like to show you. The drink with the pink petals."

Helia cocked her head, and Xelle realized maybe thinking about taking her to the Enchanted Forest had been a conversation in Xelle's head, not *with* Helia. Helia waited a moment, shook her head, and started to turn away.

"Wait!"

She turned back.

"Vessel, thawed in spring."

Helia's eyebrows raised. "That's obscure; I'm impressed."

"Do you know what it is? I found it written somewhere, somewhere important."

She giggled, and then sighed. "I should have known."

Xelle had forgotten how sweet her giggle was. If giggles could be sweet. And even if there was a clear edge to that one. She felt confused.

"It's fiction. My best genre." Helia shook her head as though shaking herself back into something. "It's an old romantic story, that line specific to a regional retelling by Bard Kalle Du'Iyero."

Ash, she'd forgotten how much Helia knew about this stuff. How could she not have written?

Helia glanced back at the Mages. "Sigh," she said, this time like saying the word sigh. "Short version, then. In this retelling, each scene is a song. This one is a particularly sad song, a promise to love someone no matter what, whatever the circumstance, whatever the weight, whatever the consequence. It's heavy on trust, like not Magey trust, but mutual trust. Deep connection."

Why Mage trust was different than regular trust sounded like a really interesting discussion.

"Anyway, it's romance. Or more than, really. And I've got to go."

Xelle was romantic. What was she implying, that Xelle didn't know romance?

She was rarely annoyed with Helia, but that bothered her. Xelle was *extremely* romantic. Just the rivers through which it flowed always ended in chasms. See, that was poetic. And romantic!

"Xeleanor. I have to go." She could probably see Xelle was in her head. "Real quick, though, how are you stuck here? That sounds wrong."

She was stuck everywhere. Welcome to her life. "Oh. Part of my weird, secret arrangement with To'Ever." She almost said with Crown Mage Avail, but she felt sure she wasn't supposed to mention him. "I have to stay here with an eye on me. Price of partial library access."

Helia nodded curtly. "You're going to have to make a move."

Oh, that wasn't the issue. It was just what move. "I will," she said.

She watched as Helia hurried away, then slowed her pace to return to Mage Kern's side. Kern had to have seen her, but he made no motion to look remotely her way.

As always, Xelle was hit with a wave of unease, on top of the undulations already pulsing in her chest. She hadn't seen Helia in, well, months now (it actually felt like longer), and she hadn't hugged her, hadn't said anything. Just like, used her. And, really, why hadn't she just asked Helia about inkbloom? She was a Mage now, she would know.

No. No, no, no. She was not going to put her at risk, not when Xelle had other paths. First, a Mage of Helia's rank might not even have progressed to those studies yet. Even if so, no one knew about her nightgarden. And she wasn't putting Helia at risk by asking her to outright break sacred protocols. Xelle could break rules all on her own.

Maybe there would be a day for those harder questions. But not now—now, she had a lead. She was going to have to think about this song and what it meant, but right now, she was rattled, she felt weird, as in totally out of sorts, and she was going to just go practice magic. Magic. Her magic. It was what always calmed her when the world spun too fast.

And she could feel it spinning up.

08 - Visiting Hours

Stuck. The word stuck was stuck in her head. She was stuck, as in stuck in this Tower. Maybe being stuck wasn't as bad when she was stuck on what to do and working on how to do it, but now she had a plan but couldn't be where she needed to be, which was frustrating on every level and in every second—and she was feeling each second, at least when she allowed herself to think about it, which was a whole lot of the time. Being stuck.

But maybe, maybe now with the inkbloom, she was not! Fira save her. What had been written was a *song*. Every time she'd been around the little buds, she'd felt the need to sing, but she'd been wrapped up in her issues. Again, that depression of absence, the sneakiest one!

And not just any song. A song of emotion, truth— Trust, connection, what she'd read about the Inkbloom. Romance, even! It made sense now. She had to *sing* to them. They had food and moisture and dark light, maybe her flowers wanted love too. Trust.

They knew they were *useful*, but they wanted to be *loved*.

And, damn, Xelle knew that feeling.

Admittedly, it felt quite silly saying that all this felt right to her now just by hearing that a note referenced a lyric, but she'd spent time around the little buds; it made sense to her in the unknowable way that phyta-things that they'd tried to tell her suddenly made sense. Like something one knew they'd heard but couldn't think of, but once it was clear, it was very clear.

She at least had to try it. Oh, and then she could make sure it wasn't still the "buds bloom in spring" thing all along. She really didn't think so but best to close that loop too, while it was still (barely) spring.

Then there was Fepa. Ash-burned ash-hole Fepa. As much as the

Mage would let her do in the Tower, he was totally uninterested in letting her leave. She didn't really want Avail knowing she was gone, so she didn't want to submit it through Tower channels as time away. (Besides, time away from what; she had no classes, no assignments, no social calendar, why was her life so ridiculous?)

On top of that, she now thoroughly detested *everything* about being an Apprentice. Basically, it made her less relevant than a Study and it kept her away from everyone and she couldn't help with projects.

Not ideal.

And totally her fault. Except, no, that wasn't true either.

Xelle nearly growled out loud the next time she was summoned to Fepa's office. A really elaborate, nice, office. That somehow Fepa had made unpleasant. She might call the décor style—hoardy. Hoardish? Hoard-chic? No, it wasn't chic. More, just . . . sad.

A mismatched, yet somehow not eclectic, array of objects sat on open (as in not glass-covered) pedestals. A statue that had that specific sheen of a high percentage of gold. An artistic structure that looked like finely-cut aluminum, meant to dazzle in the lightpod hung above it, but almost by way of assault rather than beauty. An angular crystal vase that would hold no flower Xelle could imagine.

Even his window, with a completely gorgeous view over the back forest, was mostly blocked by a richly woven tapestry depicting an Ever Mage surrounded by beams of light.

No, at least it wasn't a depiction of Fepa.

Knowing the resources and privilege of a Mage, Xelle's disdain carried no guilt. Nothing here spoke to divergence. Fepa would have been screened for disorders, for needs of comfort.

None of that. Mage Fepa was simply a spoiled jerk with connections someone wasn't willing to lose. Who wasted his resources on making one of the prettiest rooms in the world somehow unpleasant. With chunks of metal and glass that were not even beautiful; just meant to show value.

She wasn't jealous. Just tired. Something. And there weren't even guests. It was just Fepa. As if he ever wanted to talk to her alone.

"I'll be gone a few weeks," he said, wrapping a fuzzy scarf around his neck despite it not being cold anymore. "I'm in management for an important event this year, so there's pre-planning to set up. Now, I've asked you here, because while I'm gone, I need to set some—"

Nope, nope, not setting anything. "Oh, is it *the* event?" she asked with an excited grin, super fake, but not a concern with Fepa. She scrambled, quickly, for something he might be into, something that might happen in late spring. She wouldn't risk mentioning magipuck, given the strong reactions in the magesphere. She couldn't see him gardening, or—

"ROTL. You wouldn't know."

Thank you, Kwill!

Xelle's eyes lit up. "No. Way. You really do ROTL? That's so cool." She pronounced it how the larping enthusiast at To'Breath had, like row-tl.

"You know about it?" His voice lifted up a touch. Almost like emotion, heh.

She raised her hands, and gave them a big enthusiastic 'no way' type waggle. "Know about it, yeah. Best cross-Tower activity under the clouds. What's this year's scenario?"

"I'm in management." He tugged at his scarf. "Can't disclose."

"Wow! They must be lucky to have you."

Fepa did role playing? *Collaboratively?* Fepa *was* role playing. What, did he pretend to be a real per with hu empathy when they met up? Or was this still his character? Ash, Fepa had to be with the faction whose asses everyone wanted to muddy, co-op or not. She almost asked to go. How was he picked to help *run* it? Ack, she couldn't allow for silence. "Maybe you can tell me—"

He raised a gloved hand. "I need to depart. I'll resume your instruction when I'm back."

Xelle got the ash out of there before he remembered to tell her she couldn't leave, and did actually cast up to sit in a tree out front, just to watch and make sure he got in a moveroom, and then watched it walk down the street and out of sight.

Firana, Stalker of Night. Fepa-free. Time to flee.

Now. She wasn't supposed to leave the Tower, but she also wasn't supposed to have a nightgarden, let alone one filled with inkbloom buds. Eh, no one noticed her anyway. She'd missed the Ever classes once for sleeping in, and no one had so much as mentioned it. Maybe she was still a ghost. Anyway, she'd be fast. Just in case, she left a note in her Front Desk file saying she was camping in the forest for her studies while Mage Fepa was away. Better if no one asked, but at least she had some cover.

Rather than cut the path down through Mytil or risk being noticed in a moveroom on the main connector, Xelle decided to be actively seen starting off into the forest with camping equipment. A full day's trip in a moveroom, but with a little unauthorized (as a non-Mage) casting and some relaxing stops at pretty perches on tree-topped hills and crags, she made a nice few days of piecing her way directly through the forest to To'Arc, hoping the clearer mind would help her convene with the inkbloom by song, if that's really how this would work.

Xelle couldn't be seen in To'Arc either, where her nightgarden's hidden entrance waited under the staircase. Which is why she'd created a Frond rune that could be accessed from outside. *But* she was not great at Frond Magic. And so, she snuck all the way to the old stone wall behind which her nightgarden sat before even attempting to connect. She removed the little squishbottle. (Now hyper-aware of vesselcraft, she tried not to think about how plain it was.) No, she held it up boldly, like an offering. A little swagger never hurt her confidence.

Ugh, though, connecting to Frond magic was like pulling a hinge that had rusted since the rather muddled year or so she'd studied it. Painstakingly, she squeezed the juice into her palm, and put every bit of concentration into drawing the rune she'd made just inside, pulling her hand slowly through the air, filling her nose with the scent of the pungent liquid. And when, exhausted, she didn't think she could do it, she opened her eyes.

Her hands were completely dry. She was inside. In her nightgarden, standing on the rune.

The inkbloom buds were unopened, still, in their obsidian-covered beds, yet they gave the slightest of glows, enough to fumble her way to the blue lights she'd had special-made, turn them on, and plop down in her swiveling chair. The sword shined her way, reflecting the blue light. She'd actually forgotten about the bizarre huge blade, propped against the wall. Fira, it was elaborate. She didn't have space to think about it yet.

Getting out a notebook and squinting in the dimness, she made a list of things she'd need to do, as she'd never remember otherwise (or spin her mind trying to remember, which was not a good option). A hanger for the obsidian mirror, clamps for the hanger in the stone. And . . . ooh, another wire to hang Helia's mirror on the other . . . No, just the obsidian mirror, scratch that. A stand for the sword. Something appropriately stately, maybe a clean forest wood, hand sculpted; she'd save up to have that done properly. Tiles for the remaining section of floor, so also that meant a tile cutter and blades. Some more oil to preserve the protruding roots. And she'd have to see if she could figure out casts for silence (she was terrible at Breath, but it could help?), as tile cutters would be loud and she no longer had another space here.

She set the notebook, with lists and measurements, away.

Xelle was in To'Arc. She was here, in her Tower. Yet she was here for a reason, and she could no longer postpone the uncertainty pounding in her chest. This was the time to find out.

Instead of using the kneeling board against the livewalls on either side, she sat in the middle of the room, staying in her swiveling chair, and allowing it to rotate back and forth with the rhythm in her hips. She closed her eyes.

Normally, deep and new casts would take immense preparation, day after day. But she'd found her nights in the forest calming. She didn't know the vessel song specifically (not that interested; it sounded depressing, and she'd justified the specific song wasn't the point), but since it was a deep and emotional song, and about connection, that was the sort of song she tended to compose herself. Ha, she was her own frozen vessel. Actually, that was depressing.

She began to sing.

It got a little personal. Which was Xelle-speak for a lot personal. She sang about home, about not knowing where it really was, or where she should be. She sang about gratitude for her friends, wishing they weren't all scattered. Weren't all busy. About how much she missed them, about the toll it took to not think about that, about not thinking of their company, day after day alone. And then, as she tried to fold in Arc magic, she could not avoid singing the one thing she'd not wanted to address here. About Ay'tea. How he'd just left. How much she missed him. How, maybe, she always would. (Was such a thing possible? Surely . . . over time . . .) How, now, she did not imagine a close hug, but a stolen meeting of lips, the tightening of hands. Her body constricted. Xelle imagined so much more, so much that was simply not possible, and not by her own constraints. Her voice warbled, and raised, and lowered.

She sang about being alone.

When she finally opened her eyes, she'd forgotten she was even casting, or what she was casting. She felt pulled into the song, into the very fibers of Arc Magic.

The blossoms had opened.

Not fully. They peeked open. She could feel them, feel their excitement. Like children, yet also not. Like beings born into adulthood but with the excitement of discovery still new. Their presence was exhilarating; she was radiating her own excitement back and it was as though they were struggling to respond. Inherently, like the pull to greet a friend who was busy unlacing a coat, she knew they needed time.

With Ever magic she couldn't have attempted just this winter, she easily took the threads of Arc that she'd wound to the phyta, and, grasping their consent like a wood anchor, she strengthened the bond. Solidified it. Enchanted the cast, she realized with a start. Could she . . . do that? Without reagents?

Yet she had. She knew it. She would feel this garden forever. Even, as scary as that sounded when she thought it in words, if she undid the initial cast.

Deep connections could be untied. But never undone.

Sweeping into her pocket, with the Ever reagents she'd brought, she started the process, now, for enchanting the rune she'd drawn on the floor. She felt embarrassed at how she'd drawn it, in a moment, without planning. Ay'tea's funny doodle. An **X**, in frustration. It felt juvenile. But changing it now would weaken it, and so she enchanted it also. Even over years, even when trod upon by her muddy boots, this—this would stay. Should stay.

She took a huge breath, and saw where she was, what was happening around her. The magic she'd just done, reaching through at least three prongs in short space, it was like the perfect song; it was the type of magic one could only comprehend when fully immersed in a moment. Without thought, but pulled from someplace deeper. From understanding. Her blossoms glowed now, brighter, and a shiver ran up her neck. Xelle had waited so long for this moment, and everything had gone better than she could have imagined. So now . . .

Fira. All Fira.

She had not . . . made a rune to get out.

All these months, she had this rune set to enter through the outside wall, and she'd not considered how she would *leave.*

A sinking feeling plunged in her gut. Why did all her best moments have to be marred? It really was a trend.

Her mind starting to spiral, she knew she had to narrow her thoughts. Goal. What was she doing? She'd done what she could for now. Since her only way out of the room was now her old magic door into the Tower, she needed to find a way out of To'Arc, and get back to To'Ever. Before Mage Fepa completed his larp. Ugh, that Mage. She swiped away an image of his fakey little face.

Maybe she could just . . . sneak out. She was in an obscure part of the Tower; part of why she'd chosen it. It would be fine; she stopped worrying.

Carefully and with unexpected familiarity, she moved back through her stone wall and under the old staircase, trying not to think about where she was, in To'Arc, the place she'd left.

Yeah, this was not happening.

As if, now, she could slip into a crowd, no one noticing or considering where she'd been? Here, the dragonfriend, known to be residing at To'Ever? She couldn't just walk out and scoot away.

And she wasn't about to cast in *here.* Her nightgarden was at least wrapped, but in the open corridor, she had the sense that the fingerprint of a Xelle cast in Jehanne's Tower would waft its way to the Crown Mage like smokeweed.

She got out her pen and tore off a piece of notebook paper, wrote the note and sealed it, and then threw it, amagically, like a catchdisk, into the empty hallway before darting away.

Fira, Xelle.

She slipped into a closet, and arranged herself amongst the buckets, hoping this was not the moment for someone to clean a back section of the Tower. Not enjoying her churning feelings, she tried to sing something old, gentle, under her breath. To escape the drawn-out time and the uncertainty, and hope that rescue would come, and avoid, just for a while, what she would do if it did not.

Finally, as her mind was near to escaping the space she'd tried to put it in, there was a rap on the door. A moment later, it creaked open. A familiar figure stepped in, shutting the door behind her. She said nothing, and though her eyes stared with a professor's gaze, there was a touch of fire in her cheeks.

Xelle stood. "I . . . really can't get into it, but I needed to check something, and I messed it up, and . . . can you help me out of here?"

There was a pause. "You are insufferable."

She worried—if she'd finally used her last with Helia. "Never mind, I shouldn't have . . ."

Helia raised a sharp hand, and weirdly obeying, Xelle shut her mouth.

From her other hand, the Mage held out a cloak. "I cannot do this a lot, Xelle. You'll give me a reputation. Not that I care, but I do have a social life to manage. Put it on."

Grimacing as apologetically as she could at Helia, she fully cloaked herself in the rather plain and clearly amagical covering, and followed as Helia walked into the corridor.

"Talk and giggle," she said. "They'll think we're together."

Ah. So it was a known thing that some pers in relationships of various sorts with Mages did not want those relationships known in the Tower village. Xelle followed, chuckling nervously along as Helia told a funny story that was so random and not funny, that it was clear she was making it up as she went along. But as no one other than Xelle had to endure the whole thing, perhaps it worked to a casual observer.

The door clicked shut behind them, and Xelle nervously slipped off the hood to see the golden-trimmed wallpaper of the Mage's personal room.

Helia was . . . laughing. "What the ash did you do?" she chided, hands setting on her rounded hips.

"I, uh, hid a rune—you can't see it" (true enough) "to get in, so I could check on something later, which I just did, and I forgot to make one to leave."

Helia chuckled all the way over to the couch, where she fell back onto the soft cushions with the artful grace that only Helia could gather while falling backward. Bear, the cat who'd bonded to her, jumped up onto her lap.

"Hi, Bear," Xelle mumbled, walking over to give aer head a little scratch. "Yeah, I know, now it seems obvious, but I'd never runed before, and I got excited about the whole thing, and I don't know . . . I never considered it!"

"How long were you at Frond?" Helia at least stopped chuckling. Enough of that.

"A year?" Xelle grimaced.

"That's impressive." Helia nodded appreciatively. "No, really. Yeah, a one-rune network is one of the worst ideas I've ever heard, but to get Frond Magic to work like that—such *advanced* magic. You're really something." She shook her head. "Now, to get you out of here should be easy." She pointed to her balcony.

Well, yes, with Xelle's skill with the sling cast, she could Arc Magic off of the balcony and hurry off to the trees below, hopefully without being seen or sensed. Helia knew she could do that as she'd witnessed Xelle's own magical float-down from the top of the Tower. She breathed out in relief. That specific 'disaster averted' relief that left a per thrilled but shaky. "Nice. Yeah, thanks. Can I sit down?"

Helia extended a hand toward the couch.

"Sorry, I actually wanted to visit, but no one was supposed to know I was here."

"One-rune network," Helia repeated, with a very serious face.

Not as funny as she thought that was.

Realizing Helia was wearing more symbols of her Mage status and specialties than Xelle was used to seeing, she stopped. "I'm sorry, you're probably working."

"I was." Helia flicked her expression sarcastically. "But now I'm here. Afternoon cleared."

"Oh." Xelle wasn't sure what to respond. Really, after this, she'd just been going to return to To'Ever. She did want to see Helia, but also wouldn't have wanted to risk being seen. But she was here now. And while she didn't want to delay and risk finding out Fepa had been kicked out early for pretending to plan a larp, leaving now or later this afternoon wasn't important. "Want to talk?"

Now Helia just laughed. "I'd love to. Besides, if I get a reputation for bringing a cloaked figure to my room, I'd really get one for leaving this quickly."

Ok, that was funny.

"Remember that game I taught you?" Helia went to open her cabinet.

She sort of did. Helia got the rolled game mat out and spread the dice and tokens over it, finally seeming to relax. "Everyone's on edge here. I don't know how else to say it. Not because of you, but because of the Spire and the way they've reacted. Classic. Instead of clarifying why you'd arrived on a dragon, whether you were an exceptionally bizarre Study, or whether you really were one of these Amberborn or even working for Pelir, or what they might know about said Amberborn, they clammed up about all of it. Which, of course, made people think you'd been sent away. People then wondered why Pelir was still here, or if that meant you'd been on the right side of the Amberborn all along. Enter entire evenings of friends trading conspiracy theories about who the Amberborn are and who's behind them. Which turned into, either you were a villain or a hero, with pers all taking bets on which."

"Literal bets?" She was curious.

"Yes." Helia's face suggested not interrupting again.

Ugh, she was really getting Mage vibes.

Then Helia didn't say more as she sorted the game tokens into bins. Finally, she looked up. "At Ever, have you heard anything about them?"

"The Amberborn?" Actually, Xelle had tried not to worry about that part for the time being. She wanted to learn magic and get back to the dragons since she felt like an ash-swipe for asking them to leave. Kern was doing his deal, and this was Xelle's focus. Inkbloom. Then dragons. *Then* everything else. "No. They aren't even talked about there."

It pinged at Xelle that perhaps the Amberborn were the Hurts, and she didn't want to hold things from Helia. But, no, the Hurts were not Mages, or least not all? And Pelir wasn't one. Xelle wasn't one. This reminded her of all the knots she hadn't yet untied while focusing on the inkbloom. But to reach the dragons, she needed the inkbloom. She had to focus. Right?

"I'll keep trying to find out," Helia said, watching Xelle's face intently. "If I can help you in any specific way, please let me know."

Actually. "Can you do the calling cast yet? Where you see each other?"

Her face snapped up. "No, that's very ad . . . Fira, Xelle, who are you . . . You know, I don't want to know. I don't want to know. And no, not yet."

This felt wrong. Hiding from Helia, when she trusted Helia. The knots were too complicated on *all* of this. She sat back, watching her.

"What?" Helia stopped sorting, and sat back herself, onto the couch. "What is it? Xeleanor, you tell me."

With relief, she obeyed. "I have things I shouldn't talk about. I trust you. But I need to keep my projects my own for now. And that makes me feel bad. And I don't want to use you, you've always—"

"Stop!" Helia thwacked her hand against a pillow. "Just. Stop. We are not going anywhere if you're scared of me, or scared of using me, or whatever you think it is. Do I not appear to you that I can take care of myself? Did I not just bail you out from a one-node Frond network that in several months, you never considered what an absolutely crap-loaded idea that was?" Helia looked aggravated. "If you don't tell me something, I trust you. Can you ash-flamed trust me?"

That was a good question. And Xelle thought about her answer, maybe longer than she should have. And decided, this time on her own, to be honest.

"I do trust you. But I can't keep worrying that you like me and I'm using you. As a friend, or as anything else."

Helia sighed, and leaned back. She did not appear bothered, and, oddly, the tension dissolved. "You aren't using me, and you aren't using any of your friends, whoever else you're thinking about right now."

She hadn't been thinking of anyone else.

"You just . . . aren't like that. Pers care about you. And we're trying to help you, the same ash-poked way you would help any of us."

This reminded her. Something had been worrying her. Not

worrying, just wondering. Feeling unclear, she went ahead and said it. Asked it. Anyway. "Helia, why did you get me a mirror?"

Helia opened her mouth and held it, her head slowly tilting to the side. This was an uncharacteristically silly look for the elegant Mage, yet, still—still, she managed to be beautiful doing it. "Are you worried it's enchanted? Cursed?"

"No," Xelle replied, honestly. "I just didn't know what it was for."

Helia leaned in, and stared. Whatever she was going to say, she almost didn't say it. And then, she did. Her voice, normally bubbly and light, was intense. So intense. "Once the Arc Spire got their mitts on you, I knew you wouldn't stay. You couldn't. You would never put up with whatever they were messing with you about. You're way too . . . in charge of yourself. It's why— Xeleanor, I thought of the most beautiful thing I could give you, maybe to remember me a little, and it was you. You're the most beautiful thing I've ever seen. Your face. Your smile. Your ridiculous . . ."

She turned away.

Xelle felt uneasy. So uneasy. Helia was upset, and she was right, Xelle didn't stay, Xelle never stayed, but Firana Stalker of Night, this Mage was beautiful, more than anything Xelle could ever be, and her cheeks were flushed, and her gown had shifted over her shoulder as she'd twisted. Xelle's heart pounded. Go. She should go. She rose, unsteady, from the seat.

Bear, from the other side of the room, called out.

"Are you leaving, then?" Helia asked, finally, nervously shifting to look at her.

"I don't know," Xelle replied, blankly.

Helia stared at her.

Xelle stared back.

"Is pledging necessary to you? It's not to me."

She stared. Again. Finally noting the glimmer in her friend's eyes, Xelle's whole body constricted and she gasped in a gust of need. But, first, she had to clarify. And this felt important. She leaned in, her voice lowered. "It's a different type of pledge. And for that, you have mine." Seeing Helia's eyes turn to fire, Xelle pushed her back, onto the couch.

Their mouths, together, were warm.

09 - *Tall Ladders*

Turns out Xelle did not have to leave via balcony. Helia arranged a private moveroom, one that took her, again borrowing Helia's cloak (she told Xelle the common cloaks were handy to have and Helia would just buy another one) to Mytil, the least notable destination for an Arc Tower vroom—one giving away nothing about its passenger when logged.

Arc Mages had access to staff vrooms who knew better than to banter without invitation, and so the conn kept the curtains drawn, accepted the destination of the Enchanted Forest without argument, and kept xyr eyes to the road until they pulled in. Xe left without comment, and Xelle, mindful that she was now a figure of note, checked that the hood on her cloak was drawn before walking inside. Similarly, she did not linger at the bar, but instead let Klein know she was supposed to still be at Ever Tower (she trusted his discretion always), and headed upstairs with a small dinner tray including an experimental cocktail, as Klein described it.

"I haven't named it yet," he said. "You'll have to let me know what you think."

It was dark and boozy, with tastes of maple, and she sipped it slowly with and after the meal, enjoying how the flavors lingered on her tongue. Soon, her eyes grew heavy, and she lay down, grateful for the soft, if simple, bed, not needing to pull on the night ivy, but for once, waking from a long, restful sleep.

Not to say that there were not nightpaths or agitations from the storm in her mind; there always were. But a morning when she did not remember them and felt reasonably refreshed was always a cause for gratitude. Setting the dishes outside to carry downstairs, she whooshed around a quick travel cast to sweep any dust out the lovely little window of her small room. Then, putting on her cloak, she took the dishes to where Klein had told her to leave them, and moved back through the empty bar area and out to the forest.

Ah. Right. Xelle reminded herself that she'd intended to figure out some kind of secret entrance, or ask Klein if one already existed, perhaps, so she didn't have to walk through the open spaces to reach her room. If she was going to get herself into pickles where she didn't want to be seen, that would be necessary, especially since, to her knowledge, no one except Klein knew about her rented attic room here. And as Klein had offered her the spot because she was a caster, there would be no ethical problem if the secret entrance involved a bit of magic. Xelle stopped before she forgot, to add that to the list she'd made in her garden.

As for that list, she'd thought about shopping for some of the supplies here, in Mytil, as a trip to the shops sounded really nice right now, but again, she was not supposed to be seen away from To'Ever, a concept which was more and more irritating the more it constrained her. So she slid the notebook of fixes back into her bag, for her next trip to Vi'Ever, a place she was definitely allowed to be.

Inkbloom. Dragons. Then fixes.

She wondered if there'd ever again be a time in her life when fixes weren't on that list. Or when she wouldn't feel as constrained as she did in her own nightgarden. Hardly even constrained. Constricted.

Xelle caught view of a particularly tall and sturdy tree (interesting trees always caught her eye) and stopped in place, staring up at it. Definitely the sort where, as a child, she would have climbed and built platforms, working with her friends whose parents were part of the tall ladder community of her homevillage. And where she would have sat, coming up with her next big idea.

Thinking of it made her laugh. So many of her great discoveries, her revelations, had been in the company of a tree, but now she had to stay focused on the inkbloom. Inkbloom could not coexist with trees; trees needed light, and inkbloom could not endure it.

Inkbloom needed dark. And that's where Xelle needed to focus if she was going to help them to life.

The tree was staring back. What was it? *Oh.*

Xelle wasn't inkbloom.

But what did that mean? Perhaps that . . . Xelle needed both. The dark and the light. Even as the inkbloom grew, how could she really help them when she was stuffed into the dark?

A forest breeze blew past, and Xelle closed her eyes, breathing deeply into it. Into the forest. The place that had grown her, shaped her. She needed her list for clarity, to manage her scattered mind. But she'd been wrapped too into it. The inkbloom were growing. Reaching the dragons depended on the inkbloom. And the inkbloom depended on Xelle. On her ability to visit, to tend, without such stress and secrecy. On her ability to learn, and to advance her craft away from peering eyes.

The inkbloom had its space. And not only for the inkbloom. Xelle, too, needed the darkness. A space where she could stare into her mirror of obsidian and view the darkness within herself. Yet, she'd forgotten to take care of the light. As if in response, a burst of sunshine shot through the waving branches of a tree, causing Xelle to look forward, deeper into the forest.

Inkbloom. Dragons. Fixes.

Xelle.

The light.

The forest.

She knew exactly who to visit.

Her material feeling excellent, she didn't hesitate to cast her way, quickly, onward and weaving through the trees, first for a quick stop at her parents'. Being this way, she could stop by.

To her delight, Hall and his curas were already there for the afternoon, and she enjoyed the gleam in her parents' eyes—Na Vuia doing her best to act unbothered, Na Lleyx basically chortling in joy, and Na Foose unexpectedly rolling around on the floor with the kids in the silliest of ways while telling them Sa Xeleanor was here, and what a surprise it was. She tried not to dwell on the idea that she'd be the one to end it, again, and rather soon.

"I have my nopatina," Vallie whispered, when Xelle was near. Her hand reached out from a pocket, her fingers wrapped smoothly around the metal vine. "I like it."

"I'm glad," Xelle said, wrapping her young friend in a hug that would also end too soon.

This time, no one said anything to draw Xelle's angst as she nervously got out that she wasn't actually supposed to be away, and needed to go, and could not even stay the full afternoon, let alone the night, but was passing near and wanted to see them. Though they must have felt that loss, the round of hugs, and acceptance, and no words of concern felt like power itself, and she cursed her singular being, for only being able to be in one place when there was a whole world of love.

No, one Xelle was plenty, she laughed to herself, hoping to spark a little cheer as she headed just outvillage to the per she'd decided to visit. Or, perhaps, she allowed herself to think, that the forest had led her to visit.

She found him in a tree, out behind his home.

"Hallo! Kosti!" she called up, trying to focus on her aims here and not think about the whirlwind that had just happened, if it had really just happened. (Sometimes something so precious, yet so fleeting, felt as though it could not have been real, and to believe it was real would invite in uncomfortable feelings. She was being polite. But didn't want to think of them now. Also, if she were so distracted, she might act strange to Kosti, or miss something she meant to ask, and then all of that would bother her even more.)

Kosti sailed down, toward her. In a moment of distracted shock, she thought he'd learned to cast, but then saw he was gliding down a long rope. Like flying. With such grace.

"Xelle, you're back?"

Why was it always like that. She tried to smile. "Just invillage for the afternoon."

He rested a gloved hand on his thin hip. "And you swung by here?"

"I always love to see you, but this is specific. I've already been to my parents'."

Strangely, once answered, the idea that she had traveled to Tam to see him did not seem to faze him. "It's partial, but you're welcome up." He nodded up the ladder, next to the rope.

One thing Xelle had learned about tall ladder enthusiasts was to never take them up on partial anything. Whether it was a ladder leading to a plank between two branches, or an unwalled shelter, Xelle's nervousness with unsteady heights was already making her spin.

"Ground today, if you would." She gestured toward a soft patch of greenfloor, which squished the tiniest bit under her bottom, as a waft of green scents passed on the breeze. Oh, she did love the forest.

Kosti plopped next to her, to pull something out of his pocket, snap it in half, and offer the other to Xelle.

"No thanks," she said, never above forest pocket food, but generally preferring her own. (And knowing what was in it.) "So I'd like to build a workshop, and for reasons, I would like it to be up in a tree."

"You've been away too long!" he said with a chortle. "No one needs a reason to build up into a tree!"

Xelle didn't love that. She tried to smile.

"And you're an Arc Mage, right," he continued, beaming with village pride. "So you won't need a ladder!"

Yeah. An Ever Apprentice now, but she didn't need to get into all of that. "It's complicated," she said with a grin she hoped passed. "But I'd also like a way to climb to it amagically, and I thought you'd mentioned pull-up ladders once."

"Yes!" Kosti jumped up, as if they were about to build one, then realizing they were only discussing it, he sat back down, biting into whatever his snack was, and not waiting to finish it to talk again. Xelle scootched back, just a bit. "I haven't quite worked retracting to the length I'd like, but I've got solid builds for folding, pulling, even swiveling. It's kind of my specialty," he bragged, seemingly unaware that she probably already knew that, to be specifically here.

Xelle had mulled over all sorts of ideas for basic construction, ins and outs, and an amagic switch if she needed to avoid even shadows. But she saw no cause to 'reinvent the ladder' when she knew an expert who spent all day every day thinking about exactly this.

It was dark outside and the lamps of the workshop lit before she made her way to leave, a stack of drawings in hand. Kosti wouldn't hear of taking payment; he seemed honored that the Mage from Tam (she finally corrected him that her title wasn't Mage and he seemed to take it as code for their secrecy, which made him even more excited) valued his inventions.

Well, she owed Kosti one, then. And she made sure to tell him so.

Xelle's room at To'Ever looked undisturbed (including Kern's precious pendant which she'd tucked out of easy view), Mage Fepa hadn't yet returned, and without any irritated summons from Crown Mage Avail or anyone else, Xelle seemed to have gotten away with her unsanctioned travels.

Stirred up by her series of (quite distinct) visits with the inkbloom, Helia, Klein, her family, and then Kosti, she found that being back alone at To'Ever was . . . lonely. Sure, she'd been lonely before, but the layer peeled loose now, and hovered around her. Raw. Unreceding. Like she was no longer a connected person.

Mixed into that, she worried for the dragons, for whatever she was supposed to be learning and wasn't. Her mind was spinning about it. When she was supposed to focus. When she tried to relax. Even in bed, through the night ivy, when she tried not to reimagine her loneliness, tried to pull to sleep, she thought about how little she'd accomplished, all the mistakes she'd made.

She knew—she knew—she could not put all that burden on herself. Kern was working his end, and Xelle was restrained, here, but still making progress with her inkbloom, which she finally had moving forward. A tremendous accomplishment in a short time; she was doing fine. Everything hinged on being able to reach the dragons without external control; she was doing fine. Yet this didn't stop her mind, which then affected her rest, which then affected . . . her.

Xelle tried to focus on the inkbloom when the tangle grew too thick. Part of her now, in a sense, she could feel the phyta, growing each day. Thriving. The bond firmly secure, she sang through it, every night before bed (after messaging Thunder), wondering at a world where such connections were possible. The inkbloom knew her now, in the ways that they could. And—just a tiny amount, as she surmised their depth of being—she was starting to know them.

Yet, she found that the deepening connection to the phyta brought her own loneliness into greater acuity, even after singing, which should have relaxed her, except she was the only one singing and that felt lonely. It all flooded through the night ivy, releasing her control on it, and rattled around her mind. The uncertainty. The worry. The doubt. The feelings, but only from afar. These were getting to be too much. Her heart ached with longing.

She poured it into her plans.

First, she found the spot. Learning from her lesson of being a bit too specific in selecting her nightgarden plot, she leaned into the inherent richness of the high rim forest. An evergreen, it needed to be to provide cover, yet wide and strong enough to hold the beams and frames of the structure.

Next, she made the ladder. Then, moved on to the room. The storage. The windows; it had to have nice windows, even to look out at a canopy of soft needles. Especially to look out at a canopy of soft needles! Whatever pieces she could afford to commission or buy, she did, but never enough to aggregate the idea of what she'd built.

Taking the place of her previous hours in classes, with Fepa, or at the library, she worked outside as much as she could, rising with the sun, packing her meals for long days.

In the back of her mind rested the idea of wondering if she would ever again spend a summer like this, breathing the forest, sawing wood. And though she remained alone, she kept her focus on that, and on her work. On the forest. On the friendly warmth of the sunlight, when she stepped through it. On the satisfaction of each new piece, fitting together. Of the thump of her borrowed mallet and the soft ache of her arms. Of her own soft humming, as she worked, day after day, then week after week.

And just as the chill of fall began to darken the evenings, she finished the last pieces, ready, now, for assembly.

Though Ever Tower was used to (and resigned to, it seemed) her retreating to the forest to practice both Ever and Arc Magic, she limited her practical casts to avoid suspicion. Working primarily by hand, she framed the room, easily using her Arc Magic to hold and lift the wood frames as she positioned and secured them.

Seeing the shapes form and visions become real, Xelle's mood started to improve, even if the storm in her mind and the pit in her heart did not. Part of her couldn't believe the summer had passed, even though she'd certainly felt present, working through each hour of it. There was simply a peace here; she had let it carry her, perhaps. Out in the forest, shaping and joining wood, reveling in the smells of sap and musk . . . Perhaps she would always be a forestper at heart.

No. She would. Even away from them, the trees would always call her.

"There!" she said, pulling the sheet from the tall, constructed piece. Around her, a group of assembled Studies politely applauded.

"This is what you've been working on?" one asked.

Xelle nodded. "Yes, it's a multi-species birdhouse. Birds will house themselves, of course, but if they choose this spot, we get to enjoy them going about their business without needing the binoculars." She pointed at the set, looking as tired as she felt next to the large window of the Lounge.

"I've never seen one so large," another Study said. "Impressive work."

"Thank you," Xelle said.

"I think it's nice. I think they'll use it," He'milo added, from near the back of the gathering. The Study she'd first met with his parent had become sort of a de facto coordinator at what they called the Bird Window, and she now saw Ebbia and the others gathered around him, offering enthusiastic smiles.

With appreciation, Xelle nodded back their way.

While the whole project was a cover to explain (even though they were used to her spending all day in the forest) why she was seen carting lumber and sometimes smelled like a walking pine tree, she had put some serious effort into making it nice. A way to contribute here. Slightly less of a ghost.

She hoped.

And as the crowd dispersed, and Xelle returned back to the Front Desk, making a show of handing back a few woodworking tools she'd borrowed from Tower supplies, her heart beat faster, knowing what was next. Her construction had been nice, she thought, but the most complicated part was yet to come.

Sure, Xelle enjoyed the idea of hiding her treehouse in plain sight, as they said, but once she started to further develop her magic here, casts only allowed to Mages, she could not risk even casual detection.

She waited a few days—a very long few days—during which all she could really think about was finally getting this new place to . . . *be*.

It probably sounded odd to say she needed a place to know she would not be disturbed by pers when she was also bemoaning how lonely she felt.

These were different.

~

She started her casts small. To verify no one was near, no one could sense them. Sure, a powerful Mage could certainly hide from her, but if a powerful Mage had been waiting in the forest day after day watching her practice powerful wrapping magic, then that tree had already fallen.

Again, she was glad she'd kept practicing the two prongs all summer, one then the other, every day here in the forest strengthening muscles she didn't know she had to traverse them, as now what she planned to do felt strangely easy.

No, not easy, not even a little easy. Why would she even think that? Achievable.

She hoped.

The tiny runes were all set in place, traced in, day after day until cured. And her understanding of this tree was deep; she'd meditated with it day after day, at the close of her build, her daily progression of task to task as oppressive as it had felt necessary. A place to put her daymind other than swimming into emptiness. And, look, look at all she'd done.

Finding the concealed switch that enabled her ladder segments to glide down the trunk and to the ground, she turned it. Then, standing on the sturdy platform, because yes, she'd taken her reaction to unprotected heights into account, she turned the switch back, causing a tension weight to pull herself up, like a lift rather than a ladder, and onto the fenced exterior ledge she called 'the porch', which ran fully around the small rectangular building.

Carefully, she rubbed the thick sap, selected and cured just for this enchantment, fully around the platform's edge, working quickly so that it would not begin to dry. Her arms pulled in and out of the guard rail, making sure no spots along the roundly sanded sides of the base boards were missed.

She'd thought about taking the process in sections, but she wanted it to be solid (segmented casts just gave her an eww feeling in general), so she pushed on, next taking the carefully filtered powder from her envelope and sprinkling it over the sap, walking around and around, while weaving together the words of personal protection, the threads of her being, and the flow of the runes.

At the point where she had spun around, metaphorically also, and felt as though she were pulling ten thousand threads, each bowing from needles, to embroider her runes, she worried she had been too bold, too indulgent. But, like treating bare wood, there was only one chance to start fresh, and so she leaned into her boldness, imagining she had the confidence to dance through until the last thread was stitched. She pulled them together, until, like twisting a bundle of reedy stalks just so, they snapped.

She let go, her arms feeling disconnected, nearly swaying. Low material, low mind. She stumbled in, through the door.

As her consciousness gathered and returned, she nervously felt around her, felt into the air and space. This was . . . solid.

This space would stay loyal to Xelle. It would resist magic detecting it was here, or magic within being detected outside of it. And she would sense it, from near or afar. The longer she stayed here, worked here, grew an understanding, the stronger the enchantment would grow.

The idea excited her. Made her nervous. Yet, she'd plunged ahead. What she'd done; it was amazing. The emptiness inside her did not fill, but felt powerful, a tool for greatness, even if the greatness was as private to herself as the emptiness. She breathed in, feeling for the sense of the enchantment, for its depth. Yes, it held. It was so good.

Too many threads tied to a Mage could weave a life of burden, but if Xelle was going to be tied to her nightgarden, she would be tied to her daygarden as well. She hoped, being so precious to her, they would not be so heavy a weight.

She lowered her arms. Let her face relax. Took calming breaths. Allowed herself to feel the ache that permeated every layer of her being, especially surrounding the core, where the enchantment held. It reminded her of a stitched wound, but this one no magic could heal. Only time. Commitment. And spirit.

It was dark outside. She'd not slept. Hopefully, Mage Fepa had not sent for her (he rarely did now). If only she had a balcony. In her Tower room, she meant. She could Arc her way to it. Perhaps. No, not with her material as such. Xelle was too tired, now, for anything quick, or anything clever. She was a Mage who'd spent too much time in the woods, practiced a little too long, cast a lot too much. She'd Walk of Mage her way back.

One thing. First.

From her bag, she carefully unwrapped the hand-mirror Helia had given her. Yes, it was a hand-mirror, but Xelle was not one to carry a mirror. She attached it to the brackets she'd installed in anticipation of this moment.

There. Furnishings for another day, but for today, now, this was home.

A home.

Xelle returned to the Tower.

The year of Tenne's residence felt much longer at the start than it did now, at its end. While another E'lle Prize wouldn't be awarded for four more years, the annual rotation of the main gallery had moved on. Tenne gave back his fancy clothes, the common supplies. Even the tools he'd grown to love were not, they said, his to keep.

They hadn't even known what they were saying and how it stung. Not his. Yeah, never his. Owin had won, not him.

The note he'd slid under the artist's door had never been answered, but, before Tenne went crawling back to To'Arc to check on his Da, he supposed he'd try one more time.

Reaching the top of the concrete ramp, Tenne peered through the window and down a plain, windowless hall. He supposed there were windows to the outside. Supposed it'd be weird to have a view of a corridor. Pers walking by. Huh. That'd be like his own last year: a sad hu in a diorama to show everyone how well the city treated art. If he'd hoped that the populace somehow operated with whatever it was he hadn't found in the magesphere, well, he'd been wrong. And now, he was just . . . going back to the Mages that hosted him. A sad little nothing. Tenne Not'Kern.

Not even a cheat. He couldn't even be that.

He shook it off.

Walking inside and down the hall, he rapped at the loose doorframe, mostly expecting Owin to see him through the viewing lens and slam in the extra bolt. He shuffled a bit. His boots were dirty; when was the last time he'd worn these?

A creaking sounded.

There, again, was Owin, mouth turned in disbelief. "Why are you here?"

"It's my last try, I guess. To let you know I didn't want to take your award."

"After the year is over and the money's spent?" Owin laughed. It was a nice laugh, if it weren't so annoyed.

"Um, yeah. I couldn't tell them." He expected Owin to roll his eyes or slam the door again, but the taller hu cocked his head.

"Here, come in before I throw you out. If you think you owe me this story, I'll take it. Then throw you out. You've got me curious." He shrugged, then gestured inside.

Tenne glanced around the small space. Owin was apparently a good artist, and Tenne kind of hoped to check that out, but he'd have no idea what was his. While the room wasn't filled with much in terms of furniture, it was covered in art. Not fancy, framed art, but simple sketches, little paintings, tinkling strands of polished glass. He knew Owin hadn't made all these; versatility was fine, but these trinkets were not conceived of the same soul.

"Gifts and such. Over the years," Owin said, sitting on a stool against the countertop, putting one of his feet on the rung of a second stool, and watching Tenne keenly.

Feeling weird sitting on the low couch or whatever like a friend, Tenne stayed standing. Since he couldn't actually say much, his story would be underwhelming and Owin would call him a prod and push him back out in to the hallway and . . .

Whatever happened then happened and he'd go back. To whatever.

Owin was waiting.

"So I can't really tell you."

The stool grated against the floor.

"Wait, wait. It involves—" He couldn't mention Mages, he didn't want to bring his Da into it . . . Owin was glaring. He had to say something. "Someone I can't tell you who it is told me I couldn't let on that something had happened because bad pers were involved and they are trying to catch them."

Owin moved his second leg onto the rung of his own stool. "You're in, like, a sting, based on the word of someone you won't say. And you want to set my mind at ease by explaining this. Bon Tenne Du'Mytil?"

That name was a fraud. "I'm just Tenne."

"Tenne?"

He looked up.

"Get the flame out of my place."

Well, he'd tried. Tenne threw his arms up. "I get it. I get you. I knew this would happen, and I'm here anyway. I asked . . . the per . . . if I could just bail, and there's . . . reasons. Ash-wipe." He knew he was sounding irritated too, now, and needed to go before his temper got him. "I just wanted to tell you I'm sorry. If it helps, it was stuffy and weird and they watched me everywhere." That was not going to help. "Never mind, just I wish you well and bye."

He turned toward the door.

The voice nearly growled from behind. "One thing."

"Sure." Tenne turned back. Ash, this hu was pissed.

"What did you spend the money on?"

"Uh." Well, if he didn't like that, he really wasn't going to like this. "I snuck out. Cleaned up messy places. Painted cartoons on gray walls for kids and stuff. Flying frogs in pretty gowns and stuff." He shrugged. "Just tried to make pers happy." He was shocked to see Owin recoil and then grin.

"That is specific."

"What?"

"Never mind. Just, where are you going now?"

"To'Arc, I guess. My Da's there." Of course, he probably knew that and Tenne was jerkier for mentioning it. "Don't really have much. Here, anyway. They took back my stuff. The rest is outside. I'll call a vroom."

"Outside? Oh, this is artist housing. You can't leave it there; pers will think it's out to be taken."

"They'll swipe my stuff?"

"Fira, are you always like this? No, not swipe. Pers leave things out, to help each other."

"Oh." That sounded nice. "That sounds nice."

"Curse my nuts."

"What?" Tenne was already thinking about his stuff; probably needed to go get that.

"Look, I'll help you pull your things up here, you crash on my couch tonight, and tomorrow you take me to see some of these glamfrogs."

Tenne didn't want to go back to To'Arc. If he could stall a day, he would. "Sure," he said, following Owin down the ramp to help heft up his case.

10 - *Time*

It had been time for the change, if not long overdue. The new space, Helia's mirror, everything she'd seen looking into it. No, she didn't regret the choice.

The window's morning sun illuminated the shower room mirror, and Xelle stared into the reflection, unused to the shortness of her crownhair. Unused to the new color now surrounding her. Not new. Just now, exposed.

But what had keeping the longer hair done her, when no one had ever seen it? Even during her evening with Helia, she'd kept her cap in place, taking care not to disturb Hellie's either. It wasn't the intimacy that had stayed her, and Helia had made no comment about it, but the abrupt shift in the color of new growth. What she hadn't wanted Helia to see. The long crownhair she'd had, now down the dustchute, a dark rainbow based in grayed black, nearly flecked with bright colors. Moments of joy. Exploration. Grown when she'd been in her lab, at To'Arc.

The pattern had been unusual then, she knew (and thus she'd been protective of it), but, she'd thought, the array of colors was maybe a sign of her younger age. Of her joy in the study of magic. Of all the casts she'd been learning.

Then, Ay'tea had left.

It was amazing how many shades of black there were, once one stood in the sunlight. The black now, the color that remained once she'd trimmed it to a loose crop, was grim, faded, lost. No sparks of color. No light.

Well, she supposed, that was about intimacy, then. Not intimacy of body, but of soul. Of not wanting to explain to Helia, in their time of fun and joy, that everything she'd had and been had felt whisked from her, all in the day she'd made that shit petition.

When would he leave her heart? Fira, more than her heart. Her soul.

Surely, surely, in time.

The inkbloom felt ready.

And Xelle was going to meet them. No more delay. She did worry for her energy at another trip, as she'd not taken any breaks, at least not after those few days camping. But after all the work and hope and . . . *need* she'd put into these blossoms, full inferno if she was going to sleep on them now.

She, again, left Kern's locket tucked away in her room at To'Ever. The assigned room, not her daygarden. She was determined . . . very much so . . . to *never* have that locket on in the forest or anywhere near her daygarden.

Speaking of the daygarden, the success of her efforts there (meaning she'd done it and liked the result) had emboldened her. She went and asked Fepa if she could travel to To'Arc, said she missed her old home and friends and wanted to visit. He said sure, his voice oddly plain, like he didn't want to deal with her right now either. They didn't discuss how long.

She left.

This time, she took a fire-burned vroom—openly with no cloak or shadowlurking, thank Fira—down to Mytil, spent a night in her room at the Enchanted Forest where she had lovely conversations with Klein about the waterfall in her homevillage, all the events surrounding it she'd grown up with, and little stories about the pers who had shared them.

And then, in the morning, joyfully cradling a baggie of snacks Klein had left out for her (he always knew her favorites), she walked to the art district and took another vroom, up to To'Arc.

The vroomruns were annoying. The conns sharp of tone. The passengers meh. The travel bumpy and the seats worn. Same old intrusions and misunderstandings and awkward shifting about. For once, Xelle didn't even care; with all luck, she wouldn't be needing vrooms soon. (Well, she cared, she just could think her way past it this time.)

Despite the partial-relief of her open traveling, her next goals *would* require discretion. A lot of it. So, asking to be dropped off at the village, she made her way toward the Tower, stopped at an outside garden, and, struck by the incredibly lovely day, sat down on the green-floor. Not ready yet anyway for either the intense casting or the play she wasn't quite sure she should be making or the way too many feelings swirled all at once, she rolled onto her back and stared up at the thick lattice of dark verdant leaves.

To'Arc in mid-fall was the absolute best. Delightful. Warmed, but not warm. Laced with chill, but not chilled. Smells and sounds, and the vines creeping thick without any of their leaves falling or wilting. And today was magnificent by those standards. Her hands reached up, behind her neck, her fingers running over soft little leaves as she pulled them around to rest together, over her chest.

For a while, she didn't do anything. As much as her mind ever allowed, that is. But it was calming, and so she did not rush to leave.

She ordered her three intended tasks in least to most risk. This left her chuckling to herself at the idea that imbuing Frond Magic onto the Arc Tower grounds was her safest goal.

Yet feeling that assessment correct, Xelle made her way to the back of the Arc Tower, and lingered a day outside, working a second rune back onto the foundation of a long-demolished shed, broken up to allow trees to grow through (which they had), but with a few solid chunks remaining under the layer of moss that had grown over them. Making the same rune as before, she rubbed reagents into it, first a fluid type of sap, and then, the sealing dust. Even as the moss later spread back over what she'd done, which she hoped it would, the rune should stay strong. Perhaps long after Xelle was gone, a very long time from now. Working into the night, she added a common stain, one that should cover the cured reagent paint, making it look like part of the original floor, and then finally wrapping herself in her travel blanket to sleep.

The smells of autumn filled her ears as filtered light streamed onto her, and her sleep was not as troubled as it could have been.

Rolling up and getting ready for the day, her gaze drew to what she could see of the rising, domed Tower through the color-tinged trees above. There would be no changing colors inside the Ever Tower; in winter, there would be even more greenery. A boast of it. Even the forests around Ever Tower would stay largely green.

She couldn't stop thinking To'Arc felt like home, but at the same time, she pushed the thought aside. Things to do. And she did not live here anymore. Did not even know if she could. She pushed it aside.

Instead, she focused on her second task: an uninvited call to a Spire Mage, while hopefully not alerting the rest. No reason to worry. She found herself again nervously chuckling, aloud.

Regaining her countenance, she moved to the large gardens behind the Tower, the ones for growing food, not for wandering. Positioning herself against a row of tall stalks, she stopped and sat, taking a moment to collect her thoughts and peer through the binoculars (yes, the ones for the bird watching). She counted the windows. Then counted again. As she'd hoped, the outer frame was swung open. If there was any day a window would be open, it would be this absolutely perfect one. She counted one last time. She positioned her gaze.

Then, with a quick but heavy cast, she sent a whisper straight up (magic this time; no Front Desk!) to the high floors of the Tower, into the open window. She felt fairly good that it worked and that it had not been swatted away as could easily be done by a skilled Mage, but still, unease roiled in her gut with how her message might be received. Yet she had a question, and no one else she could risk to ask. At worst case, she'd be sent away, which she already was.

Hurrying now, she left the woods in the direction of the path down to the village. Her breath labored from both the intensive cast and the fast walk, she located the secluded garden, its trellises thick with fall vines around a birdbath, a swing, a pair of benches, and a distinctive statuette. It was empty, and Xelle collapsed down onto a bench. The moments passed, and Xelle clasped her own hands, to keep them from shaking.

It was *a delight* when Spire Mage We'le appeared, out of nowhere, a sheer off-white gown flowing in the wind around her, and a structured white hat set tight, and as far as Xelle could tell not looking . . . too upset?

Xelle jumped to her feet. And bowed, nearly tripping over wobbling legs. "Spire Mage We'le."

"Xeleanor," she responded calmly.

With a nervous chuckle, she thanked the Mage. "Please, just that. Or Xelle. They're calling me Apprentice Xeleanor Du'Tam, now." No way in all Alyssia she was going to tell We'le the other name she'd heard, and yes, it ended in Fepa.

"Are you well?" We'le was asking.

"I am, Spire Mage We'le. Unsettled, but well."

She waited. Apparently an elaboration was expected to that. Which made sense. "Unsettled because I've not made any progress in learning what hu did to the dragons, how to protect them, who these hu are, how to let the dragons return. But well. Well in body and mostly in spirit. And in a few small tasks I needed to set in place. For the rest, I mean."

Xelle had, of course, thought about asking We'le directly about the dragons, but she was very much getting the hint that no Mage was going to tell her an ash-burned thing on that. ('Hint' meaning they'd all rebuffed her quickly and directly.) Better not to burn that here. Still, she'd started by making it clear she had that interest, just in case.

"You're lonely?" was We'le's response.

Lonely? Before Xelle could consider it, she'd already nodded. "I'm . . ." How would she say, 'but I'm not here to talk about me.' And clearly another no-go on the dragons. She went in another way. "What are the Amberborn?"

Now We'le chuckled, and nodded her head, before walking over to sit on the swing. To Xelle's complete surprise, she began to . . . swing. Rather voraciously. "They're nothing. They don't exist."

"I was wondering," Xelle said, really to herself but aloud.

We'le, swooping upward, nodded. "Can I trust you, Xeleanor?"

Xelle stood straighter. "I hope that you can. Crown Mage Jehanne . . . she . . . told me I could trust you."

We'le about fell off the swing, and swooping a quick cast, basically caught herself before crumpling ungraciously to the ground. *"Did she?"*

Mages were always a lot. "She did." What else was Xelle supposed to say.

"Well." We'le pulled her knees up, her gown over them. As far as Xelle knew, she was in her sixties, but the way she sat on the old stone tiles reminded her of a child, sneaking from home in her nightgown to watch the moons.

"As far as I know," she went on, rocking slightly, "the Amberborn are a fictional distraction invented by someone actually close to the supremacist ideologies they sought to emulate. That said, I'm on the Sevensense, which is entirely real. Consider us oversight, and I've already said more than I should on that. *And* you will never discuss that concept with anyone, nor will you speak, write, or communicate that name in any way without our express permission." She turned a sharp gaze. "There is no 'or' to that, please understand. It will not be done." We'le waved an arm behind her, stopping the momentum of the swing, which flopped back to its inanimate nadir.

While she was sure she'd done some form of mini-gape, Xelle tried to quickly adjust to the occasion. She bowed. "Thank you, Spire Mage We'le, for your trust." Xelle also knew that every time she had a quick but important conversation, she'd surely forget what she actually should have asked. This time, a question jumped to the front.

"Who is doing this, please? All this. Pelir. The machines. Do you know?"

We'le shook her head. "No. Only that there's a network, power behind it. Same pers who invented this Amberborn rubble." She glanced up and to the side. "I don't really know that, but how else could it be? One of those."

"I get it. Spire Mage We'le," she hastily appended. "I call them the Hurts."

We'le's head cocked back around. "The Hurts."

Xelle nodded. And shrugged. "They seem to want to hurt pers." Oh, another thing. "If I may, why did you mention supremacy?"

We'le grimaced. "Well, I would have answered that a name that on the cap for some sort of original-destiny invocation would only be made up by actual supremacists but then you hit me with 'The Hurts'."

Xelle snorted, then covered her mouth. She lowered her hand, thinking a moment. "But doesn't that work? I am genuinely against hurting, so—also, bad name?"

The elderly Mage squinted, and shook a finger. "Mmm. I would love to continue this repartée, but I excused myself for the washroom." She opened her hands a touch, then joined them. "I don't know that we've helped each other much. Perhaps another time."

Was that some sort of— "Kern is working for both now," Xelle hastened to say. "The Hurts and the magesphere. They compromised him, but now he wants to help. He feels like he's . . . changing. Maybe getting stronger."

We'le froze in place. A tiny freezing; as quickly, she was standing as though conducting a springday speech, her face as placid. "Do you trust him?"

"It's complicated." For now, she did. But he'd been influenced before. And who knew what angle his 'new strength' might take.

We'le paused, her lips pulling back the slightest amount. "In that case, I will say a phrase to you one time, that you will not speak again until you are certain of your right to do so. The Back Desk."

The Back Desk. Faced with the alarming idea of only hearing a thing once and perhaps forgetting it, she repeated it several times in her mind before realizing We'le was continuing and she might miss *that.*

"This desk is in Vi'Arc. You'll need a pass, the first time." We'le took a scrap of uneven paper from a pocket and pressed it between her hands. "Later." She waved it as if Xelle were holding farts in a vial. "Take this and put it away. Now, if I don't go, they'll be sending Frond to my washroom with warmed oil." She pointed at Xelle again, sharply. "Mind your secrets. No more garden whispers. And I strongly suggest you are not seen in the Tower until you've settled. Best for you. Best also, for your friends." She tipped her head, then tipped it back, then suddenly was gone.

Fira. Mages.

Speaking of Mages, Xelle had been thinking of visiting Helia again. Maybe sending her a secret note, if not a cast, and asking whether the visit would be welcome.

But We'le had made her thoughts on that clear.

When she'd visited Helia, she'd let go and just enjoyed the time together. (Actually really enjoyed it.) And before leaving, she'd searched Helia's eyes for any shade of regret, or expectation, and there'd been none. She'd made her a spiced tea, before helping her out of the Tower.

It had felt natural. Nice. Like a tension had been lifted.

And We'le was right; she couldn't put Helia in danger. Not until she knew more, could move more freely. Or Helia could.

Xelle didn't like this feeling.

She didn't like feeling like she was always *before* something. Preparing for something. Things ahead, no idea what they might be.

She felt lost.

Overwhelmed and not ready to reevaluate her plans for the moment, Xelle walked to the village. Not to a Nook & Bunk, but the far side invillage, where they were known to not ask questions.

~

A rapping sounded at her door.

Mmm, Xelle groaned, having just laid down to sleep. Sleep was hard enough to settle into without it being interrupted, in which case she wouldn't return long after the interruption had passed. Also, she hoped whoever was here was of good intent; she felt groggy and out of sorts. But it was a full building of pers, and she didn't want to be on the bad side of any management, even ones who thought the time to sleep was not yet proper.

She rose, groaning again, and slipped on her undercap and shorts. She creaked open the door.

It was Thyra.

Thyra. From the library stacks. The Breath Mage who'd really been the only one to offer her dialogue until Xelle had pushed em away. She beckoned em in, and pushed the door closed.

E held up a tiny vial and touched one ear, as if a question. Xelle nodded, and as a light scent barely passed by, Xelle felt sure they could not be heard. Which negated any security of the crowded inn, but Xelle had felt sure, on that first meeting, that whatever Thyra's secrets, e was not a threat. To Xelle.

Secrets? Danger? Magic inhalants? Was this a nightpath?

No, if it were, Xelle wouldn't ask the question so quickly and without need. Besides, Xelle's nightpaths always came with strong emotion of some sort, not her head hurting in such a mundanely irritating way. Then, Thyra was here. Xelle was in Vi'Arc. She'd just talked to We'le. And it was fall.

"How did you find me?" Xelle asked, looking the Mage up and down without pretense of not doing so. E was not marked as a Mage; if Xelle hadn't recognized eir face and particular expression, e would have thought the hu was an outvillage shopper, or a craftsper finding a home for a new set of wares.

Thyra shrugged, still not looking quite at Xelle.

"A seat?" Xelle offered. All she had in the little room was a bed, so Xelle crawled back onto the pillow side and pulled into a cross-seat. Realizing she was tilting on the small, hard pillow, she wrenched it out and set it behind her back.

Thyra stayed standing.

"I'd like to talk," Thyra said.

Given the amount of time that Xelle had wished she'd found the Mage before leaving To'Breath, for once she was prepared with what to say. She rubbed the side of her face, a yawn escaping. "I would too. But I need to know who you work for and I need to believe it." A little direct. But so was showing up at her bed.

Thyra's face tightened.

Xelle didn't have the energy. "They put a rough bag over my head and tried to take me with them."

The Mage's head jerked around and e finally looked at Xelle directly. For a quick moment. "Wehj. The Wehj Labor Council. They have concerns. I serve them. I serve Breath." Relaxing a little, e sat, but on the floor, not the bed. "For you, this started with Pelir. For me, this started before. Do you know the Lunests?"

Xelle shook her head. "Tell me. Please." Yet, Thyra hesitated. Xelle wasn't sure what she could—

"Tell me something you know. We must both have an interest in secrecy."

Nodding slowly, as she was starting to see how such things worked, Xelle thought what she could say. "I know a Mage who is involved. If I said more than that, it would compromise my working with xem."

Working with xem! She'd said more than she'd meant to. Pretending it was on purpose, Xelle stopped and waited.

Like a merchant deciding if the offered coins would suffice, Thyra pressed eir lips, moving them slightly. "For now," e said. E sat straighter. "The Lunests. Lunest Manor, in Highponds. Este Irla Du'Lunest, she. Este Mark Du'Lunest, he. Rusted coins."

Este. Xelle didn't know pers still used that title. From what she was gathering, it would be self-declared. And to not even take the prestigious name of Highponds, but of . . . their house? This made Bon Lerf Du'Lerf look like a small potato. Well, no, Lerf did claim a whole city. And brand.

The Lunests. She remembered what Klein had told her, when first looking into Kern. "What do they want?"

Thyra's lip twitched up, like a tic. "More. Always more."

They sat without speaking for a moment. Xelle had realized before that it took Thyra significant energy to communicate (more than Xelle!) and so she didn't want to burden em. If Thyra had found her, all the way here, then e would share what e wanted.

It hadn't been much of a conversation yet, but Xelle felt a creeping feeling of comfort. Between We'le, and Thyra, and dear Helia, of perhaps being less alone, at least in a broader sense.

And not just Kern.

Thyra shifted. "They excel at covering their tracks. With coins." E made a small clinking noise. "The link between Arc Spire and the Lunests is not clear. Not to me. Perhaps to you. I believe they are at the top of this. The transfer between them and all our Towers is not clear. They don't understand," e added. "Wehj. I pledged to To'Breath."

Thyra had to know that Xelle herself had not pledged, then, or now, but, then, e'd also made it sound like a choice. Perhaps, then, they did have something in common. Wishing she had something wiser to say, Xelle searched, and settled on this. "Loyalty to more than one is complex. I know it. Yet the place where they intersect is where you find yourself."

Not really sure what she'd just said or why that was what had popped out, Xelle resolved to think about it. Later.

"You no longer know me. Nor at To'Breath."

The Mage seemed to be waiting for a response. Xelle nodded. E rose, facing the door. "I wish you sleep."

"Thyra."

E turned back, partially.

"I will not reveal you." She'd been thinking of a way to say this. She didn't want to promise absolute silence. The more pers she could trust to work with, the more complicated that would get. But she wanted Thyra to trust her. E could trust her. She hoped. "Do you remember what book I was reading, when we met?"

Thyra nodded, with a slight gleam in eir eye, and then the door clicked shut.

Xelle lay awake.

Despite We'le's cautions, there was no way she was going back to To'Ever without visiting her inkbloom. For months now, they'd connected from afar, as the phyta grew, and as they learned each other. The inkbloom knew she was near, and e felt them, strongly, now, calling for em.

Xelle made her way out of Vi'Arc, and back toward the Tower, hopefully without being seen or noticed. She wound back to the outside wall, and, not easily but successfully, runed her way inside the nightgarden.

The room glowed with the surreal light of the inkbloom.

That wasn't quite right, as it wasn't really light that the phyta reflected from the chunks of obsidian surrounding them, but more the ability to see in the dark. E knew, that sounded nonsensical, but here it was simply true.

Xelle did not have to turn on eir lights. The glow of the inkbloom would make the blue lights e'd had made look futile, like a child's chalk next to thick, cured paint. In fact, e wanted to be rid of them; add that to eir list of homekeeping needs. No, she didn't want to spin later wondering what thing she'd wanted to remember, and so she took out her notebook again, and finding that she could see better in whatever this light was than the blue light she'd used before, Xelle made a wavering note. *Disassemble blue lights. Sell? Store?*

Xelle scanned the livewalls, taking in the phyta's richness, the way the glow concentrated into each blossom, and yet how the vines were just as clear, each connecting with the next. No wonder, no wonder this could not be drawn with standard paper or ink. E started to think how one could do it, with black paper and magical inks, and—

Perhaps e was being rude.

Hello, e said, in eir mind. *I hope that I am welcome here.* No, that wasn't right, they'd been calling em there. *Thank you, I mean, thank you for calling me. If you are ever displeased, please let me know. Through our bond. I am so . . . grateful to be here, with you, physically now. You are beautiful!* Xelle cringed, imagining meeting someone and starting with that line, but the inkbloom felt . . . joyful, almost. Not hu joy, but something akin.

Were they . . . were they ready to use? Was it appropriate to use them? Was Xelle ready to try a dangerous cast e'd never learned? And what did you do? Pick a blossom? Xelle did not want to pick a blossom. E . . .

The moment had been so distant that now that it was here, she realized she hadn't prepared at all. Had she even believed?

She'd spent all her time and all her resources on this thing that no one thought she could do. That felt like believing to her. And if she didn't know how to do it, she was going to figure it out.

Xelle sat down onto the seat and swiveled back and forth. Her mind tried to catch up, not used to processing motion in the surreal, new light. Xelle closed her eyes.

E felt a . . . center. Like a crossroads with uncountable paths, but as foreign to a path as this light was to light. Yet e felt it, was in it. The inkbloom observed em, like a visitor at the door, here for an errand, but not meant to stay. As odd as an actionless visitor, was how she felt now, and as odd as walking away after the intrusion would feel, so would it here. She must do something, and soon.

E sang. Worried about the effect words might have in such a place, this time, in a low hum only, hoping the tones of the song would convey that Xelle did not know how to travel yet, that she was here, with respect and caution, yet great desire, hoping for a steadying touch.

She felt one. One, two, and many all at once.

The center drew into more comprehension, yet with nothing around it. From here, Xelle knew e could go anywhere. The entire world before em. Xelle was tiny. A point. Almost nothing.

With a gasp, she snapped open her eyes, fearful she might disappear into the speck she'd imagined, hoping the exit had not caused offense, but right now knowing she needed to tend to herself. She rubbed her hands together, feeling the softness of the lotion she'd used earlier, the ridge from where she'd scratched her thumb. The width of each fingernail, not evenly smooth, yet a pleasant feeling.

There was no scent anymore, which became its own scent. She could not smell the soil, or the bricks, or anything but peace. Her sounds were her own, the turning of the swivel joint on her seat, the stretching of her body as she moved. Her tongue ran over the back of her teeth, two tiny knobs of bone protruding.

Xelle looked, still gathering herself, at the inkbloom, traced their vines and swirls of light with her gaze as she reoriented. She felt them more deeply now. Felt . . . comforted.

There was no need to pick anything, they were there, offering partnership. No. Bond. Yet, her previous mistake with the singular rune (though it had turned out quite nice) made her pause. How, if she cast from here, following where the inkbloom led her—(The inkbloom was the teacher of the cast!)—how would she return? As little as she knew about the phyta, she'd never heard that it was like a rune, one to the other. It was the property of the mature blossom, was all she'd gleaned. Like a reagent.

This was more. Much, much, more.

She felt a tug. Like a rope. Like the way she'd learned to pull herself from tree to tree, bypassing the slow road below. What she called her sling cast.

The bond. The bond was the connection. And she felt it, that she could sling from here, hold the connection, and then sling back again.

At once, possibilities flooded her mind. Where she could travel, how far, how fast, how long. Elation. Then, fear. Vulnerability. If the nightgarden were destroyed, the phyta harmed (or upset?), her material low, her connection weakened while away, then she could find herself unable to return. And then she felt . . . love. Love? These phyta, they were part of Xelle now. Was she part of them, or was that not how it worked? Did they seek to calm her? Her heart buzzed, and she spun in non-space, seeing everything around her, knowing where she could fly, not alone, but together.

Slinging. Pulling. Bonds. *Ash-swept Mages.* They talked about this. In code. Conversations she'd caught, walked past, over all these years, suddenly made sense.

Return pod. What was that? Not a fancy vroom, she knew that. She walked over, gazing into and around each blossom. She didn't want to disturb the chunks of obsidian, or dig into their soil. She paced back and forth against one livewall, then over to the other. She thought of Mages.

No, not Fepa. Ugh.

Arc Mages. High-ranking Arc Mages. Top advisors, what about when she'd had assignment to the records room. Mages of all levels, barely staying long enough to grab a file or drop one off—

Gone long enough to eat first. Eat before you go. Why had ranking Mages chatted about getting their granola in? They hadn't.

E closed eir eyes and tried now, to ask the inkbloom if e was right. If there was something e would eat, to help return without holding the connection. A pod?

Xelle felt an energy amongst the vines. Calling it a discussion would be like calling a taut string a wave, but it was the feel e had. One of the blossoms opened up, an inner stalk swelling to what looked like a large grape. As e put it in eir mouth, it squished around and Xelle almost spat it out. But she held back, and soon what was left was hard. Like a pit. Well, it was a pit.

Perhaps it was better to swallow with the coating.

With a bit of will and much more faith, e pushed the pit down into her throat, feeling nothing left, except—

There it was. Like, carrying to grow a baby. (She had never carried pregnancy, but this was what she could imagine.)

Feeling very scared about what she'd just done and if it had been so wise to jump in this way, and what the consequences might be, and feeling like any moment she'd spiral and have a day or a month or a life, even, where she couldn't see the light for the gloom and not being able to deal with that right now, she grabbed the hand offered. A vine, not hand, and slung out and went back, not home, but somewhere she could feel safe. Then she let go.

Xelle stood in eir daygarden.

Xelle stood in eir daygarden.

She staggered to the bed, worrying that she'd done something wrong. The feelings. Something. Tired.

In her sleep, a presence.

11 - The glimmer in her eyes

Xelle awoke. She felt heavy, tired. Searching herself, her material, and remembering the first classes health checks she'd learned at To'Frond, she concluded this: She was very tired.

Which is to say, in the understatements of Xelle-speak and double-blades of magic-speak, unharmed but in utter necessity of rest.

She seemed well, in body. Some fatigue, her material low but not yet dangerously. The worst bit was her nightpaths; for the next few days they were especially intense, severe, *specific,* and completely disorienting.

Every morning she reassured herself. Where she was. Who she was. What day it was. That she had no pre-set schedule that day. That the things she'd seen and done during the nightpaths had not been real. That she didn't think them herself, whatever her mind thrust at her.

Each day, she tried to rest.

Xelle still remembered when rest was a treasured thing. A day off, a few days off. Here, under the void of Mage Fepa, she really didn't have a place to be. Not by hu standards. In any other circumstance, this would have been near-perfection. An accomplishment, and then a rest.

In this circumstance, the rest was as vacuous as it was necessary, her mind left to wrench in endless frustration. She had a way to visit Thunder and the rest of the dragons but she couldn't yet do it. She remembered Jehanne's warning, the urgency in her eyes. Watch your material. Life and death.

Xelle could not wait, but moreso, she could not mess this up. And so she could wait. Would wait. Each moment clicked by, with too much distraction to do something, but barely able to stand sitting here, letting her mind cycle over its emptiness.

Muttering grumbles, an odd comfort, she finally put on Kern's locket, and sat, waiting, in her room. He'd told her to figure out how to contact him, but she'd made a whole secret room and self-taught (meaning, no Mages) inkbloom travel in the meantime, so he could chalk his own figure onto the floor and hump it.

After a while—she was tired and not going anywhere, buddy—she felt the ringing, and answered it. Kern stepped into her room.

Not truly, but it felt that way. And no, she would not swipe her hand through the visage. She stayed on the bed, and pulled her legs in.

"Kern," she said with a slight bow.

"Xeleanor," he returned. If he was irritated by her casual pose, he did not indicate it.

"Do you know the Lunests?" She watched his reactions, expectantly.

"Lunests? Lunest Estate? They are wealthy." Still, he showed no other reaction.

"I have reason to think they are behind recent events. Will you look into it?"

He tilted his head. "The Lunests? Interesting. I will see what I can find." He paused. "Without reasons to inquire, I'll need to be cautious. But I can think of something. They are . . . not known for their warmth."

A warning sat on her tongue. Not to be found out. But was she talking to Kern, or to herself? Kern knew this; he'd just said it. 'Correct moves only,' Jehanne had told her.

No, what else had she said? 'From her position.'

Fira.

Either Mages were going to get more direct in their speech, or Xelle was going to have to get sharper at clues, and she knew which one it would be.

From Jehanne's position. Maybe from Kern's too. But what was Xelle? An oddball Apprentice viewed as mystery or chaos, very few knowing her at all. Maybe Xelle's position was different. Maybe she could misstep. Maybe she didn't need the imprisonment of perfection.

Kern was staring at her eyes. Not, like, gazing into her eyes, but peering at them. Where in Mage advancement did one gain such casts of entitlement? "What have you been casting?" He sounded like he'd found her sneaking samosas from the kitchen. Which had happened a lot at Arc. Yet this was not the scent he was picking up.

Did inkbloom leave a trace? Could he sense the pod within her, waiting to take her back to the nightgarden? She was dealing with a very skilled Arc Mage. Well, if he knew, he knew. Good to know there was a shadow. And his suspicions, she had no desire to parse. "Arc Magic, as you've previously advised me, Spire Mage Kern." She bowed again.

"You're putting us all at risk," he said, maintaining a perfect professor's expression. "It concerns me."

She shrugged. She didn't want to hurt anyone, but the idea—when they knew so little—that her experiments were more dangerous than their languid caution was irritating. Calling herself the rattle in the salt jar felt self-indulgent, but she couldn't help think they might need one. And luckily for Xelle, inkbloom were too sacred to discuss, including over this call, so he could not press her further. "If you have something to tell me, please do. Otherwise, I know that you are busy."

His eyes flared. "Yes. I am. Until later?"

The image blinked out.

Xelle waited almost a week, making herself wait until she really felt like herself again. This was a very long week, believing she could see Thunder again, could reassure them all (beyond her nightly messages directly to Thunder which she wasn't sure zhey received) that her resolve had not faded, but knowing that she could take no chance in exceeding her own limitations. She was stretching them enough.

Rather than continue to dissolve in her own muck, she started taking this time to think about how she would arrive, how the cast would work. Other precautions. Other plans. She wasn't sure how many times she could travel on the pod she'd ingested. Whether it would digest (she didn't love thinking about this) or stay there. She could be safe and go back to the nightgarden first, but then, that was extra exertion when she could go directly to the mountains. Finally, thinking about how she knew she'd heard the phrase 'return pod' and hoping some of Kern's warning tone hadn't rubbed off on her, she decided she needed to go to the nightgarden first. See how she felt from there. At least, then, she'd be at her starting point if she couldn't go further.

Yet, Xelle really hoped she wouldn't have to wait another week. This one had been endless enough, and her nightgarden was a small, cramped room, stocked with questionably old jerky. Still. She'd made her decision, she was going there first. She stood in her daygarden and breathed in. Only thinking of the pod now, feeling to sense it. With that attention, it felt like a stomache-ache, something ready to leave. She felt its impatience.

She let it take her.

The disorientation of the inkbloom's strange light felt like the realm of a nightpath, and she had to drop down and rub the stone tiles of the garden's floor, reach toward one of the curving roots and feel its tiny ridges, to convince herself this world was real, that she had traveled safely. That she was here.

Yes, she was here, but the pod was no longer within her. Not consumed. Returned, was her best word in the moment. Rising, she moved toward where it had grown before, curious if it would be in the same spot. There was no pod in that blossom, nor in the others as she searched each side.

She had no idea how that worked.

It didn't matter; she felt the crossroads even more strongly now, and knew that she could go to the mountains and sling back safely, without a pod, as long as she held the connection. That way, she wouldn't risk having to wait again, or worse. It might be a short visit, but at least she could go. Show them she hadn't forgotten, in case Thunder wasn't getting the messages she sent zhem, every night. (Or even if Thunder were afraid or otherwise not allowed to pass her messages. She had no concept, yet, of the dynamics.)

Xelle reached into her heart as if she were made of vapor, and flung her hand outward. To somewhere cold.

Used now to the delight of fall on the high rim, she was not ready for the frigid blast of fall (in a strictly temporal sense!) in the high mountains, of dry, harsh wind. Yet, she was able to push her shivers aside, because, amidst a snow-blurred background of gray rock and white ice, there zhey were. There stood Thunder.

Thunder hopped and ran in circles around her. "Ok, ok!" Xelle said, running her arm along the per's smooth shoulder as zhey bent down to inspect her.

Why was Xelle being inspected? Thunder sniffed around her, sniffing the ground, then her leg, then stumbled back, a puff of smoke emanating from zheir mouth.

"What's wrong?" Xelle asked, her teeth chattering. Thunder breathed fire to the side. Without anything to catch on fire, the flames dissipated quickly, yet the blast of warmth brought her some relief.

Thunder let a little screech. Zhey sounded upset.

Xelle could not see the other dragons, but Thunder's distress felt related to whatever zhey'd sniffed on her. Xelle tried to think what she might smell like. Other than garlic. "Do I smell like another hu?"

Zhey dipped, in the sign they'd agreed on as 'no'.

"A type of magic?" Maybe dragons smelled magic, and having a much stronger influence of Ever prong now would be notable.

Thunder nodded. "Ever Magic?"

This time, the no was pronounced. If it wasn't Ever, she doubted it'd be Frond.

"Arc Magic? . . . My inkbloom?"

It was definitely that. Thunder reared up and glanced over zheir shoulder as if worried they'd be overheard.

She thought this through. The only way Xelle knew how to reach the dragons was by inkbloom, so wouldn't that be expected? *The only way to reach the dragons . . .* "Thunder. Has inkbloom been used to hurt dragons?"

Slowly, zhey nodded.

Oh.

All the secrecy, the removal from books. Still . . .

The idea made Xelle feel heavy. She looked up at Thunder. "Is there a way we can communicate, that you can talk to me, I mean, without just yes and no? I suppose you don't speak hu."

Thunder sat back and snorted. No, zhey dipped. Then yes, zhey nodded.

Wait, zhey did or zhey didn't? Now Xelle laughed, her teeth ending in unpleasantly involuntary clatter. She was glad to see that Thunder didn't look cold. But, she'd barely arrived and she'd need to leave very soon. Unused to what she'd done and firmly holding the connection like a safety rope, she could feel the tension of the inkbloom starting to pull her back. Even if Thunder could keep her warm, here, without a cloak—why had she not thought to bring a cloak? "I can't stay, but I need you to know I'm still doing my best. To bring you back. And I really need to stick to one question at a time, don't I?"

Thunder didn't react, maybe not sure if that was the question. Xelle laughed again. "Do you speak hu language, in any way I can receive it?"

No, zhey motioned, but with an edge to it. Ah, hu language.

"Is there a way you can communicate to me?"

Yes, zhey motioned.

Xelle wondered why zhey hadn't before.

Thunder sat back further, snout scrunching, as though annoyed at this thought. "Hey." She was not taking this from a teen. "You have your dragon pers here to explain things to you. I was not taught anything about dragons; I'm figuring this out on my own. Hu-wise," she added at Thunder's narrowing of zheir eyes. "I am willing to try it. What do I do?"

Oh! Xelle fell back into a seat—perhaps?—feeling like the floor had dropped out around her in all directions. Her skin tingled and her eyes twitched, more than usual. The tastes of ash and herbs filled her mouth.

She found herself resisting, willing away the foreign sensations. But, she made herself remember, zhey were trying to communicate. She trusted zhem. Inherently. With about all the willpower and trust she could find, she relaxed. If falling backward off of a cliff based on a teenager's trust felt like relaxing.

Now, sounds in her ears. A sound; it startled her. With a yelp, Xelle flailed like a child new to water, and pushed away the noises and lights and everything that was not her.

It took her many long moments to understand that she was lying on her back in a patch of scratchy snow, and that the large dragon face hovering above her did not look displeased. "Wow," she said. "That's going to take me some time to understand."

Thunder, from what she could see of zheir bobbing face once it pulled away, was bouncing again. Clearly it had worked better than zhey'd thought, even if Xelle felt like she'd forgotten to swim and filled her sinuses with harsh sting and fear.

"Give me a moment," she waved, shooing the dragon like a climbing nibling as she crawled over onto her quickly numbing hands and knees, onto a snowless rock, just trying to regain the feelings of her body against its surface. Of space as it should be. Even the intense cold helped reorient her.

"What if," she finally said. "What if we try something simple? One sense. Something I need to know first. That would help me adjust to the rest. And quickly; I really need to go." Not just the magic; she worried for her quickly-numbing hands.

Thunder was either confused or contemplating what she'd said. As someone who had carried that unfortunate burden her whole life (one of her grandparents had long mistaken her thinking-face for annoyance, which generated a bit of annoyance in turn, until they'd worked it out), Xelle tried not to judge.

Thunder seemed to think that was funny. Xelle scowled, in mock. "Do you understand, though? Just, like, one facet of the gem this time. Only the sight, or only the sound." She pointed to her eyes and then her ears.

Now, ready for the onslaught (she could find nicer words for it when it deserved them) she laid on her back, closed her eyes, pulled her freezing hands into her sleeves, and waited.

The resistance hit as hard, but not as thick. She could see something, on the other side, not as in a wall, but a shell, around her. She flailed again, pushing through it, willing herself to ignore everything else, the discomfort, the cold. *There!*

She could see grass. Pretty, waving grass against sparkling water—a place Xelle had not seen before. Not exactly. 'Seeing' wasn't correct either; unlike her own vision, it felt harder to see up close, and easier to see at some distance, then again it blurred. And the colors were a palette she couldn't attempt to explain, as she had no basis to reference them. But, different colors. More of them. So many more.

The grass waved, then faltered. Xelle felt a horrible ache surge in her stomach, as if she would throw it up. Not like the inkbloom, like a spoiled lunch. In this world, she thought, she rolled onto her side, arms across her middle. In the distance, a dragon soared, clearly. She yearned for emotions, felt scared without them. Who was this? A friend? A parent? She could not feel, or hear in this world. Only see.

In that instant she started to hear, and like the screeching of gears falling loose, the vision wavered. The sounds dropped. Silence.

The high rim, now. She soared over it, looking down. Hu, there were hu below her, building homes. The hu all looked like Xelle. And the houses, they were all the same, a simple hut of an impractical shape.

She lurched.

Now, she saw clearly, the place in the low mountains where Xelle had met Thunder that first time. Where Thunder had lived, before zheir family (not quite family, she would have to understand better) had to destroy it, to leave.

The images stopped.

And Xelle was freezing on a mountain slope, Thunder now shivering too. She rolled to her feet, holding out shaky arms to comfort the dragon. "You keep moving. And you don't want to. You weren't always in the mountains."

Instead of a nod, Xelle now understood this was correct. Or close to correct. And being in the mountains and not by choice, would be . . . confinement. They were confined before, and now more so.

That was also correct.

But why had they stayed, for so long? An agreement, or— She remembered what Jehanne had said. A treaty.

"Did the treaty keep you in the mountains?"

Yes.

"Did hu break the treaty by causing you to leave again?"

Pause. Yes.

Well. That was something. "I want to help you return. Not just to the mountains, but wherever your home should be. I can do my best." Xelle felt sick, not from the vision, but from her own reactions about what hu had done, even without knowing more. To jump now to help when she'd lived in this world. When she was about to return to it, this felt . . . sick as well. But also necessary.

She was dangerously cold.

Thunder flapped upward, landing hard on the ground and stomping around in a circle. At first, Xelle thought she'd done something wrong, until she realized it reminded her of a child imitating a grumpy old hu.

"They're mad, the others," she tried. Yes, that was it. "They might not wait for whatever I can do. What hu can do."

While this was correct, something was not. She could warm at the nightgarden. One more thought. Thunder tapped zheir claws in the gesture they'd established as 'Ready?' and Xelle nodded.

It wasn't easier this time, but it wasn't quite as hard. What Xelle saw was the sun, rising and setting, over and over as if time were flying past. Time. The vision stopped. A feeling remained, the feeling of the inkbloom's sling, the rope that threatened to slip from her grasp. She needed to leave now; even if she asked Thunder for more warmth, all the back and forth was causing her still unfamiliar cast to strain. Yet, she thought she had it.

"Time goes faster for you?"

Thunder's snout scrunched, and Xelle felt certain it was in frustration.

"Slower. You're older. They're older."

Zhey nodded.

Xelle wondered if Thunder was trying to say not to worry, the time hadn't felt as long to them, but it seemed insensitive to—

Thunder was nodding.

Ah, yes, hiding thoughts from a dragon. She shrugged.

As if trying to imitate it, Thunder bowed zheir arms out to the side. "How would you do it? We call it a shrug, like, oh well!"

Zheir head waggled slightly side to side as zheir eyes rolled upward.

Xelle was impressed. If dragons were more internally sarcastic than she was, they were going to get along just fine. "Hey." Her mouth clattered violently, and instead of straining to form the words, she switched to thought. *That was well-done. I don't know if I understood enough, but I really think I understood some. And that means you know that I do have to go. You can feel it, maybe? The inkbloom?* Zhey nodded. *I mostly wanted you to know I am trying to help, that I won't give up. Can you tell them? The others?* Again, a nod, though slower. *And there are pers all over the lower mountains now, and I don't know if any mean harm.* That was so difficult to say. To think. Thunder needed to know. *I have to go back, now. I'll practice and return, ok?*

Thunder ran a claw around in the dirt, a low grumble sounding around zhem. While she'd expected Thunder's reaction to be sad, or resigned, or even encouraging, she had the distinct sense zhey were . . . upset. Impatient. Almost angry.

Her fingers were stinging now inside her sleeves, her cast pulsing. *This is dangerous for me now. I'm sorry I can't stay longer.*

Zhey stamped, and tapped another 'Ready?' Was Thunder saying they could fly now? More communication? "Tell me," she blurted out, regretting the opening of her mouth.

The image of soaring toward To'Arc popped into her mind.

Oh.

I want you to go with me too. But it's just . . . not set up for that. And I'm not there anymore. I'm at a different Tower and I . . . It felt unfair to suggest that her own confinement of choice was anything like this, but actually, dragons read all her thoughts, so. Eh. *We'll figure it out, ok? Hey. Can you hear when I talk to you? When I'm back there? At To'Ever.* Ah. Thunder would have to know she was staying at To'Ever, she should have realized that.

Zhey nodded. A little.

Can you talk to me? Show me things? When I'm not near? The answer to that was more confused. But the pull was increasing now. She had to go.

Thunder let her run a shaking, sleeved hand down the side of zheir face. And watched with a flat expression as Xelle disappeared.

She collapsed onto the floor of her nightgarden, winded but here. She patted herself, now. Yes, she was really here. And well. Ish. She breathed onto her fingers, wincing at the pain. Reaching down to pull off her boots and cradle her aching toes. Crawling to the closet to pull out her damaged cloak, and wrapping in it, shaking uncontrollably. And then, the reverberations of the magic hit her, causing the cold to feel unimportant.

This sensation was so different than the return pod, and, frankly, as unpleasant in entirely different ways. Instead of moving herself with the aid of the phyta, this time it felt like they'd pulled her back. She'd landed here, hard, in a non-physical sense.

Exhaustion took her again, but with comfort she realized it was not as severe as before. Whether the sling travel was easier or she would grow accustomed to the casts, or both, she didn't know. And she was much too tired to parse it. Wearily, she tried to communicate gratitude to the inkbloom. Her worries, her troubles, they were not about them. She hoped . . . hoped they understood.

There was no bed here, she realized, but she could not go anywhere without rest. She curled into the cloak, willing sleep to take her on the hard, uneven floor.

Sleep did not take her.

Hour after hour passed. She would sit up, try to breathe long breaths, but she was tired. Sleep would find her.

Late now, she knew. Late into the night. Sleep would find her. It always did, eventually.

She dreamed of an arm, reaching over her. Comfort. And she drifted into the nightpaths.

12 - Magey Riddles and other Ash

Her nightgarden had no space for a bed. So slinging back here in exhaustion was not a plausible solution, longer term. Perhaps she would strengthen at this means of travel, or determine other means. She couldn't worry about it on the first attempt. She wouldn't.

Ready to go back to her daygarden in theory, she was not yet in material. Or regular old energy. (Still not convinced those were so separate.) She did hope, with a bit of gut optimism, it wouldn't take a week to recover this time—but she knew she wasn't casting anywhere today.

She might as well find this Back Desk. Not just so it didn't linger as an unknown (Xelle distinctly didn't prefer lingering unknowns), but if it were needed in an instant, that wouldn't be the time to figure it out. Plus, if this pass was a ticket she needed the first time, better to hand that over and not potentially lose it. Or have it wear out. Or whatever magic tickets did. And she wasn't going to sit in here all day; even the inkbloom seemed to be gently suggesting to give them their space.

Oh, it was a nice walk to Vi'Arc. Xelle would never apologize for mentioning or over-mentioning (ugh, that word was apologizing—well, strike that!) the bliss of an autumn walk amongst the trees. Perhaps even more so, as there was no land of eternal fall she could live in (or . . . maybe? that she would want to?) the perfect fall day always held a specific edge of it perhaps being the last, a tiny blast of cold just waiting outside, just waiting to breathe in and add the tiniest chill, leading to the deepest cold. Deeply healing. Deeply liminal. Her life, in a day. Anyway.

Xelle was used to cold. But e really loved fall.

Not sensing anyone else around her, she reached into her pocket and removed the pass We'le had handed her. It was a rectangular-ish scrap of paper, the type some would consider coarse and impractical but was probably expensive, found only in a Mytil paper boutique or the one hu out in a mountain town who makes them, and only for certain clients.

It was blank on both sides. Standard Mage stuff, there, she wasn't worried anything had rubbed off. She brushed it over with Arc detection, expecting letters to appear, but there was no reaction at all.

Did We'le know she'd learned a bit of other prongs? She tried a hint of Breath (poorly, but enough) and nothing happened. She didn't think a rune would be involved. Well, she was the one living at Ever; was the card enchanted? It didn't feel to be.

It didn't feel like magic at all. Hilarious. Hilarious Mages.

And where was this desk anyway? Somewhere in the whole fire-spread village?

Curses, she was too tired for some Magey riddle. You know—the 'pass' referred to a cross-street, not the paper, or 'don't speak these words' meant you needed to write them, or perform a word-erasure, or, whatever. She was not going to eat the paper or stand here looking through it. No.

Xelle liked puzzles, when she'd asked to do them. Now, she was tired. So, she rather aimlessly walked the village, just glad for the regular motion in her legs and the perfection of the precious fall day, now mixed with the smells of frying or the rustling of extra canopies being added to the market stalls, or the singing of children through the windows of a village school. She absorbed it all, every piece, feeling very much here, and alive, and strangely calmed. By the day, by seeing Thunder—probably by it all.

In the back of her mind, she knew her immersion in her wanderings also sought to avoid that distressing moment when she had to decide on a next course . . . without having reached the Desk. She took the paper out again, willing it to share its secret.

"Have a piece of paper?" The tiniest whisper ran into her ear. She swatted by instinct, as though a wayward stalk of tall grass had tickled her. As grass didn't talk or reach her ears, she turned around to see a hu, standing at a distance, pushing a small cart. Staring her way.

Great, the local creeper.

She stopped. No, that was an Arc cast. So subtle she almost didn't realize it, though of course, *thinking* about it made that completely obvious. She wandered back toward the cart, hurrying a little at the relief of finding a path. "I do." The hu waited.

Fira, was there a coded response? 'Show me your wares?' She just stood there, seeing if her presence was enough. Clearly, the per knew that she had the thing. Their eyes met.

The hu waited a moment, seemed to shrug, then said, "Follow me, if you will. I have a few items you might like, but it's too windy here, on the main street."

Once alone in the nondescript alley, she felt the shimmer of magic.

"Wasn't expecting you," the hu said, "but it seems that was mutual. Can't let you in just with that. And, please, let that be for you, because I don't even know the process for a clean-up."

"What am I supposed to do?" Xelle's heart started pounding, not in concern, but in the way her body reacted to an uneasy interaction.

The hu was clearly trying to mask an expression of some kind. "At this point, convince me that's yours?" Xe nodded toward the paper now concealed in her hand.

Xelle flashed the sign of the Arc. The hu's mouth flattened a bit.

"Umm . . ." She realized she was saying that aloud. Mentioning We'le seemed wrong; the hu could easily ask who sent her and try and verify it, and We'le had seemed quite serious about her own privacy. Privacy. That reminded her . . .

Nervously, she slowly moved her finger toward her forehead, and the hu's eyes followed it curiously. "I'm the dragonfriend," Xelle offered. "Xeleanor Du'Tam," she added hastily.

Xyr eyes widened and stared intensely at the sigil. Feeling a tingle in it, Xelle wondered who this hu could be. A Mage did not feel correct, but that was absolutely a nuanced cast. A puzzle for another time, as the hu had drawn back.

"So you are." Xe said it plainly, and flashed the Arc. "Welcome. Look for this cart, even if the vendor changes. Next time, approach discreetly and ask to get out of the wind."

"Could anyone just say that?"

The hu's eyes narrowed. "No. Now, your paper?"

Reminding herself xe'd sensed it and then cast Arc Magic, but still worrying that she might have done something wrong, she nervously handed over the plain piece of paper. The hu lifted a curtain on the cart, and motioned her in.

Into the cart? This was either a way to the Back Desk or things were about to get very strange. She glanced at the low-roofed cart, trying to memorize a few key details for future recollection while fervently hoping she wasn't crawling into a Xelle-sized box to be taken, as the Hurts had tried to before, but reminding herself xe'd known of the paper. She was a Mage. If anything felt wrong, she would fight back.

These were too many thoughts at once, and the hu was looking impatient now, xyr arm extended. Xelle pushed back an involuntary moment of fear and ducked under the heavy cloth, appearing all at once inside a barely lit room, not the cart at all. A clerk sat at an old, scratched-up desk, as bothered and bored as any clerk at the normal one. Familiarity, often an unexpected friend.

"Xeleanor . . . Du'Tam." Great, now she was getting mageshamed here too. Well, she'd been invited in. Xe could deal with it.

"Call me Xelle," she said, with a friendly wave and the sign of the Arc. "So, uh, how does this work? Like, is this actually a door to go in? Can I just do that?" Then, she thought, why would pers go through all this just to end up visibly in the Tower? "I suppose you only go certain places? Are there signs?"

Based on the returned expression, the clerk and she were not off on the best footing. Well, her mind was spinning now; she was doing her best. "May I know your name?" she tried.

"You may." Xe set down a pencil. "Sec Lai Dvi'Arc, she, unless you annoy me."

Oh, not a Mage, then. That was interesting. And Sec, she hadn't heard the title. Xelle bowed. "It is nice to meet you, Sec Lai."

Her face softened a bit. "Now, there is transport through here, and then a hidden lift. Only opens to certain rooms on certain floors. You will not speak of them." Looking at Xelle, she sighed. "You're not marked for anything, and I'm strict on compartments. But if you'd like to tell me who you are hoping to see, you could do worse with your trust."

"I'm . . ." She did trust her. If they put her at this secret desk, anyway. She seemed nice. But Xelle had a feeling she should not say whom, that others did not. "One of these rooms, can I call from it?" She hadn't meant to bother We'le, but if she needed a contact, she knew of no other. Maybe she still wouldn't need to.

Lai tilted her head. "Sort of, yes. There are rooms for many purposes. I'm sorry . . . I don't remember someone of your status coming through since I've been here. Usually it's better explained to them." She considered for a moment. "I suggest you take the transport and lift to the parlor."

Transport. Parlor. Check. Thanking Sec Lai, Xelle walked back through the indicated door, shutting it behind her as instructed, and was surprised to see little seats on some sort of moving track, like a tiny train, but with the track moving instead. There was a little lever. She pulled it, and the track stopped.

Xelle sat down onto one of the seats. She started to reach toward the lever, and felt silly. If she could be trusted with this, surely she could cast. With a fling of her hand, the lever went back into place, and the track began moving again.

She wondered how the cart had worked, the seamless passage between the small space and large. She had not cast, herself, to transport into the Back Desk (which was probably still in the village, given the need for a train), but had stepped through it as though it were there the whole time. If the cart had been stationary, she could have assumed it was a false front, but she had watched it move. Not knowing gave her a new weight, another separation. Arc Knowledge that was being held from her, because she would not pledge.

Yet, she was here, in a place she hadn't known existed. That was something. Almost an illusion itself in the smoothness of motion, but clearly physical, the track continued through a wideish corridor. The sides were covered with paintings, some that looked very old. Not that To'Arc was so far away, but still, Xelle was surprised how quickly another station pulled into view. Not sure what lever she should pull here, she was relieved when the track stopped, right where she could depart. Once she was off, it began to move again.

Indeed, there was a small and weirdly posh lift, with upholstered walls and a shiny floor. A control knob could be moved next to a series of labeled locations. Seeing **Parlor** she selected it, and without much of a sensation of movement, only a low rumble seemed to tell her it had worked. The door opened, and . . . yes, it was a parlor.

Designed by someone who really liked pink and rose shades. And fringe.

There were no attendants, no clerks, but only a blank book. This, she knew, was not Arc Magic, but an Ever enchantment. Taking the pen next to it, she carefully wrote: *Here to see Spire Mage We'le.* She was nervous what We'le's reaction might be, but well, at least she could tell her about her progress? That her trust was not misplaced?

Xelle worried about all this as she waited on a short bench with wide arms, noticing there seemed to be no door. No amagic door, or at least none visible to her now.

After a handful of minutes, her worry grew. Had she done this right? Could she just . . . take the lift back? What if We'le declined to see her? Or was out at the market? (Did We'le do her own shopping?) What if someone else needed to use this room and was waiting? How often did pers do this whole thing?

She was glad (more than that, but no energy left to describe it) when the Mage entered, smoothly and with a light blue gown, seeming to walk through one of the walls.

Xelle noted which one. And stood. "Spire Mage We'le." She flashed the Arc.

"I'm not sure I meant use it . . . so soon?" By her smile, she wasn't upset. "But perhaps you aren't here to visit?"

"Yes, well, I learned some things. Sometimes I work fast." Thinking this was not generally accurate, she added, "Mostly slow."

"Oh." We'le sat in one of the poofier chairs. Xelle sat back down on her bench. We'le's thin arms were crossed over one knee, attentively. Not as though Xelle were a storyteller, she somehow thought. As though she were the student. Well, anyway.

"I talked to a dragon," Xelle began. "I believe that they used to live across Alyssia, or at least had homes outside of the mountains. Hu made them leave. First once, then twice, then again. Just as I did, this spring."

Very, very slowly, We'le nodded.

"And I've been thinking. There are so many resources out there, I mean, I didn't know about any of this." She waved around. "I've learned something concrete, too, about the Hurts."

She had considered giving We'le the name of the Lunests as well, but even though she'd told We'le about Kern, she didn't want any chance of crossing casts on his efforts. Not yet, or at least not with a Mage, when she'd decided what she needed was less restriction. And that really was it. It clicked, again. She'd talked to dragons, she'd accessed the Tower, she was learning her way, even without their help. Xelle just couldn't remain throttled. The knowledge that there was so much access out there, being kept from her, along with all of Kern's cautious tone—Xelle was feeling *restless*. If she'd bumbled her way into a Spire Mage again, she might as well take the opportunity.

She sat straighter. "I can't do more as an ignored Apprentice."

We'le stared at her, the brief joy and humor in her eyes turned off, like a lamp. She removed the hands from her knee. "This is why you're here?"

Xelle's mouth hung open, trying to—

"I pledged. To To'Arc. Crown Mage Jehanne pledged. We all pledged. It's how it works." She stood. "Honestly, Xeleanor? I feel like no matter what I give you, it won't be enough."

That hurt.

"Now, Apprentice, I suppose you should be back at To'Ever, to check in with your Mage." She nodded. "Yes, I'll send you back."

What the ash was this? Again, like she was a child. Like she hadn't been the one to talk to dragons on her own? Find dragons on her own? "You can't 'send' pers," she heard herself sputtering out.

"You don't know what I can do."

It felt like being tossed. And when her howl of protest stopped, it was taken over by a cascading rumble. Xelle threw her arms over her head as a shelf pulled down, and a stack of full boxes crashed all around her.

"In the candy pantry," she heard someone say.

Fira!

The door opened, and a kitchen staffper she recognized from Ever was shaking a spoon at her. Seeming to realize who it was, she stopped, and tightened her lips.

Xelle clambered to her feet. "I'm sorry, I was just—"

"Well I can see exactly what you're doing, Apprentice. You're from Arc, right? You can wave your little travel arm and fix my shelves and restack all this before I decide to march to the Front Desk with a report." As Xelle nodded, she stomped off, muttering.

Quickly, and trying to gain hold of a little reality while realizing she was standing, untraveling, in the Ever kitchen pantry appearing to steal . . . chocolate pretzels, she swept around with light casts, restacking the items with as much care as she could find through a shaking mind and wobbling hands.

Then she really enjoyed (meaning *not*) marching through the kitchen, like some parade of exile, with the kitchen staff lining each side, watching her leave. Some tsking. Some staring. One even whistled.

And at this point she was in no mood to sit around and wait for Kern's call. Almost slamming her own door and clasping on the locket, she stood in the center of the room and felt everywhere around her for some shadow of the connection he'd made.

It really was just a shadow. She rattled it, calling through. "Kern. Can we talk?" In alarm, she pushed herself back onto the bed.

"Better," Kern said when his visage walked into her room.

She sighed. A shaky, weird-sounding sigh. After all that, the big, fancy Mage was almost a comfort. At least *he* wouldn't *toss* her. "I talked to the dragons," she blurted. "The hu continue to move them from their homes, first to the mountains, and further up them. Whatever this 'treaty' was, I now know it was breached when I asked them to leave. *Again.*" Kern's eyes widened, questioningly. "Yes, I did. I told them to get out of there. You would have too if giant, sinister machines that made no sense with weird, non-prong shadows were tromping toward your friends." She'd said a lot there. And tried not to worry. Right now. Later. Answers now. Worry later.

Kern was pacing back and forth, and Xelle tried not to twitch too much as his leg passed right through her hiking boots. "I have an idea," he finally said. "For the time being."

Had he listened to her? Did he know all this? Why was she always the one to *not know?*

"If we close mountain access, which I could do as part of the investigation, then signal to the conglomerate that I am doing this to let them pass, then, we could see who shows up at the obsidian cliff. Once they are detected, not related to me—of course To'Arc would detect and intervene—you could signal the dragons to at least return to where they were."

Using the dragons as a lure? The automatic catch she'd vowed to remember pinged. She'd think about that later. "By closed to everyone, you mean all hu."

He glanced at her sharply. "Yes. The point would be, we could give the dragons space to return, at least from where they are now. Maybe we can get the conglomerate to show some cards."

"You can't keep every hu out. Never mind," she corrected. "I guess you just need to not get completely caught by surprise like before." That wasn't really better. "Also, is that their name?"

"No." He raised and lowered his shoulders. "Just needed something to call them."

"I used 'Hurts'."

"What?" He looked like a professor who'd just been given a terrible excuse for uncompleted research.

"I call them 'the Hurts'."

Kern's face grew rigid. "I am not saying that. Your . . . thoughts on the plan, Xeleanor."

It wasn't quite a question, but she appreciated it.

She rose to stand, just making sure she was far enough away to not get walked through. "I don't . . . Why would the Hurts"—now that he'd dissed her name, it was set—"think they could possibly get through to the obsidian in any timeframe? Under all that rubble? No one would risk casting there."

Kern pointed at her. "Grand would. And they've got someone at Grand. Not sure who, but I can tell, and the implications of that worry me. Still, you're right, we don't want to give them the opportunity. We'd have to let them in long enough to be detected, without them thinking I had anything to do with it. Plausibly long enough that I'm not a liability, but then not long enough to reach the obsidian." He lowered his hand. "I've been thinking about this, Xeleanor. My main concern is that once this plan starts, there's not a good way to stop it."

Something in that made any thought she'd held spin out. Why were they talking about obsidian? She could ask that. That would be a safe question. She thought. "What if they wanted the dragons, not the obsidian?"

"The test would parse that?"

Oh, no, teacher voice. Well, she'd been a lab lead. She had a voice too. "What's the worst thing–you know, reasonable thing–that could happen on account of your plan?"

He stared. "It reveals me. It endangers the dragons. It starts a war."

What was she supposed to say to that? She felt so overwhelmed. Out of nowhere. No, for a long time now. Just . . . And part of it, she knew, was no matter how much she learned, these ranking Mages always made her feel small. Was she small? Her mind was spinning.

She raised her hands. "Let's try it."

"We'll need to—"

A knock sounded. She spun to the door, then to Kern, but Kern was gone. "Yes?"

A voice sounded through the still-closed door. "Mage Fepa would like to speak with you."

"You have frequently not been seen around the Tower," Fepa said, his voice thin. He did not rise, but stayed slouched behind his desk, not meeting Xelle's eyes.

"I'm sorry, Mage Fepa, it had been so long since I'd seen some of my friends, and you were busy, so I took extra days." She had to get out of this. Not this conversation. All of this. It was unsustainable.

But would she pledge? To whom? She felt so . . . trapped.

"You're making me look bad," he went on. "I agreed to mentor you under an understanding that you are a regarded entity of the Crown."

"Oh, I am." That . . . was not better. "I mean, I'm grateful that you accepted me. Here. And my . . . days away have helped me refine my casting. It's been a great help. How was ROTL?" she tried.

"I am speaking to you. No more leaving without my direct consent and written time of return." He tapped his desk. "And . . . daily reports. To my office."

"Yes, Mage Fepa. I'll return right away to create today's."

He didn't chase her into the corridor, nor did any clerks, and as soon as she was sure no one could see her, she ran to her daygarden.

And started painting a rune.

13 - Runing Around

A stone's throw was the farthest Xelle had runed. Frond Magic was not her strongest prong, nor would it be. And so, she'd relied on the inkbloom as her best course of travel moving forward. But We'le tossing her across Alyssia like a sweaty shirt had been quite the awakening to what was possible in the realms of magic. All the worse if she had meant it that way.

The thing was, magic was *complicated,* and Xelle now had a suspicion she was probably linking untrained Arc Magic into her runes, and doing so without intention was pretty ash-burned dangerous.

She remembered moving the sword, but that had been with Jehanne in the room, and the sword's own magic, and it really hadn't felt like her doing. But it was. That was Arc. Of course it was. Her switching around had her mixing the prongs, apparently, without full understanding of the impact, without ever having learned these casts.

So. Should she stop and figure that out before zipping around the world? Yes. Would she? No.

As long as the dragons were away, she had to keep going.

She knew enough to sleep first. So she scribbled out a report for Fepa, walked it to the Front Desk, and then returned to her assigned room, falling quickly asleep.

She let herself be seen in the Tower, picking up a warm morning meal of soup, and calming biscuits. Thinking of Na Lleyx's lectures, she ate, and drank a solid glass of water while gazing out of a second-floor Tower window, nerves now surmounting (despite previous bravado).

Though she'd be back in a few hours, she disliked having tasks linger, and needed her mind clear. So she sat and wrote a second report for Fepa, uneventfully dropping it at the Front Desk with a clear specification for evening delivery, before returning to her daygarden.

Xelle took a deep breath. She rubbed her hands in spores, and concentrated on her nightgarden, hoping how close she'd made the other two runes would not confuse her.

It shouldn't. Her nightgarden was a specific place, and just outside of it was not. Close only in hu sense, not in the pathways of magic.

She was still worrying about it when she realized where she was standing.

"Dearest inkbloom," she said into the glowing darkness, with relief masking as cheer. "It is good to see you." She had planned to offer a song, but she had a specific feeling that the inkbloom sensed her own unease and didn't want . . . the energy of it. This bothered her in a strange way, but she didn't really want to parse that feeling while standing here amongst them. "I have a trip I'd like to make, but I'd like the ability to stay longer, until I get stronger at slinging. And . . . I have another stop too. Could I get two pods? Do you . . . do that?"

Nothing happened. One of the blossom's brightness flickered.

Well, a true relationship then. Good, that actually reassured her.

"I'm not trying to push it, and of course it's up to you." That felt right to say, also. "I just need to go see the dragons, and I've been thinking about something else, too, and I'd like to make a side stop. A friend." Images flashed in her mind, of each place.

Whether it was the mention of the friend or the dragons, two blossoms glowed brighter, each making a pod. Each seemed a little more wobbly-shaped than before, and one slumped against the sheer side of an obsidian chunk. Was this . . . sarcasm?

If one pod down the hatch was bizarre, two was . . . not real fun. Maybe this was why Arc Mages took vrooms. At least she did it this time before the coating subsided.

Xelle burped.

And before her friend here changed their mind, she put her fingers on her sigil, and plunged right to its source.

Thunder was asleep.

Zheir back legs were moving back and forth as if zhey were running, and little poofs of smoke made a trail of dark clouds from zheir nostrils. They were in the same place as before, by the frozen lake, but this time another dragon lay nearby, who looked at Xelle with notable annoyance.

"Hello," she said with a wave, deciding asking if this one would allow one of her names was best avoided for now. Her breath clouded in front of her face.

With a start, Thunder jumped up, sniffing, then charged at Xelle, nearly knocking her over.

"Hey!" She ran to lean against zheir side, as zhey rumbled. "I didn't sling this time, so I can stay longer. And look—" she patted her sides "—I wore a cloak." Yes, it was Helia's thin, hooded cloak, just in case she had issues at her next stop, but at least it wasn't Na Lleyx's patched poofcloak. (She also had the cloak she was hoping to enchant, but that she wasn't taking anywhere until she could be sure. And Jaynel's cloak just felt . . . like it needed to stay in the nightgarden, and not be cleaned or repaired. Look, she was weird.) Her arms already shivered in the cold, but not as violently as before.

"Awkward question," she went on. "Is there, uh, someone in charge here?"

The other dragon scooted, rotating against the ground before settling, so that zheir back end pointed at Xelle.

Ignoring zhem, Thunder sat back with twitching ears, like the question didn't make sense. Yet Xelle knew, from previous interactions, however brief, there was absolutely a structure here and not acknowledging that would do neither of them good. "I want to provide someone an update," she tried. "Directly."

Not looking thrilled by the idea but also, perhaps, agreeing, Thunder made a barking sound and tapped zheir claws together. The meaning now familiar, she allowed Thunder to swoop her up and flap away, over a few patches of trees to another clearing, where a dragon rested under a thin and scrappy tree.

This dragon was beautiful. That sounded condescending, but it was her reaction and oh well that they could hear whatever she was thinking. In shades of lavender with violet swirls, zheir wings rose gracefully at Xelle's arrival, generating a swirl of particles in the light breeze.

Xelle bowed. "I am Xeleanor, friend of Thunder. I lack the ability to know your true identity," (truly, she didn't know if dragons even had names) "but may I refer to you as Breeze?"

There was not a response that she could detect, but from behind, Thunder nodded, and flicked zheir head that way. She trusted Thunder, and nodded, again, at the dragon. At Breeze.

"I am working with a powerful Mage, who has proposed a plan to seal from hu access the area where you last lived. We can't promise to keep everyone away, but if you would permit the presence of Mages nearby, we could at least do our best."

Breeze did not look happy.

"I'm uneasy about it too. All of it, but especially that the pers who tried to reach you before might try to do so again. The Mage is even suggesting allowing it, to be ready this time. We'd all need to think about that."

Xelle shifted uncomfortably.

"Nothing is happening now; I'm trying to learn more first. And please know, whatever we decide, this is a temporary plan only, until I can better understand where your homelands are, and how you might return. Safely. With your consent, you could think about these options and considerations, and I would visit again once we have secured the area to let you know we are ready. And to hear your decision." Fira, this dragon wasn't responding at all. "As the treaty has been broken—as *hu* broke the treaty—this would require your trust. And . . . the more you want to tell me that can help me, I promise I will honor that."

She felt so formal. She had no idea whether dragons respected formality, or it made her look insincere. The words kinda sounded like a doorside salesper as she heard them.

Breeze snorted, and seemed to be saying something to Thunder.

Standing a little taller (Xelle had the distinct impression Thunder didn't know whether to imitate the formality Xelle had attempted), zhey nodded, hugely and dramatically.

Xelle turned back to Breeze. Look, she was awkward! Please let that not mess this up. "I want to help. If there's anything else I can do, please tell me. Otherwise, I'll return once the lower mountain area is cleared."

Breeze . . . grunted?

And without Xelle knowing what had happened, Thunder quickly clapped a 'ready', and with Xelle's return nod, flew her quite a ways away, to a gently sloping hill, a snowdrift pattern already forming a walled-in area. Xelle had the feeling zhey wanted them to be alone. She could understand that.

After setting Xelle down onto a flat area of rock, Thunder flopped and rolled onto zheir back. A plume of flame shot into the air, and Xelle scurried backward. "Hey, whoop, delicate hu over here. But, actually, do keep the air warm, if you would. This cloak isn't the best." At least she had gloves on this time.

Thunder rolled back around. More gently, zhey breathed out a little plume. Which felt really nice.

She smiled, gratefully. "We're ok? With Breeze?"

Thunder nodded.

Yeah, made sense. Deal reached, don't mess it up. But ugh, this was no better than the magesphere.

Xelle watched eir friend a minute. And something clicked. "Everything is so serious. What about you, can you tell me about your life? Like when I told you stories, back when we first met?"

This time, the communication was not as frightening. Still, eir gloved hands pressed into the tiny patch of dry, withered greenfloor as the visions overtook em, and the sensations of the ground below drew numbly distant. E saw Lightning, nudging forward a roll of twigs, then tossing it into the air. The vision was from Thunder's perspective, but e had the notion of flying up to catch it in Thunder's claws. Then, Thunder was squeezing through narrow rock formations, reaching a small pile of metal and shining objects. Next, Thunder was down in the foothills, mashing a huge pile of berries with zheir feet, glancing back nervously at moments. Sneaking out!

At once, a nausea overtook her, and she cried out, "Stop." Seeing zheir face leaning down into hers, she gasped out through heavy breaths. "That was wonderful, and easier than last time, but I think I can only do so much at a time. For now."

Feeling embarrassed, like she retched upon eating a gifted piece of cake, Xelle sat back, letting the world stop spinning around her.

"Hey," she finally said. "Hu know to never, ever cast in the mountains. Maybe, I'm thinking, that's about the obsidian, or about the dragons, or the treaty."

Thunder seemed to agree.

"But—if I cast here, is there danger?"

Seeing Thunder's waggle, (what they'd agreed served for a shrug), Xelle reached out with her material. It was depleted by the energy to travel here. Significantly. But fine for an easy little cast.

She reached out, searching the ground for any fallen twigs, and weaving them together up above her, her eyes closed the whole time.

Xelle opened them to a small, lumpy ball, not too impressive. But before she could ask, Thunder had grabbed it in zheir claws and flown up, high.

"I can't fly," she started to call, and then laughed. Firana, she couldn't. As zhey tossed the ball, Xelle slung a thread of travel upward, hooking it onto the tallest branch she could find, and whipped into the air, Helia's cloak billowing behind her—narrowly catching the ball and tossing it back before landing a bit roughly on the ground.

They did this a few more times before Xelle told zhem to stop again, but this time her eyes full of light and her rather-freezing cheeks warmed by the exertion. "You've worn me out, for now. Not just you," she amended. "My travel. And I really should go."

Thunder sat back, pouting.

"I know. Look, I need you here, so I can find the rest. I'll come back, we'll get you back to the lower mountains, and we'll take it from there. Oh," she added, the visions still echoing in her mind. "You really do hoard, then? I realized thinking about it I shouldn't assume things I learned from hu who've never met you."

A ridiculous noise sounded as a pointed dragon tongue waggled from zheir mouth.

"I'll take that as a yes. Eh," she said, brushing herself off, "well, we do too. We just call it other words. What about the obsidian? Is that a hoard, or something different?"

It was clearly different. Xelle wanted to stay and learn more, but her teeth were now chattering, her stomach queasy, and getting stranded here would do no one good.

"I'll see you soon," she said. "Always here," she added, tapping her forehead.

Xelle wobbled in place, at the imbalance of consuming one pod while leaving the other inside her. *Let's not do that often.* Her eyes opened into Kwillen's room, a pair of pants slung across the back of a chair. Fira! She covered them. Her eyes. Not the pants. "Kwill, it's me, Xelle? I'm sorry, I didn't consider the downsides of porting right in. Are you here? Are you . . . I mean you're not, exposed, right?" *Exposed?*

No one answered. Which was quite excellent, as weird as that had sounded. Tentatively, she sat down on eir couch, not thinking e'd be offended if she waited.

Kwill was sipping a tall drink through a straw and staring blankly at her.

Mmm, she murmured, pushing against the armrest and to a seat. She checked; her cap was still on. And she'd drooled a little. She wiped that off. "Oh. Hey. I didn't think this through. Is it . . . fine to be here? I'm not totally awake. I . . . cast to get here." She didn't add that she'd played ball in the high mountains, plus traveled to get there first.

Given Kwill's lack of reaction, she probably could have. "I see that," e said, nonchalantly. "A tiring endeavor, indeed! Yet, I am thoroughly delighted. At Breath, you know, most pers use the door, but I delight in your unique customs." Then e nearly giggled, uncharacteristic for the often flat-toned Study. "Xelle, how are you? Other than alarmingly skilled and . . . still not a Mage?"

Only Kwillen could get away with that kind of sass.

"I am fine." She shuffled around to straighten her cloak and twist her pantlegs correctly over her socks. "I'm now an Apprentice at To'Ever, to a total ash-pile, who just told me I'm not supposed to leave but I just did anyway, so that's a situation I will need to remedy at some point. Yes, I left Arc. For now. Maybe forever. You know how I feel about it," (not totally but enough) "but I'm sure you heard of my . . . event . . . and the stove was too hot for me. Yes, I arrived here via Arc Magic, because no matter how much I practice Ever, Arc's what I return to. No, I can't explain how. Kind of lonely, honestly. I'm this weird Apprentice and don't really have friends there."

Realizing she'd slipped down the angsty slide before even totally waking up, she stopped herself. Kwill didn't need to hear that her best friend at Arc had completely ghosted her, that she thought of him every day, her own weight which no one would ever see or understand, and that she'd slept with the other one, not that that was a problem, but—

"Fira, you need to get out more."

She grimaced. "I mean, I'm here?"

"Thank Halina! No seriously, you sound worse than my Mage greatsarents drunk in the hot springs. Can you take a break?"

"No," she replied. Seeing eir head tilt, she grimaced again. "So the part about the dragon at Arc, that was true. And me. But there's more people don't know, and not the Amberborn stuff; that's all ash." She pointed to her forehead. "Because I intervened, the dragons—yes, there are a lot of them and they all seem pretty cool—are kind of miserable up in the high mountains. It's super cold. Constantly windy. Rocky. Plain. Not a lot to do. Scant food. And it shouldn't matter what there is; it's not where they want to be and that's that."

Kwill took another sip, which made a slurpy straw noise. "I see I won't be convincing you today. Then, assuming this is not strictly a social call, what do you need?"

"It's also a social call." Realizing that came out rather whiny, she sat a little straighter, really trying to properly wake up. "It's really good to see you. But yeah, you're right, I need to get back. To Mage Nope Du'Nope. He grumbled me hard for not being around enough, and not making him important enough, I guess. Oh, and he's forbidden me from traveling." Xelle shrugged.

Kwillen closed eir eyes. "I probably do not want to ask this, but who is this Mage."

Ugh, that's right, Xelle always forgot how connected Kwill's family was. She'd learned it was one reason e didn't have a lot of friends here; pers often tried to use em, and eir prickly façade had grown in defense.

"Mage Fepa Du'Ever," she answered.

E let a long breath, setting down the drink. "Fira, even my Ma detests him." E raised one leg over the other and stretched back. "In that case, what can I do?" Switching legs, e stretched again.

"Well." She cracked a grin, both happy to see em but also very nervous what e would respond to the next. "I was going to ask if you'd join my revolution."

Eir stretch stopped cold. "Curse it, Xelle."

"Is that a no?"

Releasing, E made a rather rude and airy noise. "Not a no, just . . ."

Now, e stood and starting pacing around. "I'm a fake, you know. I don't like casting, or at least I'm terrible at it. Even if I weren't, I resent them making me do it. But, look, you're out there doing things. Taking risks. Disobeying Mages. Being absurd. Here, I'm behaving and then silently complaining about it to my sketchbook."

Xelle had no idea that e . . . drew? Wrote? A topic for another time. "Then join. I mean, what, you'd get kicked out of here?"

For the first time, her friend's placid demeanor faded, and Kwillen looked legitimately scared.

"I'm sorry," she started—

"No," e interrupted. "No, I deserved that. Or . . . I don't know. Cut some slack on whatever I'm saying; I walk into my room after a crappy day, you're snoring on my couch, I had just been thinking . . ." E stopped. "What would I do?"

She almost urged the need for discretion. Silence. But, Fira, even if Kwill wasn't the most solid Breath caster, that was one reason she'd come here. E was still Breath. The culture. The academics. E knew all that. E'd been the one to explain it to her. E was really good at explaining things! That said, she should at least set the parameters. "Without letting on."

E nodded, eyes rolling a bit.

"Yeah, I know you know but even Breath pers set parameters? I would like you to find out what the Lunests are up to. What motives they might have had to . . ." (e had to know it was about these things) "impact Arc Ascension and or harm or capture dragons."

"Oh, just that?" E squinted. "Just press on the ultra-rich a bit regarding their epic subversions?" Then e grinned. "Absolutely intriguing; you are by far my most interesting friend. Sure, I'll go to Wehj. I have excuses out of the Tower."

Xelle really had missed this per. "I'm sure you could work from here?"

"I want out. You're right. Besides, sussing around—I'm good at it. Was trained on it. Don't need fancy magic when you have Kwillen

Du'Satta." E clicked eir mouth. "And fine. I am not dealing with Ma's visit anyway. She didn't ask. I'm a grown adult."

Xelle felt uncomfortable. While Kwill normally threw jabs about eir family, e looked actually distressed.

E waved off whatever face she must have made. "Don't worry, I won't burn the sash closet yet. Like I said, I'll come up with a way to get out. A million pers would do me favors. And when I find something out, I'll show up at Ever. Old friend from Breath. A plan?"

She smiled. Not just relying on Kern for information would be such a welcome change. And seeing Kwill again. She didn't even want to leave now. But, surely e had planning to do. And Xelle *did* have to get back or she'd burn her own sash closet with Fepa, maybe before she was ready. She rose.

"What's with the spy cloak, anyway? Big droopy hood. You look like a courtesan. I mean, no shade if you are. Just guessing not."

"I would be a fine courtesan," she grumbled. "Highest rates."

That was not true.

But, she did think she'd be a decent partner. Someday. If everyone around didn't repel one way or the other. Bad train of thought. Time to go.

"I'm new to the porting bit," she said. "Figured if I didn't end up in the right spot, or something happened, I might need to not be identified. You know, you're Kwill, but now I'm dragonfriend. Anyway. I'll see you—"

Kwill raised a hand. "Xelle, sorry in advance, but a friend thing."

Now, what was this.

"You're pushing too hard on casting. New casts, tiring ones, you can go too far. I need you to take care of yourself."

She didn't want to talk about it. Hoping she gave an expression that passed as something near appreciative, she stood there. Waiting for em to what, turn around?

Apparently e was going to watch. Fine. Closing her eyes, she felt the second pod, stirring in her. Stomach didn't feel right, like ***not at all,*** and yeah, she should go.

Her mind narrowed, breath by breath, only on her daygarden.

As though distant, she heard Kwill's applause.

14 - One Other Thing

Yeah. She'd pushed too far. Maybe a break on the traveling until it was time. At least her daygarden couch flipped open to be a bed, though (shh) she flopped down without opening it.

Xelle didn't love naps. She loved the idea of them. But mostly, she awoke groggy and annoyed and with the rest of the day's mood cemented, once she figured out what time of day it was. Today was no different. Tonight, actually.

Glad she'd turned in today's report before leaving, she dragged herself up, rather miserably sipped down some soup, knocked back a glass of wine, and (this time pulling her bed out as a bed) fell again to sleep.

The next morning, needing Mage Fepa to see her around given her absence yesterday (and no she hadn't enrolled in fall classes either), she made a show of sitting in the library, helping new Studies find what they needed, and then looking like she was working out casting notes in the Atrium while she was actually doodling Breath-like geometric patterns and then swooshing them with bold, connecting strokes while humming a tune to herself and making up lyrics for it.

None of these activities brought her joy. She felt tired, and worried, and as she would after an important conversation with a hu, she now cycled over her actions while visiting Thunder, and then Kwill. Things she should or shouldn't have done, or said. Her own little songs felt like running her fingers over each other: more of an acknowledgement that comfort existed in the world, rather than finding it herself.

She spent the evening writing and sealing a few dozen reports for Fepa, enough to get her well into the twelfth month, so at least she could put off dealing with that for a while. She delivered the first one to the Front Desk, ensuring it was marked nondelay, a request the clerk side-eyed but absolutely did not argue.

Anyway, Fepa wasn't going to read them. He never even had anything on his desk except fresh polish or a new trinket. That thought did not cheer her up.

With her gloom not subsiding the next morning, either, she spent the next few days updating the birdhouse and adding some decorative paints, before the weather got too cold to do so. At least in that small act of creation, she found some spark. Some defiance. (No, she couldn't quite explain why she called it that, but then she wasn't in the best spirits.) And each day felt a little less dire.

She looked over the drying paint. "I think that's it," she murmured to herself with implied ceremonial definition, while still blowing a little warmth into her hands from inside the large window. The colors were pretty, but not obtrusive; the book's back notes, which skipped between a variety of topics (bird topics), had provided some tips on ways to decorate the structure for human eyes without detriment to its residents. What did inns call them? Amenities.

Abirdities.

Smiling at her silent joke, she glanced around at the mostly empty room, and no one met her gaze. Anyway. She'd left the brush drying on a towel by an outside faucet; might as well return it now.

Xelle walked back out, taking the winding old path to the maintenance side-door, and, distracted, nearly walked into two Mages who were talking excitedly in a plain little nook. The sort of corner the cleaning crews often forgot about. The sort of place you met to not be interrupted.

Their conversation stopped abruptly.

Normally, she would, of course, apologize and hurry past (unknowingly walking into conversations was some type of superpower she had), but she'd heard, very clearly, the name Fepa. They were junior Mages, the types she wouldn't have hesitated to converse with at To'Arc. Why was she nervous now? Fira, she had to get out of this. At least, for now, she could try and reassure them.

"I don't know what you're talking about, but my word I won't mention it. We're . . . not friends," she blurted out. An ill-advised addition, so she hurried to move along.

One Mage snorted. "Something in common."

The other glared at xem. "Shh!"

Xelle, images flashing before her of another universe where these might be *her* friends, tried to smile reassuringly. "Really, it's fine. He's horrid. I know."

The first Mage leaned in. "Did he tell you anything? About the ROTL?"

He had not. "No." Xelle shook her head. "Well, yes. That he was helping to run it."

The second Mage leaned back and crossed xyr arms, encouraging Xelle to move along.

The other laughed. "Sure. Run it into the ground, he did. Bullied his way onto the committee. They gave in once they realized he wasn't really going to help them design the scenario, and agreeing would get him off their back. Then he shows up, and makes himself some sort of divinely chosen ruler." Xe snorted.

"Not on the committee," the other clarified, monotone. "In the scenario. A self-appointed ruler . . . *in* the scenario."

Xelle processed this a moment, feeling a little hungry just to connect. Even like this. "Are you both in ROTL, then? Is that how you say it?" She tried to sound light.

They nodded, the quieter Mage loosening into a bit of smile.

"It sounds really cool. I wonder why you don't hear more about it?"

They exchanged a look. "Some Mages think it's un-Mage-like."

Xelle rolled her eyes. "Some Mages need an attitude adjustment." Seeing that the remark had not gone over with the solidarity she'd hoped, she quickly changed course. "But Fepa— If he assigned his own role, wasn't there a way for the group to overrule him?"

"Oh, sure," the first Mage said. "But this was more fun."

The second Mage practically lit up. "That thread of the scenario turned into a collective overthrow. I mean, he's just one Mage; he can't retaliate against *everyone*."

"Oh. Wow. That explains why he didn't want to talk about it. I'm Xelle," she added, trying a friendly smile. At the sudden sting of realizing they trusted her enough to tell the story (which lots of pers had to know by now) but not enough to mention their own names, Xelle realized she'd better go pick up her brush.

"I won't say anything. And thanks for the trust." She nodded politely. The Mages turned inward.

Great. They'd seemed to take that as a jab. *Fira.*

Xelle offered the Ever with one of her still-chilly hands, and then ducked away.

The birdhouse, she reminded herself. It looked nice.

Distracted by her travels and busywork, Xelle had neglected to put on Kern's locket. (This was unfair, she'd been *totally* exhausted.) When she realized the oversight and clasped it on, he called essentially immediately.

As before, she couldn't see his background, but she had the impression he'd excused himself from a meeting and was glancing around in a hallway.

His voice rang firmly. "I need you to check in more often. I could reach you directly there, but it would not go so great for you."

Not about to mention her triumph with the inkbloom or the resultant exhaustion, Xelle almost responded that she'd been balancing finishing a birdhouse and not getting yeeted by fictionally deposed Mage Fepa. A tension in Kern's eyes held her. Instead, she nodded. "I'm sorry. I will."

He clasped his hands. "I haven't found out much yet, regarding

Lunest Estate. My contacts are kept completely isolated now, something I'm hoping my plan will change." He looked sharply at Xelle. "I've changed my approach. I have risked appearing more irritated, more questioning to my contacts. I said that I was doubting their need to influence my Ascension to Crown Mage. That the Spire was starting to see me in that role, thanks to them. Giving me more access, more secrets. That I held leverage now. They may have trapped Spire Mage Kern, but a Crown Mage would not endure a lack of access, a lack of connection. If they want the power I am about to touch, they will have to offer more."

So risky. Yet, if he went along too well with everything, that would likely be suspicious too. She did not envy Kern his position.

"I told their latest messengers I had a way to clear access to the location they'd been trying to reach. This very much got their attention. But I reminded that this would put me at increased notice in Arc Tower, and so I needed to seal our relationship a bit more securely. Before they could reach to the treat I'd set in front of them, I immediately followed that I had something even better to offer, as well. I hoped this would give them reason for my newfound boldness. I waved it in front of them, said their previous grips would not hold but I was interested in a more firmly mutual relationship."

"By the grip, you mean—"

Unable to stop a quick sigh, he nodded. "I said grips, but yes. They could expose my role, but Tenne is out of the residence. He isn't talking to me. That hold has weakened. And they would lose their easiest chance at a Crown Mage, expose themselves in the process, and on a personal level I wouldn't need to deal with their troubles anymore and could perhaps repair things with my cura. So, I concluded, I was now willing to accept that risk."

If Kern had said this to his contacts with the same edge he said it now to Xelle, she could see why this would be rather convincing.

"They, of course, wanted to know what the better thing was I could offer them. I laughed and said I would not reveal it to liaisons.

Only directly to those in charge. And by doing so, I would be firmly tainted now, as a participant rather than a victim. We would both be sealed into this deal, without need for a continued dance. They could take it or leave it."

Ok. Stepping it up. But, she felt uneasy. If Kern were to ascend, he might be able to pick his own sides, truly. She knew that, he knew that, and they knew that likely too. What treat could he dangle that Xelle would be comfortable with? Involving the other Spire Mages—any Mages—without their consent was not a line she was willing to cross.

He peered at her briefly like a professor noting the progress of a new caster, without anything to add. Then continued. "I made it clear: Do not send me to a shadowy corner, or a darkened village moveroom. I am in position for the Crown of Alyssia, and I will be sent only to a place I will believe. Otherwise, my best reserve piece stays in my pocket and my plans for Ascension remain in consideration. Take it or leave it. Start over if you must."

This was really, really feeling serious now. She watched him, looking for any clues. His demeanor. His intent. Yet, he didn't need to give them, and he knew that. They'd approached him specifically because of his bond to Tenne, his insecurity as a parent. And if Tenne were now estranged, they would know the instability that might bring, to someone they'd infused with a hunger for power instead. With the offer for a new grasping point, they'd think long and hard before dismissing it.

Kern continued, "They said surely I knew I had to give them something. Some promise. Some collateral. So . . . I reluctantly, in their view, told them the nature of what I could provide. I know how to bring you a magic locator for the dragons, I said."

What? There was a locator? The only locator Xelle had thought around was—

Inferno.

"You're going to bring them *me?* Did I agree to this?"

He raised his eyebrows. "Do you have my locket on? Am I here now?" Then grew serious. "I won't let them take or harm you."

"How can I trust that?" She knew she sounded a little screechy, but really!

The air wavered around her, and, she realized, Spire Mage Kern Du'Arc was standing—in her room—towering over her in all his velvet and chains and huge finger rings. Him. Casting a huge shadow on her wall. Not a visage.

Flame him. "Oh. Oh, you think I'm intimidated?" She opened the door, and with a burst of unmitigated Arc Magic, swept him through it.

He didn't budge. And her door was still closed.

Yeah, maybe she should stop while she was ahead on this one. "Fine." She took a breath. "I do forget to think about it. I didn't grow up in the magesphere; I still see everyone as . . . pers. I'm sorry. You are a ranking Spire Mage, and I know you could protect me." She added a little bow. "But . . . They also wanted collateral. And if you're here to—"

"I'm here to remind you that a sigil and a few secrets does not make you invulnerable, Xeleanor. And you are not my collateral." His mouth tightened. "I gave them my personal chain. This—" he pointed to the polished chain holding the charms marking his pledge to Arc, his increasing rank, and his position on the Spire "—is a replica. As any Mage, jeweler, or half-high street vendor would know on quick inspection."

Wow. Her point was more how he would manage them once he didn't actually hand her over, but burn it, he could figure that out. They had his *chain*? That gave them enormous leverage. While also putting them at risk. Whose story pers would believe if that chain showed up in bad hands would not be a risk Xelle would want to take. If it were her. That must have got their attention. "And you get it back?"

"When I bring you to them."

"And that happens?"

"When they give me a location for a meeting that I will find credible."

"The Lunest Estate," she answered.

A tiny tweak of his neck and shoulder served as a shrug. "We'll see."

Ash. They needed more to go on.

"Fine." Xelle took a shaky breath, trying to firm her voice. "I'll go. And you know where to find me. You. No one else. I won't take direction from anyone but you." He'd made the same condition himself; surely he'd understand.

He nodded, expressionless.

Her arm twitched, involuntarily. "I'm jumpy. Lately," she mumbled.

"Good," he said. "Good to see some sense in you."

Well, look, they were downright friends now. Speaking of which. "How is Tenne?" she asked, trying to release her grimace. "You mentioned him to the Hurts, that you weren't talking."

"We aren't." His expression soured. "I haven't heard from him."

Tenne had made clear he cared about his Da, even if he was upset. "Oh, I'm sure that—"

"Don't need it from you. Especially with that on." He pointed to where, under her shirt, his late spouse's pendant rested. Irritating to them both, apparently.

"How's the drinking?" she asked. Making a face that might have come across a bit impetuous rather than caring, she tried to back off. Might have snapped like a dig, but wasn't meant to be. She did worry about it. Whether for himself or their plans, they couldn't afford any more uncertainty.

"Managed." Without further comment, he turned and walked openly out of her door, closing it behind him.

What, he's just walking through To'Ever now? Whatever. She had a lot on her mind. And apparently, a lot of practicing to do.

The baby pine tree she'd found growing in a crack where they would not have survived was now being sung to daily in a little corner of her daygarden. They couldn't stay there, either, but once they were a little bigger, she'd plant them outside. Wouldn't hurt to make the area around her a bit denser, besides, they were a really cute tree.

She couldn't practice everything here. Especially travel magic in a smallish (but not as small or low-ceilinged as her nightgarden!) room. But she could do a lot, and now freely and without worry of detection. This gave her a new sense of boldness, as well as comfort, and she did not delay in getting to work.

If she was going to be a travel Mage, as Kern had previously taunted (though this wasn't about him; she felt that in her soul), moving and traveling needed to both be understood and effortless. Not to say her material was limitless, but, with said limitations, she could not be concentrating into the fibers for simple lifts, nor misunderstanding the implications of what she'd already mastered. First, movement.

Taking a small pillow, she tossed it onto the couch. (Meaning, with a cast.) Onto the floor. Lifted above her head, and spun. Let it hang there. With each cast, this grew more natural. More understood. As easy as she could do it with her arms, but with a different exertion.

Then, to travel. The pillow blinking out of sight, and appearing in each of these locations, at her will, some easier, some with struggle, as though pulling a rope in the wind. Back and forth she went, day after day, until the pillow blinked around as though on its own. As though! She was still in full control of its travel. This felt good. Satisfying. Better even than the more complicated casts she'd worked through so quickly, climbing the ladder of coursework and research at To'Arc, always ready for the next.

Like her door.

Fira, now that she understood it better (and not as well!), she was horrified that she'd managed to create some sort of Ever-Frond-Arc contraption within the actual stones of the Arc Tower. More horrified that it had worked. Because, she now understood, one could not Arc travel *themself* without inkbloom, nor could one walk *through* stone without concepts much more advanced than the reagents she'd used, so what she'd likely done was actually Frond travel across the line of tiny runes she'd made to serve as a crude sort of magic wrapping, but it was such a short distance, she felt she was stepping through. Which maybe explained why she was able to rune travel again without much practice.

Fira.

She did not want to give one to the Mages for having rules about pers doing casts they hadn't learned but . . . maybe there were reasons.

With this on her mind, she moved on to practicing traveling objects through other objects, like how she'd sent the sword through the walls of the Tower. Like We'le had sent her! (As annoying as this had been, in retrospect it had not felt like turning the magic in assault, but more like a parent reclaiming an extra cookie; a nuance she hadn't yet wanted to parse. Anyway.)

Xelle sent the pillow through the low table. Then onto it. Then through it. Then, finally, she combined the two. Travel with movement. First, she took the pillow and aimed it at a second one. She traveled past it, landing it on the other side. Then, she traveled it in front, with a new thread of movement that whipped from the first cast, and sent it into the second pillow, knocking it aside. She understood the space. What belonged in it. What could be.

And this was why, according to fundamentals, a traveling object could not arrive coexistent with another, why she'd never really walked *into* the nightgarden wall. Such a cast—not something she was going to try—would, if she understood it, shock its own caster, return the intended energy without executing its intent. The same reason pers walked through open doors, and not into closed ones. Travel relied on connection, not discord, being, not unbeing. Perhaps, she could consider ways to cross entities, but she didn't like thinking about it. She didn't know if such things could be done, but this *would* be turning the magic, would cloud her clarity of space, and thus, she had no reason to consider it.

Then, her pillows well exhausted (and extra floofy) after long days spent, she thought about what Kern had done, in her room. She'd been thinking about it for days. Studying the Arc texts she'd been able to get, rereading the fundamentals like starting over in the craft.

That is, she supposed, what she was doing. But also not.

In her room—she hadn't tried to travel him (!), she'd simply aimed to move him. Catch him off guard. Turning nothing, for the frustration she felt at . . . It wasn't as though he'd resisted himself from her cast, or fought it; she was pushing him with the same consent he'd offered at entering her room. Yet, he'd just stood there like a smug-ash jerk as she huffed breath against a boulder. And she believed, after going over all the options of what he could have done, that rather than block the cast, he'd somehow removed himself from her space. As if he'd traveled, just slightly out, out of the space she understood. Disallowed her motion.

This sounded dangerous, yet he'd appeared unaffected. Her *cast* had appeared unaffected.

Yet, with no desire to enchant some sort of device to attack her or involve the very, very complicated concepts of mirrors without a mentor, she had no way to know if her daily stretches—they felt that way—would have the same effect against an assault. But whatever she did, she felt stronger. More in control.

Xelle waited, almost eagerly, for the next per to try and give her coals.

And every day, she returned to Ever casts. Knowing she should not spend all day on Arc Magic, that even Fepa would feel her energies shift, she resumed her daily practice of Ever, completed again before switching back to Arc. Besides, she had a goal.

She'd meant to enchant the cloak from the start (a forestper likes her cloaks!), but she'd been considering the possibilities in the context of the Ever texts. Durability of the cloak, unfading color, loyalty to prevent loss.

Yet Xelle's traveling, without even making it to warmer areas, had reminded her how a cloak could go from a burden to a need with one swing of the inkbloom. And so the enchantment she'd started working was one that would vary heaviness and lightness, to put it overly simply. The concept, not quite described by standard phrasing, swerved very close to, if not through Arc Magic, and so she thought it would be an ideal first try. Something she wanted. Something she could do. Everybody wins.

She was finally ready to try it. Well, on a sample, as Xelle now understood the value of knowing what she was doing (!) before doing it, and also—that cloak had been expensive. And worth it! She really liked the cloak she'd commissioned from the tailor in Vi'Ever. Not Helia's spy (courtesan) cloak or Na Lleyx's fuzzy creation, or her infamous dragon arrival cloak, but a charcoal cloak, with black accents, perfect pockets, and a few carabiner rings. At the same time, she'd asked for extra samples of the fabric, which the tailor had easily provided.

One of these scraps sat, now, on her table, along with a bottle of a light, fluid sap, and an updated version of the powder she'd spent months sampling and remixing. She reached, surprised to see her hand shaking, for the sap. Rubbing sap, however light, onto fabric seemed so strange to someone who'd grown up within the populace, but to an Ever Mage, it was like sipping on water. (And no, Xelle did not consider herself an Ever Mage, but she'd certainly given this her best attention. One didn't need to be a carpenter to learn to build a frame.)

The amagically illogical mixture of the smooth sap and rough fabric was also how she'd immediately know if the cast had taken—not if it worked, but if it'd taken. If so, the sap would imbue into the matter of the fabric, leaving behind no residue, sticky or otherwise. It didn't make sense, not in the properties of objects a school child was taught. But that, she supposed, was why it was magic.

There was an aspect of enchantment that Xelle particularly valued. Unlike a passive cast, a passive enchanted object would not give off a magic shadow. Detection could be run on it, dependent on the skill and wards, but generally, she could wear her cloak around, without most pers picking up on its powers, even unwrapped. (Wrapped enchantments were much, much more advanced than the Arc-wrapped enchantment she'd used on the daygarden though she did have another overly-bold idea brewing on that. That was getting ahead. First, the test.)

She warmed the sap between her hands, pressing, but not working it, and then slowly, like a furniture restorer (the image came to mind), began applying the sap onto the fabric. Knowing that her hands were messy, she carefully grasped the handle of an enchantment sieve (this had been way more expensive than she'd expected, but having a good one seemed advised), and sprinkled the powder evenly over the object.

Then the cast.

Unlike Arc Magic, drawn of immersion into paths, Ever Magic was . . . harder. Not more difficult, but more rigid. Finding a specific place, a congruence of angles, and sinking vectors of purpose into them.

It felt prickly, pokey. But she could manage, and she did, determined to make it through.

When she relaxed, her hands were covered in sap, and the table dusted with reactive powder, but the fabric was clean, normal again. As it had been, but only at a glance.

Not wanting to risk the interference of a travel cast on her test (it shouldn't, but why add risk), she stepped on her pump pedal and washed her hands with soap, then, taking a cloth to wipe off the table (she'd sanitize it with an Arc cast later), nudged the cloth onto the clean side, as she took care of the other.

She wrapped the cloth around one hand. Guiding it was much more difficult than she'd hoped. She wrestled (with herself, not as if fighting the object) to tell it she wanted warmth and cover, but after a while—perhaps quite a while—it warmed against her skin. Looking the same as it had, but when she walked out into the cold outside air, her hand stayed warm. She told it, this makes me feel nice in this cold. This is cold, and unless I say otherwise, this is how I'd like for you to react to cold. She didn't say this aloud, but again, in the positioning of the Ever.

Then, she returned inside next to her lamp, and coaxed it (her mind was getting so tired, and she barely realized it was she being trained, not the fabric) into lightness. Now, it felt like she held nothing. A sheer veil, an affectation only. This is warmth, I like the feeling this way. All of these reactions can change, if I want otherwise.

Back and forth she went, five times each, about ready to collapse. (After the first round, let alone the next, next, next, and next.)

When she realized how perfectly it had actually worked, not only was she too exhausted to appreciate it, but nearly too much so to destroy the scrap. No. It must be done. Xelle's cycling mind never liked loose ends anyway, but the ability to conduct enchantments required discipline and focus. Unused enchantments were bad practice, for a multitude of reasons.

Sitting at her small indoor stove—this could not be made outside where someone might detect it—she slowly built, kindled, and instructed an Ever fire. A fire of permanence. And with well wishes for the fabric returning to unbeing, she held it with a pair of wick straighteners, over the flame, and watched it float into sparks.

She would wait to talk to Kwill before enchanting the actual cloak (she had a question on that) but it seemed that she was ready.

The inadequacy of that claim set her laughing. And, she numbly trudged back to her room in the Tower, making sure to first send Fepa his pre-drafted report of a long day of fruitful practice.

"It's ok." Owin returned to his painting.

Tenne watched his partner—his love—for a minute, until Owin looked back around. "Am I supposed to say more?"

"Mmm, no, sorry." Tenne moved the little sculpture once on the towel, to detach it from anything that had started to dry to the bottom. He had liked this one, in a new style he'd been trying.

But if Owin said it was just ok, he might need to try again.

See, that was just it. Living with artists had turned out to be every dream of Tenne's. Artists strolled in and out of the complex, exchanging ideas, or bringing a round to share. He wished he hadn't won that grant. What had been the value of living in isolation? Now, now he was learning. He was living.

That wasn't fair, either. Once word got out that Bon Tenne Du'Mytil had moved into the housing area, more pers came by. To meet him. To talk to him. Owin's art was being seen now, too. He'd made enough that they could maybe even get into their own place. None of that would have happened without the grant. He paused. Oh. It would have happened to Owin. Tenne would not have been there.

Owin was back to his canvas. He wore old shorts with a bit of ill fit, enough that Tenne could see his muscles, flexing up, through his thighs. He breathed out, keeping that breath quiet so as not to disturb the painter at work. The painter sure disturbed him, he thought to himself, a wave of heat running through his body.

The figure sat on its towel. Tenne still liked this one. He wouldn't destroy it, he'd just store it, back into his trunk, with the other experiments that didn't quite pass.

Everything else in this place was still Owin's, until they moved, but the trunk was Tenne's. He'd never shared the lock sequence and Owin had never asked.

He thought back to that first day, when they'd visited the old paper press site. When he'd shown Owin one of the most colorful and cheerful murals he'd done. Owin had laughed. Had smiled.

And had showed him, that night, what it really felt like, to be loved.

Tenne had to let the figure dry. Then, he'd stow it away.

15 - *Six Months*

Rayn was lounging in the kitchen. "Xelle!"

Xelle herself had just been passing by, caught the smell of some strongly savory baking, and been surprised to see the hu leaned back in a chair, her long legs propped up on a dirty dishes cart. She blinked. "Don't tell me it's already been six months. Plus your travel?"

"Why, you wanted me tossed out early?" Her mouth crooked.

"No, of course not. I just . . . Eh, maybe it does feel so long. It does and it doesn't." She didn't like thinking about that.

Rayn swung her legs down, boots thumping against the tile floor. "That, is a song I also sing."

Xelle hoped her smile didn't show, or at least wasn't too far. She really liked Rayn slipping into hometown phrasing, but didn't want to be disrespectful either.

"What is that face?"

Caught a bit, Xelle tripped over her words, finally landing on, "I like your Sharre phrases. They are poetic."

"Pfft. And you sound like a forester calling stories up the ladder. You seem stressed."

Abrupt change of subject there. "I . . ." Fine, she was feeling the tension of many pulls in many directions. "It's nice to see you."

Rayn chuckled. "It's nice to be here, honestly. Got enough of Grand. Enough for a lifetime! What a place. Hey. You living in the Study area now? Oh." She peered in at Xelle's pin. "Still the mysterious Apprentice I see. Fix Party Fepa yet?"

She grimaced. "No. Decidedly not fixed. And, no, not near here. They stuffed me in some weird corner, it's hardly a room. Was on the way to Study Supplies to filch some refills for the clippy thing. You know, the squeezer."

By the look on the Ever Study's face, this probably did not fade her perceptions of Xelle's eloquence.

"Well, how was Grand, anyway?" she tried. "I guess they let you in. Did you get a wand?" Xelle swished with her hand.

"Shh!" She gestured for quiet.

Xelle wasn't exactly sure if she was serious as no one else was even there, but then Rayn added, "Not here. Later."

She considered this as the hu stood to check on what appeared to be a wide, flattish bread loaf. How did bread smell like this?

Rayn was now poking a stick into it. "Just about to glory."

Just then, a pair of Studies walked in, giggling, until they saw Xelle, at which point they quietly started unloading a bag of roots onto a cutting board.

You know, Xelle had had a crappy day. Fepa had criticized her fakey reports, though he clearly hadn't read them. Which caused her to tear up the last dozen she'd had stocked, and then write a new set, so annoyed by the worthless task that she'd written enough to get her well into the new year. After having to grovel to Fepa with today's 'revision', she'd spent an hour trying to use the obtained pass to get a loan text from Breath, then had been denied. And on top of that, she'd had a stomachache yet been too sullen to go find a potion, or even a chalk-tab to handle it. Walking to Supplies had been considered a real highlight. But here was a friendly face, and a mouthwatering bread, and . . . why not try.

Xelle lowered her voice. "Um, I have a place we could go talk, if you're up for sharing secrets. Well-wrapped, unknown, you'd be the first to see it, other than a baby pine tree and some squirrels. And especially if you're bringing whatever that is." She pointed at the breadpan.

"Ah. It's spice loaf. Yes, we call it spice loaf. Two words. Respect the parts." She leaned to one side, taking the chance to stretch. "Other pers claim to make it, they add spices, right. And we're fine with that;

enjoy the bread!" She leaned, now to the other side. "But it's not a Sharre spice loaf if it doesn't have *our* seasonings."

Rayn's voice having grown, the two Studies glanced over, before resuming their chopping.

All the more reason to go. But. "It sounds amazing. But, I mean, was it for something? I didn't really mean to swipe it, it just smelled so good."

"It was for me, and my dinner alone in the Study kitchen." This time, she kept her voice low. "Secret place not too creepy?"

Luckily in this regard, they were in To'Ever, and not To'Arc. "I think it's rather pleasant."

Rayn hopped over to a dish. "Got a fresh spread here, if you'll carry this." She handed it to Xelle, who curiously peeked in at a thick, light brown swirl of something that looked very good. Rayn folded a thin towel over the bread, and set it on a plate. "Do you have glasses?"

She was speaking normally now, but of course, they could be heading to Xelle's room at this point, and it was pretty obvious they were taking the meal somewhere. "I do." Xelle had been proud of stocking a tiny kitchen and enough to live by, more in case she ever had to hide there than for having guests. But having a guest sounded nicer.

"This way," Xelle gestured, as they made their way outside.

By the chill, Xelle expected to see snow, but oddly there was none. But it was that feeling—that specific feeling—that the snow would arrive soon. Very soon.

A shiver of both cold and a little excitement at the thought (if it was going to be cold there might as well be snow), they took the normal zig-zag of paths in relative silence. Xelle chilly without a coat herself, she had to imagine the Sharre-born Study was freezing, but Rayn said nothing of it as they wound through the trees.

"You're running a cast?" Rayn whispered.

Xelle nodded, then realizing she might not see that, whispered back, "Yes. I've gotten pretty good at it, I'm only slightly ruffled that you noticed. I think if I were being followed, watched, or cast upon in any way, I'd at least have the warning of it. Combines a few prongs. Sort of. It's complicated."

Reaching the tree, she ducked under the canopy of needles and Rayn did the same. "You promise not to tell?"

"A question belated?" Rayn grinned.

Hmmpf. Of course, she already trusted her. Xelle's sense of people, she supposed. But setting expectations was good?

A voice whispered in her ear. Not a travel cast, just a whisper, but it shocked her just the same. "I will never betray your confidence."

"Nor I yours," she whispered back. Suddenly, they broke out laughing.

"Well, that over with," Xelle said, "we should get into the wrapping before our giggles draw the squirrels."

"They would tell," Rayn agreed.

"Not if they like us. Just don't cross a squirrel. Are you comfortable with ladders?"

As Rayn nodded nonchalantly, Xelle reached over for the hidden switch, admittedly covering her movement slightly. It was a subtle motion, known only to herself and for now she wanted to keep it private. Sharing the secret, but not the key, she supposed. The ladder folded down, almost to the ground.

"No magic, just forest innovation," Xelle said proudly. "Here, you go up?"

Rayn seemed to hesitate. Well, she didn't want to be suspicious. "Look. I'm confused by uneasy heights. Um, terrified. Frozen. I usually ride the ladder up, so I don't have to look. So if you go first, I can still do that."

She thought Rayn might respond or joke, but she didn't, and the tall hu whisked up the ladder with surprising speed. Xelle, again activated the ladder, rode to the top, and sealed them within her enchantment—basically locking the door from this side.

"Secure." She looked at Rayn, glad to see she looked legitimately impressed by her cheery space within the tree. "Welcome to my daygarden."

Rayn was staring at the travel rune on the floor. "Was this rune designed when you were twelve?"

"No. Now, want the tour, or the secret slide back down?"

Rayn made sort of a sad balloon noise. Look, that's how it sounded. Giving up, Xelle glided the dip down onto the table with a slightly showoffy cast, and motioned to Rayn for the bread to join it. She pointed, starting right and going around the room. "Couch that also serves as bed. Storage. Little kitchen. Wash closet. Magic practice area; wish it were larger but I have limitations."

"The bread is best warm," was all Rayn said, helping herself to a glass, the water pump, and a seat on the couch. "You do what you want, but we break a piece, with this motion." She took one hand and pinched off a piece of the bread. "Then we swipe it through the meal; it's polite to swipe from the edges and wipe the bowl as you go." She demonstrated. "Aff then . . . *ooooh.*"

Clearly uninterested in hiding her true feelings about spice bread, Rayn's eyes rolled back a bit while she made some rather guttural noises.

Xelle tried to imitate what she'd done. The same hand, the same pinch, the same swipe. And Rayn said something about it, some sort of rating, but this Xelle did not hear, as she bit into the best thing she'd ever eaten and that included a Vi'Arc street samosa.

This was no small feat.

Her wide eyes turned to Rayn and seeing Rayn as smugly delighted in the response as Xelle had been about the daygarden, Xelle knew no commentary would be needed. Which was good because her mouth was happily stuffed with bread.

"You want to see it?" Rayn finally said, as they both leaned back against the cushions and the bread plate (and the dip bowl) sat empty.

"Mmm?" Xelle was in the bread zone. "Sure," she agreed, not exactly sure to what she was agreeing.

"I made this myself." From her bag, she removed the thinnest, willowiest wand Xelle had ever seen or imagined.

"That is . . . not grand?"

"I know! They were so horrified, they suggested I should destroy it. Wands are strong! Big!" She had taken on some imitation of a booming voice. "Well, that's their wands. I like mine, and I had full permission to cast one. Besides, I'm not Grand. I'm Ever. Ever forever and never to part!"

Xelle smiled, but did not comment on how she, too, had once thought that way about this place.

But had she? Eh.

"I can't demo it," Rayn was continuing. "I know you said we're wrapped here, and I believe you—saltflow, I started to try and sense how you enchanted a whole border of runes and somehow made . . . an Arc net? and now I know who I'm dealing with—but one, these are very complicated to use. Two, I don't want anyone to know I have it, and just in case a little Grand shadow sticks on my stockings, it would go poorly for us both. Or maybe I'm just . . ."

No, Xelle understood. Magic and one's loyalties was complicated. She could imagine using a wand when one had no intent to continue the study could feel like bantering with an estranged ex. As opposed to keeping a fond letter. "May I?" Xelle reached out her hand.

"Yes." Rayn still held it close. "But I should warn you, Grand Mages do not let others touch their wands. It's not like our enchantments, which are often gifted or shared. Fortunately, I am not a Grand Mage."

As she handed over the wand, Xelle saw a twitch in her eye, a nervousness. Not about the wand. "You're about to pledge?" she asked.

"Yes. I mean, yes. I'm— It's time for me." She peered at Xelle, silent for a moment. "I appreciate you kicking it, I really do. I promise, I'll kick it other ways. I'm ready to belong."

That was layered, and overwhelming, and a bit personal, and Xelle realized she was swishing the almost-Mage's wand around with the same energy Na'Vuia would silently release frustrations into stirring a fry batter. "I should probably—" She handed it back.

Rayn pulled it close, like a candle. "Tonight's my last night off. Gave me a couple days. 'For recovery.' Went into the village, to take care of things I'd been putting off. It was nice." Her speech was unusually clipped.

"Wow, two days. Thrilling."

"But see, that's it, Xelle. I get two stinking days because I'm still a Study. They give me days. When I'm a Mage, I'm not here for their pellets." Turning swiftly, she put the wand back into what Xelle saw was some sort of sleeve, then carefully positioned it back into her bag. She turned around. "Could I invite you to the ceremony?"

It looked like there was more to that question. More layers, not more question.

"Hey." Xelle tried to look reassuring. "I know I could pledge if I wanted to. They're sure wearing me down to do it, right? I mean, why shouldn't I?" No, this was about Rayn. She lifted her chin. "That would be really nice. I'd be honored to attend."

As the words came out, they did not feel strange. She felt . . . joy. Joy to be invited, to be trusted. She'd never actually seen a pledging; they kept them small. Even Helia's spots had all gone to grandparents; Xelle'd never even considered being invited.

Rayn leaned forward, waggling a quick finger toward Xelle's face. "Your tattoo, by the way— I passed through Mytil. I remembered noting it before but saw in Mytil it was the style. I'm still learning my cultures." She shrugged apologetically.

Wait, what? This was not a Mytil style. At least, it *hadn't been.* Also, should she tell her? She'd already trusted this per she barely knew with her biggest secret here. From the moment they'd met, she'd felt that. That trust. A lack of tension she wasn't used to. "It's a dragon sigil," she heard herself saying. "You know how I'm the dragonfriend? This is why. It's a mark my friend gave me. It allows zhem to communicate to me, not words, but location and urgency, I guess. Zhey can read my thoughts, either sent through the sigil, or when I'm close. And zhey can connect with me, and convey to me things they've sensed. Images, scents."

She'd been thinking more about that, how the earlier ones had differed from the others. "I think zhey can convey things they've actually sensed, but also things they can imagine." It explained why some of the images had felt inaccurate, cartoonish. Thunder had been showing Xelle something zhey'd not seen zhemself.

"And if it's a style now, they're um . . ." She couldn't quite bring herself to say 'imitating me'; that sounded ridiculous.

Rayn shifted, a bit oddly. "Makes the wand seem . . ." She gestured toward the bag. "The pledging . . ."

Xelle did understand that, kind of deeply. "It's not a competition." Not to Xelle. "The structure here, the ranking, makes us feel that way." She paused. "I think about things like this a lot."

"The night ivy," Rayn said.

Her head jerked up.

"I'm sorry. If that was personal. You told me, in the vroom that you called your distress with sleep the night ivy. All the thinking, I mean. Just . . . the name stuck with me."

Oh. If she'd mentioned the night ivy, she would have also mentioned the storm. Xelle thought. The storm was the distress. The night ivy was the hope. "Do you . . . have that too?"

She shook her head, looking a little somber. "No. But speaking of which, I'm supposed to be up early. I guess it's all about to start." She glanced away, before turning back with a broad smile. "Thanks for inviting me. This was nice."

It really was. Xelle found herself smiling too. "Thanks for dinner. I . . . will have spice bread again. The Sharre way!"

Rayn's smile broke into a full-up beam. "If you'll have me, I'll surely make it again. It's something I have here. Of home." Her eyes flitted askance, showing, now, that tiredness.

"You are always invited. And thanks for not telling. About it."

Rayn waved her hand dismissively. Then yawned. "Sorry. It can't be soon. I'm swamped with the pledging prep. But I'll send you the pass for the ceremony. You press this?"

As Rayn reached for the doorway, Xelle suddenly felt awkward taking the pass. Surely Rayn had friends here, as personable as she was. She nodded, about the doorway, and then realized Rayn had already figured out how to work the doorway and was asking about the ladder. Rayn was halfway through the door, and Xelle didn't want to be an obligation, or for showing her the room. "If you find anyone else to go, that's fine too."

"Sure. Our fortunes spin the moons. Well, see you maybe."

Before Xelle realized that Rayn had done so, the ladder had been extended and Rayn was on her way. And Xelle remembered that she'd said pers in Mytil were getting tattooed with imitations of her *sigil.*

Everything felt like a lot.

16 - *The Seven Mages of Satta*

The year was drawing to a close. Snow covered the forest and hills of Ever Region, and the skies glowed bright, day and even night, with the reflection of sun and then the moons against the glittering canvas.

Making her way to her daygarden had grown more complicated once she left literal tracks, but this had only prompted Xelle to delve deeper into the simplest casts of Arc Magic.

Instead of slinging herself around, a rather loud cast that left streaks of shadow, she learned how to cast the slightest fibers against her boots, preventing them from quite contacting the snow, as her weight pressed against the cast itself.

Enchanted travel boots? It sounded like a plan, but she'd sworn not to enchant her cloak until she could ask Kwill for eir advice, so she wasn't going to start enchanting boots, either, even if she weren't worried about managing the effects of multiple enchantments. Of course, Kwill going to Wehj and doing some investigating, and then traveling back here would take some time. It had been a month, now, and she tried not to think too much about what day e might arrive. She knew e would, though, and that lent her comfort as she went back about her days alone, practicing, sending Mage Fepa crappy reports, sleeping—as much as she ever did—and then back to the next.

Helia had sent, so wonderfully, a few notes through the post, but nervous about We'le's cautions, Xelle had not replied. She trusted Helia would not take that for more. And Rayn, true to word, was nearly sequestered in preparation for her pledging. Xelle had tried to catch her in the halls, but she'd breezed past, barely giving Xelle a look. Not knowing the same about Rayn that she did with Helia, she did worry a bit here. Perhaps she'd done something wrong. Again.

Not always. Kwill was still her friend. And surely, e'd be here soon.

Kern had not checked in, nor had she called him. This didn't concern her; he was a Spire Mage, if something had happened to him, that would quickly spread. And, truly, with someone else now working the Lunests angle, she'd prefer he not go through with his plan to ransom her or whatever it was.

That was assuming Kwill could learn anything Kern could.

And that probably wasn't true.

~

The clerk found her in the corridor. "Oh, good, I was worried. They said you . . ."

"Practice in the forest?"

He nodded. By the cut of his clothes, she'd long figured he was from Frond Region, and could see why trudging aimlessly through winter snow with a message might not be his first preference.

"I'm from Tam." She said it like he didn't know the name of the dragonfriend he'd been sent to find. "I'm a forest sort." She shrugged. While their characterizations of her were often bizarre, she'd leaned into the forester vibe a bit, knowing it gave her solid cover for her daygarden as well as sneaking away to rune back to Arc. And from there, to anywhere.

"Yes, I've got two cards." He held out . . . two cards. "That one's nondelay."

She glanced down. One, painted with lovely gold and green inks, was an invitation to Rayn's pledging ceremony. Both excited she'd really (still) been sent one and annoyed that whatever Fepa's nondelay message was was preventing her from enjoying it, she resigned to study every detail later, and instead flipped to the other.

Hastily written, it was a notice of visitation. Huh. Not Fepa, then.

Now, Apprentice Xeleanor Du'Tam knew she was not important

enough to have hand-delivered nondelay notices, so then, it was the visitor who was important. Kern? Would he approach her in the open?

Helia wouldn't use a written note. And she'd been hoping for Kwill, but they wouldn't be so huffy for a Study. She shrugged, almost slipping the cards into a pocket but not wanting to bend the invitation, and headed off toward the Front Desk.

It was Kwill. E was wearing eir normal finery; this time an off-white ruffled drape over thick black traveling pants. An asymmetrically shaped cap topped eir head, matching the shirt, neither one with dirt or smudges.

Not Xelle. The moment you put white on her, every sauce in Alyssia would compete to be the first to splotch upon it. A walking canvas for the world of sauce.

Not knowing what story Kwill'd told and thinking rushing over warmly might not fit it, she walked solemnly to face em and offered a stately bow.

The clerk standing beside em spoke. "Apprentice Xeleanor Du'Tam. This is Breath Study Kwillen Du'Satta, e. Study Kwillen says that you met on a previous exchange to Breath Tower. When you . . . studied at Arc Tower."

"Yes. Uh, yes, we did." She nodded again at Kwill. "A privilege to receive your visit. What takes you this way?"

Kwill didn't crack a grin or even a sarcastic tilt. She would have thought it was a Kwill impersonator. Did . . . Breath do that? It would be turning the magic. Anyway. This was Kwill.

"I'm taking a sojourn to rest in my choices and contemplate how best to suit the Mages of Satta."

And what was that accent? Kwill didn't speak like that. It was like . . . affected.

"Excuse me," the clerk squeaked in. "Could I . . . Which one is your parent?"

"My parents are not of the seven," e said, in the same tone, somehow dull and sharp at the same time. "I am grandcura to Crown

Mage Kwilloura Du'Grand, and guarded of Spire Mage Withrip Du'Breath."

"Wow," the clerk breathed out. "Crown Mage *Kwilloura.*" He looked at Xelle. "Spire Mage Pontacia Du'Ever was one of the seven. Since you were here, I thought— Do you need anything else?" the clerk interrupted himself, seeing Kwill's gaze turn.

"I'd like to talk to Apprentice Xeleanor Du'Tam for now; I've heard that e is dragonfriend, and my sojourn would not be complete without learning more about this unexpected turn of events."

"Yes, oh, sure." The clerk bowed at Kwill, then turned and bowed at Xelle. "If, uh, if you have issues with access, let me know."

"Thank you, friend." Kwill bowed to the clerk, who nearly giggled in delight. "Xeleanor?" E reached out an arm, and Xelle took it, walking em slowly through and into the Atrium.

E leaned a little closer as they walked. The accent was gone. "Can you get us in private, fast? Pers here shouldn't recognize me, but that clerk is going to spread the word faster than piss steams in snow."

"That, I can do. Here." She ducked through, into a hallway that wound toward the library. "This way, through the Study stacks." Weaving through the less-desirable back section, with old cast research and outdated guides, she walked them through the old, rarely-used door and into the snow-covered patio beyond. They stopped under the thick beams of a small shelter. "Can I cast on your boots?"

"Delighted," e said, and Xelle, instead of making her light cast onto herself, made it onto both of them, and they walked, hovering just over the snow, and quickly out of sight.

"Is it always this cold here?" e asked, shivering heavily.

"No. This is winter." She stuck her tongue out at em, regretting the choice in the chilly blast that found it. "But, I mean, yeah, it's no To'Breath. Here."

She clicked down her ladder, gestured em up, and without explanation, rode it herself once e'd moved into the room. Sealed. Done.

"We're fairly wrapped now," she said. "Now what was all that. Mages? Grandparents? Mobbing? I was with you all over To'Breath and you were not mobbed."

"They'd all tried already," e said, flopping down onto the couch. "Here, I'd be hot coffee on a sermon morn. Do you know . . . I've never been to To'Ever? Well, maybe, but not that I remember."

Xelle tried to imagine visiting a Mage Tower and not specifically recalling it. She couldn't. And technically e had—

"The Seven Mages of Satta." Kwill closed eir eyes.

Oh.

Xelle knew this. They'd been mentioned in most of the more recent books in the To'Breath library, when she'd been there. One family, with a Spire Mage concurrently in each Tower, and even one Crown Mage. "*That's* your family? You . . ." She didn't add that e'd not spoken particularly kindly of them.

"My family," e repeated, allowing eir eyes to open slowly, and not seeing whatever e was worried to see, opening them fully. "Sorry for the quick getaway, but since I said I was casually saying hello, there'd be no reason for us to go somewhere secret. It was easier to just go and have them assume I'm in your room, or such. Thanks for that. Hey, though. Did you make this?" E waved roughly around the space. "Don't answer. You did. Fira, 'fairly wrapped'? You make it sound like sticktape over paper. Xelle, I'm not even sure what I'm sensing, and I'm Breath. I could never do this."

She wasn't sure that was true. Or maybe, she thought, that e couldn't do something else, as impressive to her. Like whatever that voice was, she thought. Not wanting to minimize, she didn't vocalize that. Instead, she made a quick gesture of thanks.

"You're actually amazing. And what are you carrying?" Kwill tipped eir chin over. "Looks fancy."

She glanced down at the card remaining in her hand. "It's an invitation to a pledging for my friend, Rayn. Oh." What did this mean? "It says 'and a guest'."

"That's standard." E leaned back again on the couch. "This is comfortable."

"Thanks. You've been to pledging ceremonies?" Realizing it was *her* ashed-out comfortable couch e was complimenting, she plopped down on the other side. Ah, it was soft. She allowed, but didn't voice the gloat.

"Yes, many. And you shouldn't go alone. I mean, do what you want but it's kind of a sad-horn look, at something most pers are clamoring to attend."

"Huh. Well, it's tomorrow if you want to go." Who else would she ask? Especially on that notice.

Kwill leaned over to look at the card. "They sent it for tomorrow? And I thought Breath was flighty."

Realizing maybe Rayn wasn't upset at her, that she could see her pledging, and that two of her friends could meet filled her with sudden joy. "What is this feeling?" she blurted out. "I'm excited about something."

"I would repeat that you need to get out more, but last time, you ported into my room and crashed on the couch so we'd have to work on the specifics."

Xelle made a farty noise.

"Be blessed," e incanted.

"Stop that." She tilted the card back and forth in her hand, letting the light catch the golden ink. "This is pretty; I don't want to turn it in."

"Oh." Kwill grinned. "You don't need to."

"Isn't it like . . . my ticket?"

"Xeleanor. Where are you?"

Right. Mage Tower. They knew everyone who'd been invited. "Well then. I mean, if I'm taking you, I'd get in anyway?"

Groaning, Kwillen rolled to the floor with unnecessary drama.

Kicking off her boots, Xelle put her socked feet up on eir back. "You can meet Rayn, too. I think you'd like her. She's the only other one who knows about this room." She hoped they'd get along. They were both easy-going, right? Who knew. Friend dynamics could be strange.

"You win. I will suffer this no longer." Kwill rolled out from under her feet, and awkwardly propped emself to stand. With a brush-off that was more symbolic than effective, e plopped back onto the couch. "I did go to Wehj, and I admire your patience in not asking."

Oop. Actually, she'd been so excited to see em, she'd forgotten there was business involved.

"How much do you know about them?" e started.

Xelle shrugged. "I really don't."

"So, Mark, he, and Irla, she. Married, technically."

"Technically?"

"No evidence they like each other, even professionally. But they do both like the generational wealth, started by a grandparent's success making specialty lighting, which then expanded into fuelstone trade and other markets. Eventually the family built a huge house in the Highponds, that was so notable even for Highponds, people started calling it the Lunest Manor, after the company. Once Irla and Mark got control, they expanded the place into a gated compound, then started treating it like a town, with its own placename. One could argue it's still two pers' house with an absurdly huge yard, but it's so extravagant, I don't even begrudge it having its own name. Once you get that far." E shrugged.

"Got it. So they're wealthy and have their own town in one of the nicest places on Alyssia. Why would they be stirring trouble?"

"Well." Kwill picked up a pretzel stick—where did that come from?—and twirled it around. "They want to commercialize visits to the moons."

"What?" Xelle sputtered. That was . . . unbelievable. Outrageous. But Kwill wasn't joking?

"Yes. They also want to make mountain living viable. Special estates, with views of dragons and access to the moon-visits."

At this point, Xelle realized she was breathing into the back of her hands. Not meaning it to look as dramatic as it did, she lowered them.

"Clearly, this is an endeavor that requires substantial magic outside of magesphere protocols, and that's not hidden. They boast about making magic finally work for the populace, and not the reverse. This is all the open part. But." E lowered a finger firmly. "One thing Mages love to do is talk to me in private. It is my strong belief that the Lunests have influenced several Mages."

"You mean manipulated." Influenced was too nice. "Threatened."

E paused. "I do. They have four on the project now. Potentially all high-ranking. Grand. Arc. Charm. And . . . it pains me to say, Breath."

Xelle grimaced. "Well I know the Arc one."

"Of course you do. And they are not working on the other Towers. Irla has insisted that Dust, Ever, and Frond be avoided, and Mark is not at a point to challenge her. Honestly, Xelle, I don't know which of them is worse." The bit about involved Mages seeming to bother em a bit, e again leaned back.

The moons?

She glanced at Kwill's face. No, definitely not a joke. She tried to absorb this. It wasn't easy, and her mind spun. Who was worse? Was that important, even? But it could be, if strategizing. Understanding. And four Mages, on this offensively indulgent project. She thought it was. No, it must be. A valuable project would not require such deceit. Was that right? Was this even possible? All of it was stirring in her mind. She tried to settle it. Kwill, at least, seemed to see her distress (and knew it wasn't upsetting, exactly, just mental jar-shaking, which was still upsetting, but in a way that she was still fine) and was waiting for her reply. The travel. Her head snapped forward.

"How are they going to the moons?" She didn't want to think that . . .

"Do you know of something called inkblooms?"

"Inkbloom," she corrected, by rote. "It's . . . sensitive. To'Arc." She trusted Kwill completely, but wasn't ready to say more than that.

"Well, it's something they think will help them do this moons stuff. In addition to Grand Magic."

Xelle had never discussed or been taught anything about inkbloom in her Arc training, but she knew—instinctively—using them with Grand Magic would have dire consequences. She'd need to think about this more. Now, she was feeling more strange. Uneasy. Disoriented, even.

"And they're obsessed with dragons."

That didn't help.

"Xelle?"

E reached out, and nervously placed a hand over hers. It comforted her.

She closed her eyes, and slowly—slowly—breathed out, as e rubbed eir fingers over Xelle's own. Slowly. Kindly.

"Thank you." She withdrew her hand, then feeling it rude, reached out and gave eirs a squeeze. "I'm ok."

Finally, she sat back. Kwill was eating a pretzel stick. "You got your revolution." E waggled the pretzel stick, talking through a bit of crunch.

Wonderful. "Yes, it's very impressive. All here on my couch. Maybe someday we'll get a Mage." She wasn't sure why she'd said that. Felt wrong. Maybe the four Mages were still echoing in her mind.

Kwill cocked eir head a bit and pointed to the invitation. "Do you trust her?"

Rayn, e meant. "Yes. Completely."

"Revolution-curious?"

Welcoming the distraction, Xelle grinned. "Perhaps." She'd told Rayn other things. That was . . . a good idea. "Let's try and talk to her soon. Maybe after the ceremony? Or if you have to go afterward, I will."

Kwill crunched down the rest of the stick while shaking eir head. "You won't catch her soon. Mage initiation is worse than pledging prep."

That was true; she'd barely seen Helia for weeks. "I should tell you something." She'd told Rayn; it felt wrong for Kwill not to know.

"Sure." Kwill turned to face her, eir expression blank.

"The dragon mark isn't just a mark. It's a sigil. It connects me to the dragons, mentally." She still didn't feel comfortable mentioning Thunder directly. That wasn't a matter of trust. Just . . . unsurety.

Kwill's eyebrows were now raised, and e looked legitimately shocked. "Ash. I thought it was . . . ash. It's a sigil? Fira, Xelle. And I was worried pers would run after *me*."

"It's different." It was. "Kind of a repellent, honestly. At least here; I've learned pers in Mytil are imitating it." She tapped her sigil. "With tattoos, but still."

"I wish they'd imitate me."

Hadn't e always complained that—

"A hundred Kwillens running around so pers could bug them and I could go about my business."

Oh. She hadn't thought about it like that. Yet having seen how hard Kwill could spiral, she quickly steered this another way. "Art is interesting isn't it?"

Kwill nodded, still distracted. "There is so much power in magic that we never discuss."

Yeah. She thought about Thunder's fearful reaction to the inkbloom, something she'd been so excited to use. Dangerous powers, she was learning. But, they all were, if turned.

The magesphere spent so much time talking about how one never turned the magic, maybe they hadn't spent enough time considering what to do if someone did . . .

The thought was chilling. "Art. Anyway." She rubbed her forehead, not even sure anymore what she was saying. "Maybe we need one of those, too. In the revolution." She laughed weakly. "An artist."

"Know any?" Kwill bit into another pretzel.

Actually. She did.

But, oh! "I wanted to ask you something. About an enchantment."

Kwill rather rudely gestured at emself. Of course e was a Breath caster, like she didn't know that. "Sorry, I don't feed trolls," she said. "But I do have a question about an enchantment."

E waited.

"I . . . you know enchanting processes are secretive, and even being Mage Fepa's designer bag wouldn't allow me to betray them. But. I think all first classes teach the basics?"

"To'Breath learns the basics, yes."

She took a breath, and looked nervously into eir eyes. "I have tested an enchantment that will make my cloak adjust to the . . . not the *weather,* but the *feel,* around me. Whether I need it to be light, or heavy, calm, or wavy. It should even change shape, as it learns."

E leaned back, considering this. "Fine, I'm impressed."

"But I'd like to wrap it," she continued. "I broadcast enough as it is." She tapped her sigil. "I know we all have our ways of wrapping, but Arc Magic is too . . . *sweeping* for what I want here. I think it would tangle. Or something. And Ever too *thick,* even if I could learn it. I normally use Frond for a pseudo-wrapping thing since I haven't really explored the others, but I've only done that onto structures, and I don't know how I'd even start to use rune wrapping around something that would be so fluid and in motion. I wondered if there was something I could do. With Breath. Not to wrap any active casting, but just to dust the enchantment itself. Poof-poof." She flicked her fingers.

"The Seven Mages of Xelle."

"Is that a joke?"

"Was supposed to be? Anyway. Yeah. I . . . do know how to do that. One of my sarents sold so many wraps, he moved to Iyero and we never saw him again."

"I'm sorry?"

"I'm sorry he didn't leave before making me listen to his endless bragging, droning about it over family feast. But you might not like it. And I don't do it."

"Like what?"

"Breath wraps, on any cast, require you to absorb some of the cast. Instead of deflecting energy to create a repulsion, the caster trades it. For a sense of oneself. As long as whatever you're doing is transient, and you don't do it too often before you go buy an island or whatever, any residual effects are minimal."

That . . . sounded uncomfortable. "What about on an enchantment?"

"Would take a bit out of you, yeah. And that would imbue, so it'd have to be something you're going to keep using. Don't think one perma-wrap would hurt you, but you wouldn't want to waste it. Also it'd probably draw attention if someone else tried to use it. Like a bird with the wrong chirp."

"But you haven't done it? The temporary version?"

"Not . . . technically. Not in class. Not on another prong. Fine. I tried it on my own once, wrapping a small notability cast, just to see if my sarent was all the boss he claimed to be." Kwill glanced over. "Yes, it worked. But I felt sick, got very unwrapped gas for an hour, and decided I was done with that."

"Would you . . . tell me everything you know about it?"

"On one condition. You try it after I'm gone."

Xelle shook her head. "You don't want me to fart on you."

Kwillen shrugged. And they both laughed.

17 - To Pledge

The mood reminded her of a wedding. The alcove had been decorated with dark green banners, in the specific shade traditionally signifying the Ever Tower. In the early days of Alyssian unification (Xelle had spent a lot of time reading history books at To'Breath, and these little perspectives had latched onto her every perception of the magesphere, she'd found, whether she wanted them to or not) Mages had traditionally identified themselves by these seven colors. Now, Mages dressed to their own styles, but in times of ceremony, would often revert to the specific shade of their prong.

In fact, her own preference for black clothing was unrelated to the fact that it was, dyed with a specifically dark pigment, the traditional color for To'Arc. This made her think of Helia, who looked vibrant in floral shades and evening lights. She couldn't even imagine her with a black sash, truly. Yet, Helia had pledged. And today, Rayn would join her.

Xelle glanced around from her position in the doorway, curious to see visitors from far-away Sharre, perhaps dressed in the same unique style of length and pattern that Rayn wore. Instead, she saw Ever Mages: teachers and mentors. A spattering of traditional evergreen robes amidst the mélange of metallic-threaded finery.

"Apprentice Xeleanor Du'Tam, she or e, and Breath Study Kwillen Du'Satta, e," a voice boomed out, making her visibly jump.

Kwill, in gold-trimmed white robes and a stately cap, stood tall, walking with long strides, and Xelle—who hadn't thought to shop for finery—had to settle for the blackest tunic and pants she owned (with a quick Arc cast to repair a hole), at least hoping they had an air of formality (or perhaps, unintended tradition) to them. Borrowing one of Na Lleyx's tricks, she'd quick-embroidered a vine down each sleeve, which might pass from a distance as something nicer.

Xelle had no idea if those already seated would clap or anything, but fortunately the Mages stayed in place, facing ahead while side-glancing at the pair, as they took their positions in the front row.

A Study walked to the front holding a small horn. (Apparently they'd been the last to be seated?) The Study played an old-sounding melody, one Xelle didn't know, bowed to silence, and then left. The room shuffled in their seats, some turning around to look.

Rayn looked amazing.

If the town of Sharre had not showed up for her, she'd dressed for the whole town. Layers of evergreen fabric, striped with a rich, mossy green and highlighted with small, gold accents, confused the eye whether they flowed from the tunic, the train, or the beautiful high-waisted pants which flowed out into wider, lily-like shapes just above the floor, almost warning a per not to look too closely. Or daring them to, Xelle thought with a grin. Instead of her usual sewn turban, Rayn wore a high knot of fabric, with its own train in what Xelle thought to be seven wide ribbons of sheer, metallic fabric. Only the thin chains Rayn normally wore around her ears, the small tattoos surrounding her face, and the curl of her lip over an overwhelmed expression confirmed this was, indeed, Ever Study Rayn Du'Sharre. For a short while longer.

Rayn glanced her way, not smiling but her mouth relaxing a touch, as if wanting to but unsure how the Mages would perceive it.

Xelle nodded, her heart pounding a little in gratitude for the gesture. And then, Xelle could only see her back, as she took her place facing the presiding Mage, an elderly sort in a plain, green robe, accented only by a sash and chain.

As happy as she was for Rayn's pledge, she did not focus on the words of the ceremony, but instead her eyes traced the folds of Rayn's trailing fabric, the grout-lines on the floor, Kwill's buckled boots, each reaching to an exaggerated point against the cleanly-mopped tiles. To pass the time and keep her heart from pounding against the blur of ceremonial language, she thought of songs, shapes, remembered how much fun they'd had in her daygarden. Remembered the warm spice and soft texture of the bread. Wished, a moment, that Rayn were not turned away, so she could see the quirks of her expression.

Oh. It was time.

"Do you, Study Rayn Du'Sharre, pledge all to the Ever Tower, Spire of the Sacred Crown of Hallina, for as long as you live."

"I do."

"And do you do so without reservation, hesitation, or influence."

Rayn paused. Not really; it was fleeting. But Xelle caught it, and her heart leapt, and then she heard it.

"I do."

There was a long silence, as the presiding Mage leaned forward, presumably pinning on a basic chain.

The Mage stepped back. "Gatherers. Family. Friends. I present to you, Mage Rayn Du'Ever, she."

Xelle didn't have time to consider her reaction to that as the room clattered in a polite, muted applause. Annoyed, Xelle found herself clapping louder. Seeing what she was doing, Kwill joined her. And then, the rest of the room, raising their volume until the banners themselves seemed to shake.

The small crowd, looking a bit abashed at why they'd clapped so much, dispersed. Attendants had already moved in, taking down the banners.

Rayn walked over, with the illusion of gliding in her finery. Xelle gazed at her flushed face a moment; she looked so good.

"Well, there's a reception now. I'm really sorry, but it's Mages only." She pointed at Xelle. "You know how I feel about that, don't try to guilt me."

Xelle felt hurt, she would never—

"Hi, I'm Rayn."

"Hi, I'm Kwill, e. Xelle and I met when she was staying at To'Breath. I told her she shouldn't go alone. To this."

Rayn smiled warmly. "As well she shouldn't. Thank you. And it's nice to meet you. Kwill?"

E nodded. Then, leaned forward. "If you'll take my advice as someone who's been to a few of these. That Mage that just waved? Will creep on any new Mage. Reputation."

Rayn stifled a disdainful sputter. "I was wondering who the ash that was."

"They won't miss you."

She looked over, her eyebrows raising in surprise as she, and Xelle at the same time, realized Kwill's implication. "At my own reception?"

"Nah, they're going for the open bar. The few that will notice will respect you more. You're reporting to initiation in the morning, right?"

She nodded.

"Skip it. Get sleep. Will feel good, I promise. Unless you want to go?"

"Not really." She nearly deadpanned the words.

"Meet up in the forest?" Eir head tilted at Xelle, indicating where e specifically meant. "Chat?"

Rayn sighed, rather like a flag unhooking in the wind. "I'd love that. And you're sure? Sure I won't hurt my status?"

"Certain."

She looked over at Xelle. "E really knows all this?"

Xelle grimaced. "Yes. E really does. Let's talk about it . . . when we're there."

"Sounds good. But first, I'm going to change."

Xelle couldn't quite remember the last time she'd had two friends in the same place. Not labmates, or of course her Tam family, but three friends, in a room, talking with no reason to be there other than to do so. It felt . . . really good. Like, a new warmth had filled some of that empty space. And also really sad.

Why would it have to end so soon?

Rayn wasn't as surprised or amused as she was sympathetic to learning about Kwill's connection to the Seven Mages of Satta. "It's hard," she said. Their eyes seemed to meet for a long moment, until Kwill popped back into eir usual self.

"Enough about that." E twirled a pen in eir fingers. "Who wants to talk about Xelle's revolution?"

Ugh. "Kwill, stop saying that. I'm not revolting, I'm just reacting. Like any of us would."

E waved that dismissive hand again, and Xelle scrunched her face at em.

"You called it that! Now that we're doing it, all the sudden the ship has no sail. Now, how much does she know about the dragons?" E pointed the pen at Rayn.

Funny that e assumed she knew something. E wasn't wrong, of course. "She knows it. All that I do, anyway. And you." It was hard to keep track now what she'd told them both here, or what were vestiges from her nightpaths, but she thought everyone was generally caught up.

"Paint me our revolution?" Rayn asked, leaning forward. See, Rayn knew it wasn't *hers.*

Kwill answered, while she was still gloating about that. "There were rumors spread trying to keep one of the Arc Spire Mages from ascending to Arc Crown Mage, saying that Mage was with some disruptive 'Amberborn' group, that are vaguely trying to turn the magic against the populace. It's how she met me, being sent to To'Breath to look into it, just as vaguely."

"Me too," Rayn noted with a slight grin. "But, turning the magic?" She didn't have a grin for that.

"Turn the whole magesphere, they say. Again, vaguely." E wiggled eir fingers and make a spooky noise. "You know, we should probably get Xelle to tell us some of the middle story on this, but in the end she flew to To'Arc on a dragon—onto To'Arc, forgive me—everyone saw it, and now she's the dragonfriend. Whoever was behind it needed to duck under for a bit, which slowed the chaos at Arc. But, of note, they still haven't done their Ascension. Oh, but before the ducking, whoever these pers are quick-spread more rumors that Xelle also is Amberborn. Then Xelle moves—Or is sent? We don't know?–to Ever where she gets stuck to a notably unpleasant rusted coin Mage, all of which is making pers think maybe she's neither so good nor so powerful?"

Uh, Xelle hadn't heard this part.

"But Xelle has sources—I'm at Breath, we know about sources—and finds out that the Lunests of the infamous Lunest Estate of Highponds are likely involved. I go to Wehj, get out of being at To'Breath for a bit, don't have to deal with my Ma's plans, and learn a few things."

By the time Kwill had relayed the moon plans and dragon obsessions, Rayn was reaching into her bag and uncorking a fat bottle. "Snagged from the cart heading to the reception. It's my reception; what, were they going to track the sand? Anyone?"

It wasn't the best, but then Xelle was a little fussy about her libations. She kept that to herself. As Na'Foose would have said, the price was right.

"So there's someone involved at Grand?" Rayn scowled as she asked this.

"She was just there for six months," Xelle explained to Kwill.

"Really?" Eir chin snapped up. "You got them to let you stay there? I wondered why the accents on your pledging suit were grandgold. Seemed too intentional not to know. Little tribute?"

"Yeah, I'm sentimental, and I learned a lot there. And yep, I thought going as a Study would help that whole situation. It's why I put off pledging."

"Ah, the Xelle technique."

She glared—*hard*—at em, but Kwill ignored it, and Rayn was still talking.

"It didn't. It did. But not so much. They are so restrictive about everything. Everything is a big fired-up deal." She waved at Xelle. "You wouldn't be able to stand it."

Hey. Pers might be surprised what she could stand. "Oh? More restrictive than my ash-burned Apprenticeship? Have I not mentioned it? Total freedom, no lab. Except I can't do anything without someone else's permission. I can't go anywhere. I can't interact. I get stared at like an out-of-place museum exhibit. I—"

"Then pledge!" Rayn interrupted. "If you want to be a Mage, why not be a Mage?"

If anyone else would have said that, Xelle would have probably stormed out. But first, storming out of one's own secret room was a challenge. And two, she didn't . . . want to. And three, there wasn't malice in the way she said it. More . . . well, she couldn't place it. Her own uncertainty, she supposed.

By the way Kwill had leaned back against the arm of the couch, e seemed to be thinking something similar. About Xelle, anyway. Ugh. If only she had a way to—

Burn it. "I am a Mage."

Now they were both leaned back. Fira, she wasn't an oddity to be watched. "You heard me. Who says I can't be? A Mage without a Tower. And you're fired-up right. I can't stand it. And I'm not going to anymore. I'm leaving soon. I can't live at a Tower. I can't use the libraries. I can't—"

Her next swallow went down a little rough and she coughed to clear it out. "I'll figure it out. I'm thinking through how to do it. I need time."

Her head was starting to swirl. "You know this stuff is rancid?"

"I rather like it," Kwill interjected. "A nose of buffet. But I do have a potion, if you're over it." E reached from eir robe and clinked a little, plump-bottomed glass vial onto the table.

"Breath Mages," she got out, now fighting a weird burp. "Never leave your Tower without one."

Kwill tsked. "Oh, I'm just a Study. She's the Mage."

And at least for a little longer, Xelle decided to leave that potion untouched.

~

"It was so good to see you again," she said, shifting from side-to-side a bit.

Kwillen's lips tightened. "If you would enjoy a hug, it would not concern me too greatly." Eir eyes darted back and forth, strangely making Xelle more at ease.

Feeling another new warmth, Xelle rushed forward and gave em a tight squeeze, which was sweetly but awkwardly returned.

"Rayn. I like her," e added.

Xelle's lip pulled up, involuntarily. "Yeah, me too." And now Xelle would be leaving, and Rayn would be busy. The ability to travel in a moment didn't mean much when a per was too busy to see you. She pushed it away, but again, the note came to mind.

Rayn's note, that was. After the three had parted ways last night, Xelle had crashed out on her daygarden couch, not returning to her assigned room until the morning. A sealed note had been clipped to the door, thanking her for the company and reminding that she (Rayn) would be sequestered in Mage initiation for a bit. A "don't call on me" note, she supposed.

Kwill gently tapped her arm. "And it was fun to see Ever Tower. It's so different . . ." e mulled. "And I see why you love the forest."

"To me, Breath was different," she noted, a lot of thoughts in her mind. "The forest is same." She thought of To'Arc, also, but that was complicated. And she did love the forest. And had no reason to dismiss it. She just felt . . .

"True." Kwill chuckled. "On my way, then."

She watched, her mind continuing to swirl, as e walked back out into the Atrium, toward the Tower's front. And unlike when she'd left To'Breath that first time, this time, she knew she would see em again.

She'd believed it before, but believing just wasn't knowing. Her mouth turned into a small, sad but grateful, smile.

The note. On her door. The way she'd signed it, *Mage Rayn Du'Ever,* had brought such a smile to Xelle's lips. But it wasn't until she'd seen the greeting that it'd lit her whole face.

Mage Xeleanor Du'Alyssia.

18 - Happy Birthday

Thirty years old. She'd spent so much of the year mulling about this impending eventuality that now she felt it couldn't be true. In full celebration of the day, Xelle was laying back on her bed at To'Ever, the regular (assigned) bed, and staring at the ceiling. A pretty but mostly plain ceiling. One wide wood beam split across the smooth plaster, and Xelle traced it back and forth with a slow gaze, feeling decidedly glum.

Her birthday would be in the Tower records, of course. But no one would see it there, because no one would look. Kwillen was back across the world. Rayn was Maging; she'd only even seen her once, and returned a hurried wave. She didn't have a lab anymore, or classes. She had Mage Fepa, whom she did her best to avoid, and hallways across hallways of staring Ever casters who apparently still considered that she maybe wasn't a good per. "Happy Birthday, no one," she bemoaned.

Fira. She couldn't just lie here and sulk.

. . . she could.

No. Before she realized she'd done it, she'd flipped up onto her feet, and once on her feet, she felt like . . . she should walk. Her walking took her, a bit instinctively, in the direction of the forest. Well, the forest was in all directions here. But, meaning, she went outside and headed toward her daygarden. Which gave her an idea.

"It's my Fira-blessed birthday. I deserve a present," she muttered to a squirrel.

The squirrel chattered back.

~

Xelle was surprised at her nerves while laying the cloak out on her freshly-cleaned and dried (again amagically, as she would risk no shadows for this) table.

With her disciplined, daily study, her Ever Magic was flowing naturally. Maybe natural wasn't the right word. Her Ever practice was more basic and more forced, in general, but she'd built up to and practiced this enchantment very specifically and felt comfortable that she knew it. (Less comfortable that she could execute it on much more than a scrap, but there was one way to find out.)

But for this cast, she needed to cast Ever. Strictly. Except for the Breath twist, but what she meant was she could not do her usual thing of pulling in Arc to ease her way. The idea that the cloak could not be Arc to best serve Arc was probably something she would have learned in Mage workshops. If she'd stayed at Arc.

Not a good birthday thought. Besides, she needed her mind clear for this.

Maybe she shouldn't try adding the Breath wrap, especially with so little instruction. But she wanted to. She wanted to try. She thought she could do it. Now, Xelle always felt ridiculous trying to Breath cast, but this was . . . not Breath *based.* She didn't need to be a master at carving to make a wax seal, she just needed to press wax onto a very elegant envelope without ruining it. Something like that.

Now, she needed to concentrate. If this was really it.

Xelle stepped in. Metaphorically. Ever Magic always felt like . . . another place to her. Ah, maybe that was the difference regarding it being natural. Familiarity with a place didn't make it her place? Anyway, Ever Magic was a different place. And so, when she immersed in it, she could not swirl and weave as she did casting Arc. Like putting on skis kept one's boots at the lodge. Committed once out. That didn't make total sense; the boots were detachable. A gymnast who needed to glide. Well, no, that implied—

She could ponder this later. She needed to focus.

Then, one task at hand, the next in fast grip. That stressful combination of balancing on a platform while preparing to leap from it. Like applying stain on wood, getting it even, letting it soak, and wiping it before it could dry. One she started, she could not stop.

Irritated now, at her own distracting daypaths, she remembered she could do this. And jumped in, with that in mind.

First, the sap. Continuous motion. No thoughts. Just process. Then the powder. So much fabric; she could not let herself think about this. Just apply. Make it solid. Keep going. Miss nothing. Now. Add Breath. Not the breathing of air, but of cast. Like cradling syrup on her tongue while pulling licorice through her teeth, letting the syrup flow through, and then biting it shut.

If that sounded sexual, it was. But not sensual, not with Breath magic. Not with something that wasn't hers.

With the uncomfortable relief of knowing whatever was done or not done was now what it was, she found herself lying on the hard floor, hands pressed against her cramping insides. Painful burps were forcefully let from her mouth; her muscles ached.

Yet, she was . . . a little different now, inside. A piece, a shade, was missing, and replaced with an element of her cast.

Now this, this felt a little sensual. Something that wanted to be there. Something she'd help create. The feeling was . . . foreign. Pleasantly—new, full. And disorienting as it settled against newly-stirred emptiness. Sadness. Confusion. This was normal, she reminded herself. She felt out of sorts because she was out of sorts. It would take her time to adjust. She could not let these feelings panic her. She could only wait them out. Distract herself, as best she could.

As her physical discomfort eased, she rose to see the cloak, and leaned to inspect it. No sap remained. No powder. But charcoal gray fabric, draping wide with a brooding hood, soft to her touch. "Happy birthday," she whispered.

Now, to see if it worked.

~

She sat, outside, the cloak under her, over her, and around her, only a bright, endless flurry of snow before her eyes. She did not feel the cold.

Underneath her, the fabric padded like a blanket. Around her, it embraced her, filled her spirit with warmth.

What good was feeling warm . . . alone?

Sadness took her.

Xelle sat. She stared at the snow.

Her last birthday, she'd been at To'Arc. She hadn't coped with feelings of not belonging then, for the Tower had become regular, comfortable to her. Ay'tea had written her a little poem; he'd read it for the whole lab, his mouth tilting at Xelle's reactions to the references. Small things. Meanings the rest of the lab would not know. The words had burned through her, warmer than this. Warmer than a cloak.

The rest of the Studies had smiled and applauded before returning to their work, and Ay'tea had said he was glad Xelle enjoyed it, the spark in his eyes confirming. Now in retrospect, she recognized the cross-glances of the lab. The air of intrigue. Then, she'd only been focused on him, on the calm his words made her feel. A salve—a joy that ran deep and lifted high.

At the time, she hadn't understood. Or, she now knew, allowed herself to.

She'd always understood, not from meeting, but from the first time they'd talked, in private. He'd made a joke. Their eyes had met. A shiver had run through her, causing her to look away.

Curse Fira, they'd both looked away. And why, why, when now she could see the Studies, smiling in anticipation. Wondering when it would snap. Seeing a whole world of joy for Xelle that she'd thought herself too proper to enjoy.

What good that did her now.

Later that day, they'd gone on a walk around the Tower, through the snow, looking for berries. Cheerful, a little freezing. Keeping an 'appropriate' distance, even as he passed over the little paper before saluting her a quirky farewell, just for the day. She'd memorized the words from the piece of paper he'd handed her, his little symbol sketched onto the bottom.

The words of that little poem had held her, comforted her in the evenings, helped her sleep calmly through the nightpaths. Mostly. They had stayed.

She could not repeat them now. The first words leapt to mind, and she shoved them. Shoved them away. Ay'tea had left. His fault, her fault. It didn't matter; he was gone.

Words that echoed in her mind meant nothing without the care of the one who'd written them.

But then, no, then, she'd been in a different mood. Longing. Power. A need for something—to do something. She'd made her petition. She'd been sent off to Breath. And . . . he'd left. She'd been left, staring at the swirling snow.

She stared out, at the snow.

There were days now she didn't think of him. It seemed, anyway. But when the thoughts returned, they were stronger than they'd been. A confusing sensation, not joy, but also not pain. Perhaps . . . regret.

He'd left. He'd not sent her a note. Not even after she was away, her mind in a temporary spin. Not even after he was away, wherever away was. Was that wrong, or was that right? Had she been more forward with him, that last day, than she'd realized? Had she signaled the feelings that had felt so real, yet perhaps been her own unwanted fiction?

Maybe not even that day, but before. All the smiling, all the laughing.

She hung her head, eyes pressed closed, and heart pounding. She could not reject it. It had been so natural. So right. Why couldn't she laugh? Why couldn't she glow with the light of the sparks she knew she'd felt between them?

Why did the sparks have to be dulled with doubt, when

acknowledging them would have been such a simple kindness. Again, if they were ever there.

She'd known it then. But she didn't now. And none of it mattered. None of it. There was nothing now, anyway, without him. A story without hope. She'd had something special. She'd ruined it.

"How do I fix my head?" she asked the snow, wincing at its brightness as she opened her eyes.

Time, perhaps. Surely time.

Quietly, she rose, and found herself walking the Tower path. Like she had a year ago, on her birthday, through the snow. But, no, that was To'Arc. Tower of change and time. This was To'Ever. Tower of permanence.

She laughed. Bitterly.

Finding herself naturally walking back to the proper front of the Tower, she wandered in through the Front Desk as if only out for a stroll. She realized, hoping to hide any surprise from the uninterested clerk, that the cloak had shifted. Still, warm for winter, but lightened in feel, as she passed inside. The hood, which had hung low and covered her face, now pulled back, just over her cap.

"Apprentice Xeleanor," the voice said.

"Hmm? Oh. Yes?" She smiled at the clerk.

"Have a card for you; was just about to put it in a cart. From Arc."

A dagger stabbed her heart. She reached for the card, thanked the clerk, and rushed into the Atrium, her breath settling at the gold ink and flowery flourishes. Helia.

She opened the card.

Dearest Xeleanor,

I wanted to wish you the very happiest of birthdays. I know that you've not been by, but I am basing this note on my suspicions that you are operating with increased caution and, generally, my presence remains welcome. If I am wrong, I trust the candor and speed of your reply.

I do recall, though, that you mentioned a place I would enjoy, in Mytil? A drink with flower petals, you mentioned. I was thinking about the significance of bringing in the new year, and pink petals sounded like the most delightful poetry to color all the snow.

I presume it is snowy there, too.

I'm aware you won't have time to post a reply, but I'm confident in your skills of communication.

My Best to you, whatever your decision—

Helia

Xelle stared at the paper. After their intimate yet oddly separable encounter at last parting, she did wonder with all these notions of flowers and celebration if there was something she was missing here.

Then, with gratitude, she remembered this was Helia. ***Helia would tell her.*** What relief in a friend, in a partner . . . Xelle could simply ask her. Whatever it was. Perhaps the Mage just wanted to try a new drink. Whatever it was, Helia would tell her.

All clouds, that was comforting.

Asking the Front Desk for a stationery set and nearly chuckling at the stark contrast of the green-flecked but utilitarian paper to Helia's personal effects, Xelle stepped aside to a ledge, and began to write.

Hellie-

Your presence is not only welcome, it is treasured. Caution has, as you surmise, stayed me.

Yes, the place. It's called "the Enchanted Forest" up the hill from the art district, on the edge of the city. No, you don't capitalize it. Small place, but taxi conns should know the way. If you get there first, tell Klein you're with me.

I look forward to seeing you. And thanks for thinking of me. Means a lot right now.

- Xelle.

“Apprentice? I’m loading the carts now. Should I wait?”

Hmm? Xelle glanced over. “No, thank you. I’ll send it myself. In a bit.”

Xelle nodded back at the clerk, and walked back out, into the snow, and around a few trees, again casting on her boots to avoid leaving prints. Settling into deep concentration, she focused on the card. And on Helia’s room. And let it drop, onto the table.

In her mind, she thought she heard Bear. A soft meow.

She smiled.

19 - Pink Petals

Traveling to Mytil from To'Ever was a much longer trip than from To'Arc, reminding her of her much-anticipated childhood excursions to the city. A faraway place centered on art, with gleaming white buildings and shops for anything and smells of flowers and cooking and big open spaces—a place more magic than magic to young Xelle. A place, though, that Xelle had never celebrated the new year. And today, she would!

This time, since it was a significant holiday and even Mage Fepa appreciated those, she asked straight out if she could go meet a friend and if he'd allow her to arrange a vroom on his behalf to take her. In the middle of his own party planning, one with visiting contacts which didn't seem to involve showing Xelle off, he hurried her away, saying sure, tell them he'd approved it.

Settling into the vroom's space, curtained away from the conn, and all by herself, Xelle relaxed for the long run to the city. Given her own vroom like a Mage (fine, perks *were* nice) and knowing the conn was on staff, no expectation or need for tips, she was able to relax back in a comfortably padded seat, with a padded back in matching red velvet, and a swivel to look out either window. Her bag even got its own velvet seat, next to her, swiveling about as if happy. (Her bag was not alive, it just looked happy as the seat twisted and thus Xelle did not secure the lock.)

The snowy ground was a bit bright, and so Xelle mostly watched the clouds that peeked through the treetops, and imagined what shapes they could be and what such a cloud might be thinking, until each eclipse, when the conn would stop and wait, and Xelle would peer out across the darkened scenery, peering for items of interest. It was a peaceful run, and she realized, as she hopped out with a brief wave to the conn, that even yesterday's melancholy had melted a bit in the trip through the sparkling forest roads.

Yet nerves struck, just a bit, as she walked through the tavern door. Given the holiday, the space was rather crowded, but seeing her, Klein slid a couple of pitchers away from her usual spot at the bar and began to wipe it down.

"I'm expecting a friend," she said, beaming at Klein as she walked close and Klein gave the counter a final swoop.

"A table, then? One should be opening in the side room."

"Oh, no, I was hoping she could meet you. If we can sit here?" Again, it was Xelle's usual spot, right up at the bar, but she didn't want to presume they could both squeeze in, or even that Klein would welcome conversation on such a busy night.

"Absolutely, Xeleanor. It would be my pleasure." He slid a glass of what looked like citrused water toward her. "Unless you'd like something now."

"No, I'll wait. Thank you." She smiled. "How have you been?"

"I focus on my more joyful existences, and thus I am well. How about yourself?"

Xelle drank from the water, clean and bright as always. She sighed. "Is it always complicated?"

Klein smiled. "When it's right."

"I have no idea what that means." Always appreciating his assuring banter even when it tilted askew, she laughed. "Anyway, I've stuck myself again."

"How so?" He hung the towel on a peg. Klein was always doing something bartender, the familiarity of which made the next words come out a little easier.

"They want me to pledge to a Tower, to be a Mage. Yet everywhere I go, I kind of burn the bridge and run." She'd not heard herself say that before, and wondered if it was true. It didn't sound right to hear it. She didn't *like* that.

"I would recommend . . ." Klein hesitated. Xelle wasn't sure she'd heard him hesitate before. "Even a worldly bridge is not the path. It is a path. That someone already selected. And in a greater context, it is not a road at all, but an emphasis on two places."

Ay'tea used to say something like that.

"I might need that drink," was all she said.

Klein looked up to the tinkling of door chimes. "Are you ordering for your friend?"

"I am," she said, turning to see Helia standing in the doorway, framed like artwork. Her metallic cap and long chains no longer overtook her, but blended in to layers of chiffon. Ash, Magery *suited* this hu. Her sash and chain draped over elegant winter robes, with thick, perfectly fitted gloves, clasped unsurely together. And if Xelle had been worried about her reception, after, after last time (the curve of Helia's bare hip entered her mind)—this dissolved in an instant at Helia's spreading grin.

She reached out her draped arms, and without care, Xelle rushed into them.

"Is it true, love, that you are thirty?"

Xelle found herself dabbing her eyes. "It was nice for you to remember."

As if she lived there, Helia trounced (in the most elegant way of course) toward the bar. Xelle saw Klein gesturing her warmly.

For a moment, Xelle thought about getting her own drink. Her usual, or asking for something new. But she remembered now, remembered what had made her think of Helia that day when, with nowhere left for Xelle to fall, Helia had extended her arms and pulled her up. "Two Pink Petals, please. Hers sweeter than mine."

Xelle grinned at her own wit, until realizing that Klein and Helia were introducing each other. Well, she'd tried to have manners. And neither looked upset, so Xelle plopped into her seat, and swung forward, nodding again in excitement at Hellie beside her.

Klein took his time preparing the drinks, like an openly unabashed seduction. Straining a sweet berry, muddling two perfectly fresh greenleaves. His spirits were unlabeled, always kept in what looked like very old and artfully shaped bottles; this was Mytil after all, even if not *in* the art district. He poured, strained, blocked in chilled ice, stirred a long metal spoon around with intense precision, strained again, and then poured the concoction into two medium-width, plain, cone-shaped glasses. Now a smaller leaf on top. A fresh grind of some medium-colored peppergrain, and then a sprinkling of fresh petals. Then, to Helia's, he added what seemed to be a candied petal. "The longer you wait for it, the sweeter it will be," he offered with a wink. "But then, who likes to wait. Now, I'll leave you two?"

"We'd like dinner, also," Xelle answered.

"If it suits your evening, we'd welcome your company as well," Helia added, acknowledging the crowded space. "Did you know it was her birthday yesterday?"

"It's hard to keep track," he answered nonchalantly.

"Then good she has us both. Anything specific for dinner, Xeleanor?"

What was going on here? "Um, no I tend to let Klein pick."

Helia was looking at him curiously, her head tilted just slightly. "I'd be delighted for his insights. And, the bill is to me, please."

"Mage," he said, nodding in respect, and then offering the sign of the Arc. Helia flashed it back.

Klein did not return for a while, as Helia began describing interesting things she'd seen on the moveroom here. Xelle, glad to listen, couldn't help be brought back to their casual evenings together in Vi'Arc. How much had changed in this past year, yet how much had not.

Xelle took another sip. Her drink was perfectly balanced. Sweet, she realized, but without the thought of it. Unless, like Xelle, one thought of it. (She was always like this.)

Grateful for the excuse not to try and think what she might say about her bizarre situation with To'Ever, Mage Kern, Kwill and Rayn, and all the rest, Xelle found that Helia had months of stories to tell. She poured them out, from her decision to limit teaching classes, to her travails in diplomacy training, to a few dates she'd been on, to a yellow-feathered bird who'd taken a liking to her balcony. She'd just started in on stories about Bear, the cat who'd bonded with her and turned her neatly decorated room into a bit of a blanket fort, when Klein walked over, with one stone pot, two smaller bowls, and a tray carrying napkins, sticks, and seven-pronged ladles.

The dish held layers of warmth. Thick noodles. Bright, curled greens. Thin-sliced bean curd and long, stringy mushrooms. In the center rested a warm layer of curdskin, fried around the edges, and holding a thick paste that poured out when the layer was cracked.

Xelle was about to ladle some into her individual bowl when she saw Hellie's head tilt. She'd missed those little expressions.

"I'm fine to eat out of the same bowl, unless there's an issue."

"Oh," she said, feeling her face flush.

When Klein returned next, Helia pushed forward her empty glass. "The petals were wonderful. Would you be so kind to serve us two of what you'd serve her? Tonight, I mean."

Xelle wondered if it would be her special drink, the one they'd called 'an enchanted forest of my own', but whatever he mixed was done in the back, and when the glasses were set down, she was surprised to see the gentlest tint of violet, as if the angularly cut glassware were a jeweler's finest setting for the most elegant, mysterious gem.

It tasted as good as it looked. Not discernably sweet or bitter, just like a breath of evening with the hint of meadow flowers wafting on a slightly chilled breeze.

"We don't get many Mages in here," Klein was saying. "But when we do, they are the special ones."

Helia peered around, her expression keenly interested.

Xelle tracked the turning of her head. The room, like the grandest forest cabin in the daylight, now glowed with colored lightpods: purple, silver, and a few green. There wasn't much to see through the crowd of people, topped by a field of festive and garishly-decorated caps. The top of the doors to the expanded side section. A crowd gathered around the knockball table. The angled beams leading up to a line of leaded windows, streaming with moonslight. Hangings on the top of the walls, ranging from a couple of the Mytil magipuck teams to interesting, woven tapestries Xelle did not recognize. The tops of a couple of worn murals poking past pers' broad smiles and raised glasses.

A couple danced.

Small chimes, perhaps dangles on caps, or other jewelry worn for the occasion. The combined murmur of the celebratory night.

"I bet this is one of your favorites." Helia was saying it.

Klein smiled, drying off a glass. "I can see you perceive how complicated that might be." He nodded, with what looked like respect. "And this one, seems to be a favorite of yours as well?"

He winked at Xelle, but she felt no unkindness in it, no mockery. A peace, a peace she had not felt around Helia before, settled.

And when Klein moved along, Xelle decided to tell Helia about her daygarden, to invite her there if the time arose. Some talking in code, of course, but Helia always understood her. She told her, also, about what she'd been trying. She showed her the cloak, the nature of its Breath-dusted enchantment.

"Extraordinary," Helia said, running her fingers along the fabric. "Like you."

Whether it was this third drink, or the gold glow of Helia's eyes and well-oiled skin, Xelle felt that she glowed, herself.

Klein walked back, looking up, as if gazing through the slanted ceiling, past the canopy of trees and the shafts of moonslight. "It's the new year in twenty," he said. To Xelle, it sounded conversational, but every per stopped, shuffling into place, chairs grating or glasses being lifted.

"20. 19. 18. 17. 16. 15. 14. 13. 12. 11. 10. 09. 08. 07. 06. 05. 04. 03. 02. 01."

The bar erupted in cheers, and Xelle, overwhelmed by all that had changed this year, all that was different, all that might be to come, folded down onto Helia's chest, and let Helia run her hand gently over her back.

When their tears subsided, they saw two glasses of sparkling, fine wine, before them, brought without asking, so surely a treat from Klein.

"Cheers, friend," Xelle said.

Helia beamed. And took a sip.

They talked no longer, but sat, sipping, and watching the pers gathering their things, saying their goodbyes, wishing each other powerful wishes, both as great as a desired life, and as small as a wish to meet again. Or, perhaps, the reverse.

And it wasn't until they sat back, in that clear moment of mutual sigh that meant the evening was over, that Xelle considered it wasn't clear whether Helia would be getting her own room for the night. She looked at the now sleepy-eyed Mage, trying to figure out what to ask, and what it meant that she hadn't considered it.

Helia grinned, lolling her head to the side lazily. "No sex, love, you're too gloomy for it, and tonight's already been perfect. I'll keep the offer in my pocket."

Xelle hadn't— Noting the gleam in Helia's eyes, she relaxed.

Two could play at this. "What. You profess your love for me, then decide one time is enough?"

"Yeah, burned off some angst." She gave a fake, exaggerated sigh. "But it's good luck to kiss on a new year's eve. Aftereve, I suppose. I wasn't sure if there were accommodations here—you didn't mention it—so I booked a loft in the art district."

With her bag sitting on the clean bartop, Helia waited.

Xelle stared at the bag, half wondering why it wasn't being lifted. "Oh. The good luck kiss? I would never pass on a little bit of luck."

Helia's eyes lit. Well, burned. "Oh, it won't just be a little."

As soft lips turned into violet-scented breath and a merging of hot, reaching mouths, Xelle pulled her hand slowly down Helia's shapely side, feeling each swatch of expensive fabric and imagining the flushed skin beneath.

"Love you, friend," Helia said, turning and gliding back out of the door. The rest of the bar had nearly frozen, the rough, dwindling clamor of the waning party pausing just for everyone to watch the Arc Mage proceed past.

Helia left. But also stayed with her.

And if that kiss, that kiss that was surely felt across the multiverse, was a sign of her year ahead, then, Xelle, thought—she'd never stop flying.

The new year rose with thick flurries, thick for the calmer streets of Mytil. The bar was not open as she descended, but, as usual, Klein had left a simmering cup of broth that she sipped down, gratefully, taking a moment to feel the solace of the large, empty hall. Not large for a hall, of course. But larger than any of Xelle's personal spaces, and with that special feel only captured by a place that could be full, and isn't.

Even Fepa wouldn't expect her back *on* the first day, and so, asking her new hood to conceal her mark and face—not a bit strange in the cold winds—she took a taxi to Vi'Arc, and then walked, casting a bit, up the hill to To'Arc.

Traveling the runes of her nightgarden was growing easier for her, though in fairness she had only one runemark (well, two if she was right about the doorway) and was able to tune directly to it.

"Hello," she said, delighted at the bright glow from her inkbloom, blinking back what she felt certain was a return greeting.

As before, she did not bother to light the blue lights she'd had made, as the glow from the phyta was soothing and plenty to see by in the small space. She still hadn't brought in the hangers and frames yet, as much work as she'd put in on her daygarden, but she had the notes stored away, and would get to it soon.

Still unsure what deep magic the killing sword held, she nodded it a quick hello. But she needed to get back to To'Ever, and so her stay here would be short.

Xelle dared not ask for a double pod again quite yet, and the inkbloom seemed to appreciate the nuance, as they brightly grew a single pod and nearly popped it into her hand. Realizing she'd better grow used to the idea, she slid it into her mouth and then took a long swig from her flask, the water chilled by the cold walk here.

And, the inkbloom feeling receptive to some company, she sat down on her swiveling seat and sang to them a song. Not an old song, nor a familiar one, but words that flew to her lips, like a bird greeting a new day's sun.

Every breath is better
Because you spoke my name
In the days ahead I know that I
Will feel this just the same.

Every light shines warmer
Because you saw my own
As the years will go I wish you'll know
The ways that I have glowed.

Every song sings sweeter
From the time I heard your voice
In this moment now I sing to you
And will, forever yours.

20 - *Chains*

The note said to meet in Vi'Ever. A sketchy note by sketchy note standards, printed amagically onto plain, mid-grade paper, that did not just ask her to visit the village, but told her to arrive, alone, behind an old warehouse on the sixth day of the first month.

If this was Kern's attempt at subtlety, he could stick to stomping around.

But . . . what if it wasn't Kern?

Xelle stood, circling blankly on this idea that someone would deceive her, try to hurt her—no longer new but no less unpleasant. And whatever cleverness or solution she tried to grasp out of the nothingness before her, it came back to one thing. She'd be on her alert. And she wouldn't be afraid to cast. And she'd see where this year of intense, no-day-job working had got her.

She decided to wear a comfortable black tunic and pants, and minimize carrying things she couldn't afford to lose. She didn't even clip on Essie, though she did remove the sanitizing gel and a clothie and push them into a pocket. She would, however, wear her cloak, and . . . hesitating, she also put on Kern's locket, and tucked it down, under the mid-necked collar.

Then, finding her flatblade, she checked the clasp and slid it up between her undercap and cap. This was . . . pinchy, and she didn't want to go back to her daygarden for her sewing kit (plus she'd have to leave Kern's locket here then come back), so, shrugging, she slid it into the opposite pocket from the gel. Then, thinking about it, she took the clothie from the one pocket, wrapped the flatblade in it, and put it back, leaving the gel now alone.

Sorry, this was getting specific, but she'd also never been summoned to the back of a warehouse before.

Not trusting a vroom at this point, she walked, just out of sight of the road, down to the village, met there by the sounds of pleasant mid-day chatter, clanking fuelstones, and the occasional burst of pungent frying smells from the back of a café.

Though Vi'Ever was, to her understanding, one of the smaller Tower villages, this warehouse was annoyingly on the other side of it. Yet it was not difficult to find (the description clear), and, keeping alert, she backed up against the brick wall to wait.

While she wished her sense of smell didn't work so well back here, and she wasn't quite sure *what* she was smelling (Some kind of . . . gross . . . old . . . oil?), she kept all her senses attuned and on watch. The strain of this total alertness was new and not at all pleasant. She felt robbed, very directly. Not able to relax back and think wandering thoughts as if meeting a friend, she stood. Ready. Scanning from side-to-side, and occasionally throwing a slight detection—the Breath version, which no longer made her giggle, but had a particular subtlety that suited it—in the cast itself, if not in the execution.

Execution seemed less important in the face of actual risk.

Kern appeared, suddenly, in front of her, and she jumped.

If she'd expected him shrouded or disguised, this figure before her was the opposite. Regal. Powerful. Full regalia. Xelle knew his mage chain to be a replica, but it was lost among his other honors and jewels. He looked . . . a legend. Kern reached out his hand, face unmoving. Well, she was here, wasn't she? She reached out to it, and felt his huge, bejeweled fingers wrap around hers. They were large, strong, and weirdly comforting, not in a personal way, but like a strong coat on a cold day.

They appeared just outside a huge, towering gate. With a shiver, she let go of his hand, to find that her wrist was tied to his now, with a cast. She cut him a glare. Then looked about. *All of Helina.*

That such a place existed.

Sweeping, lush, green hills, undotted with dwellings or farms. The glittering of water, from small, emerald-like lakes in the distance. She turned to face a towering gate, each side bearing a huge, wrought (overwrought!) ℒ. Then, the Lunest Estate, in the Highponds. She glanced again at the landscape, so amazed that it was easy to even push thoughts of how far they'd just traveled aside. And this was the *yard.*

A guard, if that was the right word, approached. There was a feel to xem. What did that . . . ? Oh. This was a *Mage.* Without adornment, trained for muscle, but with the air of reaching only a Mage could project.

Xe nodded, unlocked the gate, and led them forward.

To Xelle's shock, a moveroom was right ahead, having been concealed with a cast. Trying to cover that shock and keep her expression blank, Xelle stepped into the plushly furnished vroom (lettered in gold with the same ℒ), and took a seat.

No words were spoken as they pushed up a long drive, the vroom running smoothly and quietly. It wasn't magic, but the fuelstones had to be expensive to be quiet compared to what the Towers used. Feeling her emotions churn, as well as the rather visceral irritation of her now-physical tie to Kern (no, that hadn't left her mind!), she did at least try to take in the view. Anything that might help her understanding.

Statues lined the drive—statues without benches or rests, she couldn't help but note. And the manor itself—holy Fira. Never had Xelle even conceived of a building so large, not outside a Mage Tower, of course.

Did a thousand pers live here, then? No, even that wouldn't be enough.

Her ability to focus degraded further as they were led inside, through austere gates, golden trim, and impossibly high-ceilinged foyers. Her heart pounded in her chest. The Mytil gallery looked like a toy chest compared to this. What was she doing here? Who would this help? They could keep her here, like a teacup, never to be seen again.

Did she even *trust* Kern? Or . . . did he trust her? Having her here? Knowing what she knew? Or did he know that her words would only be taken as lies.

There were casts for that . . . there were . . . Dear Alyssia, she had not even really thought about having the magic turned on her once here. In this huge complex, that wasn't even open to search. What was she doing?

Should she leave? Should she run now?

Almost as if responding, she felt a squeeze at her hand. Not from Kern's fingers, but as if, through the leash. It was not kind, it was not comforting, it was simply a message. Stay strong.

Just as she started to wonder how far they'd have to walk through this maze of extravagance, she was led directly into a small, narrow room. It was pretty. Satins. Patterns. Swatches of glossy black and vibrant blue, laced with white and gold.

And why so narrow?

Ah. At the end rested a stocky, curtained dais, and seated upon two chairs were two of the most annoying-looking pers she'd ever seen, dressed and fussed with every detail except any sense of welcome. A parlor for ash-holes, she thought, only built for others to be in their presence. Fortunately, she was supposed to be here under duress, so she didn't need to hide her repulsion.

A voice called out, "You are in the presence of Este Irla Du'Lunest and Este Mark Du'Lunest." Xelle believed them to be she and he, and also surmised that the lack of pronoun use was not a personal preference or shift, but a presumption this would be known to anyone here. The announcement, then, was not an introduction but a warning. Her lip curled in distaste.

"Approaching is Spire Mage Kern Du'Arc." No mention of herself. *Good. Underestimate me, spent-pods.*

Irla, who Xelle was sure insisted on always being named first, sat, one leg over the other, a bored expression on her face. She wore a soft, cream-colored blouse over matching, wide-legged pants. Her beret, intentionally oversized of the same soft fabric, slumped over to one side, and other than a few simple jewels, her main adornment was a bright red lip.

Mark, in what felt like defiantly intentional contrast, wore a shirt and long skirt made entirely of shiny black. Metal bands, perhaps steel, no, more likely titanium, clasped around his sleeves, and a long chain dangled without grace from his neck. His cap, of the same shiny fabric, was minimalist, yet he wore wire glasses with bizarre angular lenses, neither of a practical shape to be useful for his sight, nor with any reason to be tinted blue in the gentle yet illuminating (and presumably expensive) lightpods of the room's lamps.

"A hu is your secret?" Irla began. "This no-one? And you truly believe she can locate any dragon?"

Kern's head tilted as if bored. "Her sigil is authentic, as I'm sure your Breath Mage has already told you."

"But she's not a Mage." This time Mark, peering forward through his band-star glasses. "Is that why they call her dragonfriend?"

Xelle wasn't sure what move to make, so she decided maintaining her sullen glare worked best for now.

"She's unimportant. It's her abilities you need." Kern stepped forward, leaving Xelle in his shadow. "To be brought here is, I admit, a pleasure. The Este Lunests. Pers of power. Someone I can actually work with. So let's get to it, as I'm sure we're all busy. You see I have the sigil-bearer, with my word on Hullina it is authentic. You can take her if you wish, or let me keep her. But before I release her to either of our care, I require my chain, and a better understanding of what you need from our deal."

"Our deal?" Irla laughed. "We control you."

"No." Kern shook his head, and his voice boomed out in unwavering confidence. "You control my reputation. Not me. If I decide this arrangement is no longer to my advantage, I give myself over to To'Frond, live some years of isolated comfort while they sort it, and meanwhile you are exposed." He scanned the room as if imagining it were wider, and with an audience. "That would slow you down again, wouldn't it? I'm sure you'd find a way out, probably by exposing the other Mages under your . . . direction."

Irla uncrossed her legs. "Ah. So you aren't as weak as they said. But decidedly more selfish. Wonderful. Perhaps we truly can work together."

Fira. This felt like Mountains & Motes writing. Was life a game to these pers?

"Not selfish," Kern corrected. "Virtuously practical. And I am no longer interested in working for a cause whose full implications I don't understand. Consider it my Tower upbringing."

Irla laughed, a rather explosive laugh, as if she truly found the joke funny. "Sure, then, we can tell you, but not until we've escorted off our guest."

No. No no no. Xelle stepped forward, ignoring the surge of worry that shot through Kern's tether.

"Hi, yep, I'm Xeleanor Dragonfriend, and you think you can control me? Try it. I can't prove your involvement—not yet—but you keep me here and I'll figure *everything* out and then spread the news my own way. You want to put my friends at risk? You want to get dirty to do it? Then enjoy the mud. Now, give Kern back his chain so I can get his mageburned chain off of my wrist." She yanked her arm away from Kern, bracing for a tug, but her arm painlessly stopped in place, jerking back at the length of her tether to the Mage. "At least here in your . . . manor . . . I won't be tied to *him*." She wasn't exactly sure how much of her sneer was authentic or acted, but it sure came out convincing, at least to her ears.

Irla seemed to think so as well. She spoke with her hand near her mouth, and a guard walked in, expressionless with even steps, and then held out the delicate chain to Kern, who snapped it up and immediately cast something, for the chain was no longer in his hand. At Irla's dismissive wave, the guard left.

Funny. That was a bad choice.

And Xelle wasn't staying. Plunging into her material, she snapped the connection to Kern, furious when it stretched but did not break. The force of it propelled her physically forward, and she threw forward a thread of travel to prevent her face from planting into the tiled floor.

"A mistake, Xeleanor," Kern bellowed, as he threw out another tether, aimed at her other arm.

Xelle blinked out, across the space, appearing on the other side of the room. Sensing the clarity of the Arc magic he'd thrown, she grabbed it, whipped it around, and tied it, like a chokehold, over the first.

Grunting with the exertion, they walked across from each other in a slow circle, the threads continuing to pull. Xelle heard footsteps, shouts, people rushing in. Kern pulled harder, slowly, and Xelle matched it with her own resistance. The cast wasn't built for this; if they kept pulling this way it would strain and break. What would that do? He was faster than her, at casting. He could just cast again.

Fira, he knew that. She glanced over. A sea of guards were surrounding the Lunests; Xelle couldn't see much more than that. "Control her!" Irla's voice boomed over the space.

"Enough!" Kern roared.

If it was a show Kern wanted, a show he would get.

She roared right back. "You traitor. Whatever you think of my 'status' in the magesphere, at least I was loyal to it. You sold your cura. Sold your friend."

Kern's laugh was a bit pointed. "What would you even know of friends? Last I heard you were confined to being Fepa's little toy. Be grateful for this chance to be more, and stop resisting before I make you regret it."

"Confined? You're the one trapped into this now. And you will regret every. single. moment. of trying to confine *me*." With a pained grunt, she leapt and twisted to one side, as the threads snapped.

As she landed, Xelle pushed on the air between them, causing Kern's cloak to blow backward, flapping loudly, like a loose tent canopy, while he, in his heavy robes, stayed firm. Surging back her way, he reversed the current, and Xelle flipped up, into the air, throwing a web of sling casts to turn fully over herself, over a fuzzy couch, and land softly on her feet behind it. As she did, she crouched, ducking what was now a full netting of Kern's own threads, which hit the wall with such force a painting dislodged, and clattered against a glass-topped table.

Kern was stronger. Mages were watching, she had to assume. He could not just let her leave; they'd know. But Xelle was leaving. Well, then, time to turn the magic. And Kern was going to have to clean up his own mess.

She took the tiniest of moments to feel the paths around her. The long corridor, the guards, the depths of the complex. Wide, thick-forged gates. Cellars of a kind. She glanced at the entrance door.

Xelle did not reach far. Not far at all. But she was thinking now, thinking of all the ways this could go, and there were some she very much did not like. And so, focusing only on a line before her, she reached into time. The tiniest moment ago, not a moment, a sliver of a sliver of a moment, and in doing so, caused it to reach ahead. The momentary disruption caused a streak. Sharp, like that sword in her room. A thin, narrow blade of disruption.

Gasping, Kern twirled into a shield of space to avoid it, and Xelle, letting her blade snap away as he turned, instead jolted through the door, slinging with strands of travel into the neighboring foyer, and launching up toward the narrow skylights far above. Ash, ash, she thought she'd fit. She thought she would.

Speeding toward them, she fumbled for her flatblade and cursed that she'd wrapped in it a clothie for some unknown covert move. Unwrapping and grasping desperately not to drop it, she shoved the clothie into her pocket and pushed the still-closed flatblade through her fist like a tiny spike, clasping her other hand around the first. Raising her arms just in time, she smashed through the skylight with her flatbladed hand, wincing as glass shattered and fell around her.

She did not wait to hear it land or check her own injury; she slung back to the roof and bolted upward, then released the cast and concentrated with all her might on her sigil. The pod, inside her, screamed with her, and in an instant, she was gone.

Xelle tumbled down, sliding across a mass of pure ice, seeing blood streak across it. She slid directly and roughly into a soft mass. A heavy black weight. A dragon's arm.

"Hey pal," she murmured out. "I um, had to get out and only had one pod and this was my best bet of making it work." Her teeth chattered violently, a combination of the harsh chill and the shock of all she'd just done. "I don't have a way to get back, and it might be safer if I can just . . . lie here a bit." She was disoriented, her instincts were spinning. She had to escape. No, she had. She was safe. She needed to settle.

Xelle was here, with Thunder. Kern was there. With the Lunests.

She didn't know what Kern might do now. If he'd need to look for her. Where she might be safe. He couldn't take her from a Tower, could he? She couldn't port right back into To'Ever with blood running down her face? No, she couldn't port anywhere. She didn't have a pod. Cuts. She hoped they were small.

Ice. She managed to scrabble onto her hands and knees. She could not see her reflection.

Hearing her, of course, Thunder puffed onto an area near them and gestured. Xelle crawled, if her inelegant thumping and sliding could be called that, over to the roughly polished surface. If she could see correctly, there were a couple small cuts.

Ash, she had her gel, but that was going to sting. Either way, they should heal, with a cleaning and a small cast to travel the skin smoothly together. Arc was not magic of healing, but any magic could heal what suited it.

Certainly better than stitches, she thought.

And with her next slip down, where her chin smacked harshly, jarring her face but thank Fira she hadn't bitten herself, she rolled over and stared numbly at Thunder. Too cold to speak again, she thought, right at zhem. *I need to get warm. Now.*

Her cloak! It had heard her, of course—she had an enchanted cloak which thickened around her. Still, the wind against her injured face was too much and she needed to clean it, so she weakly made the ready clap with her stinging hands, understanding when Thunder lifted her, carrying her off toward a face of rock, and starting a fire there, over what looked like rocks but lit at the dragon's breath.

It took a minute for the warmth to settle, and longer for the pain to subside, but as she sat, doing nothing but sitting, she finally began to relax a bit, her cloak even thinning now, though only slightly. She thanked it. She thanked it deeply.

Thunder nudged zheir nose against the cloak.

She looked up at zhem. "I enchanted it myself. What do you think?"

Zhey puffed in what Xelle, proudly, could tell was approval.

Except, then, why was that followed by a grunt? Thunder scooted around. Xelle had the impression she was being shielded, as in physically. And Xelle could feel a presence.

"What is it? No, who is it? Thunder, you don't get to control me." The words smacked her; she hadn't meant to be so harsh. But the walls had been closing in around her, and she'd just broken them. Thunder had to know.

Thunder flapped away. Not just a little, but away from the fire and up the hill. Yet, she still had zhem in her mind. Zhey were not upset; just annoyed. Sulking, even. Not even sadness, just a big, unrepentant sulk.

Thunder practically barked, now turning away from her entirely. She'd fix that in a moment.

A face was peeking around the rock. A very dragony face, powder blue with a mostly white snout, and streaks of two different shades of pink on each side.

From behind, Thunder barked again, and the face suddenly backed away, causing a poof of snow to spray over the rock.

"Pah!" Xelle waved her arms around. "Thunder, enough! And hello, Cloudpuff."

She stopped. She was doing it again. "Hello, may I call you Cloudpuff, or do you prefer a different name?"

The dragon shifted, as if unsure.

"Thunder, please come over here," Xelle called. "We are always best friends, you know that. Right? Can I please meet this new per, and can you show zhem our signs?" She looked right at the second dragon. "Thunder is my friend."

At that, Thunder sort of stomped over, and signaled the nod and the crouch, and then the ready clap, and then a couple other signs Xelle didn't yet recognize so would have to ask zhem about.

The second dragon turned to Xelle excitedly, and nodded.

"Can you confirm, please? That that's an answer to calling you Cloudpuff. It just—it's what I thought of when I saw you."

Cloudpuff, as Xelle would now think of zhem, nodded again.

"Here, sit with me? I'm staying by this fire." She glanced over to the side. "Thunder, you too? I wouldn't want to be by your fire without you, buddy."

Xelle felt remarkably older than even her 30th birthday had made her, as the two dragons scootched in, each snapping back and forth at each other and adjusting for space.

As Xelle tried to figure out the relationship here, she realized that with two dragons who could read her every thought, her entire set of relationship management skills she'd learned running a lab were about to need an overhaul.

So, she went the direct route.

"I don't sense that you dislike each other, or that there has been a history of harm. Have either of you been harmed by the other?"

She waited, as Cloudpuff crouched a little no, and then, slowly, Thunder followed.

"I don't know about dragons, but hu like to have friends. And making another friend doesn't reduce the impact of a previous friendship; it enhances it. I don't presume to know how dragons view such things, but is there any reason that either of you could not be friends with me?"

No. And no.

"Is there any reason that the two of you cannot . . . sit and enjoy the day with me?"

No. And a huffy no. She'd take it.

Cloudpuff rumbled a little. Xelle peered over, wondering what the issue might be. Hearing that, she realized, the dragon nudged in toward her face, but not touching it.

"Oh, the cuts," she murmured. How must she look here, with a scraped, thawing face, and blood on her skin.

"I can take care of this." Except, she'd hoped to cast. Thunder had been around her casting, but Cloudpuff had not. She glanced between the two dragons, letting them hear her thoughts about growing up learning that casting in the mountains was improper, and now believing there was more nuance to that caution. "May I cast here, a small amount to help with my healing?"

Thunder nearly barked out a yes, and starting to nod, Cloudpuff instead looked back at Xelle. Zhey were not upset.

Xelle smiled. "Thunder, another mirror please?"

Zhey seemed to have no problem with the word, or perhaps the word didn't matter for the concept. With another huff, a section of ice glistened, immediately cooling to an imperfectly mirrored surface. She leaned over.

Yeah, not too bad. She wasn't used to seeing blood on her face, but what was actually there appeared not to be as dramatic as the blood had looked smeared across the white and blue of the ice. In need of tending, certainly, but not a cause for alarm.

First, to wipe everything off. Ah, she remembered shoving the clean clothie back into her pocket as she fumbled for the blade, but she had no clarity of memory whether she'd done so or just shoved it against the feel of bunched fabric on her side, to fall to the Lunests' floor. Thus, more out of just . . . irritation that they, with all the wealth in Alyssia would take her little corner-embroidered clothie, nearly wheezed with relief when she found it in her fingers. She reached it into a clean section of snow, and dabbed it over her face, bringing two sharp cuts into view.

Now for the stinging. (Thunder rumbled a bit in sympathy, which she appreciated.)

With her other hand, she reached into her other pocket.

Her fingers did not touch the tin.

They touched something metal, but with motion, and delicacy. A smooth, cool, jeweler's chain. She pulled the item from her pocket, the little jeweled charm of the Arc Spire glinting with disproportionate brightness for the small, fine-cut stones in the crisp mountain light.

"Well, well," she said, looking to her friends. "The chain of a Spire Mage."

Cloudpuff started, and, it seemed Thunder communicated something, to allow zhem to settle. Cloudpuff leaned forward, sniffing a bit, then leaned back. As if following, Thunder did the same.

Xelle smiled, then remembered again what she was holding. She thanked them, in her thoughts for trusting her. "I'll deal with this later," she said aloud, now removing the tin of gel, and very carefully tucking the chain back into her pocket.

She let a very yowly yelp as the alcohol pressed against her skin, and forgetting how *much* that would sting, she moved immediately into the cast. First, blurring the pain so that it numbed, and then gently coaxing the skin, creating waves of travel, reverberating in place like guides, to accelerate the skin's re-adherence.

When she was done, and lowered her hand, her face looked as it had before. Her cloak, she realized, would have been torn. Not really wanting to take it off in high mountain hard winter (!) she ran her fingers over the shoulder area, the neck, anywhere the glass shards had shot past. If it had been torn, as she strongly suspected, it had already healed itself.

Hoping enchantments were not truly sentient but taking no chances, she ran her hands along it, whispering praise.

She wondered where Kern was. Captured, she considered with a vicious shiver. Held in the Lunest Manor. Or, back, away at To'Arc pretending to search for Xelle as Irla steamed and Mark rambled about what to do about their breach of plans. Or perhaps even, continuing to negotiate. She couldn't worry about it now.

What she did worry about was her friends here. Letting them know what she'd been doing, her progress on their return, her need to see how things went. As she started to yawn, she thought, intending Thunder and Cloudpuff to hear, that this wasn't a good place for her now, and she needed to be back with the hu, to do any good for them here.

"Could you carry me back?" she asked, clear to direct the question to Thunder. She actually had no idea how else she could leave, an idea she tried not to dwell on.

Both dragons' heads drooped.

"What, you want me to stay a little longer?"

Thunder gazed up, at the light. Then back.

"Ah." She knew this was an excuse, and from their growing connection Thunder had no qualms about flying in the moonslight, but she allowed zhem to hear her clearly, that it was a very sweet and nice excuse, and she'd be happy to stay if they could maintain the warmth she needed. But only until morning.

"And first, one thing," she added, slowly removing the chain from her pocket. She was far away, and her material was low, but this chain had an incredible connection to that office. And honestly, at this point, so did Xelle. And so did . . .

Fumbling with the cold fingers she'd expected to keep in her cloak's pockets when outdoors, she removed Kern's locket—his late spouse's locket—from around her neck, and lovingly—for the spirit of the per inside—clasped the chain back together.

The objects wanted to return. It almost wasn't her cast. But it was her cast, and closing her eyes and thinking of the lofty Spire Mage's library office near the top of the Arc Tower, she dropped the chain and locket, so close to the surface of the desk as if she'd set the top layer of a card house, and released them.

Her hand empty, and now shaking, she stuffed it, shivering, into her pocket, and moved back toward the fire Thunder had made.

With a sigh, and a happy look to Cloudpuff and Thunder, she felt a weight lift. A tiny, but important weight. And she chuckled, feeling the relief in a physical way.

She had not known what a dragon might do when amused, but by the spray of sparks and tinkle of vocal charms that ensued, she now knew. What it meant for a dragon to laugh.

Xelle also wasn't really sure when dragons slept; it didn't seem to be limited to night. But as she grew increasingly tired, and Cloudpuff wandered again away, Thunder beckoned her in against zheir side, and Xelle, her cloak turning into a soft pad beneath her, did not even reach for the night ivy. Just for tonight, in the warmth against Thunder's belly—even if it was only for tonight—she let the rest go.

21 - A Death, Conveniently

There wasn't one leader of the group of dragons. She winced even at the term 'group' since she didn't yet have a sense of whether these were all the dragons of Alyssia, or if there were more. And if there were more, what bound these together. Thunder must have heard the concepts bouncing in her head, but had chosen not to engage on any such topic. And Xelle was not ready to ask. Prying into dragon business should at least wait until they were back into the lower mountains.

She trusted Thunder inherently, but also understood the nuances of power dynamics. Lessons, she realized, that had been subtly delivered to her through the interactions of everyday life, by Na'Vuia. And she couldn't be sure that Thunder did, a thought, unfortunately, she was sure zhey'd heard.

Emotional honesty took on whole new meaning when befriending a dragon.

It seemed that each one held different levels of authority, heavily weighted with age but perhaps other factors as well. No, she felt sure there were other factors; the hierarchy was not strict to the concept of elders. And also that the level of authority may change based on the nature of the topic.

Yet the one that Thunder decided to approach with her request for passage out of the mountains (Xelle, on further thought, had decided she would not let Thunder get into more trouble on her behalf and needed to ask permission for Thunder to leave) was clearly older. Xelle had immediately thought of zhem as 'Windy', and the slate-patched dragon with worn and scratched skin seemed pleased by the name. Not just tolerant but actively pleased. And fortunately, zhey were so focused on lecturing Thunder while examining Xelle, zhey seemed not to notice her thoughts hoping Windy didn't understand hu connotations of the term, and glad she hadn't started instead with Longwind, as had genuinely first come to mind.

Thunder was granted permission to fly her to To'Arc (she wanted to restock there before heading back to To'Ever, and no longer wearing Kern's locket she felt more comfortable doing so), provided zhey were not seen. Which meant, Xelle gently reminded zhem, not *to* the Tower this time.

It was a bit of a journey from this far into the mountains, but Thunder cradled em in zheir arms, and Xelle was not uncomfortable. Even her significant fear of heights was quelled by the security of Thunder's grasp. Zhey flew steadily, but not so fast as to cause undue irritation to Xelle's face and eyes, and Xelle let emself relax, just watching the sparkle of white palettes, the texture of eir world, and new pieces of it e'd never before seen.

As Thunder flapped down into the place Xelle guided zhem, e made sure to tell zhem they'd talk again, and please, to go back for now. Still, Thunder waited for Xelle to press close, and then twice more. Whether dragons liked hugs or whether Thunder sensed that Xelle did (but only from pers she loved!) was not a question she decided to ask. For now.

And she waited, even a bit chilled and shaken, as Thunder flapped away and out of sight. Only then did she begin to make her way down the last stretch, and toward the Tower, resisting the urge to cast out of increased sensitivity. After all, Kern might be there, inside.

Not wanting to be seen either way until she'd had time to consider it, she wrapped into her cloak and hurried ahead, whisking into her nightgarden with a sigh of relief.

She told the inkbloom everything, not knowing how much they'd sensed. What had happened at the estate. That she'd blinked across a space, and that she didn't know how she'd done it. About the slice she'd made, how it'd given her an opening to leave, and how they'd saved her. Feeling them tense, though not unhappy, she sang them an extended song. Once they'd calmed and she'd collected another pod, Xelle decided, this time, she could afford a little boldness. Or, perhaps, might later regret not taking it, now while she had the chance.

Yes, she told herself, things were about to change. And if the Lunests thought to hunt her, they would have to do so in the open.

Uncertainty, or the shock of slicing time, filled her with a new urgency. Her heart pounded like a fresh fuelstone—with the need for resolution. For motion. And now, with her inkbloom, or maybe with the new connection of sleeping against a dragon's belly, she was not passing up opportunities. Not anymore.

She was at To'Arc. She wanted to know the latest. And to gather it, herself, before she returned to Ever, unsure what would happen on her return—only knowing she would no longer endure the constraints of her arrangement there once she devised a plan to leave them.

Strolling around the Tower's exterior, and up to the entrance, Xelle did have to first take a breath. A big breath. It was . . . not easy to walk in this way. As herself. Her true self. And yes, not feeling that she belonged, when all she wanted was to belong. Just not the way they'd let her. But they couldn't stop her from being Xelle. She tugged reassuringly on the cloak, and nearly thought it'd returned the gesture.

Then she stopped. Boldness was one thing, but what Kwill had said, made her consider . . .

She was thinking too much like a Mage, or perhaps an Arc Mage. Walk right in and demand the facts. She didn't have to be covert to be strategic. If she wanted to know the latest in the Tower, she needed to go to the village. At least first.

She spun on one foot in the snow. Nearly comically. And started down the hill.

Xelle wandered through the winding village streets, taking her time under the comforting warmth of her cloak. She browsed through the market, awkwardly passing by where she'd bought the cloak and cap for her first trip to To'Breath. Then, through the shops. Finally, having noticed enough eyes on her, she stopped for a coffee in a common area, sitting in a particular open way—a way she remembered from Helia—which invited pers to stop by.

In any other time in her life, pers would not have stopped by. But Xeleanor was the dragonfriend, who left To'Arc under rumors that she was part of this Amberborn movement—a society We'le told her didn't even exist! Xelle was a mystery.

Pers who live in a Tower village? They love a good mystery.

One per stopped to say hello, then hurried away. A second per swung by, curious but also nervous. And then, seeing those two near her, other pers thought somehow it must be a thing to do, and who would judge their curiosity without even knowing what they'd said? And, so, they approached her—at first the unbothered, and then the followers, and then the fomos. Pushing away her feelings of unease, one by one, across what felt like a robes-hanging rod, Xelle engaged with the residents, merchants, and visitors to To'Arc, the conversation only pausing briefly for each eclipse, as apparently a hu could be bold enough to talk to the accused dragonfriend, but not during an eclipse. The priorities of a Tower village, she thought with growing unease at each pause, until, the light brightening again, the gatherers resumed their chatter.

Though every per said it differently, what she heard was uncannily consistent.

The big news came first and often. In the interests of an ongoing investigation into the Amberborn (and, thus implied, their potential hideaways and dangerous magic), To'Arc and To'Ever had announced today a ban on travel in the mountains, even into the foothills and few established paths. To enforce this required regular patrols, and, it was said, magical surveillance of the boundary areas, as of course the Mages would not cast in the mountains themselves.

That was fast.

Xelle could not take the time, not surrounded by curious pers and not knowing when someone might decide she'd overstayed, to parse this, but Kern must have forged a deal with the Hurts, even after Xelle's departure. And he must have had plans in place with the Arc

Spire at the ready. Then, how long would this new arrangement last? Should she risk talking to him to strategize? To know when, or if, the dragons could return there? Her gut said, let him go his way, and save that risk for when it might be needed. Another uncertainty. But the dragons—no, there was no debate. She would not let them stay in that place, the sadness growing in their eyes with each visit. She'd done what she could to clear the area, and she would create her own surveillance. With their help.

If they agreed.

So much to consider. She tried to show attention to the pers around her, to absorb what they were saying, feeling nearly intoxicated between her swirling thoughts and the pressure of so many new and intruding faces.

She forced a smile.

And what of herself, she asked, as if the idea amused her. The latest word, only spoken to her by those who seemed rather excited to whisper it, was that *Xelle* was the hu who had tried to discredit Spire Mage Pelir, which was why Xelle was removed from To'Arc. Pers, at least the ones willing to offer it, were so curious to know if it was true (to be the first to learn?), they were happy to run through all they'd heard. That Xelle had then been allowed at To'Ever, under specific watch by an important Mage, to cover up that the Amberborn were real. That, by sending her there and not to To'Frond on transgression, the truth had been swept under the rug to avoid embarrassment to the magesphere.

And that Pelir, Pelir was now strongly favored to be the one to ascend at the time of Jehanne's impending retirement. Xelle marveled at the open dissolution of suspicion around Pelir's role. It was as if without enough gossip left on Pelir, it was easier to allow the reserved Mage to return to the role of silent hero, while all the bees could swarm to the nectar of Xelle's own juicy story.

About that. There was . . . she could barely get this out . . . a *subscription* one could sign up for at the Post, to receive written updates on Xeleanor and the Amberborn. Absolutely needing to see this (whatever curiosity or abandonment of care she was experiencing, she simply could not function knowing this was out there and not knowing what it was like), she went to Post herself. (She'd never switched her registration, so her unaddressed mail and Basic were still going to Vi'Arc. On top of the weekly Apprentice stipend someone at the To'Ever Front Desk had allocated for her, not knowing how else to treat a non-Mage, non-guest, non-Study, non-staff.)

She let out a gigantic and forceful breath. And stepped into Post.

Xelle walked up to the window, hoping she looked more in control than she felt. She flashed her verification coin. "Hello, I'd like to add a sub. For Xeleanor Du'Tam. It's the one about me." No one had offered its name, as if it was obvious she knew the one. Noting the clerk's widened eyes, she offered her best attempt at a friendly smile, then gave a little wave. That turned out awkward. She lowered her hand.

"Yes, uh . . ." The clerk glanced around as if shift were ending and someone would arrive that second, allowing xem to run away. Xelle waited. "Well, is that advised?"

"Oh, are there requirements to subscribe? I heard it was open."

Eyes wide, the hu's face blanched, and xe forced out, "Take it from Basic?"

"Yes, please," she answered. "Continue the charge, and stack new issues in the box." While she reached out for the roll-printed paper that slid across the counter, she also didn't want to add any more discomfort to the per's day, so she nodded her thanks, and quickly departed.

Her eyes lowered to the page like a foot sinking into mud.

Protectors of our Populace

Confirmation found: The true escape from To'Arc.

Loyal protectors. The magesphere tried all year to keep this latest hypocrisy from us, but our agents—with your dedicated support—have excavated the truth. After the thwarted dragon attack on To'Arc and the revelation of Xeleanor Du'Amberborn's

> true affiliation almost a year ago, we've uncovered that vigilant Tower Watchers attempted to assail the hu and take her to To'Frond, where we'd likely not hear from her again. (Unless the conspiracy runs even deeper, which, with your continued support, we will continue to reveal.)
>
> To their fury, a low-ranking Mage intervened, and before Tower Powers had realized what was happening, there were enough cheering onlookers to provoke a full riot of chaos and dissent, forcing them to sweep the attack on the Tower under the rug another way.
>
> Our agents confirm that the Tower should have immediately brought Spire Mages to quell the scene and capture the dissident, but the Arc Spire is too mired in the same lies these Amberborn are sowing to be effective in these troubling days. And so they shuffled Xeleanor Du'Amberborn off to To'Ever, where, as we have long reported, she remains under magesphere watch. For now.

Well, she was officially worried about Helia. But, see—she scratched her finger inside the edge of her undercap—these Hurts (she would still call them that even if—especially if—the Lunests were at or amongst the top) would threaten anyone in their way, it seemed. And so the only way to fully protect her friends was to step out of their way. Or be fully secretive about it, an option that Xelle had already decided was not sustainable.

Despite eir private jokes about the revolution, Kwill had reminded her before parting that this was not a burden she could take on, as it was never about her in the first place. Which sounded a lot better when there wasn't a whole *subscription service* dedicated to making it about her.

She scanned the text one more time. To her eyes, all of it was nonsense. Crappy nonsense. Nonsensical nonsense. Nonsense pieced together out of crumbs of truth and validated by unsubstantiated references to credibility. Were pers believing this? The writing was . . . obnoxious. It wouldn't even sound credible if it were revealing that water was wet.

Still, Xelle decided she might just stay away from To'Frond for a bit. Though—she didn't *think* they'd do anything. Not to a former Frond Study, someone not real well known there, but, she hoped, reasonably well-liked by anyone who remembered her. Anyway, not without proof or an open accusation from a Mage, not whatever this was.

She flipped the paper over, for she could see in the light that it was printed on both sides.

> Weekly Subscriber-Exclusive Bonus: The Mages Du'Satta? Amberborn? Read this, and then decide.
>
> We have learned that Kwillen Du'Satta, a Breath Study tied in with the famously elite Mage family of that town, openly visited Xeleanor Du'Amberborn at To'Ever, after which the two were hardly seen until eir departure, except at the pledging ceremony for a new non-notable Ever Mage.
>
> We do not know what power this legendary family still holds, as legends built on access do tend to wane, but we do know they are still well-regarded amongst magesphere elitists.
>
> And while one might assume certain . . . activities were undertaken in the privacy of the visit, our agents will not be distracted by desires of flesh when they are feigned to mask desires of power.
>
> We will continue to learn more, for our subscribers. You—the protectors—are the reason the truth will be uncovered.
>
> If you'll forgive the pun.

"Fira," she muttered aloud. "Now Kwill." And Rayn, too, though at least not by name, but they'd insulted her! Could she no longer have friends? She forced a breath, and could almost hear Kwill's voice correcting her again. This wasn't about her. Friends were friends.

But curse everything, now Xelle had a *zine*?

Resisting the urge to crumple the thing, light it on fire, then stomp the ash it produced, she instead rolled it up (if not gently) and shoved it into a cloak pocket.

Significantly more informed of what she was really facing and somehow the bolder for it, she left again, this time for a tavern.

"Yes, it's me, Xeleanor Du'Tam, she or e. I'm not what they say," she'd say, introducing herself. "Sure, I can tell you more about myself, but I'm curious—what do you think regarding Pelir?"

Here, outside of the daylight, away from those who had approached her, there were less of the bland re-endorsements of the quiet Mage. Here, a few whispered ill-wishes for them both, or a lack of trust in any Mage. Some mentioned that Kern would make a solid leader, and curious others inquired why it wouldn't go to We'le, who had served longest.

But, universally, she found a rallying for stability. To figure it out and get back to normal. And in that, a prevalent sentiment that Pelir had been wronged and that Pelir would and should be placed on the Crown.

"It was an injustice to all of us," one early drinker opined. "This drama. It's unbecoming. We're not some village; we're Vi'Arc. Thriving and living in the shadow of the greatest Tower of Alyssia!" Several patrons softly harrumphed, even as one walked out.

"Then where is To'Arc?" another said. "Silent. Not backing Pelir up, nor providing us the answers we need."

"All the more reason for Pelir to ascend. I have friends at the Tower." Xe poured from a pitcher. "Pelir can't speak until this is done, you know. Pelir knows the stakes. I think we'll see a leader—a leader for us—when that happens. I've met Pelir once. A good per."

"What about Kern, then? I heard Kern would ascend. Have you seen him? Such power." The per knocked back a drink.

It struck her. Whatever deal Kern had made with the Hurts, it almost certainly involved resumed enthusiasm for his own Ascension. And they would have had to make a deal, she realized. He knew too much.

Jehanne had seemed to understand that she could not retire with Pelir maligned and the selection at risk. But now the sentiments were stirred again. Unclear. A notable swing in favor toward Pelir, but even the fastest Ascension took months, giving Kern plenty of time to maneuver. A passive ruse would not satisfy now. He would have to look serious.

Xelle took a long drink of a dark maroon wine, letting the last sip sit a moment on her tongue. With enough wine for now and a new patron staring her way, she ordered a beer, and beckoned the hu to join.

Perhaps after a little too much investigation, Xelle spun herself back to her nightgarden, awkwardly curling into her cloak next to one of the old roots protruding from the floor, and vowing to remember this wasn't a great place to sleep. The cloak responded, with fluffiness, almost caressing her to rest.

Yet, she could not rest. Not just for the night ivy, for if there were any night for it, today would be that. But the light. Something . . . off. She rolled upward, finding herself face-to-face with the obsidian sword. Cautiously, Xelle rested her hand atop the smoothly engraved blade. Designed for killing, they'd said, but to her, it looked like art. Each angle, each view of that angle, a new dimension, the sharpest edge of everything. Like a narrow tapestry made of the night itself, all the moons to its glow. She realized, then, she'd not touched it before. Obsidian, sure, but not this obsidian. Not this sword. Not the blade, she meant.

Eir fingers brushed its surface, they then pressed against it. An emotion flowed through. Calm. Comfort. Surety.

Why would a sword offer em calm? E had no idea, but enveloped by that comfort, even an uneven floor and unmitigated beer breath did not prevent Xelle from accepting the sleep that came.

The bells sounded so loudly that Xelle could hear them back here, in her 'room' between the Tower, the shed, and the thick stone wall. (And yes, the fancy guardrail.) There was no reason for the bells to ring this way. Tolling, slowly. So soon after the new year. With no event. No cause.

Xelle felt a surge of fear at the unknown of this, and tried to wake, fully, to remember where she was. To'Arc. Bells. Morning. Why? What could she do? Xelle. She could travel back to To'Ever, but not knowing what potential emergency she'd left here, with her friends, her old labmates, could not be borne. She had to know.

If something had happened—something terrible—now was not the time for her to be seen. Yet, she hadn't learned how to 'call' with Arc Magic, the way that Kern did. (She resolved to add that to her list.) And so, her best bet was to glyph outside, into the forest, and from there, send a quick element of her voice to Helia's room. If Helia was even there.

"It's me," she whispered. She remembered a place, once, they'd had a picnic on a perfect summer day. An older garden, with cracking trellises and a worn stone bench. "Summer picnic." She hoped that Helia would remember. No. Helia would remember.

She sat there for a while. She tried the cast every once in a while, nervous to surprise a visitor, but hoping with Helia's wit, she could joke it away as a glitching cast. Maybe she'd link it to her courtesan. One might think Xelle was irritated at this to think of it again, but she was not. Such notions had led to, could she just say it? An incredible evening with her friend.

Feeling the connection to the room even deeper now, and allowing her heart a little unasked-for pounding in her chest, she tried again.

Helia arrived alone, wearing a huge, fuzzy coat in a shade of softstone almost as near to white as Xelle's charcoal cloak was to black. "This is . . . not a good time for you to be here," she gasped.

As warm as her coat looked, Helia was shivering. Xelle thought to offer her her own, but, no, better to be fast.

"What's going on? I really don't know."

"You really don't know," Helia repeated. She leaned in. "Crown Mage Jehanne died in her sleep. They toll, for her."

Whatever sadness she should have felt, even only having met the legendary Mage briefly, she did not feel. Not denial. Not emptiness.

Not even confusion. More . . . fear. Curiosity. And then, somehow, perhaps the sword?

She realized what it was. She did not think Jehanne was dead.

Xelle peered into Helia's eyes, which seemed to be searching her own for a reaction. "Fira, Hellie," she managed to say. Her theory would do nothing for the Mage but confuse her, put her at risk. Xelle needed more time.

"Can you go? To To'Ever. I won't say I saw you."

Xelle nodded, then drew a shaky breath. "I was all over the village yesterday."

Helia rolled her eyes. A bit harshly. "Ash, Xeleanor."

"I'm on break. I was allowed to be!" Seeing Helia's concern, she knew the Mage needed to return. "I won't be seen again, for a while. Not here, anyway. I'll go back to Ever."

Helia nodded, her eyes for once heavy, as if poured from metal. She leaned forward, gave Xelle a quick peck on the cheek, and then without waiting for one in return, she disappeared.

Xelle needed to see. She would not be noticed; she swore it. And she would return to To'Ever. But as slowly as a Spire would discuss and select a Crown Mage, was as quickly as they would resolve operating without one.

She had a secret room. She had some stock here, if mostly jerky and dried beans. She could travel snow inside, use her small, old metal cup. It wouldn't be long. It just . . . wasn't how they'd operate. Towers needed structure. And all structure, all order, hung from the Crown Mage like the finest chandelier.

Xeleanor would stay until the Arc Ascension. Then, if all was calm, *then* she would return to Ever. And Helia was safer not knowing.

The Arc Atrium sparkled from every angle, each rising column, each segment of every mosaic. Light streamed in from varied bevels, centering into a path that led through to the wide, arcblack rug, pieced together seamlessly from its segments to create a bold and awe-inspiring stage, perfectly fitted for the occasion.

Every Mage in the Tower stood present, in neat rows, leaving the illuminated center open. Behind them the guests. Behind them the Studies. Behind them the staff. Outside, gathered, the populace, waiting for the news.

A voice carried out on a travel cast, resonating in each ear as though the announcer were talking directly to oneself, and above, on the walls, the text of the voice scrolled, a pattern of glimmering light against the gray stone. A clerk just outside the door offered enchanted scrolls that could be held in the fingers, conveying the words in touch.

"Spire Mage Awayna Du'Arc." Her chair glid forward, not on its fuelstones, but carried soundlessly by a cast, as a rough-textured black cape fell over the back of it onto a cushion of air, unencumbered by the unturning wheels.

"Spire Mage Gloria Du'Arc." E walked, slowly, stately, in long cream-colored pants and a short black jacket with pointed tails, all accentuating eir height, with the smallest flutter from a short train not even hitting eir neck from the top of a smoothly-wrapped cap.

"Spire Mage Nainol Du'Arc." As rounded as Gloria was tall, Nainol paced like an unbusy gentlefolk, in a fine, tailored suit of muted green with rose gold accents overtop a vine-patterned vest, nodding occasionally to each side at the transfixed audience.

"Spire Mage Kern Du'Arc." Nearly a diamondboard crownpiece in a heavy black velvet robe and high-staked cap, the only adornments were the jewels on his hands, and the tiny chain of his status, pinned prominently to his front.

"Spire Mage We'le Du'Arc." Unlike the others in their ceremonial finery, We'le, the most senior Mage now, walked with slow, dragging steps in a simple black dress of mourning, perfectly matched to the banners before her, topped with a simple black satin cap.

These five Mages positioned themselves around the rug, and with a nod, We'le, from the center, stepped forward.

Arc Mages did not speak of death the way others did, even, or especially the Mages of To'Dust. And We'le, her arms raising to reveal long, draping sleeves of black lace, spoke not of sadness, but of change. Of resolve. Of the endurance of good.

When she concluded, the room stayed silent, without any reaction. Without tears, without joy, without murmurs. As if . . . Crown Mage Jehanne Du'Arc had always been, and always would be.

Except. She wasn't.

The unbodied voice again spoke. "At this time, the Arc Spire, by unanimous agreement, announces their selection of the next Spire Mage of Arc Tower, Sacred Prong to the Gem of Halinia. Please, step forward."

The gathered Mages shuffled and parted as one advanced through. Medium-build, muscular, wearing a wafty black skirt over coarse black pants, and a layered blouse in varied shades of gray. This Mage emerged from the center of the Mages, and while the Mages knew not to gasp, the shade of it was felt across the room, like a wave of suggested whispers.

"State your vows," the voice intoned.

The Mage turned toward the silent audience, face younger, clothes less traditional, expression blank. And spoke. Short vows, and simple. "I pledge my loyalty to upholding the Arc Tower, its values, and its truth. In service of Alyssia. In reverence to Halina. Under the sun and the moons, and the unseen light." The figure gave a slight, yet humble bow, and then flashed the Arc.

The voice, again. "Presenting Spire Mage Nar Du'Arc, she."

Around the Atrium, each Mage and each Study raised a hand, or in whatever way that they could, made the sign of the Arc. The outer rings, the staff, broke into a wave of applause, starting with a few, and spreading to the others. The Mages shifted in discomfort but did not join.

Spire Mage Nar took her place on the stage at the end of the side she'd walked from, filling a spot that had not appeared empty until she took it.

A set of musicians entered the room. Mages, each. And with a mutual nod, they began to play a procession of muted joy. Old and familiar in Arc Region. The entire Atrium held like unsatisfied lightning.

Pelir stepped into the Atrium from the Tower's front, and through the lit center of the space. Layers of wide gown in patterns of sheer black and moonslight blue gave the slightest bounce, under ruffled sleeves, and a cloth-draped seven-pronged cap in pure arcblack, similar to the one Jehanne had worn. Pelir turned to face the audience.

"State your vows."

Pelir stood, a long moment in silence. The room waited.

"I address you in a time of grief," Pelir began. "There has not been one like Crown Mage Jehanne." A pause. "Nor an Ascension such as this, with the air as it is, and without her presence to reassure you."

The room murmured a bit.

"Uncertainty. Uncertainty grows, and I refuse to stand here, not acknowledging it. Are there any here who would speak, doubting my leadership or my intent?"

The room prickled at this unexpected turn. Each Mage glanced around, as if trying to decide who it would be to step forward. When the rustling calmed, Pelir nodded. "Silence has spoken. Then, I pledge to lead Arc Tower with every piece of my soul, every edge of my perception, and every ounce of my spirit. With power, I say to you, I pledge never to let the light of Arc Magic fade from the veins of the true of heart."

When Pelir stopped, pers waited. Crown Mage vows had gone on in cases for an hour, a speech with a pledge at the end. But it seemed to those present, this *was* the end. An Ascension, already. The ceremony as quick as its planning. A shiver was felt around the room. An energy, undeniable.

Now, the voice did not just speak, but boomed. "Presenting Crown Mage Pelir, who no longer takes pronouns, who has taken the sacred vow, affixing one's self to the Crown of Halinia until the path opens for another. Always Seven."

"Always Seven," the crowd repeated, now, with energy.

"And now, the Delegation leaves to spread the Word of Arc."

Seven Mages stepped forward, each wearing a traditional version of the To'Arc black robe, each carrying a rolled and sealed scroll. The voice did not name the bearers, but each destination, waiting to announce the next until that Mage had left the room.

"Breath Tower, Prong of Halina, With Alabaster Halls." A Mage left.

"Frond Tower, Prong of Halina, Order of Alyssia." A Mage left.

"Dust Tower, Prong of Halina, of the Barren Plateau." A Mage left.

"Charm Tower, Prong of Halina, Beauty and Trade." A Mage left.

"Grand Tower, Prong of Halina, Powerful Guard." A Mage left.

"Ever Tower, Prong of Halina, Protector of the High Rim." A Mage left.

"Arc Tower, Prong of Halina, Travel In Light."

This Mage approached Pelir, and knelt. Pelir took the scroll. The Mage bowed, and then left the Atrium.

The musicians played again, a long, wandering song, with simple solos, in turn, and then again, as the staff returned to work, and as each Mage in turn bowed to Crown Mage Pelir Du'Arc, made the symbol of the Arc, then left, as that Mage's guests followed.

The musicians concluded, and carried their instruments out.

And then, they stood, watching only each other, the Seven of Arc Spire.

22 - *Paths*

The clerk at the To'Ever Front Desk watched silently as Xeleanor approached. The kind of watching where everyone present knew something was about to happen. Xelle'd thought, perhaps, she could continue on past, just for now, after what had been an extraordinary week, but the hu held out a sealed note, not meeting Xelle's eyes.

She nodded sympathetically as she took it (wasn't the clerk's fault), but did not open the seal until she could find a secluded corner of the Ever Atrium. She sat on a wood bench, enjoying the scents of the year-round hedges and their strong, rich oils, and knowing such immersion was . . . She read the note.

> Xeleanor Du'Tam,
>
> *You have failed to deliver compelling daily reports. You ignore me and my needs. You take advantage of my generosity, leaving the Tower for longer than I have granted it for a sacred holiday. You produce no value. I relinquish you as my Apprentice.*
>
> Mage Fepa Du'Ever

Xelle rolled her eyes. "Well at least now he can brag that he dismissed the dragonfriend," she muttered aloud. "You're welcome, Party Fepa. Let's not keep in touch." With a cast not quite allowed in such a space, she flicked out a spark of fire, and burned the little note, making a half-hearted attempt to travel the ash into a dustchute.

Not yet sure what rules were for walking around the Tower as a statusless evictee, but not as worried about it as she knew she should be, she at least was not made to wonder. Before getting anywhere near her room, a clerk huffed up to her, explaining in a very guarded and uncomfortable voice that she was to present to the high floor immediately, to see Crown Mage Avail. No escort was sent, interestingly, and no one, including the silent stewards, questioned her as she ascended the Tower and made her way to Avail's room.

He was not at his desk, but relaxing—it seemed—with a glass of what looked like wine in one of the green chairs. He gestured her to take its partner. "Xeleanor, I trust you are well?"

She nodded.

"Good. After that stunt, you can't be here."

Normally, her mind would startle and spin, but she felt . . . above it, in ways right now she could not explain. "I understand," she said, really trying to sort in her mind if he meant her . . . relationship with Fepa, her investigating in Vi'Arc, or even more. "I'm just a hu trying to help."

Avail nearly giggled. "Would you be here if you were not? This is an Arc foothills wine. The kind of perk to the job I make no true effort to turn down. Would you like a glass?"

Sure. Let's have wine. "Sure. Um, thank you." She reached out for the glass, swirled it, and took her time taking a sip.

Oh, Fira, it was delicious. Sweet, almost a maple edge to the golden liquid. She sipped in silence, thinking. Then, she could not stay at To'Ever. She should still have access to her daygarden, if she kept her mouth sealed on that. (And no, she did not worry about Rayn, Helia, or Kwillen; if trusting her friends would be her downfall, then so would it be.)

But where could she go?

This would . . . not be a good time for her to attempt a return to To'Arc. Not just for Xelle, but for the stability of Arc, with a new Spire and Kern's position with the Hurts potentially imperiled. But, she could not go live in the forest, or live in Tam. Her connection to the magesphere was still important, and not through her friends alone.

Another sip. There was an element to the wine that reminded her of a drink Klein had made her once, when she'd still been hiding. A similar wine, or fortification perhaps, must have been an element, complementing the spirits. His words came to mind, from the eve of the new year. 'Even a bridge is not the path, it's a path that someone already made.' She'd liked and remembered it.

To her relief, Xelle realized Avail was not in any hurry. Or, perhaps he should be, but he'd granted her permission to think, and a Crown Mage could certainly manage his own priorities. And not just to think. To think here, to have one more chance to say whatever she needed to Avail. Yet there would be limits. A glass, not a bottle. And so, she tried to keep her mind calm (the wine seemed also a message to do so!) and think. What did Xelle need?

She needed access. She needed resources. She needed—she thought—to still be at a Tower. Not Ever. Not Arc. Not Frond. Not Breath, where keenness of perception was a priority and she would certainly hinder Kwill's secrecy toward their efforts. Dust or Charm caused no reaction to her; she barely knew of them, and they were farther away from the mountains.

This left her one option, and it was the one she'd repeatedly been told would be the least welcoming.

Where had welcome got her, anyway.

"If I present myself at To'Grand," she said slowly without looking yet at Avail, "do you have anyone who could lend some luck to my roll on getting them to let me in?"

"Oh," he said, nearly mockingly. "I'll consider it." He poured himself another glass.

"Thank you, Crown Mage Avail." She rose from the seat, setting her empty glass down on a side table. "Delicious, thank you for this also." She paused. Could she? "Is she alive?"

Avail's eyes widened, and twitched. "I have . . . always felt her presence. Every day." He glanced away, and Xelle knew that was all she would get on that.

Mages. Always this way. Brooding, obfuscating romantics, the whole lot. The aros too, in their own way, she thought, thinking of Kwill. Xelle smiled. A smile she could not control, did not want to control. "Then I presume you feel her still. I . . . know what that is like," she added, briefly acknowledging the gap in her own heart. "And I will be on my way to To'Grand, with one more favor to ask you."

He raised his eyebrows.

"I mean, am I the dragonfriend?"

Avail laughed, not a joke laugh, but the type of laugh of a grandparent at a child. This did not bother her.

"Yes, then, I'll need to know where the Ever Tower Back Desk is, and if I show up there, that you will let me in."

The grandparent face dissolved, in an instant, and Avail's eyes became serious. "Who, young Xeleanor, do you think you are?"

"I'm me," she said, straightening herself. "Mage Xeleanor Du'Tam."

There was a small crowd gathered at the Study supply room. Why was there a small crowd gathered at the supply room?

A younger crowd, at that. (The thirty thing had her in some mood, sigh.) Xelle didn't see any Mages present or any other reason for a gathering, but the on-duty clerks were peering over the check-out counter in interest, and a group of Studies were hovering around a side wall, trying to make it look like they always had conversations in the cramped supply room. He'milo stepped forward, as the rest quieted. Ah. Then they'd heard.

Her heart pounded. These kids were here . . . for her?

No, not kids, she corrected herself, but Fira, Studies were young now. Some of these, like He'milo, literal teenagers. She had to stop this. Anyway. She felt a little like a lab lead again, as she stepped forward, pushing away nerves at the idea that, for whatever reason, they'd wanted to see her. "You heard that I'm leaving?" Avail did not joke.

He'milo pointed back to the supply counter. "One of my friends works here." By the glance that she exchanged with him, friends was not all that was going on. That made Xelle happy; she'd interacted with this clerk a lot over the past months and she seemed really sweet. Xelle guessed that Ma had not been told.

And considering the notification in that context, it felt a kindness on Avail's part. The clerks here were friendly, and 'hi, we're expecting you' could be a lot less awkward than Xelle having to tell them to close out her ledger, or wondering if they'd ask why.

"The Front Desk sent word that you're leaving, and would be returning some things this afternoon. Leelee told me right away. Because of the bird book. And the house. We made a club. We were making a club. We are, I mean. And we wanted to know if that was fine with you."

No one needed Xelle's permission to form a club; it had been clear they'd been a club of sorts anyway. Her blessing? A lot of confusing emotions and little scenarios ran through her mind, until she realized what the awkward teen probably wanted.

Surety.

She smiled warmly. "It would bring me great joy to know that you are carrying on the work here." She looked around at each Study, realizing again she was using sort of a teacher face, but not amending it. "And I am so grateful to be able to tell you this in person; I was hoping you would accept my gift of the book, to the club, to keep the notes going."

That was . . . clearly it.

The Studies bobbed a little; a few poking each other behind He'milo, perhaps thinking she couldn't see.

"Oh, yes, we'll take really good care of it," he said. "We'll keep it going. And the birdhouse too; we can maintain it?"

"Of course!" Xelle nodded enthusiastically. "Both are fully under control of the club. Leelee," she offered. "You'll notify the Front Desk? Tell them I coordinated this with the Crown Mage." Knowing that comment would be relayed to the Spire staff, she considered that piece as good as done. Avail was not going to take their birdhouse. "And perhaps request a sitting area, more than the two chairs and side-table. As in, a stand for the book, drawers for drawings and notes? A gathering place with soft pillows."

"That would be awesome," He'milo said. "Leelee, you'll order it? We could call it 'The Nest'!"

The Studies chattered excitedly about their new pillow-filled nest, and Xelle moved along, carting her box of checked-out miscellanea to the counter, a fog now blurring her perception, which was fine as the clerks basically took the things and one passed her a small finalization card that they both marked.

Xelle couldn't tell them what this meant. Instead of leaving as an outcast, a blur, a confusing, unverified mark on the history of To'Ever, she had left a small joy. A bird-watching club, led by bright-eyed teenagers. Ebbia, surrounded by friends. He'milo and Leelee sharing grins. A big, colorful book, bought with Na Vuia's money. A sweet little wooden birdhouse. A clearing that might now be full.

She couldn't tell them. And so, instead, she left.

Taking a final cross-seat on the bed in the Ever Tower room, Xelle concentrated on the mark.

Thunder. Hello, friend. It might be difficult for a while for me to travel and talk directly, as many eyes, powerful eyes, are upon me right now. If I don't hear back from you, then I will go there when I can, because I need you to get this message.

I'd like to offer you, all of you, a choice, with the information that I have.

As we discussed with Breeze, the area where you lived before, near the cliff, has now been forbidden from hu access. I can't promise a hu couldn't reach you, clearly, but the magesphere is protecting a boundary and monitoring the area and, having been set up between Towers and co-signed by a Mage no longer present, the proclamation would be difficult to undo without extensive forewarning.

Also, I do believe it is the intent of the Mage we discussed, with whom I'm no longer communicating, to secretly allow in the hu who tried to reach you before. As a ruse. If this happens, the intent would be for us to learn who they are and what they are doing. If . . . if they know you are there, the odds of them doing so increase. This, of course, puts you at risk. And I would never set you out as a trap. Yet, I have set myself out a bit that way, and it was my choice to do so. And now, you could be ready. Be more prepared. And I could help you, in whatever way I could.

If you decide to stay in the high mountains, I recommend that you move to another peak. As you probably already realized, I was carrying two close artifacts of this Mage when I was there, and so, while I don't believe he would expose you, he may know where you currently are.

So I offer you that choice, for now, until I can find a better one. To all of you. Please tell Windy, or Breeze, or who is most appropriate. If I don't receive an answer, I will travel in person to ensure you got the message and know your group decision, or your requests of me. But . . . I have been straining my material and a period of rest for me is in our mutual interest.

I think about you every day and would like to play catch again. Until then, I'll think to you each night. Always with me.

They'd established this greeting, the idea of always, ever since the mark had been offered, but tonight, thinking of zheir quirky grin, sullen turns, and unfettered love of games, yet not knowing when she'd see zhem again, she yearned for more than a notion of someday. And so, regrasping the connection once more as if reaching for a departing hu's arm, e added—

Friend, I don't know if you have this concept in you for someone like me, but please know, from my authentic heart: I love you.

23 - The Long Way

The obvious path to To'Grand, especially for a travel Mage, led directly through To'Arc, but Xelle had a longer path in mind. For many reasons, not all of which she wanted to consider. Her accumulating Basic sat, untouched, in Vi'Arc, but any need for it was superseded by the sizable bag of coins she found stowed into her checkout packet. As the nondescript fibercloth pack was sealed, and thus its tightly-packed contents likely unknown to the clerk, Xelle had a good sense where it was from and why it would never be mentioned again.

So Xelle took her time, traveling openly and amagically through the three largest cities of Alyssia, taking taxis, counting tips, and letting herself be seen—and sometimes avoided—in cafés. She learned what she could, smiled when she could, and sometimes, sat alone and breathed.

She did not stop first in Tam. She longed to see her family, but she was not yet settled in these new plans, and worried about their strong, yet well-intended, influences before she was. Still, her heart ached as she set out, and, she knew, uncertainty in her decision for this unknown destination was as much a factor as her desire to see those in a place she knew well.

It was, then, the same run from To'Ever to Mytil that she'd taken to meet Helia for the new year, so she relaxed back and just let herself casually enjoy the shapes passing by the windows over a long day of travel, without the pressure to take it all in.

Xelle stayed that night at the Emerald Forest, and did tell Klein about her plans. Not that she had anything too specific yet; it would all depend on her reception at To'Grand, and the nature of the network she could pull together there. But, over a strong brandy, she told him that she planned to make her way to the Tower and conduct her investigations from there—with discretion and safety, but with the assertion of being a Mage, as well as dragonfriend.

For once, Klein seemed reluctant to talk, focusing on washing and drying glasses as he listened, which she'd realized was a way he could pretend to be too busy to answer. This didn't bother her; a good friend sometimes listened, and she had her own decisions to work out, not simply lay at the feet (or the bartop) of a willing per.

Mostly, he listened. When she was done, he softly suggested that she was doing the right thing by listening to herself. Then, they switched topics and she asked about the latest in Mytil, a topic on which Klein always seemed to know all, and about which he opened quickly up. A bartender thing, she supposed.

"Is Tenne still in town?" It wasn't her business, per se, but as Kern had said his cura hadn't been talking to him (and was understandably prickly on the subject), Xelle did worry whether he was well.

"He's here, and well enough. Not been seen much since his residence at the galleries ended, but I have it on good word that he's still in town. Happier than he's been. He's living with another artist, an Owi'neil Du'Hubo, and is quite smitten with the hu."

"Really?" Xelle was happy to hear that. She was always happy when someone found their per. Happy, just . . . "I'm glad to hear that he's well."

For all of Tenne's bluster, the one image that had stuck with her was the light in his eyes when he talked about painting happy frogs on walls. She hoped that he and Owi'neil were able to do that.

She did some shopping in Mytil, easily covered by the sum in her check-out packet. Some new, soft socks, the type that felt nice to run one's hand along and feel glad for socks. Two new undercaps—her old one had become a travesty of the world and was now incinerated in the most literal of ways. A small wardrobe, in the style of her beloved Mytil.

No, Xelle was not going to stop wearing her signature style of dark colors and prioritized comfort, but having a few layers of finery to embellish the look was probably a wise idea at a place like Grand. Besides, she felt nice in them. Despite her open plainness, Xelle was a black lace hu at heart.

She restocked on personal items, selected a few snacks. She did not replenish her spices; she knew where she'd go for those.

Returning to the galleries was, unfortunately, not in the cards for now, but fortunately, Mytil was, as always, blooming with art. Even in the depths of winter (though less harsh than on the high rim) she could stroll through the city, admiring the glistening sculptures, the triumphs of thoughtful architecture, and run her fingers through the sounds of music wafting through the thin windows of old concert halls.

And within a few days, she took another vroom. Not yet to Vattam, but a short trip to the far side of the city, and to the bridge.

Now, there were many bridges in Alyssia. But when one referred to the bridge, at least a per from Arc or Ever Regions, everyone knew which one one meant.

Heart Lake was, as named, considered the heart of Alyssia, at least in terms of the populace. For the magesphere too, though for a Mage, it was the fabled cloud city of Hellina above it that provided that sanctity. Few ever saw the city, and apparently none discussed it.

Xelle would have written it off for a metaphor, or code for a wink-wink conference room somewhere on a Lakeside high floor, but once she learned the dragons were not just real but actively harmed by humanity, she had begun to doubt the entire concept of myths.

Lies, those were different.

As for Mytil, it rested atop the great cliffs of the Lake. Xelle did not usually travel to the Lake side of the city when she was there; much of it was private land, with parks and sanctuaries a longer trip down. Yet, the area by the bridge was open to all, and the vroom took her to it in nearly no time. Xelle tried not to think about this. All the times she could have sat, and rested a while, in a place of immense beauty, yet didn't. It was too much. It was too overwhelming.

Besides, her mind snuck in, despite her need for solitude, there were some places she wished she didn't have to be alone.

Today was no different. She dismounted from the vroom, with both her bag and a proper wheeled trunk full of her new acquisitions, and settled in with a sandwich she'd bought in the city, onto the high side of the bridge. The end of the cliffs, where the road crossed from the stable upper land, over an uneven, rocky stretch, and to the flatter land leading to Vattam.

She gazed out over the Lake, so large, she could not see across it. Somewhere there, rested the infamous City of Progress, Vattam. Then, to the farthest edge, the warm clime of Frond Region, with cultures and traditions so different from this opposing edge, or, she reminded herself, the cultures here so different from theirs. Around, the Lake poured into a large river, through the lushness of Charm Region. A whole Region of places she'd never been, she considered with more than a little wonder. Back toward Mytil, the sanctuary lands, and around the city and back to Xelle.

One hu, sitting against a vast Lake, feeling entirely awed by it, yet awesome to be by it.

Water affected her deeply. It sorted her, calmed her. The forest rain. The river. The rush of Tam's waterfall. Yet, ever since leaving her first and only home, she always ended up away from water. And when she found it, it was always—alone.

Her soul ached, and drew in more thoughts she could not handle. Running her hands through the greenfloor, she tried to calm her mind. And stay in the moment. A long, precious moment—even with her own hollowness, it was. And it wasn't until she worried she might start to miss the last taxi runs of the day that she collected herself and walked back to the staging area.

The next vroom took her to Vattam's center. Even with the substantial money that she'd been given, she could not justify the expense of the Stepladder Inn, but she found a nice place to leave her trunk and bag, and allow a few days here, incity.

The first day, she simply walked.

She wasn't sure what gave her the motivation, except that her days had been filled with self-imposed order and repetition, and— Fine, that was probably the motivation.

So she walked.

Through residential neighborhoods, through business sections, past parks and trees, and mysterious gated buildings. She passed what must have been a magipuck arena, and considered the fact that she'd never even seen a game. The food stands all closed in the absence of activity, and away, now, from the markets, she didn't try to find lunch, and by mid-afternoon she was thoroughly lost in the City of Progress. It wasn't until her hunger caught up with her that she, uninterested in casting today, stopped a friendly looking hu sweeping xyr porch, and asked what way she'd walk to get to Old Vattam.

"You're a long ways away," xe said, concern on xyr face. But, when she assured xem she needed no aid other than directions, xe pointed her back through a series of steps that would lead to a main thoroughfare.

This street was as interesting as the wandering, and she found a pasty cart, delighting at the hot and spicy rutabaga filling, as she walked. Belly restocked, she moved in the direction she'd been pointed, as neighborhoods shifted, and the types of shops and hu varied, and finally she saw the hill in the distance, the one with the Stepladder Inn.

She did not head toward it, knowing now where her own inn was. But, by her calculations, if things were the same as they were before, tomorrow would be the weekly visit of the bard.

Xelle never really slept well, but a day of exhaustion vibrating in her confused and grumbling feet and legs, she at least slept soundly.

The second day, she rested.

She walked to a small market, bought a collection of short stories, and sat leisurely and unconcerned with her progress through them, watching the pers move to and fro. She thought she caught some signs of worry or recognition, but it was not like Mytil, or most certainly the Ever or Arc villages. She was less known here, and those who may have had concerns simply tried to hide their hasty gestures of protection as they moved quickly by.

This time, at the Stepladder Inn, she took a seat near the back of the room. She didn't think that Jimmi Du'Ard would notice her there, but he seemed to, as he unloaded a heavy book onto a pedestal and gave her a sharp nod.

He did not acknowledge her again, but his story soothed her, calmed her mind. This time, with less humor than the previous, he told a second-person tale of a hu who had everything xe wanted, except the fullness of xemself.

Such a melancholy story would seem to bother her, but it did not. She sat, listening, drawn into the sadness. And when he stopped, nearly apologizing for the story, her heart beat more gently, her neck eased.

Sometimes, when a hu cannot have what one wants most, acknowledging the loss was . . . not a balm, but a necessity. A dressing for an open wound, to at least stop its bleeding. From view.

Alas, this storyteller had her thinking all sort of dramatic thoughts. If he could be a storyteller, close yet untouchably far from across the room, then she would be one too. Xeleanor glowed, unseen, with her own power, her own light. This was hers alone. And she would never again hold it in.

As much as Xelle loved the idea of finding new places, she had been through a lot, and looked forward to something familiar. And so on her last day incity (for no restriction other than she'd decided it was time to continue), she wandered the shops of Old Vattam, and made her way around to Mara's bar, thrilled to see that it, and Mara, were still there.

"New cloak," Mara said, nodding to Xelle.

"Yes, Ever Region this time, as I'm sure you've noted."

Mara only smiled.

"I'm going to have to visit sometime when it's not freezing cold."

Mara nodded, glancing wistfully at the drawn outside walls. "Yes, when the summer breeze blows in from the river in the golden light of evening, it is as though I have everything I could ever dream."

By the look Xelle noted in Mara's eyes, or perhaps distracting herself again from her own feelings of need, the key to that sentence was likely the 'as though'.

"Yet," he continued, "There is a special glow to a warmed drink amidst closed shutters and hanging drapes that the summer crowd could never understand. I am glad you are here for it."

This time, Xelle noted, Mara had not asked about her Tower affiliation. But, Xelle was probably at a point of reading into everything. (If she were not always at this point, she chuckled to herself.)

A few other customers arrived, and Mara tended to them, but Xelle was glad when he returned, as she'd been pondering a few questions over her spirit-warmed coffee. The safer ones first, in case Mara decided to be done with her for the evening.

"I'm curious, if you'd like to share. I'll be traveling to To'Grand, and with your insights, I wonder what you notice about the pers who go."

Mara wiped the countertop, and finally looked up. "I think the question you're asking is what do those who leave have in common?"

Xelle, though unsure that she'd meant that, nodded, running through the words quickly and trying to catch up with this diversion.

"The grandest thing about Grand culture is not their personal egos as many say, but their belief that they are a part of something important. Sometimes, to their error, more important than the rest. When a

Study leaves, and comes here to drink about it, they are usually filled with one of two things. The first, a lack of confidence. Sadness that they could not find a place in that corner of our world. That a sapling cannot find light in the tallest forest." He looked up and flung the cloth into a bin. "This is of course not true, or how would a sapling grow."

By fire, Xelle thought but did not think it wise to say. Then, lack of confidence. That was one.

"Arrogance," he continued. "Vast arrogance that they were not appreciated, their skills and contributions or whatever else not understood." He paused. "Pers say what they will about Grand culture. That it stands alone, that it cannot see the collective. That, I am certain, has never been it. Grand stands for the forest, not the tree. For each finding their own power, and then standing together, sheltering the saplings, the brush, the ground cover, and the tiniest of flowers, as they grow. Grand is power, it's true. A true Grand Mage is a guardian, never a magnate."

That was a lot for Xelle to ponder. But more customers were making their way in, and Xelle could not lose the moment. Not and spin in the night ivy for not having tried. "The Lunests. What do you know of them?"

Mara's eyes flashed sharply and he lowered his voice to quickly respond. "That the city of Wehj and its upscale yet separate branches often take on the scale of the Grand, but without the knowledge of the forest. And," he lowered his voice again, "that the sudden growth of Lerf in the meadowlands of Vattam has likely left them unsettled."

With a lukewarm smile, Mara went to greet the new guests. And, Xelle knew, other than to order or pay, that was as much as she was going to hear from the bartender tonight.

Again, the shortest path from Vattam to To'Grand would be through the Highponds, an area so beautiful Xelle's one glimpse had felt like a dream. (A dream that immediately turned into an unpleasant nightpath, but that first part, anyway.)

Xelle did not feel afraid of the Lunests. She felt . . . gross about them. Furious, maybe. However, even Xelle felt like riding so close to the Lunest Estate would be bad energy. So, she again took a longer route and decided to see Wehj, a place she'd never before been.

Wehj was not Vattam.

There was no boast of progress here, no large glass windows and open spaces pointing to the light. The city itself, and many of the areas within it, were circled by huge metal gates and fences. Buildings rose squarely of old stone, sometimes patched with newer brick. Yet there was beauty to the starkness. Branches of rose bushes wound up and around artfully twisted iron. Large parks stretched with canopies of trees. And there was a calm to the traffic: the vrooms, the pers, the hand-pushed carts on roads neatly cleared of snow, that provided a soothing rhythm.

The city of Wehj was often described as harsh, but immediately, Xelle perceived that it could be comforting. She'd planned to stop here, see some sights. Ask more. Learn what she could. But she was tiring quickly of all the interaction (and excessive walking), and needed energy to approach the Tower. The city was not far from To'Grand. She could return.

And so, she disembarked from her taxi, but only briefly stopped for a stretch and washroom, and readied herself for the last leg forward. She paused, gazing off into the distance as she approached the waiting vrooms. Never would it be lost on Xeleanor Du'Tam that her feet now stepped over ground they'd never before touched. Her eyes rested on views only thusforth imagined.

With that rush, she resumed her travel, the words sounding strange in her own mouth as she nonchalantly responded to the conn, "Yes, directly to To'Grand, thank you."

Grand Tower was . . . awesome.

She stepped from the vroom, gaping at the structure before her. The

Tower was built into huge trees, or with them, or some combination—but to suggest it as a treehouse, or like anything near her homevillage, or anything she'd ever considered would do both an unforgivable injustice. The Tower was nearly a tree itself, though clearly not, not with its towering size, and not relying on growing life. But the feel of a tree. And unlike a Tower with a domed or pointed spire, up top she craned to see that the Tower expanded at the top levels, reaching out with a structure of tall beams. A huge, open level, likely not even with glass windows, stretched across its middle.

"Pardon?" the conn interrupted nervously, likely unsure of her title. Oh, she'd forgotten to pay. Murmuring an apology, she turned, counting a little more than she'd intended but not wanting to ask for it back, and then watching nervously (for all of it) as the taxi conn pulled away, its fuelstones clanking softer and softer in the distance as she stared.

"First time?" a voice asked. A Mage, walking past with a smile. She nodded back, politely, but not having asked for the interruption.

Slowly, she walked, bag slung on, and pulling her wheeled trunk behind her, not daring yet to cast. And she walked inside.

"Greetings, how may I assist you?" The clerk stood as she entered. Well, at least they didn't recognize the dragonfriend here. At least, she didn't think this clerk did. Too bad she'd have to ruin it. Well, at least she could say hi first.

"Hello." Xelle smiled.

"Hello." Xe gave a tiny bow.

"I'm Mage Xeleanor Du'Tam, bearing a Dragon Sigil." She pointed to her mark. "I am seeking a Tower that will allow me residence for now, as I am currently unpledged, and I had to leave To'Ever, where I was staying, on a matter of business."

The clerk stared. "Yes, let me . . . get someone on that." Xe reached back and pulled a cord. A few minutes later, a Mage, wearing a gold sash, with a long wand holstered over xyr hip, ambled in. "Hmm?"

Xelle repeated her request.

"Ah," xe said, eyes widening. "Let me . . . get someone on that." The Mage removed the wand, and swished it in a quick, nearly flippant pattern.

After about ten wand swishes, two room changes, a fresh pitcher of lemonwater and a washroom break to match, Xelle found herself in front of the Grand Spire. Not in the open platform she'd seen from the ground, but one above it, a long, windowed space that would fit at least ten of the chambers used by the Arc Spire. At least. There was no central table. Each of the seven Spire Mages, looking harried as if not pleased by the disruption of Xelle's arrival, sat in a huge, grandgold, throne-like chair, with a layered side table on one side, and a drink stand on the other. Which side was which varied by the Mage. By the Spire Mage, she quickly reminded herself.

Xelle had played a bit loose with the Spires of Ever and Arc, but running out of places she wanted to be, it might be time to iron that out. A little.

"Explain your use of Mage if you are unpledged," a Spire Mage said, ticking xyr wand amagically like a fuelchip metronome.

This, she had prepared for, though her voice still shook. "I have the training and skills of a Mage. I am unpledged, so I claim no Tower in my name, nor do I claim the endorsement of one. Yet I am marked with a Dragon Sigil, so I'm not sure my learning to be a baker would be in our mutual best interest. Or the populace's, if you've tasted my baking."

One Mage raised a hand to xyr mouth.

Another gave an annoyed tilt to the head. "You could pledge." Xe glanced around like xe couldn't believe this needed to be said. "At wherever it is you studied."

"I could," she agreed, trying to sound easy about it. "I was offered such at To'Arc. But would the Towers want the dragonfriend claimed by one alone? Is that in their interest?"

That caused a rumble.

"I think we should let her stay," one said. "Rules. Proper place. Our eye on her."

Another shifted in xyr seat, looking to each side. "What precedent would that set? Calling her Mage without a pledge? Would others presume the same? It would shatter our entire structure."

"Then, with respect, don't call me one," Xelle said, censoring a great many other considerations she had long wanted to voice. "It would not change the nature of who I am. And would you rather me leave, stay with the populace?"

A thick barrier pressed around her. Not of pain, but the direct suppression of magic. Essentially a wall, pushing her away from the Spire, disallowing her casts. It had the feeling of insurmountability, inevitability. This wall could not be passed.

She stifled a sigh, nearly bored over the expectation of such nonsense, yet fascinated by her first touch of Grand Magic. The invisible wall felt . . . big. Impenetrable. Then, she would not try and penetrate it. She willed her cloak to seal around her, just as she traveled the fog creeping in and pushed it away. She blinked, or as she now understood, the inkbloom pod coating inside her did, through the space and to the other side of the barrier.

With a quick inhale of Breath, she detected who it was who had cast, and blinked again, behind xem. She whispered in xyr ear. "I would love to learn how you did that. But don't worry, I respect the granting of wands as the strict purview of Grand Tower. Perhaps, in time, I could earn a small one, a pocket wand if you will, for protection." She cast again, just a couple of slings, floating back toward the wall, pushing it back with a broad swipe of Arc, and then resting, floating mid-air in a cross-seat.

"I wish to offer my respect, but I have never seen the Grand," she said. In turn, she flashed the Ever, the Frond, the Arc, and the Breath. Then, she released her cast and lowered to the ground, where she stood, waiting.

She knew, now, a lesson she could thank Kern for, that all of this was basic for these Mages. But they'd presented a test, and she'd met it her way. Including the respect of not asking Rayn to teach her the sign. And now they must decide.

A Spire Mage, the one who had made the cast, raised xyr hand. An old, hairy hand. Xe brought it almost to a fist but then stopped, jerking it just slightly downward.

As respectfully as she could, she returned the sign.

"You can stay here for now." It was the Crown Mage who finally spoke. "And we will decide your parameters, as well as your tasks. Return to the Front Desk for registration and room assignment. And Xeleanor Du'Tam, we do not tolerate nonsense here."

Funny, that'd just been the word she'd used to describe their Mage test, as if a quick test of cast could determine her value. She was glad, then, that hu Mages, unlike dragons, did not read minds.

She also knew she shouldn't answer. Which, maybe, was why she did. "Then, Crown Mage, we have that in common. Thank you, for your trust." Unsure what to follow that with, she gave a deep bow. And left.

24 - Seal

The Grand Atrium was oddly plain. A squarish space, with many side rooms, its ceiling held high by polished trunks of old trees. Not much of a maze, or levels, or platforms—mostly just wide benches against a mixture of tables. (She hadn't seen tables in an Atrium before, and rather liked the idea?) Pers did not eat at them, but an occasional coffee or wine, or water flask could be seen perched near a stack of books, or a sketchpad, or just a young-looking Study, staring off through the broad, square windows and occasional offerings of large, traditional paintings of historical scenes and notable Grand Mages.

Xelle was not young-looking, nor a Study, but she stared the same, thinking about last night. The dragons—she'd felt them. Her sigil had awoken her from sleep. A feeling, at first, of movement, much like Arc Magic yet not, had coursed through her trembling mind. A force, all at once, that her friends had moved, nearer now. Not near to where she was here, but away from the high mountains, and back, toward To'Arc.

Then, the vision.

Thunder soared over the mountains, landing in the familiar spot where the obsidian had been hastily covered with stone. The others made no sound, other than the flapping of their wings, and footsteps against the rocky soil, as they all landed, in turn. Each drew close to the ragged stone heap. They stood. And waited. And moved inward, forming the look of a perfect amphitheater around the focus of their gaze. Then it had ended, and Xelle had stayed, trembling in her bed.

She tossed the rest of the night, in layers of fitful sleep like thin, inadequate blankets laid over the shivering of her mind. She saw. And she heard. It arrived from afar, and like an echo, it needed, it seemed, to work its way through. Again and again.

Sights. Sounds. The silence. The sending of two senses, when Thunder knew this taxed Xelle immensely, must have been intentional. And, Xelle realized, the sending specifically of silence.

There was only one reason she could consider. That it was important. Essential. Not as a clue, but as an expression. Xelle did not receive a feeling through the call, but it stirred her own feelings, as if she had. The silence of her friends gazing at their embattled home. Home, in a way. Not their desired home, but a place they had found, to rest. Together. Home in that sense. Until the hu forced it broken, the smooth wall of obsidian likely damaged under the harshly jutting rocks, yet even the extent of that damage not known without extensive and painful restoration. Again, she heard the stillness. A few night birds, stirring, in the trees.

If a dragon cried, did zhey do so this way? In stillness? In silence?

She'd sent back a message, not of thoughts, as much as she could dampen them, but of her own silence, yet an intentional, directed silence, sent directly to Thunder, hoping the intent conveyed.

The images, the ambient sound of the scene zhey'd sent still reverberated, and Xelle glanced around the chunky, lofty Atrium, letting her hands run over the smooth boards of an old, old table, feeling her senses returning. It wasn't just when she'd awoken last night, but every time she thought of them there, their silence, her chest constricted, the back of her neck tingled, and her mind drifted, another time, from reality. From the closeness and feeling of what Thunder had sent her.

She would see zhem. She would see all of them—Cloudpuff, Breeze, Windy, and even Lightning, soon. She would meet others. She would learn what it was she needed to know. She craved to no longer feel their sadness but, perhaps, to bring them some joy.

Breathing in again, she drew her eye downward to the stack of stationery she'd bought in a Mytil shop, and a roll of gorgeous decorative paper tape she'd found in Old Vattam. (Little wisps of gold over a soft blue.) And . . . an affectation she'd wanted for a really long time, a small, custom seal she'd had made while staying at the Enchanted Forest. It wasn't elaborate or, like, the work of an expert, but it was a simple, sweet design by an earnest artist. A little slanted *X* that she could press into a seal, and send her notes with proper flair. Helia would love it, she knew. Not sure about the others.

She took a breath.

Dearest Kwillen,

It was so good to see you at To'Ever. And much has happened since.

I now have solid confirmation, having met them, that the esteemed pers that we had reason to suspect are, indeed, deeply involved. I have also learned that there is a disreputable yet popular subscription in Vi'Arc that has formally affiliated you with me. I had an imaginary conversation with you about it, and have decided to trust your imaginary guidance. So, thank you.

Not sure if you are back enduring your days as a Study yet, but know that when you see this, I will be thinking of you from my current residence at To'Grand, where I have boldly presented myself as (are you ready for this) Mage Xeleanor Du'Tam.

I will try and find a way to connect soon. I am ready to accelerate our revolution. (You can see my grin from there?)

My best,

- Xeleanor.

She was grinning, and stayed so as she folded the envelope shut, and marked it to Study Kwillen Du'Satta, To'Breath.

Next one, then, she got everything out and ready. Parent time.

Nas (and please show to Hall, when he's over) –

I have done a Xelle thing again. Long story short, I am staying at To'Grand. I am also calling myself a Mage, and . . . maybe some other news has reached you. Either way, please talk to Hall about it, and know that I'm sorry for not having been able to tell you that part myself. The true parts, of course. The lies will be evident.

Life has been a bit complicated. But I am happy, I am well, and as I am discovering more rapid ways to travel, I will try to stop in and see everyone.

If you need to reach me, a Post to To'Grand will work. Depending on the clerk, a simple address of 'Xeleanor Du'Tam' would work best and not ruffle any Front Desk Feathers. (Official cast reagent.)

Not sure what else to say now, except that I am well, and I am thinking of you all, and please let Vallie and Loren know I think of them often and look forward to playing dragon again. (And I will have more stories for them!)

All my love,

- Xelle.

This one, sealed, and marked Hu Vuia et al, Village of Tam, Ever Region.

Then, another. She tapped the pen on a scrap, and made sure the ink was running right.

Mage Rayn Du'Ever - (are you used to it yet?)

I'm sorry I didn't get the chance to say goodbye (for now!) when I left the Tower (Ever Tower, well, you know that), but I ran askance of Mage Fepa and what a glorious freedom that is. If you cross his path, you would be well-advised not to mention me. Ha.

That said, it is bittersweet not to sit down and hear all about what being a Mage is like. Ohhh, yeah. So I'm calling myself 'Mage' now. In case you . . . hear about that. It's me! You may have inspired this in me (not sure if that's 'thank you' or 'sorry'?) but alas, I will not claim your placename, and thus am now Mage Xeleanor Du'Tam. And . . . I am at To'Grand. Your descriptions helped prepare me, and I have them now tolerating me in a tenuous but stable state. Would love to talk more about it.

I should be visiting my forest home sometimes (just not for a bit while I gain my footing here), so when I do I hope that I can reach you there.

In friendship,

- Xeleanor.

p.s. I forgot to tell you that at your pledging ceremony, you looked absolutely beautiful. I mean, you always do, but you know, in the stunning fancy 'wow ok' way. An image for a tapestry! That sort of thing. Anyway, see you someday soon! Thinking of you.

She stared at the note a while longer than the others (should she have said the last part?), and then, smiling warmly, she folded the envelope. She hadn't wanted to mention the daygarden, but felt sure that Rayn would take the forest home line that way, rather than a reference to Tam.

Adjusting the pen again, Xelle almost wrote 'Study' but, fortunately, caught herself. Mage Rayn Du'Ever, To'Ever.

And now, one last one. Was it a last one? She tapped her lip, and pushed away a painful thought. Yes, last for now.

Hellie,

I had a really good time over the new year. I am ~~glad~~ grateful, wait also glad it's not like there's just one thing, that you are in my life. Anyway, just me being me, right?

I wanted you to know that I'm at To'Grand. I know, don't even. So *far*, they've actually been pretty cool to me. Also, I need to learn the Arc 'calling' thing so we can talk more often. It's on my list. Well, now you know where to find me.

I am still working on behalf of my notable friends. That, right now, is my priority. I hope that you are well, and please, always let me know if there's something I can do. And please, whatever you hear, I hope you can trust me. Well, that sounds ominous writing it, but I mean that I think some pers will continue to dirty themselves in their pursuits. I suspect moreso now.

And not in the good way. Also, why do I talk. No, but really, I just. Worry. Anyway, I'm sure we'll connect soon! Hoping the best for you, and oh, for Bear! Pet aem extra for me? And get your finger down into the shoulder blades. Both of them. (Even if one starts tight.)

With love ♥,

- Xeleanor.

Her pen soared over the last envelope, the lettering smooth. Mage Helia Du'Arc, Arc Tower.

Maybe she shouldn't have gotten into the worry or ended with petting the cat, but Helia wouldn't care. To Helia, she was Xelle. And that was, as always, a comforting thought.

She allowed herself a little travel cast to warm the dark, black wax in the rounded little spoon she'd bought, and poured it over the first envelope, pressing the seal down, waiting, and then lifting it up. Fancy. (She was proud of this.) With all four done, she marked them for special handling (this cost a little extra) and set them down.

Her friends all away in silence or sealed into envelopes, what was left for the moment, she supposed, was Xeleanor Du'Tam. Forestper. Tree lover. Mage. Not Mage. Dragonfriend. Xelle.

Like the inkbloom, Xelle was starting to understand she transcended plurality. She was one, two, and many, all at once, ever traveling. Allowing this to settle, she stayed a while longer, staring at those envelopes, at the imperfect seals of wax, at her own mostly neat handwriting. Not just connection, but being. In that realization, joy and ache swirled to form a windpost of truth. A center of calm. Whatever Xeleanor was, whatever she would be, she knew then, really knew, that her heart—her true heart—was comprised of her friends.

She sat, contemplating this warmth, alone.

Inkbloom: The End

About the Author

E.D.E. Bell (she or e) was born in the year of the fire dragon during a Cleveland blizzard. After a youth in the Mitten, an MSE in Electrical Engineering from the University of Michigan, three wonderful children, and nearly two decades in Northern Virginia and Southwest Ohio developing technical intelligence strategy, she started the indie press Atthis Arts. Working through mental disorders and an ever-complicated world, she now tries to bring light and love as she can through storytelling, as a proud part of the Detroit arts community.

A passionate vegan, radiant bi, and earnest progressive, Bell feels strongly about issues related to equality and compassion and loves fantasy as a way to perceive them while offering our minds lovingly crafted worlds in which to settle. Her works are quiet and queer, and often explore conceptions of identity and community, including themes of friendship, family, and connection. She lives in Ferndale, Michigan, where she writes stories and revels in garlic.

E hopes to write many more stories with Xeleanor Du'Tam and perhaps you will join em in them. You can follow eir adventures at edebell.com.

Milton Keynes UK
Ingram Content Group UK Ltd.
UKHW030750230724
445892UK00006B/139

9 781945 009938